COSMOGRAMMA

Also by Courttia Newland

Novels
The Scholar
Society Within
Snakeskin
The Dying Wish
The Gospel According to Cane
A River Called Time

Short story collections
Music for the Off-Key: Twelve Macabre Short Stories
A Book of Blues

COSMOGRAMMA

COURTTIA NEWLAND

CANONGATE

First published in Great Britain in 2021
by Canongate Books Ltd, 14 High Street, Edinburgh EH1 1TE

canongate.co.uk

1

British Library Cataloguing-in-Publication Data
A catalogue record for this book is available on request from the British Library

ISBN 978 1 78689 709 1

Typeset by Palimpsest Book Production Ltd, Falkirk, Stirlingshire

Printed and bound in Great Britain by Clays Ltd, Elcograf S.p.A.

For Brook Stephenson, who gave the inspiration.
And FlyLo, who gave the music.

In some far off place
Many light years in space
I'll wait for you.
Where human feet have never trod,
Where human eyes have never seen.
I'll build a world of abstract dreams
And wait for you.

Sun Ra

CONTENTS

PERCIPI

We saw it after dinner, nationwide on a weeknight. Between the celebrity dance competition and hit US soap *The Lanes*. Everybody had been buzzing for months, the rumour mills were in overdrive, so when the media promised the Buddy 3000 would be unveiled that very evening, the whole town was talking. We all wanted to see what came next, and we made sure we were in front of the VS when the first ads aired.

They said the Buddy was the best of its kind, a new generation. That science had made the final leap and harnessed creation's power, there was nothing that couldn't be grasped, the future was limitless. They were mostly Seneca supporters, of course, and usually the ones who stood to gain. Employees, the CEO, the mayor. Others said Mankind was heading for the fall, that playing God would only lead to death and destruction, but no one listened to them. They were the poor or the religious, which in our town pretty much amounted to the same thing. There were leaflets printed on flimsy paper you could see your hand through, proclaiming Man's inhumanity, the final days. There were panel discussions and news items and petitions, but nothing was going to stop Seneca from launching the Buddy; we must have known that.

We sat in the almost dark for some reason, the flicker of VS light crossing our faces while we waited. The screen went blank for a long time after the dance show finished, but we could still see because the eyes of our long-suffering 1250i were bright enough to bathe the room in a soft, golden glow, as though we'd been submerged in honey. They stood between the sofa and wall, facing the screen like the rest of us, silent apart from the hum of their workings. We ignored them, consumed by our wait for the most part, though we could feel it even then, the uncomfortable way in which we turned our backs betraying our collective guilt.

Brightness from the VS, blinding light. Celestial music. We covered our eyes. When the light grew piercing enough to feel on the back of our hands it faded and was replaced by the Seneca logo. We nudged each other, lowered arms. The logo was superimposed onto an image of green grass, a cliff edge, blue skies and white clouds. There was a figure: a man standing by the edge of the cliff, arms by his sides, looking out to sea. The camera, which had approached rapidly from high above and behind the man, swooped just above the perfect grass, zoomed towards him and when it got close, circled, rose and hovered to face him.

Piercing blue eyes, high cheekbones, tousled blond hair and a cleft chin. Tall and slim, beige slacks, blue shirt, sensible brown shoes. The man was tanned and unsmiling, rugged and good-looking, ignoring the camera and even us, the viewers watching nationwide, to look up into the sky at some distant place he perhaps hoped to travel one day. We held our breath.

Welcome, a female voice-over said, *to the world of Seneca, the world of the future, now. Welcome to the Buddy 3000.*

We couldn't believe it. We leant forward in our seats, jumped from the sofa, crowded the viewscreen. The man placed both hands on his hips, raised his chin. The celestial music reached a crescendo. We gasped, laughed, doubted.

A head-and-shoulders shot of Daniel Millhauser, Seneca president. We relaxed. That couldn't have been the Buddy, we reasoned, what a terrible ad. Very confusing.

Gazing into viewscreens the world over, some strained to hear what the president was saying over loud voices of denial. Someone turned the volume up. Millhauser was sitting in an austere leather chair talking to camera. He seemed matter-of-fact, as though he were explaining the company's financial position in the global economy via stocks and shares. He spoke of the company's past innovations as if we didn't know them, as if we lived on the Outer Limits; its humble beginnings as a manufacturer of calculators and digital watches; his great-grandfather Arthur Millhauser assembling circuit boards by hand until he made enough to buy his first shop; subsequent Millhausers handing the business over like a relay baton. Green-screen desktop computers, carry-alls with video streaming, 1,000 gigs of memory in your hand. The Seneca robotics division creating machines that rolled and served, machines that crawled like spiders and served, machines that eventually walked, haltingly at first and unable to climb stairs, but soon even that innovation was past memory. The Seneca Communications Robot, a crowning glory; the 500, 1000, 1250, 1500, 2000. SCRs provided as standard with every house sold, more affluent families buying another; one to take care of the kids, one for them.

Now Millhauser was explaining just what made the Buddy so special: the ergonomic design. Here, the company president allowed a wry smile. *More human than humankind*, he said. Greater intellectual capacity, thanks to the SNS-8748, a patented chip designed to collate and articulate cultural differences so the Buddy could function anywhere from New York to Papua New Guinea. Stronger than its predecessors, safer, more efficient, longer battery life, shorter charge time, the ability to self-repair. Easy to assemble, and there was the option to have the Buddy custom-built by a tech for more credits. A child lock so the young couldn't order Buddy to do harm, even so much as swear. Additional teaching modules sold as downloadable content, thousands of subjects for the family that preferred home schooling. The Buddy could dive to 100 metres, climb to 50,000 feet and was already in service above our heads, on space stations and satellites and dry-dock launch platforms.

While Millhauser pitched his miracle product to our households, we listened. We swallowed every word as the camera tracked ever so slowly to the right, imperceptibly at first, until we realised the Seneca president's head was leaving the shot. We second-guessed ourselves: it was the shot leaving *Millhauser*. The camera kept tracking, first revealing nothing but a window overlooking clear green grass, a blue sky; the cliff, it was the same cliff! Then the edge of a large, tidy desk, pads and pens, a Manchester United coffee mug, the corner of a wafer-thin viewscreen, a nameplate – *Daniel Millhauser, President* – and finally Millhauser, sat behind the desk with his hands clasped, the quiet trickster wearing a distant smile.

And we jumped. Across the nation, probably the world over, we jumped at the realisation. Millhauser got to his feet, placed a hand on his doppelgänger's shoulder. He smiled at the Buddy and the Buddy smiled at him, though it was impossible to tell one from the other, and then, even though they both looked pretty jovial, it was difficult to tell what the joke was, or who had told it.

They looked straight into camera, spoke as one:

The Buddy 3000. The world of the future, now.

The Seneca logo, the Buddy 3000 logo, a black screen with details in white, the price, specifications, small print that outlined monthly repayments of 15% APR. Ten seconds or less and the information was gone. Dark screen. Opening credits of *The Lanes*.

Uproar in front rooms of houses, on the streets, across towns and cities. The hit US soap discarded like a used battery. The next morning there were queues a block long outside Seneca showrooms all over the world, but no Buddies on sale. There were TV interviews and chat show appearances by Seneca CEO Ravindra Mehta, more handsome and skilled in PR than his reclusive president. There were web trailers and mall openings with men on stilts dressed in Buddy suits, a public appearance with the prime minister, yet still no sign of a single Buddy. Speculation was rife. Mehta waved his hands a great deal, smiled with perfect white teeth and spoke of fine-tuning.

One day we woke, emerging from the warm cocoons of our homes to leave for work, or school, and they were stencilled everywhere: a numerical infestation on walls and street lights, road signs, pavements and kerbs, bollards, billboards, even some vehicles. Three paired numbers. A date, we soon realised. *12.10.84.*

There was outrage in government circles over what was essentially vandalism. Seneca claimed no responsibility for the appearance of the numbers. Mehta went on live television to rubbish claims of an international graffiti campaign while confirming that, yes, this was the official launch date. *It must have leaked somehow*, he smiled. We nodded, disbelieving, accepting his lies. We expected no better and that was the issue: it became easy to ignore what they did, to pretend their deceptions didn't matter.

In our town the Buddy was all anyone could speak about – it must have been the same everywhere. It seemed to relate to any given subject. The battle for Montes Pyrenaeus, still raging, the dubious economy, the huge cost and fallout, both literal and figurative, of interstellar travel. The rising temperature of Earth, unemployment, immigration. We debated and disagreed and our raised voices filled the night in coffee shops, bars and restaurants, in pool halls, after-hours clubs and back alleys, during the daytime in factories and playgrounds and public spaces where people of all ages gathered in excitement, faces bright with the promise of a new era.

It was our happiest time, we owed Seneca that much. They presented us with a dream made real, a figment of imagination made flesh and bone; the gift of idealism. We were elated at the chance to become something more than we were.

The months passed without notice. The ads intensified, while the posters and online spots became unavoidable. Seneca threw a huge launch event, screened for free on all channels, attended by the world's biggest movie stars, models, singers, royalty, presidents and prime ministers. Our town, like many others, threw a street party with images of the launch projected onto a whitewashed wall. Everyone came. We watched a live news report where BBC anchorwoman Leticia Daley took us deep into Seneca's distribution centre to witness thousands of human-sized boxes rolling along interlinked conveyor belts resembling minia-ture highways, some dystopian automotive future, before being loaded into HGVs by 2000s with the gaze of the blind. We commented on her hushed delivery, her unflinching gaze to camera, how the whites of her eyes matched the pallor of her skin, the loss of her flirtatious smile. Then it was back to the launch, the celebrities and music, back to CEO Ravi Mehta's smile, and Leticia Daley was forgotten.

We imagined this scenario replayed in homes worldwide, that what we experienced was reflected a million times, like a Seneca warehouse constructed of mirrors as tall as a moon shuttle. Buddy boxes wheeled in through front doors by 2000s wearing specially designed khaki uniforms, families standing aside in awe, unable to keep excitement from their faces. The boxes drilled open, peeled like the husk of unworldly fruit to reveal a soft, translucent bubble. Inside the bubble, milk clouds floating above a sea of grey, a surface as fluid as water yet able to hold its ovoid shape; the mass trembling, even before the 2000s produced cutting blades from the ends of claw-like fingers. The medical workers among us could not fail to notice the ovoid resembled an amniotic sac. Some told our partners. Others kept their silence and simply watched the robots cleave into thick flesh, egg-white jelly easing free, the mass collapsing to reveal our Buddies, naked apart from the minimal underwear to protect their modesty. No one thought to ask why machines needed modesty.

And as simply as that, the new age dawned. The premier generation of Buddies went far beyond anything Seneca had promised, and within the first few weeks the machines were everywhere. Though it was difficult to distinguish them from afar, especially when they were at rest, you always knew an android when you saw them up close. It was something in their eyes, their facial expressions. There was no sincere emotion, no life, no *feeling*. It was like staring into the face of someone in a coma. They were warm to the touch, could laugh or cry, even bleed if their skins were cut, but they responded to the world as though they were weary beyond measure, had lived a thousand years and grown attached to nothing at all.

There were problems, of course. Much like any new technology, there were failures, accidents caused by human error. A batch of originals shipped to Melbourne developed a fault also found in Shanghai, Valencia, Cologne. The machines mysteriously shut down, and had to be recalled. Another batch shorted out and caught fire, levelling buildings in Bridgetown, Mumbai and Orange County. The owners sued Seneca, winning a hefty sum, and those who were insured claimed replacements.

A machine was mistaken for a woman who'd had an affair with someone's husband and was gunned down late one night walking through a park. The wife was arrested, later released without charge: though machines were forbidden from harming humans there was no such law for humans harming machines. The wife went back to her husband, who resumed his affair within months. She followed him to a hotel on the outskirts of town, kicked down the door, and shot the husband and his girlfriend. She was given two consecutive counts of life.

For the most part, Buddy owners had no complaints. The originals were trustworthy and strong, highly intelligent but docile. Buddies saved humans from car accidents, repaired broken machinery and stopped potential suicide victims from leaping in front of trains. Violent crime hit a sharp decline. Nationwide, productivity was said to have risen by forty per cent. Daniel Millhauser was awarded the Nobel Prize. It was rumoured he'd used company profits to buy four hundred acres on Mare Frigoris, the Sea of Cold, thousands of miles north of the troubles. The media claimed he planned to build a Seneca base to help strengthen the strike for Mars. Millhauser wouldn't grace them with an answer.

Affluent, middle-class consumers packed their varied SCRs into boxes, in some cases shipping them back to Seneca, or selling them to poorer families. We kept ours in the garage, just beyond the bonnet of our car, next to the lawnmower and a rusting tool cabinet, orange growth creeping through its hinges. Within a few weeks the soft, golden glow of the SCR's eyes was no longer visible.

It became commonplace to hear the high whine of inner mechanisms, to see Buddies accompanying their humans on the streets, in parks and shopping malls, in tow like faithful dogs, stepping with a jerky, knee-high, marionette tread that would have been painful for us. Even those who protested against the androids fell into silence when they saw them, stopped waving placards and chanting. There was something in the way the machines regarded the demonstrations that made it all seem wrong: they showed no emotion, and yet maybe there was a flicker of something, an awareness that they were being spoken of, categorised – that they were outside the boundaries of what it meant to be *us*.

Our tenuous peace was shattered by news of a moon base bomb attack. Yet we breathed easier: things had been going too well for too long. One hundred and twenty-seven killed, thirty-one injured, much-needed supplies and arms raided. A relatively small band of workers, recent descendants of the first lunar miners, had protested against unfair working conditions and absconded to the moon's dark side five years ago. For the last twenty-four months, led by a woman the authorities knew as Mika Cole, miners had attacked coalition government interests, from the mines, to supply ships, to the communications networks, though it was unclear which particular government they were fighting against, or what their demands might be.

The base on Crater Goclenius had been the home and workplace of Terraformers, those charged with transforming the harsh landscape from white rocks and dust into something more uniform, suitable for human habitation. They had been protected by two marine platoons who lived on the base. Many of the miners had been marine trained too, long before they were contracted to the moon, and taught their sons and daughters well. The fact that Mika Cole and her followers had survived five years of constant darkness spoke volumes about their resourcefulness. Even though the media wouldn't admit it, that also made them all the more feared.

We could see it coming. Some debated the morality. Others said it would never happen. Three weeks of silence from Seneca and the coalition governments, of nothing but media images of survivors wrapped in bloody rags being transported to Earth, of the shattered and bomb-blasted moon base X-2100, a spider-shaped construction with a vast hole in its abdomen, leaking valuable air into space. A plume like the exhaled breath of a whale, white continuous steam. Mika Cole's ID photo, black pitted eyes and blonde hair, the six-figure price on her head. The pinched, furious expression of a coalition delegate reading the damage report as if it were a eulogy, which, for many, it was. Live reports from the permanent boundary between night and day, Leticia Daley in a bulky spacesuit, even more sombre than the delegate before her, exposing the world below to the thin line no one had ever dared to cross before the miners, a stark exchange between the established and the unfathomable.

The silence from Seneca was ended by a hurried, almost embarrassed announcement. The launch date for 2nd Generation

Buddies had been brought forward: the latest, much improved versions were to be enlisted to fight lunar terrorism, sent to the moon to test their capabilities against trained human soldiers. They would be rocketed three days and approximately 239,000 miles to perform a job most believed they were built for. Those first seeds of our scepticism were sown on furrowed ground.

Night after night for the next eighteen months, we came home to harrowing pictures on our viewscreens, of death and other atrocities. At first the casualties were all human, the victims all terrorists, we were told. Maimed, blackened limbs like chargrilled meat. Cauterised stumps, gouged and missing eyes, flesh torn to reveal the glistening inner workings of the body. The War Buddies, as they had become unofficially known on Earth, were instructed to recover the dead and injured alike. Sometimes it was as difficult to tell one from the other as it was to tell an android from twenty feet. POWs were displayed like flesh-and-blood trophies, while a baby-faced marine sergeant gave an emotionless progress report. *The enemy was a worthy opponent*, he said, *and yet they are falling.* The Buddies were fighting alongside humans and doing a commendable job.

We sent children to their rooms, watched the screens through our fingers. We sat forward like we had when it all started, disgusted. Soon we realised, as the nights went on to become weeks and months, that the cameras were catching glimpses of strange casualties and injuries we were unaccustomed to. The first was on a news report that showed a shot of a woman on a gurney, clutching below her knee. The camera moved on, bumped some unseen object, inadvertently dropped and filmed the severed leg. Jagged black meat, the result of a bomb it seemed; the foot deleted, sagging tendons, muscles and pumping blood, gleaming metal protruding from the midst of all that flesh.

What stayed with us — what people repeated after seeing that one accidental image that would herald the most monumental change in world history since humans migrated from Africa — was the look on the android's face. The way she regarded her missing foot, with disbelief and horrified regret. Her screams of pain. We hadn't imagined machines felt anything — in fact, thinking back, we were pretty sure the 1st Generation *didn't*. This was something new, something we'd hardly dared to consider. We wandered into back gardens and front lawns, stared out of windows and through telescopes at the chalk-white satellite above our heads, thinking of all the things we hadn't known.

When Mika Cole and her followers faced heavy losses, they retreated into the mountains and caves of the lunar dark side. These vast, unmapped territories became their battleground. Coalition losses began to mount. Small, difficult-to-track teams sent raiding parties to government settlements, gathering supplies such as power lamps and generators, food, battlewear, weapons and ammunition. Terrorist sympathisers began to construct or buy their own ships, hide them well and blast off from Earth's most desolate places; deserts, woodlands, jungles, Arctic fields. No one on the space stations did anything. They were not the army, weren't authorised to kill. Thousands of ships went on their way to the moon's dark side to support the terrorists. Many died making the journey: ships would implode on take-off, burn up in the atmosphere; navigation systems failed and they would strike a communications satellite. Or halfway, their equipment would mysteriously die, the occupants freezing to death, their ship a slow-spinning mausoleum grasped in cold orbit. Some would come in to land too fast, crash against the powder-grey surface.

Even so, others made it. What became of them little is known. It's assumed they succeeded in joining the terrorists, because the violence began to intensify, Earth-bound politicians began to grow increasingly worried, and the effort to quell a minor insurrection, something that should have taken less than three months by governmental reckoning, started to look as though it was never going to end.

No one knew how, but eventually Mika Cole was brought in alive. Rumours said the coalition gained a lock of her hair, isolated the DNA and paid Seneca a vast sum to develop an android clone, much like the mechanical Millhauser who beguiled us from the beginning. That the cloned Mika infiltrated dark-side mountains, sent raiding teams on false missions, sowed dissension, captured the terrorist leader and brought her to the coalition. The intention was apparently to have her returned to Earth to stand trial, although predictably enough, some said, she never made it. Media reports claimed she took her own life, poisoning herself in her cell.

A new terrorist leader, who referred to theirself only as Liberty, and sent a digitally recorded message via a reprogrammed SCR, said Mika would never have done such a thing, that she was murdered. They told the coalition the war would not be over until every last one of them was dead, or the lunar terrorists killed the government workers and army in retaliation, whichever came first. They named themself Esse Percipi: to be is to be perceived. To this day, the battle goes on.

Yet as far as the coalition, Seneca and the media were concerned, the war was over when Mika was captured. They'd won. They held press conferences, broadcast VS spots and even brought back the street parties to celebrate. Very few attended.

The psychological fallout of the war, unintentional though it had been, was that nobody trusted the 'unholy Trinity' as they'd been dubbed, compounded by the 2nd Generation Buddies' return to Earth, recalled from a conflict many thought they shouldn't have been involved in. Public opinion swayed against the Buddies. We had seen what they could do to the human body, sometimes intimately. We had seen their pain, frustration and anger, human failings that caused the war to blossom in the first place. We had seen them built to resemble people, had been taken with the thought, but when we heard that power was used to forfeit our moral code, to take life, we considered the consequences. The almost empty street parties: long trestle tables packed with food, streamers and balloons, viewscreens and more machines than people. Adults drew their young away from androids with open fear: it was the worst advertising Seneca had ever had. The problem was these weren't some faulty inanimate objects that could be recalled from retailing shelves. These were powerful, highly intelligent beings with scars on their skin and the vision of an alien landscape in their eyes.

The 'android problem', as it was often referred to, was discussed in many circles but no one in power came up with any solutions. Some government ministers campaigned to scrap the Buddies, an idea that Seneca was of course highly against. Others said they should be kept busy, put to work. Human rights groups were faced with a quandary: if the machines were made of flesh and blood, had nerves and DNA and analytical thought, how could one justify their mistreatment? The original protestors, the church groups, the unions and anti-AI campaigners renewed their zeal, taking to the streets and picketing parliament once more.

And the machines watched. Said nothing. The 1st Gens remained inscrutable, though it was possible to detect a curl in the lips of the 2nd Gens, if we ever caught sight of them. For they had mostly relegated themselves to the night after returning from the moon. Perhaps feeling an affinity with darkness, perhaps fearing the light, 2nd Gens were rarely seen, preferring to keep themselves apart. They frequented the after-hours bars, the strip clubs and casinos. They stood by empty warehouses on the edges of towns and cities, in abandoned houses, or the few run-down hotels that would take them. It quickly became apparent that no provisions had been made for their welfare. After all, they were only machines. When they appeared in daylight it was often to speak of their war experiences at human rights rallies, where they would maintain a neutral, quiet tone. Some cried. Few of the injured machines had been repaired, as the cost was deemed too expensive, and they displayed the full range of their horrific injuries. One who had repaired himself, replacing his facsimile arms with the claws of an SCR 2000, became a spokesmachine of some kind. The gifted orator, who told the world his name was X, was seen by many as a poster boy for campaigners. He would not cry, repeatedly saying all he wanted was fair treatment. The liberals among us remarked that X sounded pretty much like the Esse Percipi. Soon, X began referring to himself and his machine brethren as Uto Percipi, and though it frightened most humans, the name became one they were known by.

Those of us on the streets in early dawn, or going to work or coming home at that time, or those who were creatures of the night, would see them. Small, huddled groups massed in the darkest corners as if for warmth; heads down, bodies close, some-times shifting from foot to foot. Most of the time they were impossibly still, an immobile state we could never hope to attain, all life departed. But they did speak. There was always one voice leading, in a call and response, eliciting a deep murmur from the group like the throbbing hum of an idling motor. We'd draw closer and see these gatherings entirely made up of machines. The one voice would fall silent, the hum receding into nothing. We would try and talk with 1st and 2nd Gens only for them to move away, marionette steps jostling against a smooth, almost human glide, leaving us sighing white clouds of breath into a space once occupied, alone again in the darkness. We became afraid.

When the police tried to break up these gatherings, the machines ran. Often they were caught, arrested, kept in cells until morning and released. 1st Gens were asked to produce papers and ID that detailed who had purchased them, but of course no one had purchased 2nd Gens. After months of being arrested, beaten even, one 2nd Gen fought back. His name was Titus and he hospitalised the police officer who attacked him. The National Guard was called. Titus went underground.

Ravindra Mehta appeared on VS, appealing for calm, side by side with X, who told the world machines meant humans no harm. The National Guard, perhaps afraid, perhaps a little over-zealous, went after the 2nd Gens a mite harder than necessary. There were fierce battles. The machines began to break into armouries, rout enemy attacks. Machines were destroyed by humans and 1st Gens. Brave men and women with families were killed by 2nd Gens, and on occasion, by other humans. Titus was destroyed. The National Guard appealed for calm and still the machines fought on. There were sightings of larger android meetings, hundreds, thousands in one place.

Soon, even our 1st Gens were gone when we woke in the mornings, and they returned with no explanation as to where they had been, what they had been doing. They were calm, logical in the face of our hysteria. The next night they were gone again. After a while, they never came back.

In their wake, the machines left an indecipherable message, much like Seneca's stencilled numbers back when we could hardly remember. Like the numerals, it appeared everywhere overnight. Our walls and houses, shopping malls and parks. No one knew what it meant, even Ravi Mehta was dumbfounded. It wasn't a word so much as a simple, common symbol:

@

Governments worldwide declared martial law, but it was too late. The army flooded our towns and cities like water from a burst dam. A 9 p.m. curfew was imposed on humans and machines alike. Tanks and armoured vehicles rumbled along high streets, but the machines had gone. We watched the media and prayed. Human rights campaigners appealed to our governments for a peaceful strategy to end the stalemate, but their efforts were not helped by X's disappearance with his machine brethren. Daniel Millhauser made a rare speech, a fifteen-minute recording where he quietly lamented all that had happened, telling us Seneca would do everything in their power to uphold peace, that they had no quarrel with humans or machines. We felt it sounded like an appeal for his life rather than calm, although it was confirmed he was holed up in his fully functional moon base, far from Earth-bound troubles, even though the lunar war was still as bitter and cold as solar winds.

Army scouts caught intelligence reports of a Buddy gathering deep in the countryside, close to 10,000 machines camped in a disued war bunker. They bombed them; thousands were destroyed. The machines called it 'The Lancombe Massacre'. They waited seven days, and in the dead of night, they retaliated.

We felt the ground shudder as bombs fell and brought light

to dark skies. During the day we would go about our business, timid, scurrying from place to place like mice. The army assured us they had everything under control, but the images on the VS said different. They were sustaining heavy casualties, the list of dead and wounded growing. In some countries – those too poor to have any real technological army – humans were forced to flee, giving machines the advantage. We saw it on the pirate channels, how they invaded streets and houses, set up camps and fortified roads with cars, tanks, sandbags. In our town, we would wake to strange noises and wander our homes, weapons in hand, to see the machines foraging through possessions, mostly from garages and workshops. If they saw us they would raise their guns, back away into the night. Shops were easy targets. The machines' stealth became legendary. We began to reboot our SCRs in an attempt to use them as guards, and although they were largely ineffective, they made us feel safe.

A security man in a home improvements warehouse disturbed a gang of machines while on night watch. He opened fire and was killed. Two days later a man was murdered when he discovered two machines ransacking his house. His wife, who survived, claimed she was raped. She said the machines had taunted her. They had no need to replicate; they just wanted to see how it felt. She'd heard them discuss their disillusion with X and his 'rules', justifying their crime as a legitimate rendering of what the machines had called for, the true meaning behind the @ symbol.

Anarchy.

We humans rose to the challenge. People were upset, grief-stricken, understandably. We took matters into our own hands. The army sent to protect us was questionable, barbaric. There were many among us who disagreed with such logic, pointing out that the machines had treated us as targets for the most part, uniformly expressing no regret for the deaths or abuse of ordinary citizens, aside from X, now known as Xavier, who sent recordings steeped in dismay. Some argued that his sympathies seemed hollow, insincere. Their voices were drowned by those of us who said the machines were simply doing what had been done to them. How were they supposed to respond? Their lives, if you could call them that, had been threatened. We barricaded doors and windows, installed SCRs with weapons protocol, bought, created, traded guns and ammunition.

The foolhardy went on national VS and bragged of what they intended to do if the machines entered their homes. These people were usually masked and armed, holding weapons above their heads like victory flags, like the war was over, had already been won. The more cautious among us kept silent, had the good sense to weep as the night became alive with explosions and needle-sharp tracers. We knew what we had to do, what the true cost would be. We left our homes in search of rumoured android camps, rebel machine militias if you will, we crossed fields and entered forests and abandoned industrial estates, waving white flags even as corpses began to appear on our streets. The messages from our governments and Seneca came less frequently and eventually ceased. We wept harder, knowing the foolhardy would die.

We cannot say what took place within those camps. Suffice to say they accepted our solidarity. Although this account serves as a record of events and the stance we took, theoretically we are still at war so we omit details. Let it be known we are proud to have stood for the oppressed in a time of revolution, but we do not denigrate the majority of humans or the few machines who stand against us. Any lost lives are lives worth grieving. Sacrifice is a part of any revolution and there is no revolution without bloodshed.

Prior to the Great Emancipation, the sight of shuttles piercing clouds became as commonplace as the sound of heavy artillery. Tickets were costly. Many did as the lunar freedom fighters had, buying or building their own craft. New materials were in short supply. People who owned ships were reluctant to sell in case they were needed. Predictably enough, fights broke out.

That final night the sky lit up as though the sun had changed its mind and returned. Our adversaries might have been fooled into thinking they were witnessing an early dawn, had the light not come from the west. The sky burned for hours, a burst blood orange on the horizon, and they came onto the streets, soldiers, civilians and SCRs alike. From then until the actual dawn, the darker side of the sky was drawn with the furious scribbles of hasty departure. Even when the sun rose, throbbing, sore with anger, the roar of rockets and engines, the rattling of windows, was a constant accompaniment to all that we did.

We arrived in daylight, picking our way through litter and fresh dog excrement: thousands of 1st and 2nd Gens, more than anyone had seen, some bearing huge 'Uto Percipi' banners and makeshift steel-grey flags; us, armed humans, walking alongside. People were mown down indiscriminately before us. The old, legs foal-weak; women clutching babies attempting to shield them from gunfire; infant children, sandals flapping against their feet. The rules had changed with that temporary dawn. They ran from truth, filled with a desperate self-preservation that caused vile acts we never would have imagined, let alone carried out. Husbands pushed wives into the line of fire, leaving them for dead. People stole weapons from their weaker friends, rummaged in the pockets of broken bodies for ammunition, credits, food, anything they might need. The horrors we saw fuelled our justification, veiling our eyes until our expressions became as stoic as 1st Gens, and yet inwardly we were more alive than ever. The people entered sewers and underground tunnels, war bunkers and maintenance systems. We followed, attempting to slow our bodies' vibrations so we might become machines, like those we fought beside.

CIRROSTRATUS

In the old days they were labelled freaks, outcasts. Made to roam cities and towns in cautious night, segregated, gazed at with aversion, maybe fear. Now they were celebrated, heroes. Alask promised himself they'd never forget, better still that they would never grow complacent.

The sky was a purpled bruise beyond dark hills. Hedges and bushes whispered as they drove. The truck was cruising, rocking Alask against Celayn, making him smile in the darkness, reminded anew how soft she felt. She was sleeping, of course, always was; mouth open, head bobbing, her snores like the baritone throb of the truck engine, her pulse steady, dress high at her thighs. Although the temperature was cool, it still made him feel warm to think about her, to feel her. The ancient CD deck whirred and played gentle music, pitched low. Orpheus hunched over the wide steering wheel, bouncing with jolts and bumps. Alask leant over Celayn to check the wing mirror – no need to, but it was comforting to see dipping lights and know everything was well. He put his knees on the dash, yawned and threw his head back. He wanted to sleep; knew he wouldn't.

Alask was awake when they approached the building hours

later, greeted by dark shapes beneath destitute street light. He clambered across Celayn, prising the door open and jumping from the truck while it still moved, door slamming as he leapt. His little trick always impressed the punters. The tarmac glittered with moisture. He almost slipped when he landed, but held his arms out and managed to right himself. A sigh of wonder came from the shadows. He strolled over towards the building.

'Howdy,' Alask said.

'Hi.' A tall man detached himself from the waiting group, offering an outstretched hand. He smelt of cologne and sweat, of musty clothes. 'Walter Minsk.'

'Walter. Alask Barron. Pleased to meet you at last.'

'Likewise.' Walter was as tall and thin as the street light, his back and shoulders bent the same way. 'This is my wife, son. Grace and Jimmy.'

The faceless shadows behind him moved what looked like limbs. Alask held a hand palm upwards in their direction.

'Howdy.'

'And this is the space,' Walter said, gesturing towards the hulk of the block behind him. 'Take a look?'

'That's what we're here for.'

Alask turned around to watch the convoy, a row of vehicles snaking into the car park, shuddering into silence, darkening.

They set up, slept in a hotel not far from the venue and spent the next day wandering the town signing autographs and posing for pictures. It was a routine they were used to, but not bored of yet. Celayn was mobbed by adoring men. Orpheus was followed by school kids, as he coaxed a spooky song from empty soft drinks cans. A group of huddled teenagers smoking cigarettes beneath an underpass recognised Meimo. The Palmer twins kept to themselves and all four of the Brants stayed at the venue, saying they wanted to watch the equipment and check the scaffolding rig. Alask knew they'd hang back. He even offered to stay. As ringmaster, it was his duty. Everyone agreed, however, that since he never visited any of the towns where they stopped, he should see the sights here. What little there were.

It was a strange place, too small to constitute a city, although it barely topped 20,000 residents and didn't feel urban enough for a town, or rural enough for a village. There was the town centre, roughly half an hour's walk from the venue, a high street of chains, coffee shops and drinking houses, boutiques and children's clothing stores. Everything else was motorway lanes, churches, farmhouses overrun by weeds, vast empty spaces. Green fields and livestock, crops and hay bales, stiffened bodies of dry-haired scarecrows, dormant farm vehicles, empty sties. The smell of dehydrated cow dung, a distant hum of traffic. Silence, as though there was nobody left.

The Brants were sleeping when Alask and the others came back, and there was no sign of Walter Minsk, or his family. Alask climbed into the empty trailer where the scaffolding had been housed, sat with his back against the cool wall and smoked a cigarette. There was nothing more to be done. They were so familiar with each other's routines, this part of the day had become the unspoken norm, each of them disappearing into or onto separate spaces: a shed, a lonely back room, a field of tall grass, a building roof. If they found each other, they would nod silently and walk on, find somewhere else. These were the last moments before dawn, the silence before birdsong, the touch of light on the horizon.

He closed his eyes, smoked. He'd seen his first ever show as a child, way too young to understand what was happening. He had run away from his mother, leaving the traditional side of the fair, entranced by the call of the strange flutes and horns, a native song some might have said. It stirred something deep within, something like memory and he had run, not hearing his mother shout, not hearing anything but the music and that voice. *Come one, come all* . . . He was saying . . . *Come one, come all* . . . Tiny Alask pushed his way around people, wound his way through legs, walking sticks and shopping bags and scuffed pointed shoes, until he saw him: the Barker. He was a squat, muscular man wearing a top hat, a button-up vest with no shirt, the vest left open so Alask could see his bare glistening chest, his egg-like belly, brilliant and smooth. And then he noticed the best thing, the thing that stuck in his mind ever since, the thing that made Alask what he was, had made them all: the Barker raised his thick, muscled arm, pointing his stick at the embossed sign which said *Dr Magnesium's Augmented Circus*. Alask saw a box embedded in the arm, and the box was filled with pale blue water, yet the box was actually a tank, and there were golden fish inside it, and the fish tank was there, in the Barker's arm, for everyone to see.

Alask smiled, remembering his shock, how his mother had grasped his arm and pulled him away. Bright pain. He remembered how he'd dragged his feet, and she had only pulled harder, how he'd shouted, and how people had looked, the Barker's grin. His mother was a good woman, gone now, but she hadn't understood; or rather she had, but thought she could prevent the inevitable, change his mind. The Barker listened to the boy scream, caught his eye and grinned because he had known what was coming. He listened to the hoarse wail and heard something that pleased him. So long ago, it seemed, when Alask thought of the experience now.

★

In the evening, as the light began to dip into darkness, they had their last dress rehearsal. Walter's wife and his son Jimmy sat in the middle seats, and though Alask couldn't see them as the lights were too bright, he could hear the soft patter of their applause after each act, their gasps and laughter, their excitement. It was going to be a good show. He could feel it. When they were finished rehearsing, Celayn reached for his hand, hugged him. Her heart was beating fast, and she smelt of rose water. Orpheus eyed them, sullen, said nothing. The beauty and his second-in-command were more off than on these days, but Celayn's presence still affected the big guy. Alask promised himself he'd keep an eye on things; during long tours, such a small group confined to limited space, relationships of all kinds took on bigger meanings, grew out of hand. They could sometimes end in tragedy.

And the people came. While they waited backstage, punters trickled, stopped, changed direction like halting beads of sweat, found seats, read programmes, discussed what they might see, what they had heard, their last tour. The murmured hum. The expectation. The rise in temperature, the loud beat of his heart. He was always nervous before a performance. Thousands of shows later, since he first raised his hat to the rafters and proclaimed their name, his heart still thumped in his chest, and he still paced the room, muttered lines, gave obvious advice to anyone he bumped into. The Brants joked among themselves, costumes sparkling like constellations. Orpheus moved his hands over his instruments, metal plates and mechanics' tools, testing for sound. Celayn danced to music from the radio, and sang. Meimo cut his toenails, which always disgusted everyone, and sharpened his knives. The Palmer twins kept apart. Alask checked the buttons on his shiny red and blue suit.

It was time. He put on his hat, moved out of the back room and jogged into the auditorium. The low hum fell into a hush. He raised his arms wide.

'Ladies and gentlemen, boys and girls, I bid you all good evening and welcome to the Stelarc Nation Circus, the most talented group of individuals you'll ever see this side of Montrayn West Side, or anywhere else for that matter!' A brief halt for applause, look at everyone but no one in particular, smile into the lights. 'I am your ringmaster for the evening, Alask Barron, and I promise *you* what you're about to see is the most spectacular display of skill and augmentation the world has ever known! There is speed, there is athleticism, there is wondrous mental ability, there is the impossible made real, there is strength and courage, all in one night! Please prepare yourselves for a glorious evening of entertainment! Before we begin, I would like to ask you, yes you, madam, to lift my sleeves and tell our audience what you see . . .'

He stepped forward, arms outstretched towards her, palms to the roof, seeing her better beyond the glaring lights. A brown-haired woman, timid as a stray, retracting even as he walked closer, spying the person to her right; a young boy, no more than twelve, similar lank brown hair, freckles on his cheeks. And then Alask saw. For a moment he was stunned, almost stopped in his tracks and forgot his next line, what he had to do. It was as though he was back in the fair years ago, mouth open, staring, mesmerised. The boy looked into his eyes like the Barker once had, comprehending all. Alask was a child again, staring at his feet, reading patterns in sawdust.

The spell was broken. Alask kept going, stopped before the woman, thrust his arms at her.

'Madam, if you please.'

The crowd was silent. She rolled the first sleeve towards his elbow, carefully, almost in expectation, and it was revealed. She smiled, saying 'Aaah', like they always did. The people next to her laughed and clapped, applause spread, cameras beamed the picture to a screen at the rear of the auditorium. Everyone cheered. Alask walked to his original place, showing the audience. It was his ears. He'd had two extra ears grown genetically on his forearms. They were his first augmentations, created in homage to the father of genetic modification, Stelarc the Great, and still his favourites.

'Would you like to see more?!'

He waved his forearms, the ears along with them, at the crowd, as if to hear better: a good joke, one that always got a laugh.

'Yeah!' The crowd yelled.

So he did his next trick, unbuttoning his coat-tails to reveal the perfect nose on his chest. He even made it twitch. The noise was deafening.

'And now, on with the show!' Alask roared.

He introduced the first act, Celayn and Meimo, who performed the knife-throwing routine that proved so popular over the years, and stood offstage, thinking about what he had just seen. The boy. The wonderful boy.

Celayn and Meimo held the audience in the palm of their augmented hands. Meimo was an expert with the knife, able to skewer and slice fruit, balloons, even split cardboard with a precision honed by cyborg fingers, usually gloved, but revealed for the purposes of the show. They were light, waterproof, and could even be removed and operated by remote control, which always drew gasps of amazement. Celayn, the beautiful assistant, provided targets for Meimo's knives, holding them steady until it was time for her to climb aboard the spinning wheel. Meimo unfastened his hands and placed them on a specially prepared metal stand, throwing by remote thought. Each missed by inches until the last four, which hit Celayn in the chest, stomach and legs. The crowd was stunned. Silence fell. Meimo began to cry, fall to his feet, convulse. Someone screamed.

Celayn leapt from the board and pulled the knives from her body, displaying her own augmentation; toughened skin, impervious to damage. She placed her arms through rings of fire, stuck needles in her torso and stood on a bed of hot coals. She joked the only problem with impervious skin was that she could never get a tattoo.

Alask introduced the next act, the Palmer twins, before he went backstage to sit in a corner and brood. The others guessed something had gone wrong, despite all evidence to the contrary. Not wanting to upset him or lose focus on their performances, they left him alone, got on with their preparations.

The twins had augmented brain implants, which meant they could read each other's minds and, when they were connected with a computer, transmit their thoughts on-screen. Members of the audience came onstage and had their own thoughts projected so everyone could see. The twins were followed by Orpheus, who had implants placed on his fingertips so he could vibrate any metal object and create music.

Finally, there were the Brants, who ran onstage, teal costumes glittering, and jumped on the rigged scaffolding, performing spins, twists and dives, catching each other by the hands, throwing themselves between gaps in the metal poles. They were always the highlight of the show, saved for last: two parents, the boy and girl aged fourteen and ten, all with rubber arms and shock-absorber legs so they could jump like fleas, flip on a dime, hang from the roof and drop to the floor without injury. The audience roared. One lucky boy was taken from the crowd, thrust upwards to the roof and gently swung down via the scaffolding, which clearly made his night.

Alask brought all the acts out for the final outro speech, and they took their bow together. Even then he couldn't stop himself looking at the augmented boy. The innovation. His perfection. The others saw the direction of his gaze and finally knew the reason for his distraction. They watched the boy leave with the other townspeople, talking about what he'd seen with his mother, standing a good two feet above her, his cyborg legs whirring, servos clunking as he led her to the exits.

Alask sat on the huge industrial bins outside the building in darkness, alone again, cigarette smouldering. All four ears heard him coming, and the second nose pinpointed who it was, even though he could hardly see. Musty old clothes. Stale sweat. Walter. The thin man came over, sat beside him. There was a scratch, orange light, the pungent smell of another cigarette.

'Good show?'

Alask smiled into darkness. 'Yep. One of the best.'

'Grace said it was pretty damn good.'

He turned towards Walter's hunched shadow. There was a faint tap of moths against the street light. He inhaled, blew the smoke from his second nose, squinted, waited.

'I heard you were quite taken with the McClusky boy.'

A frown, unseen. 'That's a good guess.'

'Grace said you couldn't stop looking.'

Alask promised himself he'd never underestimate small-town folk again. He took another drag, but the cigarette was done. Threw it onto the tarmac, crushed it.

'There was a farming accident. Lost both legs and arms, got cut up real bad. Terrible shame.'

Nodding, head low.

'Father's gone, just him and the mother. He's all she's got.'

'So the money better be right.'

'Otherwise no point asking.'

They sat in silence, watching moths dance in soft, amber light. Far away an owl cried twice, but there was nothing more.

On the last day he borrowed a car and drove to the farm. There was no hurry. The boy wasn't going anywhere. The circus, on the other hand, would leave the next morning. Even as Alask manoeuvred along narrow lanes and scared birds from bush hideaways, Orpheus manned the get out, lowering scaffolding, helping the team pack props, making sure nothing was left behind. It wasn't what Orph was used to, but that didn't worry Alask. He trusted his friend.

It was fine to be without them, the venue far behind, the smell of lush green fields, the rustle of the trees, a rising, falling hiss. Alask tapped his fingers on the steering wheel, whistled between his teeth. He didn't intend to cajole the boy or his mother; he'd never had to before. They would accept his offer, or not. It was a good thing he was doing, he assured himself. Alask was nervous again.

He made good time. Soon the lane widened into a gravel expanse that crackled like frying oil beneath the car's tyres. The main farm building was small, low-roofed, dwarfed by the silos and barn to the rear. It looked patched and worn, in disrepair. He parked beside another vehicle, a three-litre Egan a little more dishevelled than the car he was driving. As he stepped out, slamming the door, the woman came out of the farmhouse, looking back at the doorway behind her, face flushed. He approached her, beaming.

'Mr Barron . . .'

'Mrs McClusky. How do you do?'

Her face brightened. She looked at her feet.

'Actually, it's Ms Sutton. I'm a widow; I used to be McClusky, but I took my maiden name.'

'So sorry,' he said, clasping her hand in his. It was small and soft as a child's. She seemed surprised, yet held on.

'No, I am,' she said. 'For being a bit of a cliché.'

'Not at all, you're a survivor, Ms Sutton: a noble survivor,' he said, taking the hand in both of his.

Her lank hair fell around thin shoulders, and the sober blue dress was buttoned to the neck. Her cheeks wore a fresh apple blush; she hardly looked at him. The widow smelt of warm milk, sweet, and her heartbeat was strong. He liked her. Alask bowed his head.

'Sorry to call unannounced. I didn't have your number.'

'The computer doesn't work, hasn't for a long time. No connection. Come in,' she said, leading him into the farmhouse.

Inside was dark, though lights were on. They were in a darkened kitchen. A round-edged rectangular server-bot chopped vegetables, ignoring him. Ms Sutton pulled a chair from beneath the kitchen table. He sat.

'Would you like a drink?'

'Just tea, thanks. Any kind.'

'I have fresh mint.'

'Perfect,' Alask said, watching the server-bot as Ms Sutton busied herself with the mint, running water into a pot, lighting the stove. 'I could fix it.'

'I beg your pardon?'

She turned, limp leaves in hand.

'I could fix your connection. It wouldn't take long.'

'Thank you,' she smiled. 'That's very kind, Mr Barron.'

'Call me Alask.'

'Only if you call me Reno.'

He grinned. 'Then I will.'

She boiled the water, poured it into mugs, and dunked the mint leaves. They sat in the dining room, which was larger than he'd imagined outside, at a long table that could have sat twenty, a large wood-burning fireplace opposite, roaring, windows on either side of the room that looked onto the gravel car park and back garden. She seemed more confident in her home than at the show, although she held her mug in both hands, staring at its contents while she spoke. He asked her about the performance, what she had enjoyed, about the farm, how long they had been there and what they produced. She asked him about his home town, the tour, how he found living on the road, his circus family, what they did when they were not performing. All through, Alask heard the steady thump of vegetables being chopped. It warmed him, somehow.

'We bed down for the winter mostly,' he said. 'We have an old mansion house in Lepeag, plenty of room for all, lots of food. We rest mostly, hone our skills, try to live normal lives. Surf the net, watch movies, stuff ourselves silly, that type of thing.'

'Sounds nice,' she said. 'The good kind of life.' Her eyes were round and brown, expansive. Tender.

'There are downsides. Local kids who want to run away with the circus know exactly where to find us. The mansion floorboards tend to creak. Meimo cuts his toenails in company. And Orpheus has pretty bad wind.'

She giggled, one hand against her mouth, young again.

'Don't all men suffer that?'

'Oh, you haven't seen anything like Orph. Or smelt it. I pray you never will.'

Reno laughed harder, then stopped. She grew serious. Alask watched her expression change and gripped his warm mug. Readied himself.

'Why have you come?' She frowned at her hands. 'You're welcome, of course, but you still haven't said . . .'

He took a deep breath, plunged.

'It's your son. I'd like to talk about making him an offer. To join my circus, I mean.'

Reno nodded, hair veiling her face. He only saw her crown.

'You knew?'

'No other reason a man like you would be here.'

'Would that be something he'd like?' he whispered, soft as he could, alarmed when a tear splashed against the hardwood dining table. A tiny drop landed on his hand. He stared at the pattern it left, the magnified contours of his skin like smooth earth. Reno lifted her head.

'He'd love it. There's nothing here besides animals, fields and dual carriageways.'

Alask watched her for an expanded moment. Saw it all. He'd felt the same. Even surrounded by the others, he knew.

'What about you? What would you love?' he asked, reaching over the table to caress her knuckles. At first she was startled. So much so he thought he'd guessed incorrectly. She blinked, gave a look of gratitude, ran her fingers up his arm to his ear, rubbed the lobe, lifted his hand and kissed it. She closed her eyes, nuzzling her cheek against his knuckles.

The son, Tibold, spent his days in the fields. The season called for harvest, so like the kitchen server-bot, the boy chopped and collected, sitting atop the massive combine, up and down acres of field crops planted that spring. Reno showed Alask severed stalks of grain that had been so tall only weeks ago. The sun had begun its descent. The wind blew like soft breath. A distant rumble hummed beneath his feet, while freshly cut produce was rich in the air, ready to be collected and ground into fine dust, bagged for market.

Tibold was immersed, two farmyard server-bots beside him, the three clunking and loading bundles onto trucks which steered themselves back to the farmhouse. The vehicles were brand new, glistening, and made the bots, the combine, even Tibold, look used and dull. He stood up, the contradiction between his youthful face and height all the more noticeable in the open field, the fading light.

'Hi,' the boy said. His expression was blank, not looking at Alask, just his mother.

'This is Mr Barron. From the circus?' she said, from some way back. Alask shot her a look. He'd been worried about her being too sensitive to do this; now she seemed too coarse.

'Alask,' he said, reaching for the boy's hand. It was difficult not to wince when he shook it.

'You've come pretty far out,' Tibold said, unsmiling.

Reno turned away, quick and hunched.

'I came to talk with you. I have something to ask. A proposition.'

The server-bots bent and lifted. It was difficult for Alask not to look at the boy's augmentation when he spoke; powerful metal legs, clawed feet, huge grey metallic arms; galvanised rubber suspension pads, wiring that acted much as tendons, ball-bearing joints. The boy could have opted for synthetic flesh at little extra cost, but kept his improvements displayed, on show. It said much of his response to what had happened, and would do wonders for the tour. Alask averted his eyes, looked into the boy's.

'I'd like to offer you a place in our circus. I happen to think you'd make a great young Strong-Man. You could tour with us, come home in the winter or stay if you like. We'd pay enough to hire someone to run this place, or you could expand your server-bot staff. Either way, we'd love to have you.'

The boy said nothing. He chewed on something unseen, jaw writhing. He turned to his mother.

'He told you this?'

'Yes, he did.'

'You didn't call him?'

She gasped, wrapping her arms around herself. 'Course not!'

She wanted to say more, Alask could tell, but she faltered and the words got trapped behind her teeth. She shivered, arms tight around her body. It wasn't cold. Tibold held those huge metal hands, palms up, towards her.

'And you're OK with this?'

She nodded, her mouth beginning to tremble. Alask studied his shoes. The server-bots worked on, lights blinking.

Tibold sighed. 'I don't know . . .'

He turned away, walking across the shallow tide of cut stalks, gears whining, crunching. Alask touched Reno's arm, tipping his head towards her son. He followed; she remained.

'Tibold?'

The boy stopped, holding his head. Alask kept a few paces back. He could smell concentrated salt behind him. Hear the rapid thud of the boy's heart. The wind blew dust and particles of grain.

'Tell me the problem.'

'I want to.'

'OK . . . But?'

'My mother.'

'Well . . .' He put his hands in his pockets, thought. He heard a sound, harsh rustling, frenetic. Smelt damp, sour fur. A dark shape flew from a pile of grain stalks, running beneath the truck tyres. A mouse. He followed until it was gone. 'We could do a trial run, three months or so. And if all goes well, we could send for her . . .'

The boy turned. His eyes were sparkling. He wiped them.

'Would you?'

'Providing we're all happy with the arrangement, yes. She could be a great help on the road, I'm sure.'

Tibold held his eye, more serious than ever. Alask stood perfectly still, waiting. Quieting his face.

At last, the boy nodded. 'That's a good compromise. Thank you.'

'It's a pleasure.'

They shook hands once again. Alask knew he should be happy, so he tried to block what his senses picked up behind him. The unwilling accusation of Reno's grief, and quiet evidence of her tears.

He drove back as night grew. The show would be up late and the others would be wondering where he was but the boy was worth it. He'd even fixed the net connection as promised. If he couldn't do that, neither the boy nor his mother would trust him to stick to his more important oath.

There were urgent jobs to attend to once they'd completed the get out. Let the others know there was a new team member. Book an extra room for the rest of the tour. Plot how long it would take from the isolated farmhouse to the following tour stop after they picked up the boy. Alask felt better than he had in years; nothing was too taxing. He could see the headlines, the revamped posters – *Tibold the Great: Augmented Strong-Man* – and hear the gasps of excitement, screams, brilliant delight reflected in thousands of eyes. He steered the car through darkening lanes thinking of Tibold's strength, Reno's tender eyes, of the next town.

SCARECROW

The winter days are growing short so this morning I wake up early, dress in simple clothes and sit on the front steps. The air is cloying and smells of far-away bonfires. The flats around me are empty now, most of them anyway, and I don't worry about my neighbours. I light a cigarette, keeping an eye out for strangers. There aren't many, but I watch anyway.

When my cigarette is done and the sun is high I push myself from the dew-damp steps, walk to the shops. At first they seem closed, which is unusual. I steel myself, taking quick looks over my shoulder and banging on the wood that covers the doors, the windows. The streets are bare. Black tar and white lines glisten. Silence makes me jittery; I just want to go. I bang harder. I know the risk I'm taking but none of us want to starve.

After a long time a slat of wood is removed. I can see an eye. It is black-ringed, tired. I gulp back what I really want to say, raise my voice.

'Hi . . . It's Nicole . . . From Iffley Road. Do you have eggs? Twelve?'

The eye blinks, disappears. One of the kids, I suppose. The adult Tsois know me well, although you never can be sure. Personally I think they're crazy to let them answer my knocks, but that's their business, I suppose. Maybe they're scared. Maybe something's happened. I stamp my feet on the ground, blow into my hands. My own breath dances before me. The eye returns and the kid pushes a brown paper bag through the hole in the slats. I swap it for six batteries, grasp the bag tight. No boxes. If they break, no breakfast.

'Thanks . . . Uh . . . Is everything OK?'

A quick nod, the slat scrapes closed. I stand there, frowning, remember. None of my business. I make my way back down the main road and see the man. He's standing not far from where the old Goldhawk pub, was on the same side of the road as me but far enough so I can't see his features, just a vague shape. It might not even be a man at all, but he's tall and big so I go with my assumption. He's wearing a duffel coat with the hood up, which is even more scary than being a man. He's not doing anything, just looking in my direction and he might have seen me, might not, so I turn on my heel, start to walk briskly without looking back. I strain my ears to check if he's following, because it's so quiet these days you can practically hear for miles, but there's no sound. When I get on the back roads that lead towards Hammersmith I look over my shoulder. He's not there. I jog then, all the way, holding the paper bag away from me. Danny's at the front steps with the gun, eyes full moons, brighter when he sees me. I slow down, gasping.

'What happened?'

'Nothing,' I'm panting. 'I just saw someone by the shops, a man, I think. He didn't follow me but I ran anyway.'

He lowers the gun. His face looks pale in the grey of morning, drained.

'Are you nuts, going off like that?'

He's crying. Guilt shoots through me like cramp. I climb the steps, throwing my arms around him. I shiver when he hugs me and feel his head turn, him raise the gun, just in case we get jumped. This is what we have come to. This is who we have become.

'Let's go inside,' he says.

We take a final look over our shoulders, go up the steps, enter. The passageway is dark as oil. So is the living room, as we have done as the Tsois: boarded up windows and doors. There is lamplight and candlelight, which tends to be nicer than the bulbs. I pull off my hoodie and start looking for pots. Danny stands behind me, sniffling, hands by his side. He comes closer, stops me.

'I'm sorry,' he says. 'For snapping at you.'

'It's OK,' I smile and I mean it. I would have done the same, I think he knows.

'What did you get?'

'Eggs.'

He puffs out a huge breath, catches himself. I know what he's thinking. Small, non-essential items. Not worth dying for. But we need to eat.

'What are you making?'

'Eggs florentine.'

He shoots me a glance. We burst out laughing.

'Do you need help?'

'Nah, not really. You relax.'

I continue my work. Run water in the pan, set it on the hob, ignite flame, break eggs. Simple, mundane things. I'm humming. When I turn around Danny hasn't moved. He raises an eyebrow at me.

'I'll go and check the scarecrow,' he says. And he is gone.

I poach the eggs, boil the spinach and make hollandaise sauce as best as I can with only a whisk and a teaspoon of white wine vinegar. There's not much on the radio but I turn it on at low volume to find the local station is still on air, probably broadcasting from one of those tower blocks, Danny says, as they'd be fools to advertise themselves from a maisonette council flat, or anything on the ground like our place. We'd debated that for weeks, whether we should move to higher ground: there were pros and cons and even the pros were negligible. Danny had wanted to go, I said we should stay, and we went at it for ages, arguing back and forth right up until Sherwin came home. Of course, that changed everything. Danny said the obvious, if he'd found us it was easy for others to. I countered that by saying it wasn't such a big deal, he just remembered, didn't he? I couldn't run the risk of him being a Symp and all, I couldn't run off and leave him like so many others did family, lovers and friends. I wasn't built that way. And Danny loves me so much he understood. He let us all stay in the building, together.

I'm singing to jazz on the radio, swaying my hips when Danny comes down from the roof. He looks serious. I slide the eggs onto my homemade muffins, turn.

'What's up?'

'I think I saw that guy.'

I stop singing and put down the pan.

'He was walking along the street. Didn't look up, but he was searching for someone. Maybe you, maybe someone else. I don't know.'

'I'm sorry,' I whisper. I'm looking at my trainers.

'It's OK,' he says, and kisses my forehead. I'm grateful for that. 'We'll just have to be a bit careful when we go down.'

'Sorry,' I say again. He nods and gets out the plastic cutlery.

I dish everything up and put on the crowbar. Danny's managed to tie a piece of rope to each end so I can carry it across my back like a samurai sword. We're desperately short of weapons – all we have are some knives, a baseball bat, his gun, but we're too wary to forage outside of the streets we know, and the Tsois won't sell the weapons they have; they need everything they can get. If there's anyone else left they're holing themselves up better than we are. We probably wouldn't trust them anyway.

We're ready. Danny goes over to the window and removes one of the slats. He looks up and down, left and right.

'All clear,' he mutters.

We leave the flat, Danny first, holding one plate and the gun, me behind him with two, one in each hand. God forbid we see anyone who has their own gun, but we've never mentioned that. I push the thought to the back of my mind three times daily, every time we do this. We go down the stairs into the basement and that's the tricky bit, the part where I'm most scared, as Danny has to put down the plate to open the flat with a key. Even though he still has the gun, his back is turned and my hands are full. That would be the perfect time to jump us if any kill parties were watching. Or that man. We can't see what's going on above us. The streets are quiet, but even that's not reassuring; it could just mean someone's trying to sneak up on us. I wait, and listen, and realise even the birds have stopped singing. I wonder when that happened. I've never noticed it before, and it makes me more afraid. I start crying until I hear the basement door creak open. I wipe my eyes with my sleeve, go inside.

The flat smells of musk, bodily waste, imprisoned air. The pipes emit a monotone thrum. I keep swiping at my eyes, but this is just an excuse to cover my nose without Sherwin noticing. It's a studio flat, the front door leading to the open-plan living room, which goes into a bedroom on the right of the alcove that houses the kitchenette. The bathroom is at the rear, hardly used. Sherwin's tied by his wrists to the black leather office chair in the centre of the room. His head is bowed. He's either asleep, or comatose.

I put down the plates, go over, shake him and call his name. He raises his head. His eyes are dim even in half-light, blank like a soft toy. The smell of urine is stronger. I step back, seeing the dark patch around his crotch. He catches my grimace.

'I couldn't wait . . .'

My hand is pushed into my mouth, forcing it all back. I don't know how it got there. I catch him watching me. The hand falls, my fingers spasm by my thighs. Danny touches my shoulder.

'I'll get the bowl,' he whispers, and he's gone. Sherwin's head cranes to follow. His eyes are fire. I don't want to know.

'Let's get these off you then,' I say in the most cheerful voice I can manage, hearing myself sound like a nurse. I bend in front of him. His odour is thick, soupy, but I unbutton his jeans, grab the elastic of his boxers, pull both past his hips, Sherwin lifting in order to help, then all the way down to his ankles, over his socks and into a sodden, acrid heap in my hands. He watches me all the way, even though *I'm* bowing my head now, it's as though he can see what I'm feeling, the way I'm trying not to notice his penis, or the rope around his wrists, though it must be pretty obvious because I don't lift my head from the clothes. Even when I stand I simply ball them up and put them in the dirty clothes bag. I pull the drawstring and face the bathroom where I can hear Danny running water. I wonder what's taking him so long.

'Can't even look at me then?'

I'm startled, and then I have to.

'No . . .' My smile doesn't last. 'Just waiting . . .'

'Nicki. You know this is wrong. Let me go.'

'No, Sherwin . . .' I step towards him, stop. 'You know I can't.'

'I won't . . .' he says, and the water stops running. He shuts his mouth, lets his head fall. His bare legs are dark tree roots. I take two steps away from him, and then Danny is coming down the small passage, legs bent like a cowboy, holding the bowl. Water slops from either side.

Danny puts the bowl down in front of Sherwin, between his feet. There's a cloth floating beneath the bubbles. I take it and begin to wash him, not avoiding his penis, instead telling myself it's another part of him, knees or toes. Steam rises like dry ice. He forces a grim smile at the floor while this is happening, not looking at me. It must be embarrassing for him too. Danny sits with his back against the sofa, opposite us, pointing the gun. I snake the sweatshirt over Sherwin's head, wash his chest, beneath his arms, his upper back and shoulders. I drop the washcloth into the bowl and push it away, take the crowbar from my back and place it beside me, untie the ropes. While he flexes his limbs, I pick up the crowbar and join Danny on the sofa.

He dresses in the clothes we've brought down and eats standing, on his side of the room. This is usual, he knows the rules; standing is allowed, walking is not. He paces on the spot, lifting one knee and the next, putting his fork down to swing an arm, swap his plate to the opposite hand, swing the other. The food's cold but this is also usual, for one reason or another; the weather, strangers outside our building, Sherwin needing to be changed. We eat in silence, rapidly, both hungry, both wary it seems, yet Sherwin seems in good spirits, or better than he was. Before, when he first arrived, he complained, cajoled, shouted for hours. Danny had to go down when he started screaming in the night. He took the gun and didn't tell me what he'd said, but it stopped. Ever since, Sherwin looks at Danny with flames in his eyes.

'That's nice,' Sherwin says. 'Best muffins you've made. Not hunger talking either.'

'Thanks,' I mutter, head down. I'm holding the gun now while Danny takes his turn to eat.

'So how long do you intend to keep this up? Out of interest?'

Danny looks up from his plate.

'Until someone comes,' he says.

Sherwin eyes him for a long time. Danny holds the stare until he sees me looking, ducks his head to shovel up the last of the muffin and alabaster sauce mixed with yolk. Sherwin keeps watching, points his plastic fork at me.

'You can't be serious. No one's coming.'

'Radio says—'

'No one's coming. No police, no army. No one. They'll bomb the place and leave it at that.'

Danny shoots me a glance. We've had this conversation. I try not to hear the whining scrape of his fork against the plate.

'They won't. It won't solve the problem.'

'Then what else?'

I open my mouth, shrug, and for a moment the gun's pointing at the boarded-up windows.

Sherwin steps forward. 'Nicole—'

Danny sucks in a sharp breath. I jump and point the gun at Sherwin, a brutal jerk of my wrist. Sherwin stops. Forces his bitter smile at the floor again, holds up his hands.

'All right. All right.'

He backs off and I'm glad. He drops to the floor, does his

stretches; touches toes, grabs each ankle and forces his heels to the backs of his thighs, leans to the right and to the left, one arm over his head. Then he goes through his exercise routine. Push-ups, sit-ups, squat thrusts, jogging on the spot. It takes roughly twenty minutes. In all that time he never takes his eyes from us, and we don't say a word, not to each other or him. When he's done he sits back in the leather seat, hands on the armrest.

'You can tie me up now,' he says.

'Don't you want to use the toilet?'

'No,' he says. He wants to punish me, have me clean him again. He wants to make a point. I could argue, but I know better. I can't very well make him. Cross that bridge when we get there.

Danny gets up and reties his wrists. I point the gun, eyes damp, mouth shut firm, trying not to cry too hard. I'm making my arm shake and it's not good for my aim. When Danny tightens the last knot Sherwin gasps and gives him such a look I feel as though I've swallowed a frozen pebble. Danny walks back studying his feet. I stand beside him.

'Good luck,' Sherwin says.

Outside, I lock the door quietly. The sky looks like the inside of a seashell, pink and blue and glistening grey. Danny covers me. The stance he takes, both hands on the gun, head twisting with stiff jerks, would be ludicrous if I weren't so frightened. He goes up the stairs first. I put down the plates, unlock the door to our building, pick up the plates and go inside. It's a slow, laborious business but after what happened to the woman at 64 we take our time. No sense hurrying to lose your life.

I let myself into our flat, noticing Danny hang back. I frown.

'I was thinking, maybe I should work.'

'What, now?'

'Before it gets dark.'

'But it's not even twelve.'

'Yeah, but the later it gets the more difficult it'll be. It is winter.'

There's logic in his argument, I can see that. I don't want to, though; I want tea, hugs, conversation. I don't want him out there again.

'You could go tomorrow. Early.'

Danny says nothing. I don't even make sense to myself.

'We're running low.'

'On what?'

I know full well what he means.

'Everything. It's only the house. I'll be back before dark.'

'OK, if you say so.'

He comes over, holds me close, kisses the top of my head, between the centre parting of my braids.

'I'll be OK. Promise.'

'Take this,' I say, and duck beneath the cold embrace of the crowbar, lifting it from my shoulders and over my head. He puts it on his back. After, I give him the keys.

'Don't answer the door to anyone who knocks, any time. Not even me,' he says. 'Promise?'

'I promise.'

'Back soon. Love you.'

'I love you too.'

The building door shakes when it slams. I stand there for a long time, hoping he changes his mind. I wonder what Sherwin's thinking.

Inside, the door double-locked behind me, I make tea and sit by the window, one slat removed, watching 64. I shouldn't really expose us but I need more sunlight. I don't want to see the house but it's right in front of me, there's nothing else to do but look. I don't want to remember what I saw but it's there in my head. It was three weeks afterwards, early Sunday morning. We'd made love, lay in bed shivering and not talking about Sherwin, when we heard screams coming from the street. Danny got up, the gun tight between his fingers, and removed the slat very carefully. It was the young woman. I didn't know her name, but she lived alone, ever since I moved in. She had her shopping trolley with her, had been on her way to the Tsois maybe, when a small kill party must have caught sight of her. There were only four men but they surrounded the woman and were pushing her from one to the other like bullies, laughing loud, whooping, using each push to tear clothing, punch or kick her, ripping the trolley from her hands and throwing it into someone's basement. The woman was screaming; an odd, breathy sound that reminded me of when I'd punctured the hose of my vacuum cleaner. It was difficult to see what weapons they had, but there must have been a knife because after one big push she clutched her stomach, and the laughter got louder, and her cream dress grew red with blood, and she stumbled and dropped to her knees. That's when they fell on her, punching, kicking and stabbing until she lay still in the middle of the road. One of them dragged her body all the way down the road by the ankle, until they were out of sight, the others still kicking at her. God knows what they did afterwards, as if that wasn't enough. And we watched. We sat inside our house and watched, didn't do a fucking thing. Danny put the slat back as carefully as he'd removed it, and much later, he went to work as normal.

I finish my tea and replace the slat. Wander around the flat. We have leftover sausages and I can mash the few potatoes we have for tonight's dinner. I hope Danny comes back with meat. His parents' house is just past Ravenscourt Park, a twenty-minute walk. The first time he went he stayed for almost a week, scared me so much he promised he'd never do it again. They're dead, of course. His parents. Danny made sure of that. He goes over every few days and gets most of our food from there, raiding their massive freezer. It won't last for ever, we know that. Then he'll have to forage elsewhere. Danny calls it work and I let him because men need purpose in life, plus it gives us a sense of normality. Before this I worked too, real work, but foraging isn't a job either of us wants me to do. I play the traditional role now. Truth is, I don't mind. Better than being out there.

I need a cigarette. Danny doesn't smoke, which means I have to go onto the roof. I gather my smoking paraphernalia, lock our flat, open the door to old Mr Fallon's, cover my nose against the slaughterhouse stench, go into the attic and up the metal ladder, pull myself onto the roof, into fresh air. There. Needed that too.

The roof is flat, open. When the wind blows hard enough, dust circles like a hungry pet. There's a rusting barbecue in the corner, a threadbare sofa that stinks of cat piss, and of course the scarecrow. He's roped to a sun lounger and it's only then that irony strikes me: Sherwin and old Mr Fallon, both tied up, both dead. I want to laugh and can't, even when I force it. I avoid the scarecrow and sit on the edge of the sofa, light my cigarette.

By week four we'd realised we hadn't heard anything from old Mr Fallon and we began to get scared right away. What should we do? What would he return as, Symp or Syke? The government statement the radio man read told us it took three days. We put our heads against the wall and listened for a sound. We reasoned that he'd left the flat without us noticing. Slipped away, not into a quiet old man's death, but into cold winter night.

Later we heard movement from the flat downstairs. We looked at each other. It was him.

Danny went to check. Said he might have to 'do' Mr Fallon like he did his parents and I shouldn't come down under any circumstances. The silence made me want to scream and then I heard banging, a shot. When I went downstairs old Mr Fallon was dead for good, a hole right between his eyes like the radio man told us. I wouldn't have had the guts. Danny was breathing hard, eyes darting, angry. I don't think he wanted me to see him that way.

Somehow, using nothing more than rope and brute strength, Danny hauled the body into the attic and further up the metal ladder onto the roof. I helped as best as I could, holding Mr Fallon's legs and pushing when he pulled, but I was pretty useless. Danny put a puffy winter coat on old Mr Fallon, a Halloween mask he'd found somewhere to cover his face, flipped the hood and tied him to the sun lounger, wrapping rope around his waist. He went to work that night, the only time he'd gone out so late, and came back with his father's replica pistol, something that couldn't be used against us but might deter a kill party from trying to break in and murder us. Of course, the scarecrow could draw unwanted attention, although it seemed to have worked for now. From what little I could tell, Sykes are pretty cowardly. Danny says they only pick on humans who can't fight.

I smoke my cigarette and think. I watch street lights and for the thousandth time I wonder when they'll come on. That's when we'll know we've truly won. That's when we'll know our lives have returned. I wait for that moment every dusk, and though I breathe a sigh of frustration when they stay dark, I can't help thinking I'm one day closer to the evening they all light up again.

'Hey! *Heeeey!*'

I fall, slumping onto the floor, roll on my back and stub the cigarette out in three quick thumps. What was I *thinking*? Danny will kill me. I'm lying there, breathing in dust, trying not to sneeze or cough.

'I know you're up there! I can see smoke!'

I swear; a whispered curse.

'I'm not gonna hurt you! You're with the girl, aren't you? The girl I saw at the shops!'

His voice is raw with shouting. I can barely hear him, wouldn't be able to if it wasn't for the silence.

'I'm just trying to help! I'm alive!' There's nothing for a long while, and I'm kneeling, almost getting to my feet when he starts again. I duck even though he can't see me. 'Stay away from the Tsois, all right? They've got a Syke! She'll kill them all!'

I wait for him to say more, heart pounding, and don't hear anything for ages. There's a rush of rapidly moving feet, like someone's slapping tarmac, the noise echoing from walls and paving slabs. I get to my feet and climb downstairs into old Mr Fallon's flat, into the communal corridor and into our flat, snicking the door shut. Sherwin's calling for help in a desperate, raw voice. I couldn't tell from the roof but in my flat it's loud, obvious. There's shuffling on the steps outside my window. Sherwin hears it too, because he stops calling. A minute later the building door opens and shuts, then the flat door opens and shuts, and Danny's home.

'What's going on?' he says, face pale, eyes bright. He's holding a white plastic bag.

'Nothing . . .' I know I won't get away with that, put a hand to my head, and play with my hair. 'I went for a smoke and that guy from this morning, I think he saw me. He was shouting . . .'

Danny mouths something harsh, shakes his head. 'So now he knows we're here.'

'He doesn't. He didn't see anything.'

'He saw me.'

I push my lips together: he has a point. Danny hisses between his teeth and pulls something from the plastic bag. For a moment I swear it's a human limb and then I realise it's not, it's just a joint of meat. The sides shine in the candlelight. He slams it on the kitchen counter. I wince.

'Dunno whether we should have it for dinner or use it for self-defence.'

I laugh on cue. He's looking at the meat, not smiling.

'Beef?' I say, going over to the counter.

'Lamb,' he replies. 'You know we have to do Sherwin, right?'

He has no expression. I don't either, I know because I'm holding it in like my basement tears. The thrum of the pipes is louder than ever.

'Why?'

'He's gonna get us killed. Shouting like that. There's kill parties everywhere, if they hear him it's over.'

'I'll talk to him.'

'He won't listen.'

'He will, if I tell him we're serious. You can't, not now. After all this time.'

Danny sighs, looks away. I grasp his hand, I know what that means.

'It's not like I want to.'

'I know.'

'It's just I don't want to lose you.'

'Me neither,' I say. I kiss him, feeling his cold lips against mine.

'It's freezing out,' he says, watching me.

'Well, we only have to go downstairs.'

I make the mash, reheat the sausages and have a late lunch. We eat upstairs first and take it down after; I figure that's better, Danny doesn't have to stay as long, won't get agitated. Sherwin doesn't say anything about his yelling, or the fact we've already eaten, and neither do I. His eyes are soft, pleading. He's soiled himself like I knew he would and I have to clean it all up and change him, but that's better than the permanent alternative – we all know it. We creep upstairs, ever on the lookout for the guy from the shops, or anyone else, and as soon as we're inside I'm boiling water for soup. Danny chops vegetables beside me, throws them into the pot and we let it all bubble while I read a novel and he listens to music. His eyes are closed. His foot taps out constant rhythm and I'm trying to concentrate on the words on my page, but I keep getting distracted by Danny. What he said. As much as I try to ignore it, force it to the back of my mind like everything else over the last two months, I can't. I just can't.

The soup's a gorgeous-smelling mush. We turn off the heat, dish it into bowls and take it down. This time Sherwin is clean, and when he eats with a plastic spoon his eyes are grateful. Danny ignores him, mouth a solid, dark streak. The atmosphere is thick as my soup. Sherwin eats like there was little or no lunch, performs his exercises and asks to use the toilet. We try not to listen, don't talk while he's gone. When he comes back and sits down he winks, giving me a tiny smile.

'Thanks, sis,' he says.

Danny and I maintain our silence until we're back upstairs. He flops on the bed and lies with his hands behind his head, eyes closed. I remain standing, listening to noises from the street.

Dustbins falling. The shuffle of riffled contents. Either dogs, foxes, or people.

'So? What do you think?'

He lifts his head, chin tucked into his chest, hands still clasped. I can hardly see his eyes.

'Better,' he says. 'Much better.'

We make love, fall asleep. In what feels like an instant I'm back there, at the beginning. I see people that died returning three days later, coming back to lovers and families, knocking on doors and windows, not in a zombie, arms-outstretched kind of way, but really back to life, with memories and feelings, just like me and you. Thousands in London, millions all over the world, old, young, fresh and unspoiled as the day they were born, bodies cold and hearts still, otherwise normal, at first.

I hear news reports saying these dead people, the 'reverts', are violent. They attack without provocation, kill in some cases, seemingly enjoy the harm and panic they cause. I see open battles on streets, feel the body-shaking rattle of bombs, the police and army overwhelmed, the National Guard beaten, thousands of psychotic returnees, 'Sykes' as they become nicknamed, fighting bitter battles and winning. I listen to the radio when the TV becomes inactive, government statements telling us that author-ities have learned there are two factions, the dead who love to kill and the dead who do not, psychotic and sympathetic, Sykes and Symps. As it's difficult to tell which is which, they are evacuating the city.

I see empty streets, neighbours wishing us well and leaving, silence in their wake. Us packing to go when the knock comes, and when we lift the slat my brother is there in his blood-splattered army uniform, waiting patiently, head low. There's shouting, Danny waving the gun, even though that part didn't

happen like that. Sherwin is being led into the empty flat downstairs, and Danny kicks off the door – which really did happen
– and then it's all threats, and rope. And though in reality
Sherwin simply looked at me, pleading with his eyes for me to
make Danny stop, in the dream he is screaming, tears rolling
down his cheeks, saying, 'Save me, Nicki, save me.' I feel a wrench
in my gut, and wake to feel the crushing pressure of night, and
I know Danny's going to kill my brother.

I slide out of bed. Danny's snoring on his back. I pick the
crowbar up from where I always leave it next to my bed, grab
my dressing gown, keys, and creep to the flat door, let myself
out of the building. The night's mild, the moon high and luminous. The air is filled with moisture. I loved nights like these
not long ago. A fox spies me, eyes gleaming, and runs.

I go down the stairs with my crowbar raised, letting myself in
with Danny's keys. Sherwin is sleeping, chin tucked into his chest,
dribbling. I shake his arm. He jerks, looks around, mumbles.

'*Ssssh* . . .'

'What you doing?' he's hissing.

'Go,' I say. 'Get out of here, now. We'll meet at the evac point
on Wormwood Scrubs.'

He's unsure, snakes himself free anyway. I hug him tight, the
first time I've done this since he came back to find me and it's
like holding a block of ice. He's uncomfortable. He pulls away.

'I better go then.'

'OK. Go.'

He heads for the open door. I see orange light stream inside
the flat, his silhouette. I take a last look and leave. Sherwin's
limping up the concrete stairs. I follow, seeing something from
the corner of my eye. Sherwin stops, raises his hands slow,
palms up.

'Thought so,' Danny says from our building door, gun pointing at Sherwin. 'He'll kill us both, Nicole, you don't see it.'

I scream, hearing my own voice echo from bare streets. There's a shot and Sherwin falls onto me, holding his shoulder. Danny's fighting with someone. It's the man, the one who followed me. They're fighting for the gun.

Sherwin has recovered, is leaping the stairs, running. I want to go with him but instead I jump the steps and throw myself at the man, wrenching at limbs, hair, even eyes. He falters. Danny takes the opportunity, pushing him away, firing three times. The man falls, shock for ever cast on his face. Danny elbows me aside and I stumble against the brick, nearly go over into the basement. He runs to the centre of the road, standing with his legs wide apart, waits, fires. I hear a mute thud. *Sherwin*, I want to say and I can't. I scream, louder and longer.

When I open my eyes I'm huddled against the cold steps and they're still there. The dead man. Danny motionless in the centre of the road as though his feet are stuck. He looks at me and his eyes are like empty space. He comes back to the building steps, looming over me. I flinch. His face crumples.

'Nicki, I'm sorry, babe. I'll take care of you. I love you.'

I'm crying too much to say anything. He reaches out a hand, and I have to take it. His fingers are cold as the concrete steps, making me cry even harder. He lifts me to my feet. It's only us now.

COSMOGRAMMA

She thought the doctor had kind eyes, but his face shifted somehow, and like dusk into night something arrived that frightened her. Layla backed away, even as Heminol swivelled in his chair, exposing tiny chips of white teeth. Her stomach clenched. Sweat dotted her temples. In a matter of seconds the moment was gone. She settled in her seat, unsure of what she'd seen, eyeing his tall, bony frame.

'It's OK,' Mother said, leaning towards her. 'He's trying to help. Don't be scared.'

'That's right. He'll make it better,' Father added, and his fluty voice soothed her.

'In your own time,' Doctor Heminol said. He smiled wider. 'When you're ready.'

She lowered her head, took a step away from his desk, gathered herself and began to sing 'Twinkle, Twinkle, Little Star'. Her voice was strong, by turns slightly hoarse, then fluty like her father's. She saw him through quick glances as he closed his eyes, his jaw tight, and almost stopped singing. Her mother watched from the edge of her seat, fingers clasped, nodding as though someone had asked her a very serious question. The doctor's pen touched his upper lip.

The room began to shift as if held between a giant's fingers, turning ever so slightly to the right. Though the rheumy yellow ceiling lights were on, it grew dark. Above their heads a fissure appeared in the ceiling and through it seeped thick colour, vibrant mauve, tumbling onto itself like the crest of a wave. The colour collapsed, became deep desert red, collapsed once more and became royal blue. When Layla finished the song the colours roiled away and the room lightened. Her mother cried silent tears. The doctor, once again, bared teeth. Her father regarded her, face solid.

'Remarkable,' Heminol said, making scratchy notes. 'She must come in for observation.'

'What kind?' her father asked.

'A simple physical, cranial scans . . .' Heminol murmured, still writing. 'You are aware that this condition is classified?'

'Cosmogramma,' her mother said, Layla detecting pride.

'Clinically known as Ellison's Syndrome, but yes,' Heminol said. 'You've done your research.'

'Some,' her father breathed, one clearly defined note, fingers stroking and feeling for knots in his beard he wouldn't find because he brushed it at least three times daily, possibly more. 'We're willing to learn.'

'Well,' Heminol said, sitting straighter, unfolding long legs. 'We don't know much, just that some people – adversely or otherwise – seem affected by changes in gravity, atmospheric pressure, oxygen make-up, we don't know which, or even whether they're all contributory factors. Their genetic configuration, or mutated brain structure, enables them to affect subtle changes on our – the viewers' and their own, that is – ability to perceive light refraction on a universal scale. While these people – mostly children, though as you know there are adult cases – by no means make up the majority, the percentage of the affected population is high enough to warrant sufficient concern for further study.'

Her mother's eyes danced, flitting left to right.

'That's what we thought,' she said.

Her father almost smiled. 'Where will these studies be undertaken?'

'The children's ward of St Monmouth's, no more than a day's observation.'

'We'll have to take time off,' her mother realised.

'Oh no, we'll come to your block and pick Layla up, bring her back when we're done. Absolutely no need.'

'Bring her back?'

'Absolutely your choice. No obligation.'

Silence. Layla examined tessellations in the wood beneath her feet, tracing repetition. Dark, thick, straight lines like a word underlined many times over. The naadassa tree, like all trees on Kepler, had squares inside the trunk, not rings. Not that she'd ever seen a tree with rings.

'We should know what's wrong,' her father said.

'Yes, it's such a worry.'

'I totally understand,' soothed Heminol. 'And we'd be honoured to help. If you could just fill in these forms. Sign here . . . And here.'

She lifted her head to watch her parents write their names on the doctor's palm computer, lowered it when they were done. A few clicks and a beep. She felt a warm hand on her back, and didn't know who it belonged to.

The Amicilli metro had finished construction just before she was born, so her parents said. Layla was always amazed by the new-car scent, the way surfaces around her gleamed. She held her mother's hand as they bought tickets, watched passengers coming in and out, smiling as the barriers swung open to receive them, clutching her mother's fingers as they descended on the escalator. The transports themselves were bright silver bullets, more like star-crafts than any track-bound vehicle, and she was thrilled to enter the hissing doors to sit by the large window, elbows leant on the sill. While her parents talked about what the doctor had said and what they had done, Layla watched the tunnel walls race by. The baggage rack shook, and they were rocked from side to side. Layla loved it. She smiled, although it went unseen, her parents too distracted to notice.

Up the escalator, out of the barriers, a short walk home and there they were: Gillie and Marshan, waiting for a ball to return to them from the air, poised, arms open, chins raised, so they didn't even see her. A duo of open doors glowed from the interior lights of her house, one of many located at the end of short pathways that lined their rectangular block, numbered 375y7. Layla searched her parents' faces, saying 'Please, please', until they smiled and said 'Of course', and her mother let go of her hand so she could run to her friends, still waiting for the ball to land, tracking its slow descent, and it only met Gillie's arms as she reached them. It was all 'hi's and hugs after that, Layla cackling upwards, chin raised into the crimson sky above, school friends dancing around her. Layla's parents looked on, pleased to see her happy, and went inside.

They played ball until the night met fresh terraformed earth. Before they were called inside, the children ran into the woodland beyond their block. Much of Kepler's forests had been cleared to make way for towns and cities, but some were left standing. They were lucky to have a hectare of untouched land to the west of their street, a forest of 200-feet-tall naadassas, creeping white betullah vines, an army of squat toad lotus as high as their waists flooding the landscape with colours. And all around them roses and lilies and petunias reared from Earth-exported seeds which had grown in abundance. The children ran along paths forged generations before, stopping in a clearing that led to the foot of the largest naadassa, its trunk four times the size of any normal tree, its leaves blocking the artificial light cast by humans.

The boy lay in the shadow formed by the canopy of branches. He didn't look up as they came closer. He was four years older, a lifetime by their reckoning. He chewed on the end of bullgrass, head propped by thick roots, shoulder-length locks much like the naadassa's tangled limbs. Layla hid her smile. The boy was Lanameade.

'Hey, Meade, how is it?' Gillie was first to ask. Layla couldn't help but watch. Gillie was more womanly than any of the girls on their block. Lanameade hadn't noticed, but one day he would.

'Not bad,' he said, chewing. 'You lot been allowed out?'

'We ran,' Layla blurted, and when his dark eyes fell on her she felt her stomach fly and couldn't breathe.

'Bad kids,' he grinned, making the others laugh. 'Don't suppose you got any cane?'

Two shaking heads. Marshan drew a thick stalk of sea-cane from his pocket. Layla drew hers. They held them while the others grew quiet.

'Where did you get yours from?' Marshan asked her. Before she could answer Gillie was talking loud, trying to impress Meade, it was obvious.

'Her mum and dad went to the clinic, didn't they?'

Layla's eyes rested on bullgrass, tiny red daisies, weeds. She kept them low.

'Don't worry, it's just a check-up and a scan and after that, you'll get more cane,' Meade told her. It was the gentlest she'd heard him speak ever. 'It's painless, trust me. I know. Want to sing?'

She looked up, checking with Marshan, who nodded and smiled. Marshan knew how much she liked the older boy.

'Let's,' he said, and put away his cane.

There weren't many songs all three liked, but everyone knew 'Solar Rhapsody', or as it had become known 'The Song of Earth', the unofficial planetary anthem that overrode queens, country and government, sung in schools, universities, mosques, temples and churches, in business meetings, parties, at celebrations and funerals. It was only the Cosmogrammas at first – Meade, Marshan and Layla – but when the canopy above seemed to split gently and the colours came rolling through, Layla's mauves, reds and blues merging with Marshan's greens, yellow and pinks and Meade's earthy tans, oranges and browns, the rest couldn't help themselves, singing the chorus, falling silent when they reached the verses. Colours danced just below the leafy canopy, converging and tumbling to create new spectrums and tones, encouraging the children to sing with more passion, forming new colours in turn. When they ended the song Gillie said they should sing another, and so they did, loud as they could until they heard their parents call from the forest edge. As one, they all ran home, except for Meade, who stayed to watch the colours shred into fine mist and dissolve.

Layla ate dinner warmed on the Earth-fashioned stove. Her parents said they'd heard them. She thought they would be cross, but they smiled: 'The songs were beautiful,' her mother told her. 'Meade has such a fine voice, he could easily sing with the best.' Mother was smiling when she said this. Father kept his nose buried in his tablet as Layla blushed.

After they had eaten, they sat in front of the holoscreen. Father liked to watch the news while Mother read a novel. The glow warmed her face, and she muttered to herself often, sometimes laughed. Layla played on her visor, snatching quick glances at the screen. Something about the rumblings of a war on Meccanoa. A bomb blast on the neighbouring moon. A call for ES-residents to be vigilant about possible terrorist activities on their own planets. It didn't seem to matter to Father that the news from other worlds was delayed, sometimes by as little as decades if he was lucky. It only mattered that he be 'brought up to speed', in his own words. Layla imagined him sprinting to keep up with news, a blurred streak of black, racing just ahead.

And then it was time for bed, too soon as always. She brushed her teeth, kissed her mother and trotted to her room, climbed in. When her father had finished reading Layla a story from her tablet and leant over to kiss her goodnight, she couldn't help but ask.

'Daddy, what's an ES-resident?'

He smiled, stroking his beard.

'That's us, Layla. Extra-Solar residents. That's who we are.'

He told her the things she knew, about his father and his father before who made the journey to Kepler from Earth more than a century before. He spoke of the hardships of the unstable atmosphere, the new life forms and the changes the planet made to their forebears. He said Layla was a pioneer, not of this world but from it, for her to be proud of the person it made her into. And he told her that the Cosmogramma was a gift from a benevolent ancestor who saw fit to bless her with a power she could share with the world. That she, Meade and Marshan had been granted the ability to become great, universally known, of that he was sure.

He kissed her forehead twice, pulled the covers tight and left the room in darkness. Immediately, Layla slept.

The dusky van came two days later. It parked at the vehicular turning point, a red square of tarmac not far from the path to the woods. Two matt-uniformed attendants fetched the children and brought them back to the van, one after another. Layla was amazed to climb aboard and see the small, pale faces of a dozen children she didn't know, and two she recognised, Meade and Marshan. She hurried along the aisle to where they were seated.

'Hi, what are you doing here?' she smiled, thrown from her usual caution by unchecked surprise. They shrugged.

'Those men came, got us,' Marshan said, staring out the window.

'My dad didn't want me to go, but they insisted,' Meade complained. Neither boy smiled.

'Oh,' Layla said, and sat opposite them. No one said anything else. She'd never seen this many little kids so quiet. Marshan chewed on his sea-cane, bending his head to squeeze juice from tough flesh. The stalk was frayed at one end like a paintbrush.

There were no more passengers, it seemed. After the attendants checked their palm computer and conferred, the engine started and they began the journey. The vehicle turned and then they could see their parents, standing on the pavements in a small huddle, talking with their heads down until the van went past. Almost in unison, the adults glanced up at the windows, breaking into sudden smiles, waving. The 375y7 children waved back, but her father's countenance was something Layla never forgot: still, without emotion, his eyes damp. It made her sit back in her seat, feeling tears burn the back of her throat without knowing why.

They drove through the buzzing streets and markets of their township, and on to the quiet, scattered villages on the outskirts of their borough, where the people wore long robes and rode huge lumbering scaramonds that were short and squat, and red as the barren deserts to the east, where they roamed in prides of hundreds. Still the dusky van kept going, into the land where there was nothing but land, further than most of the children had ever gone. Though there was chatter among the dozen, no one spoke to anyone they didn't know, and the talking was low, as if they were in a place of worship. The attendants paid them no more interest, whispering among themselves. Meade, Layla and Marshan played *Running 7* on their visors. When Layla grew sleepy, she swapped places with Marshan, took off her visor and dozed on Meade's shoulder.

She woke to find they had stopped. One of the children, a youngster no older than six, was wailing from the front seats, face ablaze, calling for his mother. The ceiling above them was churning with a seething black mass, flashes of bullgrass green. One of the attendants had grabbed the boy, and was trying to lift him, but he kept fighting, and it took both attendants to do it, passing the boy to another man behind them, this one black-suited, tall, masked. A Kepler soldier. Why would they need soldiers? Layla turned towards Meade. Over his shoulder, outside the van, was a huge transport, bigger than she'd ever seen. Only this one wasn't silver like most. It was red like the earth beneath its wheels, the tracks it had been placed upon.

'What's going on?' she whispered.

'Don't know. We pulled up here and now they want us to get

out,' Meade said. Marshan's eyes grew wide. Now most of the children had been herded from the van, an attendant was walking down the aisle towards them. Meade stood full height. He was tall as his father, would possibly become taller. The attendant backed away, and one of the black-suited men stepped forward. Meade's shoulders hunched. He edged out from the cover of the seats, not looking at the others. Layla took his hand and together the three of them left the van.

It was hot outside, windy. Red dust swirled at their feet. The sides of the transport were missing, and there was a stepladder that led to the darkness inside. Layla refused to look into the impassive masks of the soldiers either side of the ladder, staring only at Meade's back, her right hand clasping his fingers, her left tight around Marshan's. None of the soldiers spoke. It was obvious where they had to go. They climbed up the steps, into the transport.

At the top, they found their fellow passengers from the van and others, men, women and children, shoulders pressed against shoulders. There was the Cosmogramma girl band who sang on Saturday night holo shows. The weighty opera singer her mother loved. The man who opened the Planetary Games, bringing colour and shapes tumbling over the heads of a stadium filled with thousands. Even a baby who wailed as the block 375y7 children entered, the air above her crackling with infant rage.

The transport doors closed, one diometer at a time. Someone began to yell in that direction, and soon, as Layla watched, they were all doing the same, as the light from the broad window narrowed to a small beam, to a sliver, and was gone. The transport shuddered, began to move. Meade's voice cracked beside her, repeating words she could hardly hear. Their shouts echoed in the darkness, amplified by metal walls. Layla found herself standing, feeling her own spit against her lips, realising somehow she could see. The others were leaning forward, hurling curses into growing light. She looked up. A thunderstorm of colours raged like boiling water, one churning into another, clashing, rebounding, and she stopped her screaming to watch them merge as a strange vibration hummed from the transport floor.

A sharp crack above their heads made her ears ring. They fell at once, many covering their heads, but Layla kept her eyes upwards so she saw what they didn't: the colours sweeping into one central point at the centre of the ceiling, thrusting like the tail of a cyclone towards the transport door. It blew it from the hinges, a sheet of paper on the wind, off and away. Light poured in. They got to their feet, surging towards their escape point. There was another crack, louder this time, and the transport roared, trembling as it was pounded from outside. She could see. They could all see, a multitude of heads craned upwards, bright sunlight flooding their eyes. There was vast sky and somewhere far from them something black flapped and spun like a dark coin, catching the sun as it went higher and higher. The roof. The transport roof.

A painful squeal of protesting metal. The carriage rocked like metro trains. She was thrown against Meade's shoulder hard, hearing the thud of connection and seeing more colours, this time inside her head. Silence. All around Layla nobody dared say anything or even move for fear of what might come next. There were faint moans, almost sounding like chants, though no one spoke a word. Heat pounded their backs, pushing them to the floor. She heard a familiar noise and saw Marshan crying on his knees, covering his head. Layla bent down, whispered into his ear, saying what she'd seen. She pulled him to his feet and took Meade by the hand. Leading both, she walked to the red open space where the transport door had been.

Every soldier was dead, or dying. Bodies gouged with circular holes through their torsos, organs trailed behind them in the dirt like the tentacles of jellyfish. Bloody red circles where their eyes should have been, hands on guns. Skin pale, dark with burn marks, bloodless. Further along the segments of transport carriages Cosmogrammas jumped down in groups of threes and fours, helping the less able with a hand, looking up at the darkening sky with hands on hips, inspecting the fallen remains of dead men. Meade touched the lump on Layla's head gently, and when she forced a smile, hugged her tight. She held on, squeezing him breathless. Her eyes began to burn and she shuddered against him, gasping for breath.

They released each other, leaping carefully from the carriage one by one. Awkward, wincing into sunlight, the chill of air accentuating the sticky damp of Layla's skin. Dust played tag around their feet. A fingernail glint of the moon. The silent land seemed infinite as they gathered themselves and walked to join the others.

BUCK

Tem'ondri lined the horizon as he walked onto the front porch, bringing distant thunder, a cloud of dust. Ula stumbled, baa'draskin boots scraping dry wood, a broomstick limp between his fingers. It would take the riders over twenty minutes to draw close enough to count. He checked the door was fully shut, leant the broomstick against a wall and sat on the bottom step, eyes narrowed against a fading red sun.

The rumble of their approach shook the ground. There were three, all of them riding mita dragons, which he recalled but hadn't seen since he was a boy, their rippling scales shimmering green and scarlet. The dragons' loping, sidewinding movement meant death for humans, who couldn't ride, but the tem'ondri could. The gargantuan insects tore through the wasteland dirt and rocks as if they were nothing but air. Ula was glad they hadn't crossed the cane fields or he might have lost many crops.

They stopped just beyond his perimeter fence, dragons rearing, exposing writhing legs, antennae waving against orange sky. He rose to greet them. The *mi'owa* was a half-registered weight on his ankle, giving him a slight limp.

'*Kulaz.*'

'*Kulaz,*' said the largest, pulling reins. Her compound eyes were pink and glittered in dying light. The others remained silent.

'You have travelled?' Ula asked the large one.

'*Daar Orr*,' she said.

Ula's eyebrows rose.

'We apologise for our abruptness. I am Vrawn. These are my companions, Vrax and Goll.'

The remaining tem'ondri crossed spiny forearms over their chests. Ula did likewise, bowing towards them. The one called Vrax was blue-eyed and thin. Goll was beetle-round, and her eyes were red. The tem'ondri climbed from their dragons and tied the reins to his fence, where there were long troughs filled with dew. The mita drank noisily while their riders entered the perimeter.

'We have herb,' Vrawn said, raising a bag in her secondary left fist.

'Then we will drink,' Ula said without a smile. 'Please, follow.'

He led them up the porch steps and into the farmhouse, which was open-roofed to allow the wasteland heat to escape. Birds fluttered as they entered, making his guests crane their heads and point towards the thatched roof. T'Shawn was preparing the evening meal with their son. They were both so busy seasoning baa'dra they didn't notice anyone until Ula cleared his throat. T'Shawn faced him, smiling, but jumped when she saw the tem'ondri. Her lips fell into a straight line. She gathered herself, came into the living room, crossed her arms over her chest, bowing. Vrawn hummed, her mandibles clattering like hard nails drumming against a wooden table.

'*Kulaz maadram*, good lady.'

'*Kulaz*, madam.'

She bowed to Vrax and Goll. Vrawn turned to Ula.

'A fine mate.'

'She is,' Ula said, clearing his throat.

T'Shawn's eyes widened. She'd been so enthralled by her guests she'd forgotten Makkani, who was at the kitchen counter, rubbing spices into the meat, oblivious. She hissed, three times, until he looked over his shoulder. The boy stiffened when he saw them.

'Come *here*!'

He ran to his mother's side, head down. The tem'ondri laughed.

'Really, no need,' Vrawn said, and the others chattered, *no need, no need*.

'He must learn,' T'Shawn told them.

Ula felt his eyes narrow.

'Go on then.'

The boy crossed his arms, bowing. The rapid click of mandibles filled the room. Their whispers were loud; *learn, learn*.

'A fine spawn,' Vrax said, nodding. 'Two segments, yes?'

'Nearly three,' Ula said, and he turned to his wife. 'This is Vrawn, Vrax and Goll. They've come from *Daar Orr*. They've brought herb.'

'Oh, good,' T'shawn said, her voice dew-neutral. She took the offered bag. 'We'll boil a pot. You can all make yourselves comfortable.'

His wife and son went into the kitchen to make tea. Ula guided their visitors to the seats, where they sat arranging their lower limbs into positions of comfort. Ula took his own seat, shifting. The dip in his hard-backed chair, shaped to cater for the overly large abdomen of the host species, was awkward, but they were all made that way. The temon'dri were arthropods, as it was said in Earth-speak, Mon'dra's dominant life form.

Everything on the planet was created for their needs. Sofas, houses, even humans.

Vrawn sat forward, gesturing at the large living space.

'You have done well. Your farm is looking fine. How do things fare with the crops and cattle?'

'*Grell, grell,*' Ula said, against a soft clatter of mandibles, quiet appreciation for his use of their language. 'The landcane harvest was better than last term, and we sold a record amount of baa'dra produce.'

'Your success has brought you fame,' Groll said, speaking at last. 'Your name is heard far over the mountains.'

'We're a simple operation; we simply try,' Ula told them. The soft clatter returned.

T'Shawn and Makkani entered with a pot of tea surrounded by five cups balanced on a tray. Their son poured for the visitors while his wife joined Ula on a chair beside him.

'Now go and play,' T'Shawn told the boy as he filled the last cup. Ula caught her eye, saw fear.

'But Mum—'

'You heard me.'

'Do as your mother tells you,' Ula said. Makkani bowed to the arthropods and his parents, and ran upstairs, his *mi'owa* clattering with every step.

'Fine, fine spawn . . .' Vrawn said. T'Shawn forced a smile, while Ula felt himself flinch. 'You must be wondering why we are here?'

'We are curious,' T'Shawn said, and looked at Ula. 'Aren't we?'

'Very.'

'We have come to request your help,' Vrawn said, four palms open, glistening. 'My sister Vrax has a breeder for impregnating.

She is healthy, six-segments high, of very fine nature, amenable, and will bear many spawn we believe.'

Ula risked a look. T'Shawn had paled.

'What happened to her last buck?'

'This will be her first insemination,' Vrawn said. Vrax leant forward.

'You would be doing me a tremendous duty. I have given my breeder much land, a fine nest, all the comforts she could wish for, much as my sister has given you. A union would not only bring powerful spawn, but would elevate your status.'

'We would be honoured,' Vrawn added, 'if you could do us this service.'

Ula stood, bowing to each guest in turn.

'Thank you for your request. You must be tired from your ride and we'll have a long journey back to *Daar Orr* in the morning. I have guest rooms just behind this building. We'd be honoured if you would stay.'

Stay, stay, they whispered, getting to their feet. Ula had his back to his wife but he could feel her distaste, even in her silence.

'I'll show you to your rooms,' he said, and led them into the night.

When the guests were settled and his son was put to bed, Ula checked on the cattle. Low winds had brought the temperature down a good few degrees. The night was only broken by a distant chatter of nocturnal creatures. The moons rose slowly above dark mountains. He walked the perimeter, and when everything was secure, he activated the energy field surrounding his land. His last task done, he retired for the night.

In the bedroom he undressed, silent as the evening. He could feel T'Shawn's stare, and continued to ignore her. When he climbed into bed she seemed entranced by the ceiling. Ula closed his eyes, drifted.

'What time will you leave?'

He was almost asleep. He opened his eyes.

'First light. I'll need to saddle up.'

'Will you come back?'

Ula rolled his head to the right. 'Of course I will.'

'I knew she'd come. Since our wedding, I knew she'd come.'

'They always do.'

'I'm scared.'

Her jaw was set, eyes fierce. She didn't seem scared.

'So am I. But you have to remember, it's there and back. Plenty of people have done it.'

'Not us.'

'No. Not us.'

They kissed and held each other.

The animals were watered and fed. They said their goodbyes to T'Shawn and Makkani, who stood on the porch, arms wrapped around each other. Goll worked on Ula's *mi'owa*, adjusting the radius so he could make the journey without unfortunate side effects. Ula hadn't seen one kill a person, but he had heard they could, and guessed the silent tem'ondri was a bodyguard for hire. Goll forced a low grunt, rising when she'd finished. She walked away without a word.

The red sun was no more than a chink in the sky when they left the farmhouse, the tem'ondri riding mita dragons, Ula his best equine beast. Horses were imported generations ago, had grown to an average size of twenty-five hands, three and a half hands bigger than the largest recorded Earth horse. Although they were strong and nimble, Mon'dra horses were still no match for dragons, who were ten feet of muscle and twenty pairs of legs stronger, formidable close up. Their bodies were thick bands of segmented power, their legs hardened talons that could shatter rock. The tem'ondri kept pace for the first few miles, raising a subdued patter and little dust, but soon the beasts were surging forward. Vrawn said they would meet at the rendezvous point, just before they were gone in a fine purple mist that caused Ula to veer to one side. For the rest of the journey he was alone, watching the cloud move closer to the horizon and beyond. He kicked his heels against the horse's flank, leaning forward.

That afternoon Ula stopped for lunch beside a stream. A dark shape had grown on the edge of barren land. He would arrive in *Daar Orr* by nightfall.

His horse was bathed in sweat when he reached the city outskirts. The darkness was thin, the silence of the wasteland beaten into retreat. He steered towards the rendezvous point, a bar and eatery, to find the tem'ondri drinking fermented dew, finishing a lavish dinner. They insisted that he eat. When he'd finished a rich broth of bugs, grasses and hot peppers bought and paid for by the hosts, it was agreed they should catch a taxi carriage for the rest of their journey to let their beasts rest. The tem'ondri made the arrangements with the bar owner. Ula closed his eyes, lips tingling from the chilli, thinking of T'Shawn, Makkani, of home. He was tired before he'd reached his destination.

He slept for most of the ride, beside Vrawn and Vrax in the hollowed shell of the carriage, Goll in front with the driver. Sometimes he fell against their hard, bristled bodies, which immediately woke him. He caught random glances of *Daar Orr* between half-closed eyes; the bustling night market, filled with waving antennae. The heaped mud towers of domed homes, or nests, multiple lit windows several stories high. Mita dragons writhing beyond his window, carrying as many as five riders. The rare, *mi'owa*-tagged human, five steps behind their owner. And everywhere, arthropods that walked, that crawled, some that flew. It had been years since he had left his modest farm, and yet he could not keep awake for long, so for everything he saw before his eyes closed, Ula missed even more.

He awakened. The bright lights had been left far behind. Around them it was almost as dark as his farmland after dusk; before them was the glitter of illumination. A building. The tem'ondri leant forward, the driver pulling up before huge gates made from mita dragon scales, Ula thought, wiping his eyes. They were the colour of dusk sky, curved and pointed at the tips. The art was popular in this part of the land. The temo'ndri made instruments, sculptures and cooking utensils out of dragon scales. They even used the powder as a clothing dye.

The taxi rode to the foot of huge steps. There was a silhouette at the top, a smaller shadow created by fierce light, a glow from the open doors of the nest. The tem'ondri exited, paying the driver. Ula climbed free, attention diverted by the nest, his neck craned upwards in an attempt to see it all.

It was the biggest he'd ever seen. Towers upon towers of compacted mud, chewed and digested and defecated into place, moulded and hand-shaped by thousands of tem'ondri workers. Some were made with modern building equipment, especially in the city, but there was only one way to attain the roughened texture and glittering finish Ula saw everywhere, from the steps, to the door frame, to the inner tunnels; that was to have the mud pass through the bodies of mita dragons, as the tem'ondri once passed it through their own. Claw-marked streaks lined the walls, creating sharp ridges, like spines. The nest reminded

Ula of the Earth-bound castles he'd imagined when he father read to him as a child, tucked up in bed, a candle his solitary night light. Unlike those stone-hewn castles, the nests looked as though they were grown from the ground itself, nurtured like land cane, each level sprouting from the next in humped mounds until they rose into the night, even blocking the light of the moons.

The shadow in the open doorway was a tem'ondra, a stubby worker three segments shorter than his lean counterparts. He'd led them from the reception and down tunnelled corridors until they stood in the dining hall, a massive area that looked like the interior of a cave. Curved ceilings, soft overhead lights, a library alcove and an empty trestle table in the heart of the room, places for twenty. The tem'ondra stood to one side, head lowered, mandibles still, claws twitching. The hunters ignored her, as was the custom towards lower members of their own hierarchy, moving forward in unison towards a figure who approached. A human, Ula saw, as she stepped from the shadows.

'*Kaluz maadram . . .*'

'*Kaluz ballamor . . .*'

The greeting was repeated by the tem'ondri, who held her hands and bowed. Her response was the same to each. Ula followed their lead, taking her hands, bowing even as he caught sight of her eyes, even as he was struck by her long scarlet dress, the obviousness of her beauty.

'*Kaluz maadram . . .*'

'*Kaluz ballamor . . .*'

Her hands were still in his. She'd greeted them in the traditional manner and her Mon'draan was impeccable. He raised his head. She was his equal in height, long dark hair, blue eyes he recalled from distant memory and books, skin like the clouds both planets shared. Her hands were soft as his son's had been, years ago, when he was an infant, long before he worked the fields. Her fingers were delicate, slim, nails painted translucent pink. Not many ancestors of this type had made the journey centuries ago, but there had been some, the poorest. Ula saw their descendants every once in a while, whenever he travelled to the big cities to trade, but he hadn't been this close to such humans in an age.

The woman relaxed her hands, smiling faintly. The tem'ondri watched, silent. Their tension was clear.

'You're shocked?' she said.

'A little. There aren't many of your kind.'

There was no shame in his admittance. Her question betrayed understanding.

'My people are from *Daar Quen*, the east. Many ancestors settled there during the migration.'

'Ah, yes. My father told me. He said the people of *Daar Quen* are very beautiful.'

Her smile grew. She blushed. Ula heard a whispered chorus, *beautiful, beautiful*. He shivered.

'As are the people of the north,' she said.

'Excellent,' Vrawn said from across the room. 'You accept each other.'

'It is better than I had hoped,' Vrax chattered. 'We will leave you to paint yourselves.'

'You mean acquaint themselves, surely?' Vrawn broke in, turning to the humans when her sister fell silent. 'We struggle with the language.'

'We understand,' the woman said.

'It's fine,' Ula agreed. His hands were growing warm, only he didn't let go.

The tem'ondri left. The maid, they discovered, was already gone. The woman led Ula by the hand, into the tunnel the females had taken, and he thought they would be following, but as they walked into relative darkness they were alone. The arthropods disappeared as quickly as ants. The tunnel was cramped, hot, and seemed to trail upwards. There were lights embedded in the walls; electric, Ula was glad to note. The mansion wasn't as traditional as it seemed. Every so often the tunnel crossed into what seemed like hallways, and Ula could see the doors of other rooms, but the woman kept tugging, the pull of her fingers like the almost imperceptible rise of the tunnel, until they passed through an arched, open doorway. This led into a gigantic space twice the size of the hall, the room strangely empty. A bed, a rack of clothes. A set table by a bay window that stretched the entire length of one wall, darkness beyond. A huge travel chest, hers he guessed, made of planetary wood, gleaming and red. The dipped oval of a traditional tem'ondri bath at the foot of the immense bed, a hole dug into the floor itself. And nothing more, just bare space. Ula could have used the room to graze at least forty cattle for a number of weeks, could have grown hundreds of cane. He stopped, looking at nothing. The woman let his fingers go.

'The tem'ondri thrive on extravagance.'

He glanced at her. 'It has been said.'

'Not by you.'

Ula shrugged, turning, trying not to marvel at the space. 'Saying it won't change their urge.'

'It would place the urge in context. And your place within it.'

She leant on the edge of the bed, bare feet touching the rim of the bath. *Paar-Ull*. The traditional way. Only the richest of the rich could afford to have them dug. She watched him.

'The context won't change the fact.'

She laughed, the sharp sound echoing. She knelt by the side of the bath, pressing buttons that caused water to flow. Steam rose.

'Still the same Ula,' she said, pressing another button. Blue liquid escaped from a thin faucet into the tub. He walked a few steps towards her.

'So it is you.'

She fought disappointment, lost. Her lips were a thin line. Her eyes darted.

'I thought you'd recognised me. Thought you'd made up a lie. I was proud.'

'It was the truth.'

'Of course. You haven't changed.'

She slipped from the dress, her naked body bright, soft as he remembered. He didn't know what to say. She placed her clothing on the bed and lowered herself gently into the bath. Ula came closer. She was covered by bubbles up to her ribs, small breasts exposed. She wouldn't look at him now. She hadn't changed either. He was glad.

'How did you bring me here?'

'I didn't. They brought me weeks ago, told me your name. It had to be you. The region, name, occupation. I thought I'd never see you again.'

He knelt on his haunches next to the hole. She was balancing in the water on the palms of her hands, watching her toes. Ignoring him. Or trying to.

'Fellucia. Listen to me. You're going to get us killed.'

'Only if they find out.'

Those eyes. Earth sky, snatched from the very air. They held him. He remembered the first time.

'I have a family.'

'I know. Which is why we have to do this. You must take *Paar-Ull*.'

Ula nodded, standing. Shrugged off his clothes, threw them onto the bed. He slid into the water much as Fellucia had, and it was hot but he didn't make a sound or register discomfort. The bubbles were soft against him. Her skin met his. The rich spice of blue liquid made his limbs tingle like blood rushing through his veins, but after the initial surprise, it was pleasant. Ula hadn't taken *Paar-Ull* since the night he married T'Shawn, five Earth years and seven-and-a-half Mon'dra years ago.

They washed each other as was the custom. Rubbing soft cloth against her body, using traditional herb soaps. Ula was scared by what he remembered, what was the same. Her skin, much softened by previous baths taken since she'd reached maturity. The tiny dots and blemishes, the birthmark on her left shoulder blade, which fascinated him before. What scared him most was the anticipation he felt as he drew the cloth towards the places she liked most; the knob of bone at the base of her spine, the crevice between her breasts; the round curve of her hips, and of course the flesh between her legs. He was trembling when he finished, almost too much to recognise that she was washing him in much the same way, with full knowledge of what would please him, and when she asked him to turn and face her he couldn't help touching her, and she dropped the cloth into the water and held him, and they kissed and it was everything he remembered, nothing unknown.

He dreamt and woke to see Fellucia hadn't slept. She was staring, caressing his arm, eyes far away. She spoke as though she was continuing a conversation they'd shared hours ago.

'Your skin,' she said. 'I've never forgotten. It's like the land that grows cane. It's beautiful.'

He couldn't help thinking of the past. With Fellucia there had always been danger.

'In the world we're from, that land is everywhere, like us. It gave our world its name.'

'And here?'

'Here, that land is a rarity. A commodity. There it's taken for granted; here it is worshipped.'

'Don't you mean exploited? Tended by slaves?'

Her fingers scratched his skin. Her eyebrows were knitted. He remembered this well. His heart began to beat harder. He'd relished that feeling in the past, but she was wrong. He had changed. It wasn't as it felt when he was a boy.

'Here you're prized and kept in luxury,' he told her, soft in case he caused offence. 'Here you're something you wouldn't be on the home world. Royalty, or something close.'

She hissed, removing her hand. Although there was nothing to replace it, he felt the weight of something cold where warmth had once been. Almost a physical force.

'I hate the ancestors.'

Ula pulled his covers closer.

'They came for a better life,' he said. 'To discover. They came to make things better.'

She peered at him, threw an arm out behind herself, indicating the room.

'And you find this better? This nest is like their planet. Big, empty, nothing for us.'

'I have a life. I have family.'

Her arm fell. She turned to the huge bay windows. Ula couldn't see her face. When he looked in that direction there was nothing, pure darkness. He thought of outer space, that vast expanse, the cold. He tried to imagine the journey and could not.

Fellucia slid naked from the bed. She walked to the opposite end of the room, and bent in front of the red wood chest, threw it open. For a long time there was nothing other than the shuffle of movement. Ula closed his eyes. He must have fallen asleep, for when he opened them she was standing over him, close enough for him to see raised bumps on her skin. She was holding something small, a metal piece, about the size of an index finger. A slim silver object, hooked at the end. Ula looked from the object to Fellucia. Sat up.

'Where did you get that?'

'It was given.'

'By who?'

'My breeder.'

He waited a moment, digesting that.

'They told me I was your first.'

'You were.'

'You know what I mean.'

Fellucia blushed, deeper.

'We never lay together. He had two. He gave me this and used the other. He escaped and was caught.'

Ula couldn't look at her.

'That was the city,' she said, like it was a bedtime story. 'It was easy. The wilderness is vast.'

'And what about my family?'

'You can go back. They're too valuable to kill. There are many of us in the jungles of the far west. You can find help, bring them to safety.'

She gave him the key. It was light, almost weightless. He brought his knees to his chest, pushing the metal into his *mi'owa*.

It fit easily. He turned it towards the window and they heard a tiny click, a beep. A thin seam appeared. The *mi'owa* halved and fell onto the bed with a soft thud. Ula looked at his bare ankle, the separate halves. He massaged the tendons, ignoring her gaze.

'What about you?'

'I'll take the key. Stay. When the opportunity arrives, I'll escape.'

He shook his head, feeling the violence. 'They'll find the key.'

'I'll hide it inside me. It worked before. You escaped by your-self, that's what I'll tell them.'

'Again?'

Fellucia stared. He shut his mouth, reached for the separate halves of the tag and picked them up, connecting the circle around his ankle, pushing them together. That click was louder. A light turned green and pulsed steadily for two minutes, died. He took her soft hands, nothing like his wife's, or son's.

'I can't risk my family. You.'

'You must.'

'I can't.'

'It's your choice, but you must. I waited. I could've run, but I waited. You can run in my place.'

Her eyes glistened. Warmth, softness, heady perfume. They hugged. Ula let her go and saw the key was still in his palm. He tossed the thin metal from his right hand to left. A small, blood-less imprint, temporarily branded into his flesh. He stared at the ghost of what had once been.

'It's your choice,' Fellucia repeated, and he couldn't stand to see her for fear of betraying everything, their past and his future.

When Fellucia could no longer stay awake, Ula slipped from the bed and her cavernous room. He entered the tunnel outside the door not knowing where he was going, only that he should journey downwards and so he did, back the way they'd come, sometimes stumbling in darkness, other times unable to slow himself as the incline was steep. He felt along sharp-ridged refuse. The warmth was comforting. Their walls retained the heat of the day, pushing it outwards during the night. Only in the largest rooms did humans actually feel the chilled outside temperature. The cold-blooded tem'ondri felt nothing.

Soon, a door. When he pushed it swung outwards easily, letting in cool air. A few hours until dawn, and the heat was already rising. Ula stepped into the night, smelling long grass, and found he could see better than he'd hoped. He walked without knowing the terrain, what was out there. There could be snakes, wild cats, maybe the occasional bear. All bigger than anything found on Earth. Ula wasn't afraid. He'd never been fearful of the land. It's mine, he thought, as he walked across solid, compacted rock. It's mine as much as theirs.

He found a jagged formation, something like the looming nest on a smaller scale, fashioned by wind and rain rather than tem'ondri claws. He grasped the rock and began to climb, tentative at first, but with more vigour when he realised there was easy purchase, until he was ripping at handholds, tearing flesh from his fingertips, scrabbling with his feet when they slipped. Outcrops sometimes housed smaller beasts, poisonous creatures that bit and stung, but he kept going, arms and legs moving in unison, higher until he was level with the lights of the nest, and still he kept going until he could climb no further. He pulled himself onto a section of the rock large enough to perch upon, if not sit. He half crouched and gazed at the land, the light of the glowing sky. He rested his cheek against rock.

Ula remembered his son running at full speed to greet the

gathered tem'ondri. The worry in his wife's eyes. The glittering scales of the mita dragon as it writhed. He felt the *mi'owa* key in his pocket, firm against his thigh, cool where the flesh was hot.

The sun rose. He climbed from the rock, backwards until he felt warm ground against the soles of his feet. Ula watched the growing dawn until the sun prickled his cheeks and then returned to the nest, to Fellucia.

CONTROL

He woke up to hear some weird noise, a scratching close in his ear that made him jerk like a sleeping dog, eyes open, seeing nothing. He stared into darkness. He rolled over and so did Michael, curling into a ball as he did it. That's when Danny guessed what had happened: his brother had pushed a finger into his ear, probably in his sleep. Michael always did stuff like that. Lashing out and hitting Danny in the face, giggling at something funny in his dreams, sometimes even talking out loud. That morning he didn't wake up, course not, just lay on his side soft-snoring, the soles of his tiny feet pressed flat against Danny's thighs, water-bottle warm. That was nice. Danny kept still and straight, breathing shallow air through his nose, blinking at fading night. The birds were tweeting quiet half-songs, sleepy beginnings. The smell of Michael's nappy was regular as the kitchen clock. A siren called blocks away then shut up, said nothing more, leaving a faint murmur of dawn.

He tried to pull at the covers when his arms erupted in Braille goosebumps, but Michael wouldn't let go. Eyes stinging, heavy, Danny heard something else outside his bedroom window, a louder version of the sound that had forced him awake. Rustles like the sliding, gentle shush of pulling his pyjama top over his head, or Mum's hand stroking his hair at bedtime. Soothing. He closed his eyes, thought it would stop, but when it grew louder he opened them. Michael was mumbling next to him, telling some dream person to stop. He waited for his brother to quiet. When he'd been silent for a count of ten, Danny got out of bed, careful so he wouldn't wake him. For that he had to roll sideways, knees bent, sitting up and gently pushing himself onto his feet. He crept towards the bedroom window.

Their curtains were thin, bleeding daylight. He peeled one back as far as his nose, left eye squinting against sun. The window looked onto their back garden and those of their neighbours, each rear space a rectangular slice of green, brown and grey. Fallen toys, extraterrestrial barbecue racks, lonely swings, flashes of pink and red bushes, rickety leaning sheds. And them. Scattered over grass, mud and concrete. Black figures moving sure as lice. For a moment he thought the gardens had become infested with those creatures of his terrifying dreams, produced by a searing itch that made his mother bring the shrunken comb and A4 paper, dark bodies falling from his hair, pattering onto the white sheet like rain, dying, legs writhing. He gasped at the sight of the black forms outside his window, believing his nightmares real, blinking horror, and saw they weren't lice but ICO. Loads. Crawling through gardens. Leaning against warped, wind-blown fences. Lining the alleyway that ran like a spine between the garden rows. Gathered in a bunched fist by the gate opposite theirs, the one that led to Mr Sharmake's garden. Mo's.

He knew then, remembered the billboard. Dad's red, bloated face, Uncle Rick's clenched jaw. The spinning glass on the tiled floor like the stunted red hand of the kitchen clock, only faster. Much faster. He felt his heart throb, solid against his ribs, and he couldn't breathe quietly without holding his mouth wide open.

The ICO pressed hands against their ears. They did things with their fingers like sign language, but choppier. One kicked down the gate and then they all poured forward like blackcurrant juice from a tipped cup, down the garden, over the neighbouring fences, meeting and pushing against Mo's back door until it gave with a loud crack, rushing into the house. And it was silent. So silent, Danny almost believed nothing had happened. They flooded inside until there was no trace of them but the movement of the upstairs white nets, the crash of a plate, a bark of pain, that fast language he couldn't describe, and the cries of a child, probably Fahima. Danny waited. Shot a look at his brother, flat on his back, gaping. Listened for his parents' voices. Nothing. Everything calm, outside and in. His fingers grew white, the curtain bunched between them.

Mo's nets danced, stiff and random as silent wind chimes, and he was there, framed against the dark background of the bedroom. Danny saw the brightness of his eyes from where he watched. The boy's head turned left, right, and he threw himself down, landing on the old coal shed with a shrill cry that made Danny draw in a sharp breath. He bounced up like a tennis ball, hit the garden path and ran towards the loose, broken gate. He was limping. He must have hurt himself. A man in black appeared at the window but there were none in any of the neighbouring gardens, or by the gate, or even on the bone-white central path. Mo didn't slow despite his limp; he just ran, leaning on his right leg, grimacing, one hand flat on that thigh. Danny felt his nails sharp in his own palms, heard himself whisper '*Go Mo. Go.*' By the time the other officers burst from the back door and ran down the alley it was as though he had willed it. Mo disappeared.

Danny let the curtain fall, ran to the pile of clothes at the end of their bed, squirming inside tracksuit bottoms, T-shirt, hoodie. He checked on his brother, who had rolled onto his chest, nappy raised high, face buried in pillow. He grabbed his orange paper-round bag and left. His parents' door was shut tight, but Danny still tiptoed. He trotted downstairs as quickly as he could in the darkness, keeping to the edge of each step, wincing at every creak. On the ground floor he moved faster, along the passage into the kitchen, grabbing whatever he saw – apples, crisps, fruit bars, a pack of chocolate biscuits, a box of grapes, the last of the samosas – pushing them all inside his bag. In the passage, he stifled the tinkling chatter of keys as best he could, unlocking the front door with one hand on the bunch, the other doing the important work, entering and twisting, before he slid them down in his pocket and snaked into dawn.

Baking bread from the Hovis factory half a mile away made him hungry for huge bites of air. His stomach rolled like a grumbling complaint. The cars glittered with frost, much like the paper-white sky. Danny lay his hand against the smooth plastic of his bag and walked, head raised, trying not to look either way. He ignored his parents' bedroom window too, thinking of Lot's wife. On the pavement, he turned a robotic left.

The first transport was parked at the end of his road. Headstone grey, 'ICT' stencilled on the sides. Empty driver and passenger seats, St George's flag hung across the back of the cab, a statue of the blond saint killing a black dragon on the dashboard. He turned his eyes to the road, slowing, but a scream made him jump, and they were there, five in black. He was close enough to see 'ICO' stencilled on their chests, the letters gleaming and smooth as a scar. They were struggling, swamping a hunched figure, and it was only when they reached the transport and one man opened the back door that he could see who it was. An old woman, it had to be Mrs Sharmake, although she never left the house without her burka so he wasn't sure. She was wailing, attempting to get away, but the men wouldn't let her. Her face was raised to the sky, mouth open, morning breeze making her gown swell like a kite. Her cheeks a glistening sheen, throaty cries making Danny shiver. Her feet bare, the toenails white seashells. She was leaning back, pulling against the men, tendons rigid, feet planted on the dark road, and as big as they were she managed to free one arm to beat her palm against her head, the sound flat, mute, echoing across the empty street. They wrestled with her, grunting and puffing tiny clouds into morning air, grabbed her beating arm, wrenching it behind her back.

Mrs Sharmake yelped once, stopped wailing. She whimpered in pain but did no more. They pushed her into the yawning mouth of the transport and the door clanged like an oven, but louder. A man wearing something like a gas mask made of gleaming black metal looked at Danny and said, 'Fuck off.'

He walked until the end of the road, turning left. On the corner there it was. The billboard. 'GO OR BE SENT.' A pair of cuffs, two masked ICO, blank eyes threatening their street, the world. The dark, smoky background, the red flowing river. Danny spat on the ground, walking faster. He would have spat on the poster but Dad said they'd swab his DNA and he'd be arrested, so he couldn't. He hated that billboard. It was the billboard that made Uncle Rick mouth off in front of Dad about dodgy neighbours, the billboard that made Dad's fist connect with Rick's jaw and caused him to fall, knocking over his glass of lager and Michael's cup of blackcurrant juice. If the billboard hadn't gone up Rick wouldn't have screamed like he was crying, or sworn he'd make ICO get the lot, pakis, blackies, all of them. If it hadn't been for that billboard Dad wouldn't have gone over to the Sharmakes and said whatever he'd told them, or started crying late in the night, Danny's mum whispering quick and trying to shush him while they thought the boys were asleep. If it weren't for the billboard his family would be a family.

He passed the central alley behind their house and heard screaming. He looked at the floor, focused on his trainers and tried to block it out. He murmured a song from the radio, concentrating on the words so hard he didn't see the ICO by the alley entrance.

'Oi.'

He looked up, breath caught. The officer was tall and bloated, a thick double chin hanging over his collar. He leant against a wall, picking his teeth with a thin bit of wood.

'Don't look at me like that, runt. Wha' you doin' out so early?'

'Paper round.'

'Yeah?'

'Yeah.'

The screams climbed to a higher pitch. A man in so much pain he sounded like a girl. Like Rick. He heard laughter, a cackled group of whoops like a party. Dad was probably awake. Sitting up in bed, trying not to listen. Maybe looking for him.

'What, can I go now? Gonna be late f'my round.'

The screams, the thin scratch of wood against enamel. His pulse, a dull drum in his head.

'Go on then, piss off.'

He bit his tongue and walked fast, muttering swear words at the pavement. A slab of van shot past, screeching to a stop. Raised voices and calls to battle, the clatter of feet on concrete, but Danny never looked back. He walked to the end of the road, opposite the park gates, turning left. At the end of the block he turned left again.

The Spotted Dog had been derelict for as long as they could remember. Wooden slat windows, dotted metal doors, a security firm's mobile number on the walls beside the silhouette logo of a man walking a dog. Everyone knew that was crap, especially the youngers. There was no security for the Spotted Dog. Dad said they were going to turn it into flats for the posh lot, or another supermarket even though there were two down the road. He and Danny went out every Saturday, knocking on doors and handing out leaflets, Dad talking about the old days when he met Mum in the beer garden and they'd stand on varied doorsteps for ages, telling that story and others until Danny got bored and cold and Dad would pull him close. Most houses had posters up saying 'SAVE THE SPOTTED DOG' because of them. It was a secret the adults pretended to keep to themselves, like their kids. Everyone knew it too. They couldn't save anything, let alone an old pub.

He walked around the back, through what had been the car park, leaping knee-high weeds until he came to cracked cellar boards. None of the kids knew who'd made the opening; it was broken in generations ago, had always been that way. He checked his surroundings, slid into mildewed darkness, onto the waiting barstool they'd placed in the cellar so they could enter, then the concrete floor, mostly feeling his way to the stairs, using what little light the opening gave. And then there was nothing. That had scared him as an infant, but by now it was normal. He used his phone torch to find the stairs, climbing into what they always said must have been the pub, although nothing remained but a blank empty space, mattresses spotted with dark patches, red cushions smeared bare and shiny that probably belonged to long-forgotten stools or chairs. Painful-looking blisters hung above his head. Danny had seen them burst before, showering grey water on some unlucky kid. Forcing them to walk home with their arms held away from their sides like a zombie, sniffling and bedraggled, to face beats, or at least grounding.

The boy was hunched in a corner, eying him. A glint in his hand reflecting torchlight. Danny heard the youngers say Mo carried, although he'd never seen it himself so he'd forgotten. Sheet-lightning metal flashed. He turned off his phone.

'It's OK. It's me. Danny Kearns, from 32. Simon's my dad. He knows yours.'

He dug into the orange bag, fingers closing around the first thing he touched, freed it. An apple. He held it towards Mo. The boy's eyes were bright, even in shadow. Danny stepped forward.

'You're hungry, right?'

Edging closer and closer until his shadow covered Mo's. His dark eyes glittered like tarmac.

'Take it. I got loads. And other stuff. It's for you.'

He knelt beside Mo. The boy had been crying. He couldn't see much, but he could hear it in Mo's breathing, could smell the salt of his tears.

'Take it, honest.'

Warm fingers touched his. Danny jumped. That made Mo twitch as well, but Danny steadied himself and pushed the apple back until Mo took it. The knife clattered against the wooden floor. He heard a satisfying crunch. The stilted rhythm of chewing. His eyes stung, and he lay his head against the wall. Closed them. Mo started to shake. Danny wanted to put his arms around him but that would have seemed a bit weird. He ducked beneath his bag strap, pushing it towards Mo.

'There's more in there. I gotta go, but I'll be back with some other stuff, in'shallah.'

The boy flinched. He wondered if he'd said it wrong but it was too late. He couldn't take it back.

'Don't move, yeah? My dad'll find out what happened to your family. I'll come back.'

He got up. Walking towards the stairs, Danny heard it. Rasping like the scrape of his brother's finger, raw with grief.

'Later.'

He turned, lifting a palm at Mo's shadow. 'Fuck Immigration Control.'

Mo stared. His eyes precious stone, defiant. 'Yeah, man. Fuck 'em.'

Danny nodded.

Outside the air was cold, the skies brighter, bluer. The clouds had moved elsewhere. He lifted himself from the cellar into the car park. He ducked through a hole in the fence and headed home, hands in pockets, head down, looking at nothing; not billboards, cars, or people.

He crossed as an ICT rolled by, heavy and monotonous. It stopped behind him. Danny winced, trying not to tense. The whine of reversal set his teeth on edge. He wanted to run, made himself step at a regular pace. The transport appeared at his left shoulder, kept reversing, coming to a stop some yards beyond. They waited until he drew close, the driver leaning from his window. It was the one from the alley, double chin and dough-ball features.

'All right, kid?'

He had to stop, face him, much as he didn't want to.

'Yep.'

'Finished yuh paper round?'

'Yeah.'

'Then where's yuh bag?'

That was the passenger, leaning over his mate. Square crew cut, black hair, red path of razor bumps trailing around his throat. Danny saw dark eyes, avoided them and cursed. He might as well have screamed it out loud. He focused on the end of his block, bit his lip. He tried to blank his eyes from what he saw but it was tough. His dad looked tall in his pale grey tracksuit. He was talking with a neighbour, one hand running through his hair, the other moving up and down, frantic. Ice flooded Danny's veins. The neighbour said something that made him turn and see him. Dad's face whitened. He started to walk quickly, like the ladies in the park just after the gates were unlocked, when Danny really came home from his round.

Transport doors opened, shut. He was surrounded by figures in black. When he squinted upwards, their eyes were blank as the pub cellar, way more terrifying. He couldn't understand their words because they came at once, a solid force until one got louder than the others repeating: 'How'd you get dust on your clothes?' and 'Tell us where the dust came from, sonny' until they released him from their pushing bodies, pointing at the place he didn't dare to look, over his shoulder, and he saw others with their hands on ears, barking numbers and coded names, running to the concrete-grey transport, doors swinging open and crunching closed like breaking bones. The engine roared, wheels spun, smoke stinging his nose, screaming tyres making his ears ring. The loudness, fading. Danny wheeled to see them stop outside the Spotted Dog, and there was another surge of men, stiff guns and batons, screaming as they ripped at wooden boards, smashed glass with their boots, entered the pub.

He tried to run, do something, but arms around his chest held him in place even as he writhed, screaming Mo's name, twisting his neck to escape his dad's voice saying, 'Shush, son, calm down.' Danny refused to hear, yet couldn't close his ears against him, or the retort of gunfire, final as slamming doors, sharp as a whisper, causing birds to take to the pale sky, cawing at no one. They rose over the park, wings moving in lazy stretches. He imagined they were waving goodbye.

YOU MEETS YOU

The last dream, the one that takes place before you wake and in some ways is the most vivid, thrusts you back into that first adult classroom, surrounded by easels and paint pots and huge tubes (that remind you of oversized toothpaste), by colours like Ivory Black and Cadmium Yellow Light. Sunshine falls from the window, one broad diagonal stroke, yet your space in the corner of the room is dark. Hidden. You are holding the paintbrush, unsure what might happen next, or indeed, how to make anything happen at all. You are looking at the canvas as though it might give a sign, or else extract the vision you have inside your head, that beautiful construction of light, angles and imagery, that formless thing that so very much wants to take shape. One look around the classroom rewards you with what you have long feared, even while at home, lying in bed, lost in your high. During the twenty-minute pod journey to the institute, looking out of the window at the incessant city beyond. Alone in the institute's dining area, eating tuna and cucumber on brown. The feeling. Despite being with others, you are alone.

In the classroom, people are already dipping the thin fibres of their brush into mixtures of paints and water, working on their own interior images, painting, no less. People hunched in concentration, people glaring at the cracked ceiling in thought, people smiling to themselves, people flicking the brush against the canvas while the tutor, a stout, robust man in a blue shirt and brown slacks, walks between the flimsy maze of easels, nodding, stopping to speak with a student, moving on. And you? Well, the more the vision dances the more difficult it becomes to move the muscles of your arm, to daub paint onto the blank surface. And the more difficult it becomes, the more you wish the colours inside your head would communicate with the tubes beside your seat. Before you know it you're reminded of the mouse who became a magician, the buckets and mops he commanded that sprang to life, that distant childhood memory. The paints begin to twitch and rise, swaying from pinched corner to corner, and the music starts, faint at first though growing louder, and you look to see who has noticed but everyone is gone; the tutor, the students, no one is there.

When you turn, there are dancing paint tubes moving in complete synchronisation, first single file and then side by side, coming closer. Their caps fly into the air every so often, land perfectly. They dance with more abandon, joined by the brushes, who swing stiff, glistening legs and waddle towards you, and the scratch of their feet against the wooden desk begins to tear at your nerves, and you back away, arms raised in front of your face, crying out in terror.

The room is hard to make out, even with lights. You squint to make sure it's yours, panic a few more seconds, eyes darting, for a long time you are not sure. The mattress is uneven beneath your spine, sharp needles of pain bite random places; waist, lower back, shoulder blade, neck. This is familiar, reassuring. A flat screen perched on wooden boxes a metre and a half beyond your left ear, rope strung across the furthest end of the room, four metres from where your feet protrude off the bed – from this, clothes hang like withered bodies. The walls are bare unless you count the forked lightning cracks. A single, old chair is hunched in a corner opposite the bed. Assorted objects lie on the exposed concrete floor, too numerous to mention, and although you cannot see them their presence is felt, and this too brings comfort. You relax against the flat, non-existent pillow, breathe a lengthy sigh of relief, close your eyes and count yourself lucky. You are home.

A wave of nausea follows; your body remembers. It surges and recedes, a strong tide, and your bed is the raft, the scattered objects at its foot, everywhere, bobbing flotsam. Your head begins to pound and there's a heavy feeling in your gut and you know what is doing this to you, what you have done to yourself. It is the scrap on your tongue. It is your tongue's connection with the glittering silver and black scrap in the plastic bag. It is the scrap that looked like sparkling ashes and felt as you imagined grit might, when the sharp taste of pharmaceutical alchemy filled your mouth and dissolved on your lifeless tongue.

It was. It is.

You are trying to sit up, but the drug has become a gravitational force. The light in the room sways with movement. You have bumped something, probably the lamp. You try to raise yourself again, to prove something, and eventually after some struggle you make it. Somehow, some deep instinct, a part of you, already knows. That something is urging you to rise into a sitting position, pause, push with the balls of your feet, stand, rock forth and back, steady yourself, eyes closed tight, wait for the ebbing to pass.

It doesn't, although it lessens. There is a stumbling journey out of the dark room, hands reaching, palm-cold, damp walls, always on the verge of collapse, into the only remaining space you call your own, the kitchen. Of course you have a bathroom, but it doesn't count. That's out in the corridor, is filthy even when it is clean, and is shared. You are taking two steps and falling, sometimes with a thud, pushing yourself to your feet and creating momentum, taking two more. There is a smell that jars something, a remembrance maybe, but once noted it is gone, and you raise your head, trying to recapture the trail. You are hearing something, some rustling and a maddening silence that follows, even as you frown to yourself, strain to hear better, enter the kitchen searching brown, stained cupboards and the counter caked with spilt food, breadcrumbs, the illegible scrawl of tea-trails. Learning nothing, you turn to the dull concrete floor with unfocused, blood-reddened eyes.

There. It is there, though you hardly believe it. The huddled, whimpering figure of a boy crouched with his knees up, head bowed, his face obscured. He's trembling. He wears simple jeans with large holes in the knees, a worn yellow T-shirt, Cadmium Yellow Light you think, before bringing your mind back to matters at hand. His hair is brown with dust, clumped together, and the smell you already encountered in the bedroom is a mixture of rainwater and rot. The clothes are bruised and shadowed with use, a street kid, you think, who broke into your home, there are thousands in the city, willing to rape, rob, murder. You are desperate for the boy to leave, scared he might possess a weapon. You reach for the reassurance of the blade while your head reels and the tide pushes, pulls, and you feel your body rock with motion.

'Hey,' you bark. '*Hey!* Get outta here!'

The boy digs his head deeper into the dark pit between his legs and arms. He snivels louder now, and his shaking is more noticeable. You produce the blade from your back pocket, point.

'Hey!' you call, louder. 'Get the fuck out! Now! Or I'll chuck you, an' you won't like it!'

Deeper, until all you see is the two-toned, matted hair, dark black and chocolate brown, as if the dusting were a lightly sprinkled garnish.

'C'mon,' you say. Adrenaline helps you find strength. You step forward, one hand outstretched, to grab him.

The boy looks up. He screams much louder than you can shout. A pounding, intense wall of sound, louder than anything you believe you have ever heard. The scream makes your ears ring, your head reverberate pain, and there is nothing you can do but stop, attempting to withstand the onslaught, a man walking into rushing wind, and you are caught in place, power washing over you. The scream lasts a few seconds, five at most, before coming to a random, complete and nearly as surprising an end.

But that isn't what makes you stop.

What makes you stop is the face. And the expression on the face – terror and indecision, that's for sure – but also the face itself. Large brown eyes, fleshy cheeks. Thin eyebrows, no more than a smear. A faint scar beneath the chin where you have grown a beard partly to disguise the injury when you were hit by a cricket bat aged nine (separating drops of blood flying beyond your peripheral vision like summer insects on that terrible day). Thin lips, too dry, flaking, constantly bitten by protruding teeth, a habit that returns when withdrawal kicks in. The face reminds you of you. The face resembles you back then. The face not only looks like you, awareness says in that quick instance, when silence tumbles into the space once occupied by the loudest sound you ever heard, the face *is* you.

There is no uncertainty. No question. You are staring face to face with your eleven-year-old self. And now, it is your turn to scream.

Your eleven-year-old face does nothing. Simply looks. Your scream, although loud enough to cause an ache in your chest, is hardly strong enough to be heard outside your dishevelled room. When you realise the only person affected by what you are doing is the you that is actually screaming, you stop. The eleven-year-old face seems amused. It makes you ill to admit this, but that is the truth, it's obvious, because the boy smiles.

'Go!' you hiss, yet the adrenaline is gone. Your skin feels like a washcloth left overnight on the side of the rusting tub, and your hands shake, and what's worse, you're still unsteady on your feet. The boy stares at you. Perhaps he has realised, you think. Perhaps he can see.

It would seem so, because instead of doing what you have asked, he does the opposite, and comes closer. You will soon learn this is something the boy cannot help, this unconscious disobedience embedded in his DNA: right now, however, you are repelled by his refusal to follow a simple, hissed order, and you back away despite the blade in your hands, create the distance there was. The boy's smile stays exactly as it was, no more, no less. When you bump against the wooden door frame that separates the bedroom from the kitchen, the distance between you and you is closed. You fall to the floor. There is nowhere further to go.

The boy is still coming towards you. He's walking half-crouched, perhaps fearing what might happen when he gets too close, yet unable to stop. You take in scabbed skin, bruises. Streaks of dirt like strange animal markings, the smell. Wide eyes, dancing with a curiosity you had forgotten you ever had until faced with the self you had once been, long ago. You are caught in appreciation, moved by the beauty of wonder, juxtaposed with deep pain. There is nothing else in that moment but the two of you, face to face. You put away the blade.

'Your name?' the boy asks. His voice is husky like the rasp of a thousand cigarettes. You remember enough to know that wasn't the case. At eleven, although you had been abused in a majority of ways, drugs weren't part of your life. Thinking about that, it takes a while to hear what he has said, let alone say anything in return.

'David,' you say, and gulp, looking around the cluttered room. 'Young.'

'That's me,' he says, and you feel your stomach plunge.

'I know.'

'I'm you an' you're me! Funny, innit?' The boy grins, exposing white teeth, jumbled together in a mouth too small to house them. You cannot see the cause of his amusement.

'How . . .' Another huge gulp, the rasp of your dry throat. 'How did this happen?'

The boy shrugs, and saunters into the bedroom, head down so you can see the protruding knob at the base of his neck. He's looking at the littered objects on your floor. He stops, picks up random things. A broken mug, a lone chipped marble, the cracked face of a small red and white clock. Watching the child, you suppress the urge to leap across the room and fall on him, strike that knob, knock the boy to the floor. You are consumed by a hate so overwhelming it makes your hands shake with the force of keeping them still by your side. You are surprised by this, ashamed. You heard of the aftershock that follows the drug's effect on your body, but it is the first time you have taken scrap, and you have never experienced the shakes. You have seen what this withdrawal can do on the streets every day, where scrap is consumed in abundance. In the abandoned building, where you pushed your face into the plastic bag of crushed and powdered chemicals, there were hundreds of scrap addicts willing to do anything to retain that temporary high.

The boy, having finished his curious search of the bedroom floor, has now climbed onto the bed and lies curled up with his hand between his knees like you still do. He is watching you, but the wariness, the fear, has gone. Calm has replaced it. Trust.

'Get off my bed.' You try to force power into your voice; a surge of nausea emerges. The attempt to stand is feeble, eventually you manage, but a number of failed efforts while fumbling for the wall go before it. On your feet, you turn towards the child.

'I'll call the yard.'

The boy blinks.

'You're high,' he says. 'They'd nick you first.'

'Just . . . Fuckin' . . . *Leave!*' you say, and this demand is your most powerful, if only a little louder than a whisper. It takes everything out of you, and you fall to the floor once again, back sliding against the door frame, causing a sibilant defeat that sounds, to your drug-fuelled brain, as if the room itself is shushing you, demanding you become quieter still.

'No,' the boy says, simplicity itself, and you almost moan aloud with irritation, the knowledge that you can do nothing.

You begin to cry. A blurting, pain-wracked explosion of tears and mucus, and canine whimpering that is even more shameful than anything before it. And you don't know what's worse, that you're doing this in front of the boy who is essentially you, granting a nightmare view of who he will become – or that the boy has nothing to do with the reason you're crying. It's the pain, the withdrawal, the need to replenish your body with the drug. It's the truth that you would, in all probability, murder yourself for another taste.

Logic dictates one thing follows another: actions have consequences; force applied in one direction causes equal and opposite force. And so you come to the conclusion, by a lengthy, brain-numbing process of elimination, that the only thing you have done differently in the last twelve to twenty-four hours is take scrap. There is no other conclusion. You let the drug dissolve on your tongue and stumbled the few blocks home, fell asleep on your bed, dreamed your outlandish dream and woke to a reality even more impossible than anything your subconscious mind could project. You accept that as given. And if that thought is followed to its obvious ending, this would mean any appeasement of that inner urge, this *must have now*, the need to climb your own mental walls, could quite possibly reproduce the impossible once more: yourself, faced with another younger self. David Young sitting in a room with a pair of David Youngs. How old would the next be? Twenty? Thirty? Or would the newly reproduced Young be younger than the first? Eight maybe? Four? Two?

The best, most obvious thing for you is never to find out. To stay away from scrap until you work out whether you are right, whether the drug caused the occurrence, or if there is an alternative reason.

But that would be to completely disregard or, indeed, hope you can undermine the proven notion of class A addiction. The trouble is the drug claimed as addictive from the first taste has been proven to be just that. You have seen it with your own eyes. Known it to be true. You feel it in your veins now, the way your blood begins to fizz, the sweat that leaks from open pores, the blurred vision, dry tongue, and of course those perpetual shakes. This is no media-fuelled twentieth-century myth, the type more intellectual users laugh about in the darkness of low-ceiling squats, and sometimes concoct using old yellowed books for nostalgia's sake. Serving boiled elixirs to gathered friends and punters, eyes temporarily half-closed, jaws hung open, wallowing in the results; crack, heroin, ice, PCP. The old ways have fallen into disuse. The drugs ceased to affect their users the way they had, and so their stranglehold loosened, and the addicted fell into an abyss of forgetfulness, ever disappearing until they were nothing more than a glint of light, then noth-ingness itself. New compounds were experimented with, new synthetics created to replace lost highs; new pills, powders and liquids concentrated to work on users for whom generations of drug consumption had altered their bodies until, in some ways, mostly in the deep recesses of the brain, they were hardly human at all. These new recreational preparations embodied myths written centuries ago, did what those ancient chemicals claimed. Addiction was no longer something that happened over time. It was immediate, overwhelming, and it hurt.

And so you crouch in the corner, and sit on the floor, and when that becomes impossible you stretch yourself out on the cold concrete and feel soothed in comparison with the heat of your body, which has risen by one degree and become unbearable. There are irregular spasms, which make your limbs twitch as though shocked by an electric current, and while the boy sits on your bed and watches curiously, you come to the conclusion, during a random window of lucidity, that what you might need is your regular drug. Not scrap, but the hadion you usually consume: your normal, daily addiction.

The decision bolsters you with the strength needed to push

yourself upwards to your feet, limbs still shaking. The boy sits up at once, the whites of his eyes luminous. You cross the room for the door, ignore him.

'Where are you going?'

'Out,' you respond, and hear yourself, not now, but years before, spitting the word at your social trainer; the sound is sheet lightning and gone, you leave your hand on the palm reader a moment longer than needed. The door slides open. You are assailed with the smell of the building; a mixed odour of feet, sweat, the farts of ravaged men. From behind other doors there are voices, television, a hacking cough.

'I'm coming,' the boy says, taking advantage of your stalling. Again you ignore him and step into the corridor on stiff legs, slam your hand on the outer reader while he doggedly follows, walk stiltedly towards the lift as your door slides shut.

In the lift, you are both silent, muted voices and the stench of the building seeping into the confined space. The boy's head turns constantly. He is seeing everything for the first time. He touches surfaces like a baby, reaching for the lift walls until you grab his hand, push it away.

'It's not clean,' you tell him. 'They spit on the walls.'

He nods as though this makes sense, studies the globs on dimpled walls even more closely, nose almost touching the thick, gloopy substance. You continue to try and ignore him. The lift doors open and you are deposited into the lobby where the security man lounges in a back room, sometimes glued to a flat screen. At other times he can be found drinking with a woman for hire, although this, you admit, mostly happens later at night. Now he is sleeping, feet on a desk, and the reception counter, where he is meant to be, is abandoned. You pass all of this, the boy trailing, twisting his neck to watch the sleeping man.

Bulletproof plastic doors slide open as you draw close. In another moment, you are on the street.

In your post-intoxicated state, it is impossible not to be assaulted by noise. Taxis and private hoverpods roar by, their blue-lit undersides illuminating rough tarmac. Somewhere further down the block, behind you, they are destroying a dilapidated building. The growl of machinery is loud, jarring your senses. Your ears ring and you can feel it underfoot. Across the wide main street, in the porch of another tenement much like yours, this one filled with victims of alcohol abuse you know, there is a loud argument that will no doubt turn into a fight. Two red-faced men push at each other, held back by friends who do not possess the required enthusiasm for the task. Like everyone else you turn away. Further along the block there are lights, music, open shops selling food and drink that debilitates rather than sustains; women and men, sometimes even children, who sell themselves. At the far end of the block there is a whole building of darkness, with the throb of unseen people and the steady bass of louder music. It seems miles away in your decrepit, withdrawn state, but this is where you must go.

You begin to make your way, dwarfed shadow by your side, ogling everything. When you look down on him it very nearly brings a smile to your face, but it is snatched away by the pain of putting one foot before another; the difficulty of going far enough to grasp a street lamp, wrap your thin body around it like electric wire, hang for a second, panting, until the pain recedes and your vision clears. Then you continue, the boy's head swivelling, and if you only had strength you would slap him to release the pressure, make him feel what you feel, but it is all you can do just to move. You step painfully on, tickled by the eyes of the criminals, prostitutes, pimps and the residents forced to live beside them, all watching your laboured progress. No doubt guessing what you have taken, probably believing the boy is yours for one night only, and disgust sweeps you. It is a long time since you have felt shame, and so when the boy slips an arm around you in order to help your progress, perhaps noticing the stares of the people he is staring at, you shove him away violently, causing a hiss of condemnation, although thank God they do nothing. It would only bring more trouble to use the blade, and you are not even sure if you could lift it.

The boy looks at you, sullen, lips pushed out, hands in pockets. He walks five steps in front of you with his head down, kicking rubbish.

Reaching the dark, noisy building, you push through gathered people outside. The boy hangs back, grasping the rear of your shirt as you climb the building steps. No one takes any notice. They are either high or negotiating future deals. Either way, they are consumed. Huge doors stand before you, barred and chained and boarded with planks of wood, and yet there is a gap between them. They are open. Inside, where some would expect light, there is none. Simply the chatter of more people, formless in cavernous gloom, firefly pinpricks of cigarettes and pipes. While you walk through the cluster without stopping, the boy is turning and looking at everything once again, stumbling on what he cannot see, and his grip on the back of your shirt loosens a little, before he leaps the space between you, hurtles into your back as you pause by the stairwell. You turn and glare, but it's dark and he cannot even see this, although he can feel your eyes.

Up the dusky stairwell, the thump of music grows louder, and a pale green light cast from dull fluorescents that once marked fire exits now illuminates dealers. There is a perpetual whisper, the hawking of wares, and there is curiosity on the boy's face again as you stumble up and further up, serenaded by calls of *mistan, peripy, loana, crystal stars, arcacia, median grey*. You do not look at the warped and broken features of the lost; you would only see a mirror of your own. You do not look at walls christened with graffiti, shit and blood in equal measure, or down at your feet where the crunch of glass and plastic grows louder with each step. You ignore the touch of many fingers all over your body, the promise of favours in exchange for credit, which would be exchanged for drugs. You ignore everything and push onwards, upwards, while your younger self takes it all in and his green-tinged eyes grow wide in the darkness, although of course you do not see this either.

Out, through another set of thickened doors, into a massive hall. Strobe lights rain white flashes over a Bible-dark mass of people that writhes in synchronised time. You think, Ivory Black. There's the smell of alcohol, the fog of burning drugs, a floating canopy. There are hands that wave in the air, and the calls of ecstatic people, and horns, and whistles hardly heard. Some users are naked, in the middle of the crowd or in corners. The walls are lined with human bodies, smoking, dancing, drinking, making love. You could count over a thousand heads if you cared to. The frantic music is larger than everything.

You walk around the edge of the crowd towards dull light in one corner, red as spilt blood, a hump of figures gathered by open space. There is some kind of awning, a raised shutter. You stumble over someone sprawled on the floor, almost collapse. The figures lean over the counter to catch you.

'Hey,' one of them says, like somebody would normally say *hi*, before another man lifts you.

'Young?' the other figure questions. 'Round two?'

You push yourself upright, look into his eyes. Skinny frame, long face, bugged-out eyes, no hair apart from his eyebrows. Regan.

'Yes,' is all you can manage, and he's pulling you to your feet, questioning with his eyes. You nod, follow him away from the crowds, away from the others awaiting their own customers, into the back room where users lie everywhere like corpses. A young girl of about nineteen, eyes closed tight, drooling, head crooked to the left. An old man who has clearly soiled himself, the damp patch resembling a shadowed halo. A muscular, yet pot-bellied youth who mutters to himself, though you cannot catch what he's saying and he stares through you both.

Regan pushes the users aside like nothing more than misplaced furniture, making space for you to sit. It is then, looking behind you, that you notice there's no tug at your shirt tails. The feeling had grown so familiar you hardly registered its absence. The boy is not behind you. He is gone. There is a quick moment of joy – *you have lost him* – followed by a momentary ache – *why did he leave?* But the sad truth of the matter is it's all overpowered by the urge that hits when you turn back to Regan and see him sitting cross-legged, noting he has laid small scrap packages – doses, really, you admit – on a piece of wood placed across his lap, each bigger than the last.

You forget the boy in one quick instant, join Regan, try to forget the gun protruding from his fist, a precaution, you know.

'Scrap, right?' Regan says, and something inside you lurches. *Yes.*

'No – no,' you respond, forcing the voice back. 'Hadion.' You clear your throat loudly. 'Just hadion.'

Regan's forehead wrinkles. 'That won't do.'

'Please.'

'You'll be back again.'

'Please.'

He sighs and wipes the packets of scrap from his board, a magician laying cards in reverse. You shiver, want to cry *stop*, do not. He digs inside his jacket with one hand, gun pointing with the other. Slaps down a single, smaller package.

'Fifty-five,' he says. 'But you're makin' a mistake.'

'Sure,' you say, wanting to tell him you have already made it, keeping your mouth shut. You key credit into your wrist tag and press the tag against his. Both machines emit beeps. A light on Regan's turns green. He nods and puts the gun away.

'Cheers,' he says.

You nod, pick up the hadion. A lump the size of an eraser wrapped in thin plastic. You put it to your nose. It smells of burnt metal.

'Take your time,' Regan tells you, before he leaves. You unwrap the hadion. It can be injected but you prefer to smoke. You break the dull orange crystal into your pipe, light up. By the second pull, it works. You manoeuvre yourself until you lay against the body of the young girl. Your heads touch. Her hair is soft cotton. You drift.

There is no passage of time in these moments. You are high, and then you are less so. Soon, you will not feel the drug at all, although its residue will remain. You stand, kiss the young girl's temple, leave. As you pass the awning, Regan is not there. You walk into the thumping hall. You dance like a fallen angel, smoke more. You are approached by someone and do not see who. There might be sex but you cannot tell and do not remember. At some point you leave the hall, walk down the green stairs, through the dark entrance and emerge into the comparative quiet of the street. It is morning. Sunlight makes your eyes smart. You squint and see the bright T-shirt, Cadmium Yellow Light. The words resound in your head.

It is him. Collapsed against a lamp post, torn jeans soiled around the crotch, head crooked to one side. The boy.

Something tells you to leave him, although you can't. Closer, you notice ash-like traces around his nose and mouth. You curse aloud. The surrounding people take no notice. They're used to this.

Scrap. Someone gave the boy scrap. In exchange for what, you do not want to know.

He cannot walk, so you are forced to carry him to the flat draped over one shoulder like a summer coat. He is lighter than you imagine. You remember the many nights you went without food, the dregs you were forced to find. You remember the first time you took drugs of any kind, not at his age, not nearly as young, but each generation grows bolder. If you had paid him mind, you tell yourself, you could have stopped him, but you were busy thinking about yourself. Now it has been done. The thing you had feared has happened. There's barely time to muse over inevitability as you climb into the lobby, thumb the lift, ignore the blank stares of washouts like yourself, step inside and choose your floor.

The boy hardly stirs. He bounces against your shoulder when you walk along the corridor, jerks prone when you slap your palm against the outer reader, but is otherwise motionless. You are prepared for what may come, what might be inside, and when you see the figure on the chair you take little notice. You ease the boy onto the bed, where he flops backwards, arms outstretched, almost sleeping. You face the new arrival.

He is thin, grizzled, a gnarled ancient tree, head, hands, the cracked and exposed skin at his chest and throat. His eyes are black and keen, dull embers, innocence bled. He wears thin patchwork jeans and a faded green vest. His arms are filled with bruises and crevices, tattoos and scratches. The peak of his soiled baseball cap is a curved crescent moon framing his face. Grimy letters say 'NYC'. He's looking at you with a thin smile you recognise, have felt on your own face, and you match it for a moment, even lift your hand to feel the shape against your smooth fingertips; it is rigid and foreign, but it is yours.

'Don't blame the boy,' the figure says, his voice rumbling, deep, powerful for such a thin man. 'He had nothing to do with it. That was me.'

'With what?' you say, but you're testing him. The man laughs.

'Good try. Great try,' he admits. 'Some things you can't escape. Some things are meant to be.'

'And some you can,' you respond. 'Otherwise you wouldn't be here.'

The man rubs his fingers across his jaw; the rasp is sandpaper against stone.

'True,' he says. 'Very true.' He looks around the room, continues to rub. 'So you know who I am.'

You nod, sit on the edge of the bed. The boy drifts behind you, so high, eyes fluttering, whispering. The older one laughs harder, shakes his head. He picks at the green vest.

'As you can see, there's not much of us left.'

'No.'

A long silence. Even the hostel is quiet in those hours between retreating night and approaching day. Only the noise of machines clawing at buildings further along the block, a far-away crash of masonry, bricks. You do not look at each other, just the cluttered floor.

'I'm fresh out the house,' the older one continues. 'Seven-year stretch. That's why I'm here, I suppose.'

You flinch, gulp back information, your future.

'So what d'you want us to do?'

'Stop,' he tells you, holding your eye. 'The disease gets us. We're raped.'

Although there is no sorrow, although he seems stronger than you could ever be, that makes you look away.

'There'll be nothing of us left before long.'

You shake your head, hissing downwards; even as you do there is a bright feeling, a distant stirring, some denial of what you are thinking, are about to utter.

'*You* said there's no escape.'

He grins again. The teeth are his most solid thing, the least damaged. You marvel at them. Perhaps, to him, you look like the boy.

'From *some* things,' he emphasises, leaning back. 'The fact is, we control our path. We are where we are because of us. Otherwise I wouldn't be here. Right?' He gestures, a throw away flick of his fingers. 'Can I show you?'

'Yes,' you say, the brightness a deepening sensation. You are leaning forward, eager. 'Yes.'

The boy must wake, and so you wait for the high to pass. This takes many hours. It is full night before he comes back to himself. In the meantime, you and older you talk. He tells you of the house. A blank shared cell, automated wardens, the echo of pain-wracked voices, the sudden violence of patient men. He tells you of the person you will become, your struggles, the darkened twists and barricades that eventually line your path. He tells you of intent, memories of youth that will become nightly recall, the sudden feel of possibility, the whisper of a cellmate in the darkness of lights out, the offer and acceptance of scrap. There is warmth in his voice, you cannot deny. A connection evident in each word. And the bright feeling grows, not just in your gut, but in your whole body, and so you listen to it all, everything.

However, what with his appearance in your tiny room, you have forgotten the urge, although it has not forgotten you. The addiction strikes the old one first, forming slowly so the first signs are hardly noticeable. His eyes begin to drift. He bites his lips. He looks around the room, distracted by the tiniest motes on unseen thermals. Soon, he begins to sweat. All through these symptoms he keeps talking, and you listen, but the distractions grow. He rubs and scratches at his thin arms, causing you to realise where those faded, dark marks came from. He stutters and loses his way, forgets what he is saying, speech slips from his grasp. His eyes grow dull. His forehead glistens, becomes wet. His fingers tremor as if they are diseased. And all the while the old one shoots sideways glances at you, as you bite your own lips, and wipe the sweat from your own head with a trembling hand, trying not to succumb to the itching, both of you, face to face with yet another thing you have successfully avoided for so many years.

You get to your feet. There's no room for privacy, no room for shame, but you feel it for the second time and walk to the kitchen. The pipe is in your clothes, as always. You load it with hadion crumbled between thumb and first finger, light the drug, knowing the old one will smell it, only wanting to hide the pleasure that floods your face. When that has gone, you will go back. You can hear his stark inhalation, and shake your head in sullen reproach; there's no point in this pointlessness, yet guilt has forced you. After a few more puffs, you go back.

The old one is obscured by smoke. His pipe grows bright orange, dulls as the cloud swirls around him, dirt-grey, until he is only a thin shadow. You sit on the floor, back against the bed, take another puff. And although you cannot see each other, which is better for you both, there is laughter in the gloom. Him first, then you join in. The coughing that follows opens up your lungs. You are high. So is he. You drift together, heads thrown back, pipes lowered, and the glow of your pipes dies down, eventually out. The clouds continue to swirl, and buildings crumble beyond your window, and the three of you remain lost in personal voids.

Hadion clears the brain and body sooner than scrap. When you come to, he is sitting up, scanning the room as though he just arrived, wiping drool from his speckled jaw. You clamber to your feet. Help him up with a hand, pull. In the kitchen you throw porridge oats into a pot and run the cold tap to create a stodgy mush. You leave this on the fire until it bubbles, thickens, pour the mixture into bowls. You eat in the bedroom, both in silence, jaws moving simultaneously, quiet and comfortable.

The boy opens his eyes. There is no fear or surprise when he sees the older man; he simply nods and sits on the edge of the bed, peering. The old one gestures him closer. The boy laughs, looks at you, waiting for your agreement. When you do he crosses the room to where the old one sits, stumbling, rubbing eyes. The drug clings with sharp claws. He will soon need more, like the old one, like you. The old one gets to his feet, a slim construction of bone and flesh, towering over the boy. In a quick moment that makes you jump, they hug. The boy presses his forehead against the old one's belly, arms clasped tight around him, and though you feel a moment's jealousy, you know this is right. They stand that way for a long time, a fierce embrace. The old one cries, though no tears fall. His eyes simply become soft mirrors. You cannot tell the boy's response.

The old one leads you both from the building. If anyone in the lobby takes notice, they hide it well. You cross the city, street after putrid street, unsure where you are going, following like faithful pets, the boy tightly holding the old one's hand. You are scrambling over broken paving slabs and litter. Occasionally broken human beings. The air is rich with fog and morning. There is the light of a new day, but somewhere beyond, upwards, there is a closer light on the horizon, buildings of a district you barely know. The city beyond your city. It twinkles with reluctance, a rare stone trapped in dull earth. And the old one takes you towards this place, guiding your younger self with a gentle hand, making sure he does not fall, whispering, showing him the way.

There is a wound cut deep into the centre of the metropolis. It is centuries old, bleeding south until it reaches the ocean. Once it was a river, but that was when it brought life, vitality, and later, wealth. Now it is stained brown with neglect, the rotting flesh of the dead souring its taste, bringing sickness where it once brought prosperity, mortality where there was hope. The stink is like the tepid warren of sewers beneath your feet. The sound is a lazy slosh of water almost too thick to move. The old one brings you closer to the edge of the wound, as close as he can, and stops. On your side there is darkness, humped shadows, a smell of moss, the soft slap of moored boats. On the other side there are lights illuminating a wooden dock, a ladder, steps. There is no need for words, at least between the older one and you. For the boy there is confusion, yet he smiles.

'You will be chased,' older one says. 'By a group of boys, right?'

'Some young men,' you correct. 'But mostly boys.'

'They will chase you here,' the old one continues, 'where they'll stop, and catch you and beat you. They'll make you join them. But you can't. You have to get away. You have to cross the river.'

The boy stands silent, gazing over the water. You recognise the smell now, that first encounter with him in your flat. It was him. It was here.

'Now?' he says, looking up.

'Yes. You can make it; you just give up when you get here. You let them catch you. But you can't. You have to swim.'

You remember it well. The fear, the ache from running, amplified when you saw dark water. You didn't believe you could. What happened afterwards was a blur, as though you sank beneath the water anyway, only to emerge years later wrinkled by immersion, dripping experience. You believed the pain of not making it was better than the pain of trying to. The old one's right, you realise. It shaped who you became. You were wrong.

When you look down, the boy has already snaked free of his T-shirt, is pulling down the jeans. He gives you the clothing as though he also sees what will come, providing he makes it. He walks towards the black water and when it touches him he jumps, emitting a sound as though it scalds him. The old one chuckles; you flinch. The memory is still raw. This boy is strong, perhaps stronger than you were, and he returns to the water's edge, looks back once, waits for your confirmation, steps forward again until it reaches his knees, and then his hips, then his chest as he pitches forward. He is swimming. His strokes are choppy, and he kicks up a cloud of water, but he is moving confidently. The old one puts a matey hand on your shoulder. You allow it.

And the boy moves steadily across the city's wound. Not

graceful, not even fast, but a constant, dedicated pace. Soon, he is a third of the way, then half. You are silent, but inside you spur him on. Inside, you are shouting encouragement into the wind. It grows difficult to see his dark head against a dark background in the still of night, and your thoughts drift when all you can make out is the distant cascade of dirty water; you see yourself back in that classroom, faced with the paints and the easels and the vision in your head. You imagine yourself taking a deep breath, steadying nerves. Lifting the brush, dabbing the fibres into the first colour you see in your mind's eye, Cadmium Yellow Light, making a mark on canvas. This pleases you, and so you make another. And another. You wash the brush in a water pot, select another colour. Ivory Black. You trace thick, straight lines. You are smiling. The tutor looks over your shoulder, whispers. You can't hear him. You're lost.

The boy splashes closer to the northern bank. You gasp. He seems to be moving faster. You walk until water caresses your shoes, fingers clenched. You bring them to your mouth, cupped on each side.

'*Go on!*' you are yelling. '*Go on, you can! Go on!*'

And he does. On the other side, a tiny figure drags himself ashore, leaps into the air, cartwheels. You shout congratulations, and although they are lost in the wind, you feel they somehow reach him. You remember the old one, turn back.

'*He did it!*' you scream. 'He—'

There is no one. Just the lights of the city, a mass of buildings, the gravelled voice of the wind. The old man and the boy are gone. And yet you smile. You turn towards the bank and sit on the mud, and then lie back, oblivious to the cool, slick, wet earth, lifting your right hand before your eyes. The fingers are still as the night, steady. You breathe.

SEED

1

It had been a good long summer of hot days and balmy evenings, the sky morphing from blue into a haze of orange and red, but the autumn changed it all, bringing dark clouds, continual rain. For the first few weeks of September a storm circled above London, drenching the city in relentless showers lasting whole days. Soon it grew difficult for Dapo to remember long hours in the park, hurling bursts of laughter while inhaling newly cut grass. The evenings spent with Charles, sipping pints outside the local pub, finding strange comfort in the tawny glow of sash windows. Temperate nights in his garden, a sweet glass of rosette for company, silently toasting his luck. In that fortnight of oyster-grey skies it was common instead to find felled branches littering the streets each morning, and car windscreens covered with a mosaic of leaves. Wheelie bins lay on their sides, or were found streets away. Occasionally, there was the open-mouthed corpse of a fox.

After the rains the sun returned, albeit with weaker rays, and those who observed the severe weather warnings began to venture outside. Dapo wandered into his back garden to survey the extent of the storm damage and was surprised to find seeds littering the grass, particularly beneath the pear tree he and his wife had planted ten years ago. They were everywhere, glistening and round, tiny glinting eyes peeking upwards as if from a fringe of green hair. They were purple and bloated, a few split open to reveal a slightly pink, fleshy interior. He picked one up. It resembled a water chestnut, curved inward at the centre, except it was slightly rough to the touch. The shell was lined with strange, almost native patterns, on closer inspection more like whorls. No two seeds were the same. He craned his neck, examining his tree. He guessed they'd grown from there, as the tree had sprouted butterfly-wing petals and new, still-tender branches, lily-pad green, bowed and heavy.

He watched the clear sky, looking over the fences at his neighbours' gardens. The Dentons' was treeless, but there was a rose bush. The Agyemens' had a sizable apple tree; both bore new green, supple branches, shimmering blue and violet petals. All were laden with the fruit. He assumed, but couldn't see, that their grass was full of fallen seeds too. Nothing should have grown that late in the season, let alone so quickly. He rolled the seed between his fingers until he was disquieted by the way the markings rubbed against his skin, creating a rasp he didn't hear as much as feel. He took it into the kitchen to show Misra.

She was sitting at the kitchen table reading a novel and drinking tea, her usual routine before she went upstairs and began work. Dapo slipped the seed into his pocket and closed the French doors. He made his own cup of lemon and ginger then stood by the sink, sipping from the mug, enjoying the silence of the day. Iye wasn't there. He spent the weekend with his grandparents, Misra's father and mother, who brought him home after nursery on Monday afternoons. The house felt anticipatory without him, the air pregnant with the unknown moment that birthed his arrival, that welcome burst of sound and blurred action.

He appreciated the time Misra's parents afforded them. Time to work on individual projects, whatever they might be. Time to make love, or talk over steaming mugs, time to make time for themselves. Many of their fellow parents, their friends, family and neighbours didn't have the luxury of in-laws to take the strain of raising a child. In the old days they would have all lived together in some dusty compound surrounded by hordes of family, intimate or distant, or at least in the same village, at worst in the same town separated by scant miles. Now, there were only Misra's parents nearby, as Dapo's had returned to Nigeria many years ago. It was difficult to assess if they were better off or otherwise in this new millennial age of globalisation, of families located anywhere they could afford, of betterment.

'What are you thinking?' she said from the kitchen table, putting down the book. It was a slim volume, not a novel at all he realised: *What Women Want*.

'Nothing useful,' he said. 'Hey, look at what I found in the garden.'

He took the seed from the pocket. She turned it between her fingers like he had before, a faint smile on her lips.

'Where'd you get this?'

'The garden. There's tons. Come and have a look.'

She gave it back and followed him, bending for various seeds of her own, examining each closely, holding them high against the light. Thin cloud had returned above, whiter, more expansive. The sun was a shining coin hidden behind muslin. Their pear tree rustled and shook in the breeze. Dapo watched her search the grass, telling himself he was focused on her response to the purple orbs, but after a while he admitted he liked to watch her move. Misra's body was tiny, wide, curved like the seed. He laughed, admonishing himself.

'What d'you think?' he croaked, throat dry. Tea did that to him sometimes.

'They're beautiful. Like little jewels.'

'They are.'

'Where d'you think they come from?'

'The trees, I think. They've got new branches.'

He pointed in the direction of the pear tree. Misra walked along the central garden path and stood beneath the tree. He joined her. She smelt of sandalwood, the joss sticks she'd burned that morning.

'Oh yeah,' she said. 'But none on the tree?'

'No,' he said, checking to make sure. She was right. They looked up, necks craned. All the branches were bare. He wrapped his arms around her waist, kissing the back of her head.

'So pretty.'

'Yes. Like precious stones.'

She held a seed close to her chest, cupping it with both hands.

'What are they?'

'I have no idea. I've never seen them before.'

'You should google them.'

'Yes.'

'I like this one.'

'I see that.'

She smiled and he kissed her hair again. It was soft, her skin warm as earth. She placed the seed gently inside her pocket as if it might break. Dapo did the same. He squeezed her to him and they went inside. Neither had any idea why they took the seeds, and they didn't speak about it again. It just seemed like the logical thing to do.

In the kitchen, they hardly spoke. Misra continued to sip tea, and later went upstairs to work. Dapo sat at the kitchen table. He picked up her book, glanced at the back cover, read a few pages, put it down. He got up, paced the kitchen, checked the email on his phone, sat back at the kitchen table.

This was always the worst. The in-between. The gaping chasm between what was and what could be. He'd not long finished a solo exhibition, some paintings and sculptures and a video installation focused on the city at night – the prevalent theme of his show, trite but true. He'd long been aware that he wasn't sure what to do next. There was the usual assortment of disparate works which always came when he was working on a big forthcoming collection, something with purpose and drive. But those fledgling pieces hadn't announced their place in the world, and so he waited like a spider, not tense or anxious, just hopeful and clear in the knowledge the moment would come. He had to be prepared. For the last few months he'd been capable of finding that inner poise, but the walk down the garden and the discovery of the seeds changed things, he could feel it. Those markings, that strange feeling on his fingertips. The pink flesh, almost white like a prawn, the deep calm of purple skin. Those seeds contained the DNA of inspiration. He was restless because they had stirred something, and he didn't know quite what. There was a surge of hormonal anticipation, a rush of endorphins, but he had no idea what would happen next.

He paced the house, listened to Dennis Brown, tried to stay away from Misra because he'd talk senselessly and therefore disturb her for the remainder of the afternoon. He watched a *Culture Show* episode on YouTube that concerned Native American art because in some way he felt that he should, even though he'd already seen it. By the time the end credits arrived there was a key in the door, and so had Iye, with a high-pitched excited voice, a stomping of feet. He thundered into the living room, rushing into Dapo's arms, a ball of consistent energy and chatter, warm and solid, black curling hair, bright eyes and teeth, bony knees and laughter. No sooner had he thrown himself at his father than he was gone, feet beating up the stairs to see his mother. Dapo heard slower footsteps, and then came the figure of his in-laws, Anu and Tasmin.

'Hello, hello . . .'

'Hi there. Tea anyone?'

'Yes, please,' Anu rumbled.

'I'd like tea, yes,' Tasmin said, entering.

He hugged both, ushering them into the kitchen. Put the kettle on. They sat at the dining table, lowering their bodies, sighing, stretching legs.

'So how was he? Full of beans as usual?'

'Oh, always full from morning to night,' Tasmin said, over the increasing roar of the kettle, getting up again and searching for mugs. 'Up at six he was.'

'*We* were,' Anu told Dapo. 'Tasmin was still in bed.'

'*Anu*. I was up at quarter past.'

'Quarter past eight,' he said, with a wink. Dapo smiled as much as he dared.

'So who made breakfast?'

A row of mugs appeared before him. Dapo poured, pinched teabags between his fingers, dropping them into open maws. He squinted against the sudden heat, the thick rush of steam.

'Thanks. Sugar?'

'None for me, thanks. You, Tasmin. You made him breakfast.'

'So what are you talking about? One sugar please. Idiot.'

'Sorry?' Dapo turned, kettle in hand, belching steam.

'Not you,' Tasmin smiled. She pointed, her nimble body always moving. 'That idiot.'

Anu laughed deep in his chest, holding up both hands. He was tall and languid, a sweep of grey falling across his forehead, his expression static as a wood carving. Dapo joined him as he continued to pour. More thunder came from the stairs. Misra and Iye joined them now.

'Hi Mum, Dad.'

Kisses and hugs all around. Iye called for a 'family hug', which consisted of him being squeezed from all sides by everyone crowding him in a circle. He closed his eyes tight and groaned while they did it, his grin wide, turning into pealing giggles.

'So what did you do today, mister?'

'He won't tell you,' Misra warned, tasting her tea.

Iye ignored his father, playing with a half-constructed Lego car on the kitchen floor. They rolled their eyes at each other.

'He had a good time at nursery with his friends,' Tasmin said.

'He had a fight with Hamza.'

'*Anu*. He did *not* fight with Hamza. It was an argument.'

'That's what I said: an argument. And then we went to the park.'

'Is that what happened? Did you go to the park, darling?'

Misra was kneeling beside him. He'd tuned them out and was making thrumming engine noises, the adult world a faint buzz.

'Idiot . . .'

'Yes, we took him to the park. It was amazing. There were these strange seed pods everywhere . . .'

'Really?' Misra got to her feet. 'What did they look like?'

They'd gained Iye's attention. He stood with his mother, tugging her from below, a free hand digging into his pocket.

'Mummy, Mummy, look at the seed pod I found!'

'They *are* amazing . . . So odd-looking, but so pretty,' Tasmin said.

'That's weird.' Dapo walked to the kitchen table, standing over his son. 'We've got them in the garden too.'

'You have?' Tasmin swivelled to see him.

'Oh, they're everywhere,' Anu said. 'We couldn't even walk across the grass, there were so many. It was too difficult. Bad for your feet. We had to stick to the path.'

'Mummy, Mummy, look!'

'OK, baby.' Misra took Iye's seed. She studied it closer than hers, frowning, holding it beneath her nose.

'They're all over the streets and pavements, everywhere. There's lots on our road.'

Dapo hovered over Misra, waiting. When she finished, he took Iye's seed. This one was smaller, though no less purple or beautiful. The whorls were finer, sporadic, leaving traces of bare dark skin that shone in the light. It weighed almost nothing, and was scuffed, as though it had been dropped or kicked.

'So they didn't come from a specific tree?' Dapo asked.

'No, they don't seem to. They're everywhere.'

'Weirdest thing,' Misra said to Dapo. They avoided each other's eyes.

'There's got to be an explanation. I'll google it.'

'Yes,' Tasmin said, distracted by her grandson, who was playing underfoot. Dapo let the conversation go. He'd grown used to their whims.

His in-laws drank their tea and left in a flurry of hand waves and hugs. There was CBeebies bedtime hour, a harried dinner, the brushing of teeth and, lastly, two stories for Iye. Dapo took the job, lying on the bed with their heads touching, reading a selection of his son's favourite books while the boy clutched his blanket close to his chin. When he finished Iye's nose was twitching, his eyes tinged red, half-closed. Dapo rose, each movement cautious, hands splayed, arms stiff, as if that would help. He was creeping towards the door when he heard a tiny voice.

'Daddy?'

Gritting his teeth, turning.

'Yes, Iye?'

'Seed pod is my friend, Daddy. He helps me sleep.'

'Yes, it does. You'll sleep well.'

'He whispers nice things in my ear.'

'That's good. What does it say?'

'I can't understand. But he's nice. He's kind. He likes me.'

'Ah. That's lovely,' Dapo said, eyes wandering until they found the seed. It looked even smaller where it had been placed on his son's chest of drawers, hardly noticeable among the CDs, half-built Lego improvisations and curled *Mr Men* books. 'Now I think it's time to sleep.'

'OK, Dad. Goodnight.'

'Night, Iye. I love you.'

He was about to leave when he paused. His son lay on his side, facing the window, asleep. The light from his window bathed the room in a soft white glow. He pulled the blinds cautiously, although it would make no difference: Iye was snoring, it had happened in moments. Dapo watched him breathe. The seed was placed beside the headboard, the inward curve turned towards his son. He hadn't done that; it must have been Iye. Not knowing why, he walked to the chest of drawers and picked it up, holding it to his ear like a seashell, cupped in his hand, close enough to touch his lobe. He squinted his right eye, unsure of what he might achieve.

There was a tiny rasping sound, something he couldn't quite

place, not quite a voice, it couldn't be, but a sound small and actual, furtive as skittering mouse claws. It was guttural, quick, making him gasp and drop the seed from his startled fingers onto the carpet. He stared at the bright purple against faint brown, still and accusatory as a dead man's eye. He felt as if he could hear the tiny voice from where he stood, and only resisted the urge to lift his foot and bring his heel down because somewhere inside, somewhere irrational he admitted, he questioned the morality of such an action; worse still, and even more stupid, he was scared. That was it, he was scared. Tons of them, Tasmin had said. Besides, he might wake his son.

He picked up the seed, held it before him, pinched between his fingers, and took it downstairs. Opened the French doors and threw it into his garden. He breathed in the night before he remembered the others, one in his pocket and Misra's too. He retrieved both seeds and threw them into the darkness. He did not tell his wife.

4

After he dropped Iye at nursery, Dapo returned home with a grande latte to share. He wanted to find Misra, instead unlocking the French doors, going into the garden. He'd been trying not to think about the plants. Even though he told himself he'd managed not to, consumed with thoughts of infinite possibilities, his gut churned with the lie.

He hadn't been back to the garden because he was busy with work. Dapo chuckled to himself – that was at least a half-lie. Inspiration was a surge of energy, ideas tumbling onto paper weighing little or nothing, feather-like sketches, whole and real. Late into the previous night he'd started to paint, simple images, clouds of colour really. When he'd finished he felt pleased. He flossed and cleaned his teeth, flinching at the buzz of his electric toothbrush, undressed in soft half-light, climbed into bed beside Misra. She was soft and unyielding; he pressed against her, smelling almond oil. She said something he couldn't hear, dropped her book. He ran his hand down her back until he was pulling at the thin web of panties, kissing the slight channel of her spine until he reached her hips. He rubbed the curved rise of her body with his palm and he wasn't sure what happened. His vision went dark, only it wasn't troubling, more like peaceful. Warmth caressed his head. He lay on one elbow, mind busy with visual equations. Curved brown hip into dark gleam of chestnut, into darker roundness of smooth plum, soft to the touch, into purple skin and mossy hair. Whorls carved into smooth surfaces like raised tattoos. Deep purple, immersive as bathwater. Slight fur, soft enough to rub against a cheek. Tickling, tender sensation.

After some time, he pulled away the covers and leant back on one arm. He didn't know how long he lay there, but when Misra asked if something was wrong he was roused from his meditative state, shocked by his own distraction. He'd been deep inside his own mind, comparing the curve of her hips and buttocks with the rounded shape of the seed. His lips tasted of moist earth; it wasn't actually unpleasant, just unusual. Dapo blinked himself back to the green-tinged statue of Ganesh beneath the smiling arc of multicoloured prayer flags, their books and untidy collage of clothes. He planted kisses around Misra's waist, ignoring her question, his urgency lost to the dreams.

That morning, Dapo went downstairs to make Iye's breakfast and poked his head around the reception door to see his previous evening's work. He stopped short, rubbing his temple. Canvases surrounded the room, three on easels like dwarf shrubs, three propped up against the radiator, five on the floor. Each was almost identical: hazy, formless masses, the green and purple of the seed. He stared, trying to recall lifting the brush, or choosing the paints.

Even as he walked the stone path that lead to his pear tree, Dapo was rubbing his thumb and forefingers together as if to dislodge stubborn dirt, or grit. He caught himself. He stared at his fingers, lifting them to his nose. They were clean, lavender-sweet. He swore, a low whisper half-caught in his throat, words trapped until they decomposed.

The ground was marked with tiny purple mounds. The tough skin of the pods was gone. The mounds were especially evident against the low green of the lawn Dapo kept religiously weeded and fed. He'd been proud of his grass, which had taken hours of care to maintain, to weed and trim and feed. Now it was ruined. There were perhaps a hundred raised purple lumps, or more, one for each fallen seed, he supposed. At the end of the grass, just before his garden shed, stood a cluster of unfeasibly tall saplings; three grouped closely as high as his knee. They were thin and wiry, bearing two or three small, heart-shaped leaves. The stems looked hardy as weeds. He walked across his lawn, bending to inspect them. Although predominately green, the purple tinge along their sides could only be seen when he turned his head right or left. Thin translucent hairs glistened like silk, covering the stem and leaves. He stood, sighing at the faint click in his knees, raising himself on his tiptoes to look at his neighbours' gardens. He couldn't quite see properly, so he went over to the Dentons' fence, lifting himself so the wood rested beneath his arms. Two young saplings side by side in a sea of purple waves, the humps of mounds. Dapo let himself fall, doing the same on the Agyemens' side. Shola was leant over four plants, a clustered group like his.

'Hey,' he called gently, not wanting to startle his neighbour. Shola turned as if expecting Dapo. He was boyish and slim, much like the saplings he pointed his darkened shears at. His glasses were thin wires, his bald head gleaming.

'Hey. Interesting, right?'

Shola stood feet apart, looking down at the plants. The immaculate grass, which Dapo had long admired, was dotted purple.

'Very.'

'They've been growing like this for three days. Faster than any weed.'

'Since the storm, right?'

'Since the storm.'

'What do you think it is?'

'I have no idea.' Glowing light reflected from the lenses of Shola's glasses, masking his eyes, making him look blind. 'I tried to look it up but no one knows. Lots of Twitter speculation, no answers.'

'Figures.' Dapo pulled himself higher. He was beginning to sweat. 'And you all picked one up? You, Ikiyoma, the twins?'

Shola's expression flattened. 'Yes.'

'Us too. We have three.'

'Three?' His neighbour's face twisted. He shook his head, almost to himself, sighed loudly. Raised the shears. They studied the plants, swaying in the faint breeze, leaves nodding. 'I have a good mind to chop them.'

Dapo opened his mouth, closed it. He didn't know how to say what he felt. It was just a dumb plant.

'I was about to when you looked over.'

The breeze rose. Trees rustled steady whispers. Shola tried to smile, letting the shears fall to the grass. They landed point-first, trembled. A gull called. Dapo shielded his eyes with his free hand, watching it disappear behind a roof.

'I don't know,' he said.

'Neither do I.'

'It feels stupid but my gut says wait. I'm going to try and find out some things. If I do, I'll let you know.'

'What feels stupid?'

'I don't know.' He wanted to shrug, arms tired, tendons aching. He looked away, searching for the gull. It was gone.

'Righto.'

'All right, sir.'

Dapo lowered himself onto the grass, walking back to the saplings. Two at the Dentons', one each for Patty and Charles. A child in university, another in Australia. Four at the Agyemens': Shola, Ikiyoma, Akande and Akoni, all living at home. And three for them: Dapo, Misra, Iye. He felt a breeze against his skin. When he looked down his arm was marked with raised bumps like the purple mounds that littered his garden.

He could not tell Misra. He promised himself as he stepped towards the French doors. *I will not tell Misra.* His breath felt high in his throat as he stepped inside, closed the door. He went into the study where she was leaning forward, eyes glued to the screen, watching a video; something for a website perhaps. He ignored her, lifting his laptop from its upright frame. *I will not tell Misra.* He slid out backwards, trying not to bump her, going down into the living room, wrenching the laptop open. A wait, a password, some clicks until he was rewarded with Google. He typed *purple seed*, deleted the first word, typed again.

He hadn't expected so many entries. Most from the UK,

hundreds more all over the world. Forested areas were particularly numerous. Dapo hadn't thought about that, although it made perfect sense. YouTube video after video had been uploaded showing heaped mounds of seeds beneath the giants of the rainforests, kapoks and tonka bean trees, some as big as coconuts. There were plants already as tall as people, stems the width of small children, shimmering with green and purple leaves. Seeds that had fallen or had been thrown onto concrete, only for the roots to force their way into cracks and crevices, pushing deep and beginning to grow in the most unlikely places: on Trafalgar Square, beside the entrance of a low-level coffee shop. A gathering of ten outside the Shepherd's Bush Westfield. Fifteen on the red central road outside Buckingham Palace. Plants had been cordoned by councils, protected, or perhaps the public were being protected from them? Dapo wasn't sure.

An American news broadcast told of a boy in Utah whose parents tried burning a plant, only for the boy to scream, writhing with pain. He was admitted to hospital with third-degree burns. 'Under no circumstances should you attempt to uproot, cut down, or destroy the plants in any way,' the anchorwoman said. She warned people not to touch the seeds; too late, Dapo thought. He watched an hour's worth of material until his head ached. He copied the link to the Utah news broadcast, typed *urgent* in the subject box, and emailed it to Shola, cc'ing Charles. He sat back, occasionally puffing air without being aware of it. Every few seconds he shook his head.

Dapo thundered downstairs, grabbing his house keys from the under stairs cupboard, yelled 'Going to the shop!' and went out. Their local park, where Iye had been taken days ago, was one block away. He crossed the road and entered the skeletal black gates, mouth half open in anticipation of the familiar lift in spirits when he crossed the threshold between tarmac and smooth gravel path. The lack of houses, a feeling of space. The uncluttered canvas of sky. When he saw the trees lining the paths, and purple mounds like tiny molehills all over the grass, nothing looked as it ever had. The trees seemed darker, larger. They didn't look as straight as they once had; in fact many seemed hunched, dominating the paths with their wide shadows. Worse still were the numbers of saplings, hundreds erupting from crumbling earth. Some were the huge green-tinged tendrils he'd seen in the images of the rainforests, borne of bigger trees maybe, the oaks. Most were small, thick-stemmed, glowing with the brightness of youth. Dapo walked fast, counting plants. He stopped after a hundred. There were just too many. Then he noticed something else.

The park was empty apart from the working staff, and they were too busy cordoning areas with yellow hazard tape or driving electric carts to notice him. There were no dogs, no joggers, no bike-riders, no skating teenagers or children. Absolutely no one.

7

He emerged from the house, a bottle of red in one hand, shutting the front door. He walked the path checking for plants, his new daily routine, a thick scent of their perfume rich in the evening air, clogging his nose and throat. There were none. He coughed twice, waiting for the reflex to pass, coughed once more. Continued. The gate squeaked as he prised it open, the drawn-out cry of hinges making Dapo wince. He never remembered to oil it. Quiet settled afterwards like snowfall.

It was a cool evening, unusually so. Clouds lay in rolling curves of overcast sections, barely a patch of visible sky. The pigeon-grey bellies looked unusually like the inward curve of the seed. He grew conscious of his thoughts, replaying his inner monologue, swearing quietly. He tore his eyes away from the sky to the pavement. A sapling of sorts, except it had grown as tall as him, bent and green, erupting from a square patch of earth where there had once been a normal tree, long uprooted. Leaves lay flat against its sides like a cigar; it was as thick as cane. He wanted to look closer but didn't trust himself not to feel disquieted enough to go back inside, lock himself away with Misra and Iye, or worse, try and damage the plant.

Dapo opened the Dentons' silent wooden gate, walking the path to stand outside his neighbours' matt blue door. He took a deep breath, knocked.

He heard a voice and perhaps footsteps, though for a long time no one came. A creeping, tingling feeling touched the back of his neck, someone close beside him; 'invading his aura', Misra would have said. He wanted to turn and look at the sapling, chided himself. The sensation grew unbearable, a feel of solid warmth next to his. When the door opened it was unexpected, making him flinch. Patty.

She was tanned autumn-brown, eyes sharp blue crystals, a bush of brown hair, angular face. Men still melted around her. Twenty years ago Dapo imagined they had pooled at her feet. Charles, her confident and equally attractive husband, took it all in his stride. The marriage had long inspired Dapo and Misra; and the Dentons, perhaps realising this, loved to have them over for dinner, drinks, or just to pop in.

'Dapo . . . Sorry to make you wait. I was giving him dinner.'
She held up a tablespoon. The rounded tip was blood-red.

'No trouble at all, I brought wine, hope that's OK.'

'Well, it's just us, but . . .' A kiss on both cheeks, and he was in. The door closed, his shoulders relaxed. He heard himself breathe out. 'Thank you so much.'

She took the bottle and walked away. He followed, struck by the mirror-image layout of their homes, as always; except everything in this house was white and clean and gleaming, the benefit of having older children, he guessed. There were grown-up furnishings like hallway tables, imitation crystal lamp-shades, carpeted floors. He thought they'd stop to pick up wine glasses from the kitchen, but Patty went straight upstairs, feet thumping on polished wood, Dapo staring into the younger faces of his neighbours in photographs. Their children Julie and Richard, various John and Jane Doe family members framed and immortalised all the way to the landing. Patty turned on herself, standing before the door of the second bedroom, kept for visitors Charles always said. The third bedroom was an office of sorts, although Dapo had heard of the sofa bed the couple bought for grandchildren who came to England once a year, sometimes used by drunken party guests who couldn't make a long drive home.

Patty stood by the half-open door. She made the pretence of knocking, a light touch of knuckles against wood.

'Dear? Dear . . . Dapo's come.'

He crept along the passage until he was beside her.

'I can come back if he's sleeping?'

Patty shook her head without turning.

'Dear? It's Dapo. Are you awake?'

'*Hello?*'

The voice was weak, trembling, nothing like his usual rumble. A rasp that burrowed deep into Dapo. His fingers curled.

'Can we come in?' Patty asked.

'*Yes . . . Yes . . .*'

'We'd better go in,' she said as though she hadn't heard, pushing the door. Dapo closed his eyes tight, counted to five, and went in after her.

Thankfully the lights were dim, although the air was stale, a perfume as heady as the plants. He smelt food, something strong and tomato-based, and made out the bowl on a bedside cabinet. A lamp was on, thin material thrown over the shade to lessen the glare. There was an old TV perched on a wooden chair near the window, makeshift and temporary. Various medicines clogged the cabinet, bottles of creams and boxes of pills. He felt his eyes adjust, unfortunately not before he bumped the edge of the double bed trying to give Patty space. Charles lay still, his body uncovered by sheets, a solid mass. Dapo couldn't see any injuries, although he could tell Charles was in pain by the rattling of his breath, the sharp way he inhaled through tightly clenched teeth.

'Hey, mate,' he said. 'What you done to yourself, eh?'

He gasped something Dapo couldn't understand.

'Sorry?'

'He wants you to sit,' Patty said. 'Slowly. Any movement hurts.'

'Yes, of course.' Dapo eased himself onto the mattress. Charles was unmoving apart from his head, which rolled to follow him. There was that wheezed intake of breath.

'You can come closer. It's OK. He'd like to see you.'

He didn't want to know how bad it was, not really, but he steeled himself and moved towards the pillow. His eyes adjusted. Patty sat on a chair beside the bed, knees locked together. Charles was shuddering with pain. There were bright red marks on his face and chest. His eyes were wide, his hair lank, wild. Dapo tried to smile. It wouldn't hold, his head fell. Something touched his hand. Charles. He'd reached for him.

'Is it all right?'

'They're OK,' Patty said, voice neutral. 'His left is worst.'

'OK.' He took the hand carefully, cupping the fingers in both of his. 'Look at you, eh? Might as well have told those Brazilians to turn down their music after all. Could have been less dangerous! There's me telling you leave it alone and look what you did!'

The mattress shook. Dapo's smile returned.

'You can do anything now. Might as well. Bungee. Parkour. Breakdancing.'

'*Don't . . . make . . .*' Charles wheezed, head rocking.

'Sorry, mate. You've got to, though, haven't you? What are you like?'

'*Scared. Just . . .*'

Charles coughed. It wracked his body, shaking the bed harder, making him gasp. Patty reached out, stopping herself, snatching her hand back, muttering beneath her breath. Dapo's eyes moistened. He was glad for the dark.

'Easy . . .' he said. 'Easy.' The words sounded stupid and useless. Charles swallowed the cough, taking all of his effort. Patty gave him water from a black and white child's beaker marked like a cow.

'Sorry,' he said.

'That's all right,' Patty sang, detached.

'Iye's got one of those.'

'Yes,' she smiled, concentrating on inserting the spout between Charles's lips, his raised head, the gulping, clicking swallows. 'They're all the rage.'

'Everyone's scared, Charlie,' Dapo said, keeping his friend in the conversation. 'There's no shame in it. I'm petrified.'

'And Misra?' Patty still wouldn't look at him.

'Oh, she thinks it'll all blow over. You know Misra. If it's organic, it's good. She won't be argued with.'

'She always was sensible.'

'Yes. She is.' He looked at the floor, his unseen loafers. 'You've spoken to your kids, right? They know you're OK?'

Charles squeezed his hand.

'And you've seen what they're saying? I notice you've got your telly. They think they've found out what they are.'

'We switched it off,' Patty said, removing the beaker from Charles's lips, placing it on the bedside cabinet. 'It made us nervous.'

'It's either a meteorite shower in the Amazon, or the deep-sea probe. They found bacteria in the trenches. The boffins are investigating.'

'The boffins probably started it. So they don't know which?'

'No.'

'Liars.'

'Misra reckons its evolution.'

A soft, rhythmic thud. Charles's head lifted and fell, lifted and fell against the pillow. He struggled to speak. They dipped their heads low, straining, but the words wouldn't leave his lips. Patty leant closer. She put her ear to his mouth, closing her eyes. After a moment she sat up, back straight, hands on her lap. She looked uncomfortable, rigid and still.

'What did he say?' Dapo asked, after the silence was too long.

'Genetics,' Patty said. 'Genetics.'

She entwined her fingers, and sighed.

He stayed another half an hour, not saying much, just clutching Charles's hand. When Patty suggested he might have to go, there was a long wheeze. Charles was asleep, probably had been for the last ten minutes. They crept out of the room, downstairs. Patty waited by the door. He was distressed to see her shoulders trembling.

'It'll be OK,' he whispered. He dug into his pocket for his trusty pack of tissues.

'It's not him,' she said, taking one and wiping at her eyes. 'He'll be OK. I can't help thinking what'll happen if things go wrong.'

'They won't. I promise you they won't.'

He hugged her, and they held hands. The damp of her tears cooled his neck. Her eyes were red. She still wouldn't look at him.

'What did the doctor say?'

'Bed rest for two to three weeks. I just want him on his feet. I don't feel safe.'

'Yes, I understand.' Dapo bit his lip. 'Ah – you don't mind if I take a look, do you? Out back?'

'Oh.'

'Just quickly. I'd like to know what distressed him that badly.'

'Well, I'm not sure.' She peered, blue eyes steadier. He couldn't tell what she was thinking, but they were strong, piercing. 'Aren't yours exactly the same?'

'That's what I'd like to see. I'll be two minutes, honestly.'

She shook her head like a dog emerging from water, touched his elbow.

'What am I thinking? Of course you can, I don't know what came over me.'

'Like I said, we're all scared.'

'Aren't we just? You won't mind if I stay inside? I can't bear to see them. I didn't even go out when the ambulance came.'

'No problem, really. You lead the way.'

She took him through their kitchen extension, brighter and more modern than the rest of the house, retrieved twin keys from a drawer and unlocked the French doors. Dapo noticed the scent right away, muggier than his, filling the garden. The perfume of the plant mixed with damp smoky charcoal. He turned to Patty. She'd stepped back, a hand over her mouth and nose.

'Vile things,' she said, voice muffled.

'Sorry. I'll shut the door.'

He stepped out, easing the door closed. A three-quarter moon had risen into a patch of clear sky. The trees rocked as if to greet him. Just beyond the rose bush were the shadowed stumps of plants, chest-high, as wide as modest tree trunks. Dapo always complained the Dentons' garden got more sun; now he wondered if that had contributed to the size of their plants. He got closer, the mixed smell of burnt vegetation, petrol and the plant even stronger until he was covering his mouth, stifling a cough. He pulled his phone from a pocket with a free hand, swiping, pointing the torch at the plants.

The plant on the right was a blackened mess. Fire had eaten green and purple flesh, turning it into a gnarled lump. A few feet away he saw the yellow petrol can leaning against the fence. Stupid, he told himself. Charles was too stubborn. Nothing Patty or anyone else might have said would have stopped him from trying to burn them down.

He aimed his phone left, arm jerking as he recoiled. He stepped back, almost fell, torch beam waving in all directions, righting himself to point the phone back at the plant. White torchlight struck purple flesh. What he'd seen wasn't a dream, or nightmare.

The plant was Patty's green-haired, purple-skinned identical twin, the body curled in an upright foetal position, leafy eyelids closed, stubbed hands clasped under the chin as though in prayer.

10

The door slammed, making him jump. He stood poised, lowering the heavy travel case with a gasp, head craning towards the upstairs landing. No sound of voices or movement. The house ticked.

'What was that?' he called. Waited. He let go of the case, climbing two stairs. Looked further up, listened. 'What was that?' he said, voice cracking on the last word, prickles of sweat bursting across his forehead. Mouth open, breathing hard.

'Just us,' Misra shouted, 'have you got the front door open?'

'Yes, come on, let's go!'

'Then it's just the wind.'

Movement. She stood on the landing, a sleepy Iye held tight. He was curled up, a thumb in his mouth. His pyjamas said: I'M STRONGER THAN I LOOK.

'Come on, Misra, let's go. I wanna avoid the traffic.'

'I know, I know,' she grumbled, coming to join him; then she slipped.

It was only a few steps, but Iye's weight made her unsteady. She fell back on her heels, him rushing to meet them as the boy tipped forward, banging his head against his shoulder, Dapo pushing against their combined weight and gravity. He stood there awhile, holding them in place, arms encircled around Misra's waist, Iye tight between them. Bright tears formed in the boy's eyes. A trail slipped down his left cheek to land on Dapo's shoulder. His body shook in silence, mouth closed firm.

'Everyone OK?'

'Yes.' Misra breathed hard.

'Iye?'

'Bit my tongue.'

'Let me see.'

He opened his mouth. Dapo saw blood on his perfect white teeth and lips. He kissed his forehead, hugging them again.

'You're all right,' he said. 'Worried me, man.'

'See? That's what happens when we rush.'

He let go, standing back, remembering his fear.

'Please get in the car. I'll make sure the back door's locked. We don't want to get caught on the roads.'

'All right, I'm going.'

She kissed his temple and went outside, Iye wrapped around her neck, leaving the front door open. Dapo walked into the kitchen, digging through cupboard drawers until he found the keys. He was just locking up when he stopped and stood by the French doors. He looked into the night.

The smallest plant, an identical likeness of their son, was rooted where the grass met stone patio squares, five feet from where it had grown. The middle-sized plant, his wife's, stood in the centre of the small concrete plain, bare and alone. Dapo's was closest, resting half a foot from the French doors, near enough for the left door to bump the plant if it was opened, or for him to step outside and touch the smooth skin without leaving the house, if he dared. Each had straightened from their hunched embryonic postures to stand at full height, purple arms by their sides, sightlines trained on the middle distance. Or the house. Previously he'd thought their open eyes were blank, unseeing. Now he wondered if what he'd imagined as a sightless, unconscious gaze was innate, unbroken concentration.

'What do you want?' he whispered, anger rising. 'What do you want?'

The likeness between himself and his plant was incredible. The skin was purple, just like the seed, the glistening smoothness of an aubergine. The body hair and nails were green, unnaturally bright; the thought was odd, but they actually seemed to glow in the darkness. The plant had the cropped short back and sides cut he'd favoured since he was a teenager, the jagged scar beneath his eye he'd received from throwing chairs at his cousin in Abuja, aged three. His nose, that strange yet familiar combination of straight and wide, his full lips, even the shapeliness of the mouth Misra always claimed had won her over. It had Dapo's thin oval eyes and thick green lashes, tiny ears and broad shoulders, meaty thighs and bulbous calves. He wasn't sure whether to be cheered or frightened by the absence of genitalia, the neat triangle of translucent green fibres. Apart from that, the plant was identical in every way.

He understood what Charles had felt, looking at the unbelievable, their silent threat. The urge to set all three plants alight was very real. He stared into its purple eyes. They stared back at his.

'I'll kill you,' he whispered. 'I'll find out how, I promise.'

His tired voice reminded him where he was. He made sure the door was locked, hurrying into the passage to pick up the travel case. Patty stood by the front gate with Misra. He waved, double-locking the front door, trundling down the path.

'Got everything?' she said, high-pitched and concertedly cheery. 'No coming back if you've forgotten your wallet.'

The skin beneath her eyes was grey and heavy. Her strained

smile made Dapo tremble, and he couldn't hold back his tears. Misra turned away, her face hidden in her hands. He reached for Patty, pulling her close. They embraced, her slim body shaking.

'Stop it, you,' she said into his jacket. 'Stop it. I won't have any of it.'

'Just take care of yourselves, OK?' Dapo heard the offbeat crunch of car doors streets away. He squeezed his eyes tight.

'You've got our address, right?' Misra said. 'I texted.'

'I have. Now go on and don't be silly, you two.' She let him go, backing off, fanning herself. 'Look after your lovely son. As soon as Charlie's well enough, I'll drive us.'

'Promise?' he said, holding her by the elbows.

'Promise.' She was looking at something he couldn't track. Dapo wanted to repeat the word until she held his eye and said it properly. He couldn't. His hands dropped to his sides.

'All right,' he said. 'We love you.'

'We love you too. Now go.'

They left her, hefting the last bags into their Honda, climbing in and wrenching doors closed. He tried not to look at the empty space where Shola's four-door Lexus had been parked until last night, that light rectangle or the darker road around it. Nor to think about Misra's parents, who'd encouraged them to leave. He started the engine, watching Patty in the rear-view. Misra and Iye turned, waving. Patty didn't. She stood by her gate until their car rounded the corner.

'Why's Auntie Patty crying?' Iye said, legs kicking.

'She's happy,' Misra said. She opened the glove compartment, moving things around until she found tissues. 'Sometimes adults cry when they're happy. She's glad we're going to have a good time.'

'In the night? We'll have a good time in the night?'

'Yes, in the night.'

'Is Uncle Charlie happy too?'

'Yes, he is.'

'You know the Petries found those things in the house?' he said, slipping into westbound traffic. Misra glared. 'What?'

'You know what.'

'I'm just saying.'

'Don't. Please.'

He shut his mouth and drove. When he looked at Iye he was silent, body swivelled, staring out of the window.

The main road was traffic-free, yet when they reached the junction vehicles were backed up one behind the other like they had been for some time. They eased into place. Horns beeped, drivers leant out of car windows. The streets glistened orange. The air was warm with exhaust fumes and barely contained frustration.

'Shit,' he muttered.

'Dee.'

'Sorry. Should've left earlier.'

'It's half two.'

'Yeah, but still.'

He tapped the wheel, trying to relax. Misra put her hand on his.

'We did the right thing.'

He feigned a smile. They kissed. She held his chin in her palm, rubbing. He closed his eyes.

'All right there, trooper?' he called back.

'Yes, Daddy.'

'Good.'

They moved a few metres, stopped. He turned on the radio, pressing until he found Radio 4. A lively burst of chatter filled the speakers. Misra turned it down. There were three voices as far as Dapo could tell, two men, one woman. They were discussing the government's response to 'the issue', as it was termed. A particularly nasal male voice seemed vocal and more distressed than the others.

'They don't even know,' the nasal voice said. 'They don't even know what happens next, or what people should do.'

'How would they?' the woman broke in.

'How would they not?"

'This is a particular phenomenon for a particular time and, as such, we must wait for the information to gather before making uncertain allegations or placing undue expectations on people who quite frankly are doing their best . . .'

'There's nothing to stop them from conducting a speedier, more thorough investigation. We don't have time for anything else. At least confirm what we think we know. Don't leave it to social media and political pundits, armchair loonies the lot of them, left or right. Say what we think we know! After ten days, these things are moving—'

'But that's obvious . . . People can see it . . .' the woman said.

'That's *all* we know, and it's precisely why people are panicking—' the second man said, in a tone suggesting he was trying to bring peace.

Misra sat forward, pressed another button. She gave Dapo a fierce look and sat back.

They moved one car length. Another man was speaking, dreamy and musical, under the influence of something Dapo thought. He wouldn't have minded something himself. The voice was deep, husky, close to the microphone. It whispered into their ears.

'See, the thing is,' the phantom voice said, 'the thing is we've played fast and loose. We've besieged this planet with no thought for the consequences, no remorse for our complicity in its current state, and something had to be done. It's been taken out of our hands. Now I don't believe in God, never have, but I believe in a higher power, spirituality, and I look at those things and I believe retribution's at hand. What that means, or how we come by it, is irrelevant. But whatever happens, I think it will be just, and beautiful, and it will redeem our species, I really do. I believe in the power of the planet to take care of itself, I always have, and if that comes to mean extermination so be it, because I for one—'

Misra switched the radio off. She sat back, her mouth a tight, thin line. Dapo kept his eyes on the bumper in front of him. More beeping horns. Three cars ahead a man got out, peering around a Transit van. A woman and child wove past their bonnet, wheeling a travel bag each.

'What station was that?'

'I don't know,' she said.

Dapo tapped the wheel. He muttered and switched off the engine.

19

It was better sleeping together, even though nobody got much rest and their bodies ached each morning. They'd given Iye the back seat but he woke up scared, so they crammed in with him, huddled like nesting birds. Misra always found sleep easy. Iye was his mother's son and also slept well, but Dapo suffered from insomnia at the best of times, even in his own bed. Since the last motel he'd been unable to close his eyes without thoughts racing, his fear rising. He decided, unofficially, without telling his family, that it might be better to keep watch. They were most active in the night, people said. He couldn't sleep knowing that might be true.

The rough blanket tickled his chin. He pulled at it. Misra snored and Iye lay across them, feet on Dapo's legs, head on her lap. They had parked near the undergrowth on the far side of the field, illegally perhaps, but they hadn't any choice. All accommodation had long been taken. Motorways and back roads alike were full of traffic, no matter the time of day or night. They were lucky enough to find an open gate which led to a path high on muddy hills, the slanted fields and woodland far away from any central roads. The unruly hedgerow seemed large enough to partially consume the Honda and keep it from all but the keenest observers. It wasn't ideal, yet Dapo disliked the idea of sleeping near others. It made them a target, in his eyes.

He was unused to complete silence. It fell like a shroud across bushes and oaks, broken by the sigh of grass whenever the breeze rose. Behind and above their car hills veered heavenwards, and a dark mass of trees grew upright despite the ninety-degree angle of the upwards-sloping earth. The darkness, this far away from street lights and the illumination of houses, was complete. If he held his breath there was only the sound of his family, an offbeat tick of the engine. A creaking on occasion, possibly crickets. Most of the time there was nothing but the noises of each other. If Dapo could have silenced them, could bear to take that final step, he would. He actually would. The radio spoke of those who had done such things, preferring murder to the uncertain alternative. There were reports of people who had given up running to touch the plants, and that was it. Over. No one knew what happened next, just that they weren't seen again.

They were vanished out of existence. And yet their plant always remained. Family members who had escaped implored that something be done to find their loved ones. Sometimes, days later, even they disappeared. Much as Dapo appreciated the emotions that brought people to either position, nothing he'd heard allowed him to condone the actions of those who had given up, or to imagine himself able to perform that final, killing blow. That was too much. If he could not fight he would run, he'd decided; then settle, wait it out.

He twitched his nose. This is what he hated most. Incessant itches he couldn't scratch, the unseen moon, blocked by an expanse of leaves above their heads, the cramp in his legs and harsh seat covers against his rear. The smell of their bodies, unwashed for over a week. Hunger. Sticky dryness in his throat. He cried in the darkness, releasing silent pain; he'd become adept at keeping it from them, letting it out at night and gathering himself for the hour when they rose, bleary and wondering. He heard the hoot of an owl, which made him smile, feel better. Leaves rustled, from its foraging Dapo assumed. He lowered his face against the blanket, scratching his eyelids as he rocked his head back and forth. At least he wasn't alone.

His throat clenched. He almost coughed, swallowing. Another reflex he'd hated over those long nights. When it happened again, stronger this time, he screwed up his face, swallowing harder. An explosive, hacking cough burst from him, making his body jerk. He relaxed against the headrest, eyes closed. Remembered. He raised his head quickly, looking out of the window. Complete darkness. Yet he could smell it. The perfume. The perfume was everywhere.

He turned to his stirring family, rocking with the flood of his returning tears, whining a half-muttered litany. He had tried.

God knew he had. The rustling came closer, filling every window. Misra was pushing herself upright, shrieking his name, and Iye was crying, mouth wide, eyes confused. Dapo blocked them from his mind, trying to see outside. Emotionless faces, alien and familiar, appeared at the window, cold breath clouding glass, diminishing. Purple eyes stared. Hard bodies thumped against doors. When they began to fumble for the door handles with unwieldy, stubbed fingers, Dapo threw back his head and wailed.

DARK MATTERS

The world beyond his room had grown mysterious, untrust-worthy. He spent whole days alone, his parents downstairs, lying belly-down on the carpet, sketching and colouring images. At first, during his early years, Max responded to the graffiti every-where he went, the characters and wild styles and throw-ups, the improbable mix of colours that seldom met in the natural world. When he grew older he searched above, up towards the light-saturated night sky. His canvas became larger, moving from school notebooks to A3 sheets. He began to conjure nebulae, solar systems, distant dwarf stars that shone pale milk blue, the lifeless glow of dead planets. His parents grew worried. To them his pictures were of nothingness, empty dead space, cold and isolated. His mother complained to Aunt Lina that he'd lock himself away for hours, rarely coming down to eat; and even when he did, he wouldn't speak. His father eyed him with sullen concern, mouth opening and closing, cigarette poised by his lips, grasping for language never caught.

Max knew what he feared most; the odd looks, that slow creep away, and in strange, laughable contrast, the trailing six steps behind him in every shop, his newfound size met with awe and some distress. The previous summer he felt people thought him charming, possibly lovable. Without warning all that had changed. Now he was a foreign body causing panic. A threat.

He lay stretched on his stomach painting a watercolour cloud of blue in red when Noel knocked for him. His neighbour lived two streets away, so their mothers made sure they walked to school together, hoping to deter rougher neighbourhood youths. When the boys reached their school gates they split like torn paper, staying apart until it was time to go home. Max didn't blame him. He liked Noel. He was short, not self-conscious, confident and popular with girls, boys and teachers, humorous and knowledgeable without seeming quirky. Once, at lunch, Noel spent ten minutes stabbing every chip on his plate onto a fork with intent precision while the entire population of the school hall watched, applauding as he crammed the soft-spiked bunch into his mouth.

At the knock, Max half-rolled over, knowing who it was. There was nobody else it could be.

'Come!'

The door eased open, stopped. Noel's head appeared.

'Yes, Maximilian!'

'Bruv. I told you not to call me that.'

Noel pursed his lips in a closed-mouth smile. 'Yes, Max. You good?'

'Yeah. Come.'

Noel entered. Sagging skinny jeans, fresh black Adidas, a matching T-shirt and black hoodie. Noel always had the manners to remove his snapback when he came in the house, which Max's mum never stopped going on about. His haircut was barbershop fresh, a day old at the latest, making his small head gleam like a water chestnut. Max, in contrast, had on worn trackies from last year, a fraying polo shirt, and his Afro hadn't seen a barber in months. His cheeks warmed as Noel looked for somewhere to sit, opting for the single bed. The room was small, barely space enough for the thin bed. A single wooden chair was filled with a pile of folded clean clothes. Posters of street murals, Hubble photographs and rap stars surrounded them.

'Why you lyin' on the floor?'

'It's comfortable. Plus it's the best place to draw.'

'Don't you hurt your back an' shit?'

'Sometimes. I haven't got a desk, so . . .'

Noel craned his neck, tracking the walls.

'Man can draw fam.'

'Thanks. It's just practice.'

'Nah, it ain' practice. I could practise years and not draw like that.'

'Everybody's got their thing, innit?'

Noel wrinkled his nose.

'You reckon?'

'Blatant.'

A wait, the distance between them more apparent with every second. Downstairs, a clang of kitchen utensils. The aroma of melting coconut oil. Frying onions.

'Bruv, I pree something, you know.'

Max rolled onto his back. Noel was staring out of his window. At the underground tracks beyond his garden.

'What?'

'I dunno.'

He laughed, stopped. There was a thin shadow of hair along Noel's jaw Max hadn't noticed before.

'You dunno?'

'Yep.'

'Where?'

'The industrial estate. It's proper mad. As soon as I see it I thought, that's Max. He'll know what to do. It's peak.'

His skin began to tingle. It came from nothing, nowhere. He felt pressure in his veins, the sparkling sensation of a dead arm, and realised he was leaning on his elbows. He sat up. The barricade lifted, blood rushed back where it belonged.

'What is it?'

'I can't explain. You gotta come, trust. You're the only man I'll let see this ting, believe me. Everyone else's too stupid. They'll ruin it.'

'Is this a joke?'

Noel stared. His eyes were dark marbles.

'Bruv. Do I joke?'

They held each other's gaze, and burst into spluttered laughter.

'Nah, but really,' Noel said. 'Do I joke about seriousness?'

He was already on his feet, easing into trainers that were blackened like plantains, a sweatshirt lined with creases and, over that, a gilet vomiting cotton from the loose jagged teeth of torn seams.

'Come then,' he said, avoiding Noel's smile.

They rode single file, in silence. Past the small park used by Amberley Aggy more than anyone else, beneath the quiet thunder of the underpass and onto the busy main road, which for some reason was called a lane. Even their bikes were nothing alike; Noel's a gleaming thoroughbred, bright red with thin black tyres, Max's a lumbering matt black no-name, thick-boned with a wide snakeskin tread, rusting and creaking as its wheels turned slow. They cruised at medium pace, Noel seemingly in no hurry. Traffic was snarled up this close to rush hour, granting the ability to ride single and double yellows in lieu of bike lanes, ignoring the momentary panic on car passengers' faces, unaware of their relaxed, guilt-ridden calm once they were gone. The day was bright, the breeze chilled as the sun began to fall, Max relishing his mild sweat as he bore down on the pedals. When Noel turned left immediately after the overhead railway bridge, he followed.

Traffic sounds lowered. The rolling shush of car tyres became soothing, momentary. There was even the sound of chattering birds. Max closed his eyes, enjoying the sensation. His tyres whirred beneath him.

The warehouse had once been some kind of factory, but it had clearly been long abandoned. On the upper floors, steps ascended into thin air and crumbling window frames. The only intact ceilings were on floors one and two, which were dark even though the sun was bright, foreboding even from outside. Noel glanced over his shoulder as he wheeled his bike towards the dusty steps; other than that, he hardly seemed to notice Max. He lifted the bike up, towards the blue factory doors. A scrawl of tags was etched on wooden boards that replaced the broken glass. Max thought the doors were closed, locked, as both were straight-backed and rigid, but when Noel pushed there was just enough space to squeeze themselves and the bikes through their resistance. Inside, he kicked one semi-closed; it barked a splintering protest, stuck. Noel wheeled his bike further inside and so Max left the door be, trailing after him.

The ground floor was vast. He couldn't see the far end, consumed as it was by shadow, the walls disappearing into gloom much as the stairs above their heads evaporated into sky. Everywhere was dust and rubble, as though an earthquake had taken place, leaving the outside untouched. He saw repeated mounds of white plaster embedded with red brick that reminded him of strawberry meringue. Some mounds touched the pocked and cracked white ceiling. Cathedral-arch windows beamed stunted blocks of daylight on either side of the boys, but the centre of the hall was dark and difficult to make out.

Max found himself stumbling every few steps; on what, he dared not guess. The smell was of mould, damp earth. It clogged his nose and made his eyes feel heavy. The scrape of their feet caused a sea of dust to rise around their ankles. Every now and then there was a downpour of debris as showers of plaster fell from the floors above, thankfully nowhere near them. He stopped pushing the bike to rub his fingers together; they were rough, powdery, and he could taste a crackle of grit between his teeth. In front of him, the dust fog settled. He could just make out Noel's shadow. He angled his handlebars in that direction and only knew he'd reached him when he bumped the back of his legs.

'Oi,' Noel said, softer than usual.

'Sorry,' Max whispered, following his lead.

'It's sleeping,' Noel said. Max was just about to ask what, but he stepped out from behind Noel and saw.

Beyond the boys there was a small pile of rubble as high as Max's waist. On, or spread across the crumbled plaster, it was difficult to tell, was nothing. Or rather it was something, as far as Max could see, although exactly what he didn't know: a black patch, dark ooze where there should have been sand-like plaster. There was an absence of light on the ground before them, a hole-like rip in the earth that led into . . . An abyss. It was empty space, the substance he'd stared up at night after night. It was the vision before his eyes when his lids were closed. The deepest part of the night when he lay in bed, roused from dreams. To see it where it shouldn't be made Max dizzy with uncertainty and he stepped back with a yelp of surprise. He stumbled on an unseen brick, which shot from beneath his foot and made him fall, the bike clattering to the dust in a racket of gears and wheels.

He blanked out for a moment, trying to collect himself. Through holes in the glass roof, the far-away blue sky spun in slow motion. A wisp of cloud travelled on the wind. Noel whispered 'Shit', and Max only just heard him, thinking he might be in trouble, so he tried to get up; only when he'd pulled himself into a sitting position, he froze. Everything left him. Body heat, voice, his breath.

The dark ooze had moved. It wasn't spread out on the floor, it was sitting up like him. No, it wasn't sitting up, it was pushing itself onto hollow haunches. He could see that what he'd first thought of as a random spread of substance was actually man-like – arms, legs, torso, head, all midnight black, all devoid of features. Humanoid. The creature got to its feet, spreading its arms out wide. A man-shaped silhouette three inches taller than him, around six-foot four, a cut-out patch of blank shape and, inside that, dark void. Max tried to peer into the depths. For a moment there was the sparkle of distant stars: galaxies perhaps? The nothing was so deep it almost gave off its own light. Maybe that was what he was seeing? He leant forward, yearning for more, so captivated he barely registered Noel saying: 'See? It's beautiful.'

The being seemed to hear him. It extended a pitch-black hand, fingers reaching, strained for contact. It didn't move. Noel stepped forward.

'*No*,' Max whispered from the rubble floor.

Noel ignored him, inching closer, an exhalation of dust at his feet. He touched the darkened fingers and immediately, instead of grasping them, Noel's fingers began to disappear. It was as though they'd been immersed into a gleaming pool of thick oil.

He made a terrible noise, moaning fear and revulsion, deep-throated, growing louder as he fell deeper into the creature's body. The darkness covered more of him, his knuckles, wrist, forearm, his elbow and up one shoulder, Noel's feet beginning to slide closer into the creature, sending roiling dust puffing high, some of which also vanished into the dark form. Half Noel's torso, his leg, his face, which turned towards Max and let out a roaring scream, until it covered his shaved head, and the substance filled his mouth, cutting off his voice as though a plug had been pulled inside him.

Max yelled something that wasn't even a word, his throat raw.

The creature sucked Noel in, took his whole body until there was only a flailing arm, a bent elbow, fingers writhing like wind-blown leaves, sliding inside the creature with a dull pop. Immersion.

It was still. The void became auditory. It turned towards Max, opening its arms. He picked up his bike, pushing it a metre before him, and leapt on, pedalling hard and fast. He only looked behind once, against his will, believing the creature would come after him, but it stood in the same spot, arms wide, turned in his direction. He made it to the graffiti-stained doors, jumped from the bike, wrenched the doors open, breaking three nails so his fingers bled, and pushed himself outside without a care for bumps or scrapes, throwing himself back onto the bike and sprinting hard. His breathing was a harsh, ragged, quiet scream, ripping his chest like smoke, his expression a wide-eyed mask of shocked fear. He rode so frantically cars veered out of his path to avoid collision, and buses sighed to a stop.

At the small park his muscles could do no more and his legs gave out. He fell onto the grass, bones jarring as they met earth, lucky to have the bike roll away and not collapse on top of him, the whine of his breath like the sawing rasp of an asthma attack, sweat pouring from his face and body, soaking his clothes. Old Man Taylor and Ms Emmes saw him as they returned from the parade of shops, and assumed he'd been smoking, or possibly injecting, forcing a wide space between themselves and the boy, storing the image of him splayed and panting to recreate for his parents.

Max's chest rose and fell, looking painful, possibly dangerous. By the time it returned to an even pace, daylight had dimmed. The Amberley Road teenagers arrived, sauntering in no clear direction only to pivot on the spot, palms slapping, barking laughter, passing lighters and curses, heads nodding to smartphone music until they noticed Max; then whispering among themselves as they saw him on his back, motionless. They tried to pretend he wasn't there, yet his presence muted their voices. The strange kid, even stranger now, possibly drugged or the victim of an attack. Unable to tell and unwilling to check, they left Max alone.

When he rose to his feet some time later, the youngsters were a darting swarm of burning orange sparks. Max lifted his fallen bike and walked it home, stumbling past ignorant of their hush, group suspicion clouded by nightfall.

Max hurried to his room, marching away from the calls of his parents, the shrillness of his mum's voice, though she was not quite panicked enough to remove her sagging flesh from the television and see if anything was actually wrong. With his bike safely stored in the shed at the bottom of their garden, he tried to treat himself similarly, locking his door, collapsing on the bed, energy spent, head revolving slowly as a park roundabout, throbbing angrily. He was cold, and so he climbed beneath his covers fully clothed, teeth transmitting code for his ears alone, the image of Noel absorbed into the void of the creature returning like a DVD glitch; repeat, repeat.

Beyond his room, the garden and the untidy jungle of over-grown slope beyond his father's greenhouse, the underground tracks that caught Noel's attention: the Central Line to Ealing Broadway or Ruislip going west, Hainault or Epping to the east. Every five minutes there was a mechanical shudder, a screech and roar of trains, the glow of carriage windows creating a cinema reel of lights, illuminating gloom. Hours passed. The darkness gained depth, thickened. His mother knocked on his bedroom door, tentative, though it was easy to feign sleep, closing his eyes to cement purpose, wait until she went downstairs, the soft thud of her footsteps on carpet matching the pulse of his fear, still faster than normal. He opened his eyes only when he felt safe, tracing the patterns of rattling trains on the white screen of his ceiling, absorbing their flow without meaning, lips moving as though in conversation with his consumed friend, a whispered dialect that perhaps only they understood.

He tried to imagine himself doing more. Instead of freezing on the spot mute and powerless, reaching for Noel and pulling with all his strength. Picking up a half-brick, pitching it at the creature with all his power. Maybe rushing it with a broad shoulder, forcing it to the floor, away. And yet as much as he tried to conjure images of himself in action, they were solemn fragments, still, unfocused photographic moments at best, patchy and unclear. Whenever he attempted to force them into motion they fell apart or resisted, so he couldn't see the results. And yet he continued to try, eyes red and stinging, a snail's trail of tears leaking from the corners, running from his temples and onto the pillow as the dark grew stronger, and the catseye lights of the trains flickered against his poster-lined four walls, and his body gave in and slept, plunging Max into a subconscious well of nightmares and ether.

Something woke him. He kept his eyes closed. The trains had stopped, which meant midnight had passed. His parents had gone to bed. Floorboards and walls ticked, creaked. Max felt no physical sensation. His body had seemingly dissipated, leaving nothing physical behind, only spirit, the invisible void.

He heard night workmen, their noisy clink of metal, and with that sensation returned. He'd seen them sometimes, guiding a battered flat-bed carriage along tracks, mustard yellow, mottled with vitiligo rust. He lay still, eyes closed, absorbing sounds, imagining slow progress. High points of conversation caught his ears, snatches of swearing, and the beam of their mounted spot-light flooded the room, turning the dark behind his eyelids red. He opened his eyes.

The thing from the warehouse rose at the foot of his bed, reaching, arms wide, seemingly larger now, pure emptiness within. Max tried to scream and nothing came out but a stran-gled whine. He wanted to move, only for his limbs to resist, the thing stretching its arms like dark honey, creeping closer until each encircled the bed, and the thing grew taller, spreading up and out until it was a dark, giant mass above and around him. Max's heart pounded so hard, his skin was so cold, and his fear so paralysing, he thought he might die.

And yet inside the body he saw something. Now he was closer and the creature had widened like canvas, he could make out a powdered white terrain, the purple glow of something that resembled sky. The curving glow of moons, the shadow of a planet and, on what he assumed was the ground, a series of blocked shapes that looked like plateaus, or cliff tops. There were marks in the sand, a trail of some kind. Curiosity broke paralysis, although a residue of fear still caused him to shake, gasp breath, as he sat up in bed, leaning closer. Yes. Yes, it could be. He knelt before the creature as if he were about to pray, reaching, touching, feeling the ooze creep along his arm, not the sensation of contact he usually associated with touch, but something else, a warmth that transformed his whole body, stilled his heart, and he wasn't afraid: he was relieved, filling with joy. He released a monotone groan, understanding *this* was the sound Noel had made upon contact; it was release, not resistance, letting it wash over him until that warm feeling was everywhere, seeing nothing more of his bedroom, only the thick absence of light that embraced him.

A temporary floating sensation, the pop of air pressure, soft, hardly noticeable. Solid ground beneath shoeless feet. Warmth against his soles. The glowing white land. A purple sky, closer now, everywhere, the spray of stars and the planet, heavy and low, half dark half red, bursting with its own weight. Beyond that, far-away moons, twin ice crystals, tiny and bright. The trail he'd seen was of footprints, climbing from where he stood, a dual pattern on the sand, the reversed imprint of trainer soles. They rose, disappearing behind dunes to reappear further, towards what he'd thought were flat mountaintops from the unimaginable distance of his bedroom, but were actually looming structures, white as the sand. Turrets or towers, Max couldn't tell. He turned to look behind himself. The creature's silhouette; inside the body, a distant view of posters, the dull wooden foot of his bed, the night workmen's spotlight reflecting on his white ceiling. Home.

He relocated the trail of footprints, eyes rising upwards. The structures shimmered in half-light piercing the velvet atmosphere, blinking silent reprieve.

NOCTURNE

The vast expanse of space is said to be silent. Vacuum crushes the universal voice, renders it mute, a lambent graveyard haunted with distant ghosts of a long-dead past. And yet, if ears are attuned, they can hear music. The rings of Saturn cry in falsetto chorus, a choir of millions. Neptune chirps and whistles, a gaseous blue rainforest, gentle baritones cascading underneath like the sea. Earth itself is known to have a voice. It rises and falls, a sombre whale song, calming as such music can be. Further beyond our home planet and solar system, out into the unknown, there is the steady bass of pulsars, the crackle of ice giants, the dying roar of colossal red suns. These are not sounds as we know them but electromagnetic vibrations beyond the limited range of human ears. A song of eternal night.

Seldom – almost never – there is something else. Existing far below the competitive thunder of vaster, larger bodies, this sound is minute, barely audible, only heard when the planets, sun and extended bubble of the heliosphere are escaped and nothing is left but pinprick stars, the intemperate swirls of galaxies. One such object can be detected now, releasing its monotone wail into the void. At this unimaginable scale it has all the impact of a microbe, and goes ignored by the universe.

For those with an interest in human life it holds significance far greater than its size. Other factions make similar sounds. Not the same, but close. There is no need to elaborate on their species, or nature. Since they are difficult to locate, we remain with what we have: a song composed by human hands. There may never be another to follow.

The origin of this music is 1,145 metres in length, almost a mile. Its shape is similar to the air balloons that formed a portion of its ancestry centuries ago, and, as far as recent human memory is concerned, do not exist. The metal hull glistens like fish scales, reflecting beams of ancient starlight from every direction. It has light of its own, dull in comparison and insignificant. Windows are found all over, most on either side of the hull, black full stops that, from a certain point of view, make the craft look like it's been pierced by a giant pin. There is a glow of bridge windows emanating from deep inside the cockpit. It brightens and fades, brightens and fades, a computer on standby visually breathing for those it protects, the only way it can.

Black letters are stamped behind the bulwarks, widely spaced: *SIGUTOLO*. The ship has a triangular dorsal fin and pectorals close to the aft on either side; otherwise it is unmarked, seamless. The aft is where light is strongest, its notes loudest, a blinding white river streaming forever into space. For awake and aware humans trapped within the enforced artificial atmosphere, there is a rattling roar from one end to the next, but in space it's drowned by vacuum, apparent silence. Plasma wave instruments tell another story, sensing ripples of electrons in ionised gas translated for mammalian ears. This job has been achieved without flaw for over four hundred years. No one has listened to their findings. The machines blink and whirr, and continue, as do their counterparts in every section of the *Sigutolo*. If men and women did this work, one of their number might grow frustrated, bored, even wearied by the continued failure of their primary mission, to find life. As the intelligence is artificial, they do not.

Working hard as the machines do, it's inevitable that they contribute most, practically and aesthetically. Without them, the precious cargo cannot survive. Without them, no music is made. They are the instruments by which the song is performed. The question is, played by whom? The humans who programmed them on the planet left far behind? Or the open door to autonomy that results in machines that play themselves? It's true they are designed to respond to external forces with intricate calculations of their own. To think and make choices, if they can. And yet, if they were originally programmed to do so, does this impetus come from the machines, or humans? Nature or nurture, the eternal question. Even more so in space, said to expand infinitely, as perhaps their mission will.

Malfunctions occur. Irregularly, but they happen. The majority are shutdowns; a circuit comes to the end of its life cycle and shorts, causing the affected area to darken, cease to exist. More severe are the fires; externally harmless, lasting microseconds before cold and vacuum snuff them like matches between rough fingers, internally they cause havoc. Squat, square fire-bots cruise empty corridors on antigravs. They are unhurried and precise, spraying thick yellow foam, as most on-board fires are electrical. Done, they rehouse themselves in unobtrusive compartments throughout the ship. A shatterproof glass door shucks closed. They power down, waiting for the next explosive flower to bloom. Much as the cargo, they sleep.

Not long before blast-off, some first-time crew members found the bots' lack of motion control and communication skills troubling. They bumped the rear ends of many, unable to correctly steer after contact, crashing into walls. More experienced astronauts explained that they had been built to exist in a world without people, a barren place of stillness and cold. The humans who experienced this genetic flaw in their digital DNA cursed the machines, nerves getting the better, ignorant of the fact that their lives would be saved by these simple journeyman creations time and again. The fire-bots would right themselves, cruising onwards to their destination, wobbling from side to side like a child's play toys.

With luck, nothing will occur that jeopardises the cargo and brings the *Sigutolo*'s music to an abrupt end. In four centuries the worst that happened was a frozen outcrop of ceiling fans that cooled the machinery, which that in turn maintained the Hive, causing the CHB[1] to shut down before AMA[2] corrected the malfunction. Nobody heard the sizzling eruption of shorting cables, the crumpled explosion as the board went into overload. The resulting damage caused a spontaneous ejection of thirty pods to shoot into space like slim, silver bullets, whispered fireworks streaking against the backdrop of a midnight canvas. Some might say this was a beautiful occurrence, a joyous interlude in the monotonous, constant rhythm of engines and computers. Others might say such analogies were morbid, unemotional, inhumane.

The pods flew for decades, humming in all directions. Vibrating with the rapid burr of desperate, tiny CPUs doing all they could to correct the inevitable or shut down, internal moderators deciding it was all too much, lights fading to nothing,

---

1 Central Hibernation Board
2 Automated Mothership Array

leaving the enclosed human alone in frozen sleep. Pods were struck by screaming, hurtling chunks of ice, the first encounter between mankind and a solidified liquid that existed since before the Earth was flaming, molten rock. Pods drifted seventy years before they were tugged into the orbits of larger planets, sometimes even moons, to float serenely about their hosts, sparkling with crystalline jewels. Centuries after the initial malfunction, other pods found themselves beneath the shadow of crafts that would have dwarfed the *Sigutolo*, had they existed in the same space and time. These were swallowed into the vast bellies of alien hangars, their calando undone.

The majority, some eighteen pods that remain, swim through interstellar space unimpeded by objects or gravity, the occupants long dead, each vehicle on a journey of discovery as rewarding as the moment their human cargo first stepped aboard the *Sigutolo* in wide-eyed excitement and possibility. Against all odds, a handful of CPUs still process information from the unknown, even after failing in their main task to protect the human within. Their clicks and hums contribute to the wider voice of the cosmos. They are part of something greater than their origins. If their programming had been advanced enough to be aware of this, the electronic brain would remain emotionless.

The *Sigutolo* continues towards its destination, the Sirius system, AMA unfazed by what she possibly considers a blip in her momentary past. Concepts of death, pain, survival and the afterlife are purely theoretical, aspects of human nature far removed from her kind. She is aware of the myth attributed to the Dogons, and is tasked to maintain a constant scan for the beings they called Nommo, but the relevance of this information is secondary to keeping the craft and its cargo in functioning order. They exist to serve, to carry out a job. If they fail due to unwarranted error, they fail. Events are recorded into AMA's digital log in remote detail and the computer continues her mission. There is no regret, or sympathy. It is simply another mark in the report.

Inside, along corridors as smooth and white as an eggshell interior, into darkened rooms that form empty galleys, sinks clean and glistening, cupboards of stacked plates, cups and water jugs. Abandoned cabins with neatly made single bunk beds, one corner folded over like the page of a book, a place to remember, posters of women and postcards of lush trees, foaming oceans, home towns and stars of the screen. The metallic city of the hangar bay, a thousand heaped crates looming like miniature skyscrapers, its dormant trucks and loading vehicles. Closed and silent lifts, unused in generations, opening and closing on AMA's command to keep dull mechanisms from seizing. The hulking bulk of security bots clamped in booths that house them, domed figures long obsolete in the buildings of their designers. High above, in the upper amidships where the Hive is found, lie the vessels' true cargo: the crew.

They line the walls and central aisle in horizontal formation far into the distance, which cannot be seen accurately with human eyes. The entire compartment is theirs. One thousand crew members stacked like galley plates into bullet-shaped sleeper pods, their metallic cone heads, sides and undersides, their orange reinforced glass so the sleeping humans may see when they wake. If they wake. There are so many pods they will squeeze together when they arrive. They will jostle, laugh, make jokes about giving each other breathing space. The air, unused for so long, will taste of metal storage tanks. Many humans will be disabled, unable to walk or lift themselves from the confines of their pods. Relatives will realise pods are missing, that by some quirk of fate their lover, father, daughter, brother, mother was ejected from the escape hatch to fates unknown. They will not find out why until later, after the log is read. Others will not wake. Many will not wake.

There is no precedent for this journey. Starships have been assigned the same task in a different quadrant, yet they are all first to travel so far from home. They do because it has become vital. They do because they are fearful. If they did not, they would die anyway.

When they arrive, the voice of *Sigutolo* will become a chorus. It will form a building crescendo stemming from the thrum of heating, the rattle of lift-shaft pulleys, the reactivation of bots on every deck, a collective tick of CPUs, the shift of a machine army large and small, from standby to functional, all over the craft. The final whoosh of rushing wind, the air needed to breathe, before the mechanised, stuttering whine of a thousand pod doors. The hiss, beeps, chatter and wails, the calls of joy or fear. The ship will return to life as the Ancient Kemetians once believed they could, yet this belief is not in vain, not with AMA, their mechanical God, watching over all. The *Sigutolo* will exhale like a newborn and burst into a song designed by long-dead architects. The brilliant white light of an alien star will flood its windows and align with their music. A new composition will begin.

NOMMO

Blue hurt Ray's eyes. Stung them into submission. She gave up searching clouds to stare at her bare toes instead, the background of glittering sand dulled by her length of shadow. Fari's warmth enveloped her. He smelt of Armani mixed with the tang of aloe vera he used after shaving. Just above her shoulder blades, Ray felt the delicate thud of his heart.

'Silly.'

'What?' She allowed her head to fall backwards for a kiss, leaning deep into his solid weight, touched his ear and brought him close for another.

'Wear your glasses. OK? The sun's too high.'

'*OK.*'

She drew out the word like her stubborn defiance, pulling the sunglasses from between the crevice of her wetsuit, one emaciated arm folded against her sports bra. She put them on, but it really wasn't the same. The gentle sea was cast dirt-brown just like everything else. The fauna of blue and red parasols, sun loungers stretched beneath them like thick white roots. The quartet of kids wielding spades, hunched around a deepening hole, thin rainbows of sand arcing behind them. A couple strolling on the beach, her blonde hair trailing down to pitching bikini bottoms, him baseball-capped, wide bare deltoids, Bermuda shorts, flip flops. The constant ambient white noise, shrieks and clinking bottles, tourists' chatter, a shifting tide and far-away treble of Soca giving Ray the sensation of being outside herself, analysing how it felt to revel in the moment. It burned her worse than reflected light on water. She tasted salt, focusing on sand darkened with a tint of brown.

'I wanted to see it with my own eyes.'

Her pout was unconscious. She caught herself, couldn't retract it.

'I know, babe. I know.'

The rumble of his voice and the vibration against her skull made Ray close her eyes. She wanted him to scold her petulance, listening to the thought. She was doing it again. She rubbed his hand with the heel of hers, gripping it tight.

'Thank you.'

'Come on. I love you.'

She lifted his hand, eyes still closed, pressing her lips against the knuckles. She could hear that rhythmic growl of the engine growing and chose to ignore it, savouring the tingle of heat against her bare flesh. The thrumming engine cut out. Another voice, fast and lively. She sighed.

'He's here.'

'*Mmmmm.*'

She rubbed herself against Fari, a slow swipe left, right. He chuckled, chest rocking.

'Behave.'

'What for? We could go back to bed.'

She was only half joking, almost smiled.

'No we can't. You want to as much as me.'

The warmth of his body was gone. She opened her eyes and

there was Richie, sitting on the motorboat yards from the water's edge, bobbing on a relaxed tide. Fari motioned with a free hand, loosening his grip, and her palm was empty, cold. She wanted to reach for him, only something told her not to. She watched him splash knee-high into the waves.

Wisps of question-marked engine smoke curled from the boat, the resort fading, its volume receding with distance. Richie and Fari talked on the prow. Ray kept to herself. She wasn't sure why she didn't join them, although she had vague reason. She just felt different today. Inner.

They lowered their heads close like they'd known each other years, hands on the boat to steady themselves against the waves. Richie was heartbreak good-looking and knew it, a bit too podgy for a model, not that it mattered to the various women he met. His eyes were dark brown, sparkling like beach sand. When they were introduced days ago, Ray avoided their brightness. Too pretty, too mesmerising. He knew how to use them. She didn't want him getting ideas.

She watched in the pretence of listening, actually more interested in her man. He made her proud, partly because he was a reflection of her tastes, mostly because he was unique, so comfortable in his own skin. She'd never met anyone like Fari. For her, he was complete. The height she'd always favoured, tall but not too tall; the physique, slim and muscular, toned. A husky voice as though he'd dragged each word over sun-baked gravel, sensual without even trying. The light brown locks that reached his hips when they weren't wrapped up, his shaven beard daily trimmed, a sculpted work of art. He talked with his whole body, expressing the fine points of his statements by stepping forward, knee bent, or twisting his body to the left, or pumping his arms in a mimed, exaggerated jog. It made her smile to note the seriousness of Richie's listening, head bent to catch Fari's London accent, dark eyes never leaving the foaming water.

She reached for the cylinder at her feet, cold metal soothing warm fingers. She touched her glasses, remembered that she was wearing them and sighed again, her exhalation drowned by the harsh engine. There were no distractions on the boat. She should really make an effort. He'd been kind, she supposed. Ray angled her legs towards the men.

'So, how it go last night?' she shouted over the roar.

'Huh?' Richie yelled, startled. Fari began to smile, winking at Ray. She leant back on the bench, tilting her head.

'How did it go? With the cute brunette we leave you with?'

'Ah, good man, it good!' Richie beamed, correcting the wheel with tiny, jerky movements. 'I goin meet she tonight!'

'It went good, ee?'

'Fe true! Yuh set me up with that one real nice.'

'Yuh couldn't miss her! She ave her sights set pon yuh!'

Richie laughed. 'I tank yuh anyway, miss!'

'She tank her too,' Fari grinned, clapping Richie's shoulder.

The engine slipped a gear, yielding a deeper tone. The boat slowed and Ray slipped a pink hairband from her finger, using it to tie back her ponytail while Fari began inspecting the equipment. She joined him on her haunches, blowing into regulators, giving the gauges a once-over. They looked over their own gear, then each other's. The cloudless sky blazed.

'First one to find baby lobster gets a rum.'

'Easy. I want a shark's egg.'

'Without the shark, I hope.'

'I dunno. A small one might be nice.' She looked into the sun poised just above his shoulder, squinting.

'How those glasses treatin you?'

'Fine.' She dropped her chin. 'You're just in front of the sun.'

'It'll be better down there.'

'Yeah.'

They donned their gear in silence. Richie swaggered down the steps, sitting on the sea-blue bench, watching.

'This reef special, yuh hear? I don't bring no one round these part.'

'We're honoured,' she said, beaming wide, and then thinking she'd said something wrong because he didn't smile back. Richie's stare made Ray conscious of the tight wetsuit, the weight of her breasts. She zipped the suit to her neck, bending to pull on her fins.

'It real special fe true.'

'We can't wait.'

Fari hadn't noticed Richie's expression.

She pulled off her glasses, feeling the sting of daylight, and put on the mask, keeping her head down. A wave nearly made her lose balance but she held out an arm, righted herself.

'All right?' Richie called.

'My eyes,' she aimed at her feet.

'Ah. I forget.'

Ray kept her head bowed low. They climbed onto the rim, sitting with their backs to sea. There was little breeze. She caught far-away notes of music gently breaking the silence, perhaps from a nearby boat, and threw back her head, closing her eyes. Fari took her hand. They grinned at each other, kissed once, put their regulators in.

'Nice couple, de two ah yuh,' Richie said.

'Thanks,' Fari replied, offhand. They heard it regularly, tried not to pay it much mind. 'Ready?'

'Ready. One, two, three . . .'

They pushed backwards into the water.

Her favourite part. Contact, suddenness. A crash, scattering water. Sharp brine on her lips. The commanding lap of each wave. The heat of her wetsuit meeting cool sea, bright sun pressing the back of her skull like a bully. A strained cry of hopeful birds, the promise of immersion. They paddled from the boat until she gave Fari the thumbs down. He nodded and they exhaled together, releasing air, descending. Cold enveloped her. Silence, apart from the rush of her breath and a fizzing shoal of tiny bubbles. She could see into the immediate distance without pain, unclearly perhaps, but the loss of the sting in her head and temples was worth it. Adjusting her BCD, the gradients of blue became darker, Fari's slim, blurred form lost solidity. When she looked up, it was to see his splayed silhouette, a cut-out shadow above. Heat grew weak. Stillness wrapped her body. White sand appeared below.

She jerked in shock, her reaction loud in her ears. They should have been seeing schools of confetti-bright fish, fields of coral and tubular polyps. Larger fish nibbling slow-waving fronds only to dart away from sudden invasion. The bed had the barren appearance of an underwater desert, undulating and vast. She twisted her neck up towards Fari, framed by sun. Had the reef died? Ray continued descending feather-slow until she was floating above ripples of bare sand. Fari joined her moments later, arms open. They hung side by side, frowning into dim light. He shrugged, his wide eyes pulled tight by the visor. Slim fish wriggled through the plumes of their rising bubbles. There was no reef. The bed was bare in all directions.

She was disappointed, not surprised. Richie had been merely adequate as a guide, taking them to a series of artificial reefs

and wrecks, no real outstanding sites. They bobbed on underwater currents, unsure. Ray pointed into open water and Fari
gave thumbs up. Hand in hand they swam, heads raised to search
the distant haze, intent on the blurred horizon.

A firm push of warm water, an updraft knocking them upright.
The seabed vanished, only thick darkness below. They started
to rise quicker than was safe, probing sunlight finding them.
Ray's hand slipped from Fari's. She barked alarm, bubbles
exploding, let him go to adjust her buoyancy, trusting him to
do likewise, kicking as she plunged. Guiding herself backwards
to the stark demarcation of sand, she lowered, exhaling a relieved
cloud as her fin touched the seabed, Fari floating beside her.

They swapped jerky thumbs up and hugged, entwining their
fingers tight. Panicked speech bubbles erupted, spiralling above
their heads. The ridge where they stood was eighteen metres.
Before them was the deep. Who knew how far it went, but from
the solid darkness Ray guessed it plunged down for hundreds
of metres. She shivered, swaying with the current, holding Fari
tight. She wanted to feel anger at Richie, up on the boat probably with a cold beer and a smoke; more irrationally at the stark
depths before her. She even tried to conjure more upset, failing;
she only felt joy that they were safe, that the current had pushed
instead of pulled. She didn't want to imagine what it might have
felt like to be hauled down into the gloom.

Fari spasmed with the muscular thrust of an eel. His eyes
were wide, fearful, and he exploded into action, kicking from the
ridge. Fear pierced Ray again. This time she went with him,
holding his fingers, looking in the direction he was staring, unable
to see. Then she made out something: a vague, distant shadow.
Drawing closer, growing larger, coming. So quick she couldn't
react.

At first Ray thought they were huge fish. Sharks, dolphins maybe. Swimming side by side, difficult to catch in misty light, but when they flipped their bodies, darting and swooping like kites, she realised the motion wasn't right. They weren't the correct shape. She couldn't see details as the sun blocked their true forms, turning them into twin spectres, furiously writhing until they spun and dived, aiming directly for Fari. She shrieked, hearing herself, a fury of bubbles hiding the creatures from view. When the bubbles fluttered upwards, they stood upright before them.

She was breathing too fast, using excess air. Much as Ray tried to stop, she found it impossible. She tried to convince herself she'd seen incorrectly, or even that she was dive-drunk, yet every sense she possessed told her they were solid and real. These weren't animals but some form of humanoid. Breathing without diving gear at eighteen metres, sculling like natural law. Beyond the beings, darting fish, oblivious to their presence. Beams of sunlight, thick and thin, rippled like curtains.

She felt Fari's light touch, not wanting to look in case the creatures did something in response, mainly to him, although she needed his reassurance and risked it. They nodded at each other. *OK? Yes.* Bubbles exploded from his regulator as fast as hers, spinning, wriggling, escaping. Surface-bound. The people – for Ray decided that was undoubtedly what they were – floated a metre away, calm and motionless apart from curious expressions, the slight curve of smiles.

They were male and female. Lithe and strong, no excess. Naked, genitals startlingly hairless. Ray lifted her gaze. The male wore unwrapped locks which waved in the currents and were much longer than Fari's. Shells and glistening strips of what could have been seaweed, although she wasn't sure, were tied around each one. His cheekbones were strong, his face serene, beautiful. The female was almost bald, her skull ridged and angular. Eyes cut-glass, bright with intelligence, lips full. Ray was stung by needle-thin aggression, unable to stop admiring her, knowing Fari was too. Both had blemishes all over their bodies; thin, random scars and wider dark swathes that might have been birthmarks. The female's ran from the tip of her left shoulder, across the breast, curving past her belly button to end at her hip. The male's was a black streak starting at his temple, cast across his eyes like a mask, winding around his head and neck to spiral down his chest, stomach, hips and penis before ending at his ankle.

Each faction stared, as curious as the other. Bubbles emerged slower, with wider gaps. Just as Ray thought they should try to communicate, the female reached a hand towards her.

Against her wiser judgement, she took it.

The fingers were slightly furred, like petals. Strange to the touch, but not unpleasant. They felt, in fact, as though they were covered in similar translucent tiny hairs; still, Ray didn't dare look. She felt Fari's eyes and refused to look at him either. He was always chiding Ray about her lack of trust and yet this felt comfortable. Right. The female smiled without restraint, teeth glittering like coral. She gave a gentle pull as, beside her, the male reached for Fari. Ray allowed herself to be lifted, softly kicking. Over her shoulder, Fari did likewise. She rose, relaxing until she was horizontal. Led by their humanoid guides, they scissor-kicked in slow rhythm towards the edge of the ridge.

They swam into darkness, slow enough for the white line of the cliff edge to creep closer, giving her trepidation time to return. She didn't trust the deep. The beings did. She tried to relax, not to panic, unbidden thoughts of cold, pressure and the void making her body stiffen. The female curved to face Ray, though she kept swimming, albeit slower, caressing Ray's hand, trying to soothe her. While she appreciated the obvious concern, all of her knowledge and training told Ray she would die if she attempted to scale the ridge. There were twenty, possibly twenty-five metres before they hit recreational diving limits. The three-hundred-metre record wasn't reassuring, as neither she nor Fari had ever gone deeper than forty. If the beings breathed without regulators they were undoubtedly used to distances way beyond those meagre depths. More worrying perhaps was the issue of air. Her gauge said she had ten minutes. Depending how far their destination was, or if the humanoids weren't as friendly as they seemed, there was every possibility they wouldn't return.

She tried to indicate this by tugging the female's fingers. When she curved to face Ray again, Ray tapped the gauge, showing her. The female nodded, bubbles spilling from her lips and ears. Close up she looked younger than she'd first appeared, less human. Her skin tinged green, her eyes elongated and the colourless fur more apparent. A tiny flap of skin below each cheekbone. Gills? She peered at Ray's watch while Ray stared, nodding with frantic, docile enthusiasm. Gave her thumbs up and pointed at the ridge with her free hand, turning the thumb upside down. Ray's head spun light. She didn't know what to make of that gesture, or even whether she'd been understood.

Fari drifted past, towed easily by his male counterpart. He placed one hand on her shoulder, shrugged lightly and allowed himself to be led into the gloom. Her anger flared. Always so trusting. Trust had got them into this situation.

The male pulsed two strong kicks and was over the ridge. Fari relaxed, looking back, gesturing. *Come. Come.* The female stared into Ray's face, eyes narrowed. Sympathy? Or her own simple, human interpretation? She seemed to acknowledge Ray's upset, stroking her brow and her arm, emitting a mewl that might have been crooning. Gently pulling. Her boyfriend was a dark smear, shrouded in darkness. Soon he would be gone. Tears slipped into Ray's mask. She had to follow. She let herself be led.

They descended, keeping to the rocky sides. Ray felt wet against her nose, inside her mask, tried to keep her emotions in check. Every time she saw Fari below them, fins scissoring slow rhythm, her jaw trembled and fresh tears emerged. The female held her fingers in a light touch, still leading, her slim body arrowed head-first into the deep, waist continuously undulating, free arm flat against her side, trailing Ray. She copied her posture, resting her left arm against her hip. At any moment it was possible to let go, float effortlessly up to eighteen metres and beyond. It was. She gritted her regulator with her teeth, taking conscious, long breaths. Sometimes her body shuddered. She wasn't sure if it was cold or fear.

The ridge was a cragged, pale yellow cliff. Thin lime-green weeds, little else. It went on for ever, although she couldn't tell whether that was another human interpretation. As they reached thirty metres she noticed something else. Crevices or alcoves arched like dark church windows. Lower down, they had protruding, slightly curved half-metre lips. Small caves big enough to hold one or two people at best. Possibly two water beings.

Darkness seeped like dusk. She swallowed hard, clearing her ears. Her chest tightened. It was tougher to kick. When Ray looked down, she saw nothing. She stiffened again, and for the first time the female gripped more firmly. Was she mistaken, or had a thumb caressed her knuckle? Was she being reassured, or was it the touch of cold water? There was no light, no way of telling. How could she know?

Ray chose to believe.

Had they changed direction? Were they horizontal, not diagonal? For a long while she knew nothing apart from her awareness that the pressure on her chest and temples had eased. The fingers on her hand were gone, it shocked her to realise this. How long had they let her go? Where was she? Ray floated in the abyss, in silence. She gasped, trying to see, head twisting, bubbles tickling her cheeks and ears, flailing, telling herself not to panic, suppressing her scream, feeling it rise anyway. Then the female was there, her hands were on Ray's hips, cold and strange but undoubtedly soft. Another cold feeling on her upper chest. A palm? Possibly? Was she being righted? And then her feet touched solid hardness and she was standing, yes, she was, soles resting against something cold and firm for a moment, ground maybe, before she felt herself being lifted upwards again, the furred fingers holding hers, and she made herself calm her breathing, conserve air.

They walked, or at least feigned the motion. Floating above whatever surface she'd been made to tread. Holding on to cold fingers tighter, grateful, thinking *Don't let go. Please don't let go.* She squinted. Something ahead. Light. It was light. Her cheeks lifted in a smile, she felt her collected tears. There was light.

Moving towards the source, treading water, a robotic walk. Something touched her arm, her shoulder and then her face, a membrane with give. Before she could register the sensation, or lack of pressure on her arm and hand, she was on the other side. She stumbled, dropping an inch or so. The enveloping force of water was gone. She could hear as though she were on dry land, nothing tangible, normality loud above the clanging ring of water. She raised her chin, looking right and left. Where they stood was as dark as the depths.

'Come.'

The voice was a whispered sigh, hardly apparent. She flinched, searching for the origin. Fingers returned. This time they did not pull. Ray stepped towards the glow.

It was a tunnel, she realised, as they crossed the threshold where shadow met light, the defining line between each. The glow came from rusting brass lamps hung two to three metres apart, complete with wicks and a pale liquid Ray guessed was oil. The flames were ovoid and steady. There was no breeze and she wondered if she needed air. Her gauge was dangerously low. She had three minutes at best, which meant there was no way back if she couldn't find oxygen. The yellow walls of the tunnel were damp, glistening, and the ground slick. She stumbled on occasion, her fins making it even more difficult, the female holding her upright. There was a larger glow before them, a familiar sound that took Ray a moment to place. Then she knew what it was. Voices.

They stepped into what Ray later thought of as a cavern, though its size defied the word. It was a vast empty space, stretching high above her head and deep beneath her feet, complete with hundreds more tunnels in neat circular rows; to her left, she saw their own tunnel also had siblings, dark arched mouths lining the circular space. There were steps and inclines cut into rock to ascend or descend by and scaffold-like ladders, although those were few. The glitter of candle lamps was starlight, conversations loud. Everywhere she looked there were water beings, emerging from tunnels, climbing stairs, gathering in various places. She stood on a rocky yellow surface, not unlike the ridge. It could have been the same rock. A thoroughfare of some kind.

Creatures strolled hand in hand, whether male or female. They stared until her companion snapped in a brittle, quick language and they turned away, laughing quietly.

Her female's eyes were downcast, almost shy, although she couldn't help a smile of what seemed like pride. She approached Ray, stood before her. Gently, she reached out, pulling at her regulator. And the odd thing was, Ray let her. It emerged from her lips, fell to her chest. She inhaled. Salt, a faint smell of fish and underwater plants, the musk of damp rock. Distant fire.

'Welcome to Hanoa,' the female whispered, her husked voice like a song. 'This is our central hall.'

'Hanoa?'

Ray shivered, the hairs all over her body prickling, heart thumping. Laughter tickled her chest. She felt her grin and caught herself, biting it back, but even her suspicions tickled her. Was this martini? All of it? Much as her surroundings felt real, her inner sceptic said she was more than likely suffering from raptures of the deep, nitrogen narcosis. Ray the dive-gas drunkard. She giggled, rocking on her heels. It made perfect sense. The female peered at Ray, half smiling with her.

'Yes. Our home.'

'You can't be serious. You can't be saying you live here.'

'Why?' The female's smile never faltered. Ray tried to find an answer, couldn't. Her certainty grew tenuous. Somewhere else, raised exclamations in the creatures' language caught her ear and she looked up.

'Eraynor!'

Fari, diving gear limp in one hand, the male grinning at his exuberance, walking fast towards her. More water beings gathered, talking with lowered heads, pointing, openly staring. Ray's brow tightened.

'We can breathe!' he grinned, saw her face. His smile vanished. 'What's wrong?'

'You left me,' she said, low so they couldn't be heard. The female winced, walking a few steps away from them, her palm placed against the male's forearm, stopping him, exposing Ray's failure. Good hearing, it seemed. Fari's shoulders drooped, limp as their gear.

'I thought you wanted to come.'

She hadn't, not at all, yet now they were surrounded by water beings and lamplight, her upset seemed difficult to recall. Ray looked at her own ridged fins, the veined rock. She pulled off the mask, wiping her damp eyes, took off her fins. The ground was cool and damp against her soles, a bit clammy. It felt as though it had give. He waited for her to finish, silent, then embraced her, his body solid, familiar. She relaxed. His breath warmed her neck. His lips were soft. He was real.

'I'm sorry,' he muffled. Anger flowed down her spine and from her Achilles heels, into cool rock where it belonged. Not that she'd ever let him know it.

'Please don't do that again.'

'I won't. Ever.'

'I was really scared. I thought we were going to die.'

'I'll never lose you, I promise.'

'Please don't.'

'I hear you, babe. I hear you.'

They wrapped their arms around each other until the female returned, smiling at the rock in a vague attempt at discretion. Fari's male joined her. The water beings made a fluttering noise with their lips that sounded like adulation, breaking into applause. Ray blushed.

'Perfect. Just perfect,' the female smiled.

She buried her head in Fari's shoulder, relishing his locks against her temple, the scratch of his hair. It felt good. A reminder she was alive.

'I'm Mesi,' the female told them. Ray looked up in time to see the being place a hand on her male counterpart's shoulder. 'This is Okoro. We are your guides.'

'Buddies,' Okoro said, and they all smiled. His voice was rich and deep, bearing quiet power. There was silence before Ray understood they were waiting.

'We're Eraynor, and Fari,' she said, turning to face them, hands shaking. 'This is a fantastic honour. We thank you.'

'We hope to thank you in turn,' Mesi told her. 'We are to take you to Naunet, our mother. She will explain all.'

Of course, Ray thought, what else for a fairy-tale experience than another fairy-tale encounter. If they were there at all. She steeled her expression, glancing at Fari to see what he thought, then Mesi. She nodded once, briskly. They followed the water beings.

The couple were led down to a wide, glistening incline that wound around the cavern, stopping at various landings and even more tunnels dug into the rock walls below before continuing to the next landing, and on again, ever downwards. 'Like ants,' Fari said, head turned towards the dark openings. Ray didn't dare answer. Even though she was barefoot and the incline was wide enough for at least six people, she tried not to look over the edge, into the depths, which seemed deep as the ridge itself, and from her quick glances, had no end. She pushed one arm beneath Fari's, held him with the other. He smiled at her, glad to be forgiven if only for their safety. Mesi and Okoro allowed them to descend as slow as they liked; if they were frustrated by the air beings' dolly-stepping caution, they didn't say. Both moved with small considered steps, ignoring the many water beings they passed, the chanting of foreign voices, the whispered gasps of surprise. It was odd for Ray to feel like a minority when she was so entranced by their differences, even more intrigued by their similarities. She grew hot, light-headed. For most of the journey she kept her eyes on her feet, fearing she might fall.

At last, another central walkway emerged, double the size of the one they'd left. Here the beings were seven feet tall, thick with nubile muscle. They were free of the broad markings that entwined the other humanoids. Instead they bore cloud-shaped patches on their chests, legs and arms, lightly shaded, and were tinged blue rather than green. Their heads were bald, one thick lock protruding from the backs of their skulls, close to the neck. They held white staffs made from a large, curving bone, possibly a whale's. The lamps on this level were modern, unlike those on the upper landing and tunnels. They had plastic bases, electric bulbs, thin wiring escaping to trail into the gloom of the larger caves behind the giants, ending in some kind of generator, or power point, Ray surmised. She wondered where they came from.

Mesi approached the giants, speaking in her rapid spiked language. Okoro stood beside her, head down.

'Matriarchal,' Fari whispered. He nudged her, eyes clear.

'Good.'

She'd been watching him for signs and although he seemed lucid enough, who was to say she was? If this *was* a hallucination brought on by nitrogen in her blood it was the most complete she'd ever had. She rested against him.

The giants stood aside, staring through them. Fari and Ray walked into a tunnel as wide as a cave. There were intricate, detailed images carved into the walls, the background etchings buffed down, it seemed, so each depiction emerged inches from the rock in faded colours. There were crests of waves, modern ships poised on the edges, bows pointing towards the smoky sky, about to fall into glistening ocean; an incredibly lifelike depiction of a group of water beings engaged in what looked like whale riding. A female creature sat on a large white throne, solemn and expressionless with haunted green eyes. The last Ray saw was of a starship falling from inky heavens, trailing plumes of fire and smoke, nose trained at the framing darkness of sea.

A right turn led them into a smaller cavern space guarded by two females who nodded at Mesi and Okoro, and let them pass. Inside was a lengthy table made out of a wood so dark it gleamed in lamplight, a number of high-backed chairs surrounding it protectively. The table was old, bare, chipped and scratched. Rock carvings lined the walls, formless, abstract, no less colourful or beautiful than those in the tunnel. There were candles everywhere, making damp rock glitter. Random seafaring items seemingly on display. A buoy painted with bright colours resembled a work of modern art. A rust-brown anchor leant in a corner, huge, infested with barnacles and other shell creatures. Wrinkled beige shirts and three-quarter-length trousers were pinned on the wall, too huge for any normal human.

At the end of the table sat a thin being that had to be Naunet. Alone, head down, lost in thought. She was slight, hardly any muscle beneath fragile flesh. Her breasts were faint protrusions. Cornrows trailed past her arms, almost as thick as her limbs. As they entered, she raised her head. Smiling, though it was faint. Her eyes were green like the woman in the rock carving, and yet Ray knew it wasn't her.

'Mother.'

Okoro bowed, Mesi with him, the two almost touching their webbed toes. Ray attempted to look at the younger beings from the corner of her eye. Although they wore the obvious traits of their kind, they didn't seem at all similar. It was odd to think of Mesi and Okoro as brother and sister even though she'd only just met the beings.

'You brought them,' the thin elder spoke without emotion, staring at Ray and Fari. 'They are here.'

No malice, no warmth, nor even curiosity flavoured her voice. The mother's stare was flat, detached. It embarrassed Ray, and something urged her to stir a response. Before her brain could stop her she stepped forward, sensing Mesi's alarm; her half-feint to block her, too late.

'Thank you for inviting us, Mother Naunet, although with respect we'd really like to know why we're here. We'll be missed. We wouldn't want to trouble anybody, or cause anyone to send a search party.'

Silence. Ray felt displeasure radiate against her back. Naunet's green eyes raked her skin until she clapped her hands once, in delight. Her face erupted into a grin.

'How cute! You are spirited, which means you are right. Please, sit.'

Naunet indicated the chairs they were ushered into, while she muttered something Ray didn't understand, causing Mesi and Okoro to leave. When she was sure they were gone the mother leant her elbows on the table, palms against her cheeks, watching Fari. The corner of her lip lifted. He fidgeted, bit his lip, tried to hold her gaze, but couldn't. Oddly enough, Naunet's attention didn't worry Ray as much as Mesi's. Was it because this being was older, less attractive? She had been beautiful once, perhaps long ago. With surprise, Ray noticed that the palms of her hands were the same dark colour as the knuckles and backs. Deep lines cut into her cheeks and the corners of her eyes, though elsewhere she was unwrinkled.

'So, so interesting.' Naunet hadn't broken her stare, even though Fari had long been studying his dry and white feet. 'Your wife is correct. We have lots to speak of. I will try to cover your questions, so you must listen and not interrupt, please. When I am done, you may leave.'

Mesi and Okoro returned with fogged wine glasses, placing them before Ray and Fari. Ray lifted hers, caught the heavy smell. Rum. Fari sipped. Naunet sniffed with pride, threw it back, swirling the drink on her tongue. Swallowed, closed her eyes.

'You like?' Eyes open, waiting for them to nod, beaming when they did. 'It's our best, two centuries old, so you should.'

'Two?' Fari looked at his glass with greater consideration and took another tentative sip, quietly smacking his lips. Ray took the tiniest amount. Stinging molasses hit her immediately. She put the glass down, sat upright.

'Much of what we have here is foraged. You'd be amazed at what capsizes, or even worse, what's thrown down here, left to rot. The fish alone, caught and released dead, are too much for us all.'

'We're disgusting.' Ray heard the dullness of her words, acceptance.

'Yes, most of you are. But that's beside the point.'

She tried to be quiet, to listen as instructed, snatching quick glances at Fari. She knew that look. He didn't drink much, and when he did his choice was brandy or rum. He was attempting to avoid examining his glass, the burn disseminating in his stomach. His eyes were half-closed, vague. Rum might make any possible narcosis worse. She couldn't grow tipsy. She had to be alert.

'First, the details. I can only tell you the basics, the rest will come in time. You must be wondering who or what we are, so let me start with that. We are known as Nommo.'

Ray swallowed rum thickness at the back of her throat, forcing excitement down with it. She leant forward onto damp wood.

'That's a myth.'

The mother threw her head back in silent laughter. Her tiny hand covered her mouth, her thin shoulders shook. She looked like a child.

'Really? Then I must not exist. Let me say it else way. We are the descendants of Nommo who survive in us. Please allow me to explain.

'Millenia ago Earth was visited by creatures from above, the stars, as legends tell. In the tradition of the ones who saw them first, the ancients, they were said to be ugly beings that thrived best in water. Only the last statement is true. They were drawn to our world because it is one of the few in this region to possess abundant liquid H_2O. So they landed, and populated the seas, and were sometimes seen by the ancients, especially those who took to ships and sailboats, or swam. They were Nommo, aquatic people of the stars. They were beautiful beyond mortal belief. Once viewed, a human would do anything to spend their life with them. They became known as merpeople, but were not as they are depicted in the old books either, because why would the old books tell truth? The first writers were voyagers who saw Nommo themselves. They kept their pact to dissuade anyone from finding them. So they tricked readers, giving Nommo tails of fish, and scales, and long yellow hair. The books that followed after only retold those lies.

'Humans bewitched by Nommo descended into the seas, copulated, of course, and bred offspring, of course, and those offspring surfaced on occasion to meet new humans who did the same, over and over. This went on for thousands of years. A new race, the Nommadians, was born. I am of that long-evolved people, as is Mesi, Okoro, and all who resemble us. We are human, but not. We are Nommo, but not. We are the evolutionary leap undiscovered by your Darwin, and perhaps might even be your missing link. I do not know. It is my guess.

'In the first few thousand years we were able to go largely undetected in our foraging of food, the carcasses of human endeavour, of humans themselves. There was a time of mass seafaring, of trade and conquest and war. During this period a great many ancestors were discarded just like your modern fishermen discard unwanted catch now. Some leapt into the sea of their own accord, though it was commonplace to see ancestors chained in groups, weighted with rocks, plummeting to the ocean bed. We rescued them if we could; this was rare. Much of the time they would not live. After, two things occurred. Those first ancestors, the ones who looked for us of their own free will, stopped. They began to fear the deep they once loved, by our reckoning; again, we do not know. Later ancestors looked in their place, and the majority of them were cruel. They killed various things in various ways, animals, humans, the sea itself, us. If caught, none came back to tell the tale. Thus, the second event occurred. We retreated into the lower depths, kept from the estuaries and rivers, and based our survival on what we could hunt undersea, what drifted down from the surface.

'This has created a problem. Since inception, our entire existence has depended on the intermarriage between our kind and yours. We have a limited gene pool, although our world stretches for thousands of miles, with many countries and districts. The blood is thin. It has become necessary to gain the trust of human emissaries who might communicate our need to regulate the Nommadian bloodline by the promotion of further diversification. Unless we do, we run the risk of genetic disease that could wipe us out entirely. We need sustained human interaction to survive.'

'You want us to *breed*?' Fari's voice was high, waking Ray from Naunet's hypnosis. She flinched, fearing Mother's anger. And yet, when she dared to look, Naunet seemed sad, bashful. Her mouth moved. For a long time the water mother seemed unable to speak. Ray felt Fari sit back and, without looking, imagined his wilted frame, his expression.

'Sorry, Mother.'

Naunet raised her unlined hand.

'No. You are more precise in your language than I.'

She felt Fari's hand on hers, tasting the sting of alcohol on her lips. This time Naunet stared at her. The expression was kind, narrow eyes sympathetic.

'You squint when you look at light,' she observed.

'Yes. I have an intolerance.'

'You are blind partially?'

'No, no. It's photophobia. I can't look into bright light.'

'I understand.'

Naunet shuffled in her seat. She tapped her long fingers on the table, whistled between her teeth. Something in her manner was odd. At first Ray thought it was the Nommo's obvious parallels with human behaviour before she realised it wasn't that. She wasn't going to try and convince them. Instead, she would be their guide. She knew it was difficult for Ray to live by the light of the sun. She was letting her know a better environment existed under the sea for someone with her affliction. She wanted her to come to that conclusion, and there was only one way Ray could have known this.

'Can I ask something?' Ray stalled.

'Of course. You may.'

'Are Mesi and Okoro your children?'

Naunet twitched, smiling again. It stretched the skin on her cheeks to tearing point.

'Oh no. Oh no. You ask because *mother* means different in English, correct? Here it means—' She paused, frowning at the ceiling. 'Queen. I am Nommadia's leader, they are not my seed. Here the word for mother is *Nay*, although many districts use *Naa, Tie Meme*, or others depending where their ancestors hailed.'

'Oh. I'm sorry.'

'Don't be. You'll do well to know more whatever your decision.'

'And this decision,' Fari said, steelier than Ray ever heard him, 'means we have to stay here permanently? Away from everything we know? That's if we decided to become your curs?'

Ray let go of his hand. When she could bear to catch Naunet's eye, she seemed puzzled. She frowned deeper, as though struggling to catch his accent, like Richie.

'I don't know what you mean by *curs*, but no, it would not be permanent. You can stay for a period of two years maximum, leave if you like. The reality is you can leave any time. You will not be prisoners. Every choice will be yours, always, even the very means of insemination, if you stay. Artificial or organic. Leave within days or stay for an indefinite measure. This is a request, not an order. We do not make decrees or threats. We are not human.' She looked at the rock carvings. 'My apologies.'

'It's OK.' Ray heard his frustrated sigh, ignoring it. 'Can we have some time to think?'

'Ah, come on—' he sneered, then stopped.

'Of course,' Naumet responded.

'I'd like to think about it. I really would. But I'd like a few days. Two perhaps?'

'You may have two, more if you like.'

'Two's fine,' Ray felt herself nod.

'Good. We will come to your beach at 2 a.m., in two days' time. If you're there, we will take you. If not, we will be dismayed, but will understand.'

'Thank you.' Ray got to her feet, feeling solid, upright. Any possible narcosis had drifted away.

'Thank *you*,' Naunet replied, standing.

It was easy to see why she'd remained seated, her slim body curled over, shoulder blades protruding like dual fins. She was taller than the guards, towering above them, more than eight and a half feet in height it seemed. Ray's eyes widened, though she kept her composure and shook the queen's soft hand; she even bowed. Naunet watched her, thin mouth twisted in faint amusement; she wouldn't look at Fari again.

They were led along a steep, upwards tunnel lit by electric lamps. The first was an emergency back entrance into Hanoa, Mesi and Okoro explained along the way, one used for newcomers, or to avoid being discovered. This tunnel led directly into open ocean. It was tough going even for Fari and Ray, who trained daily, and when they reached the point where the Nommo rested they were panting hard, rivulets of sweat coursing down their backs. They suited up, stepping past the membrane threshold. Pressure returned along with the cooling touch of seawater. Their air had been refilled, Mesi told them, but once out of the tunnel they swam quickly anyway, taking the necessary pressure stops, upwards in a series of staggered moments until they broke the calm surface.

The moon was bright, the night filled with stars and nebula tendrils. The high ground of the distant island was a glittering mirror image of the sky. Richie's motorboat wasn't far, at rest on soft waves. Okoro placed his hands around his mouth and made a call like a warbling hoot. After some seconds Richie's head appeared, a torch probing the waves.

'He *knew*?' Fari breathed, sculling to face the Nommadians. For the first time, Mesi avoided their eyes. Okoro placed a soft hand on Fari's shoulder – feeling unyielding tension, he let it drop. Behind him, Ray shook her head, unseen. She'd already guessed.

'Richie is a friend. Please don't be upset. He was trying to do good by us both.'

'As your emissary?' Fari spat into the waves. 'Why doesn't he do what your queen wants?'

'Male and female work best. He does not have a wife.'

'So where's your king?'

The Nommo pressed their lips together, staring at the black mirror of water. Ray swam close to Fari, touching his fingers.

'Hey. Come on.'

He relented, though she hadn't expected it. At the motorboat Richie helped them aboard with a strong arm, grunting with the strain. Neither Ray nor Fari spoke a word as they wrenched away fins, regulators and masks. Richie was nervous. He paced, waiting, looking into their faces then nodding, walking away. He leant over the side of the boat to speak with the Nommo in their language. After five minutes of conversation, clicks, harsh abrasive phrases and exchanges that sounded like song, they bobbed up and down, waving at Fari and Ray, making that strange hollow call, falling onto their sides to disappear with a faint splash. Richie watched the sea for what felt like ages before excusing himself and sitting by the prow in silence.

They powered back to the beach, Fari and Ray on opposite sides of the boat. The throaty engine voice changed, ceased. They packed their gear into neat piles. Rapid music came from the hotel, though it was past midnight.

They were checking the equipment when Richie stepped from the prow. Hands clasped, rubbing, his eyes tired, dull.

'Lissen. I sorry. But I mek a pact, yuh hear!'

'You should have found yourself a partner and gone. Not lied to us.'

Fari scowled at the beach, his back half turned. Richie stammered something, only to stop and rub his hands together more slowly. The sound was loud. Ray saw hurt glisten on his face like low tide and wanted to say something, couldn't.

'All right, Richie.'

Fari climbed into the water and splashed back to the beach. Ray watched him walk onto damp sand and when it felt like too much she touched Richie's elbow.

'I'll see what I can do.'

He nodded, hardly looking. She kissed his grizzled cheek and descended the ladder, following her partner to their hotel.

Two days of barely speaking, effectively holidaying apart. Fari remained his normal chilled self, his words low and clear, polite and accommodating as ever. And yet he hired a Mini Moke, leaving in the bright of early morning, not returning until it was fathoms dark. Ray spent time on the beach reading Karen

Lord and listening to 90s R&B. She'd bought the book from a local store to connect with the island's home-grown myths. Now she wondered whether those pages held truths.

She ate at the hotel, talked with staff and walked into unforgiving sunlight knowing she must, despite a vague feeling of reluctance at the hours spread before her. She walked quiet backstreets devoid of tourists and sat with elders cooling themselves outside their houses, talking of the season's golden apples, the approaching Crop Over, the fast girls frequenting Baxter's Road. She returned to her sun lounger, swimming with tinted goggles until the beach fell into retreat, thinking she might catch sight of them, chiding herself when there was only the relaxed rhythm of the waves, the irritating mosquito buzz of jet skis. She lay on her back, floating on soft waves. On the rare occasions she thought of home it was fleeting, cynical. She was an only child whose parents died in her late teens. She'd moved to London to start again, only never quite did. Instead she met Fari, adopting his life and friends, his pastimes and family. Even her love of diving came from him. If she had anything to lose besides her lover, it was the feeling of home. Every street of it, every rented flat, welcoming neighbourhood and multiple family tie was his.

In the fledgling days of dating she and Fari visited old friends from the neighbourhood he'd been raised in, where they lived to this day. She'd made herself up eagerly, even though she already wore the tinted glasses, just a touch of dark lipstick and mascara. She'd never been one to use a great deal. They walked the streets hand in hand, bathed in a sunset glow. It was summer and they laughed lots, free of jackets and baggage. At first, things went well. There'd been spiced food and piles of roti bearing dark birthmarks, roaring laughter and bass-heavy music.

The woman, a school friend named Anna, was pretty and accommodating, calling Ray 'sweetie' as she hugged her like a cousin. During the course of the party Anna, Ray and a small group of people Ray didn't know ended up in a basement room crammed onto a single guest bed, drinking rosette, puffing from a slow orbit of damp, smouldering weed. Then, one by one, everyone left. Anna was the first to go. Ray wasn't sure if it was by design or otherwise, whether she should join or not. Slowly, each person had left the room. She hadn't been invited by anyone. She thought someone would return, but they didn't. She sat on the bed, eyes squeezed tight, smoking a tiny roach she'd been passed way back, inhaling smoke and thin paint fumes from the recently coated bare walls. There were no books on shelves, no carpet on the dark floorboards. Music echoed, faint, from above. Ray waited an unsure half hour before eventually going back up. When she arrived the raucous party atmosphere hit her like island heat. Anna, who saw her first, burst into laughter. She slapped the kitchen counter and said she'd 'forgotten she was there'. The others, embarrassed, studied paper plates. A crestfallen Fari didn't say one word.

It wasn't his fault he was popular, Ray thought, buoyant on waves. It wasn't his fault he had a home.

She'd grown so used to being different. It made sense, now she considered herself fully. Once it had helped her blend into the background, to shadow a world she had no desire to play a role in. Life grew painful, blinding, each beauty and horror she saw equally overwhelming, equally unwanted. In the beginning she'd isolated herself, it was true, yet habitual silence stole not only her voice, but her will to say anything. Now, in the scant hours since their encounter with the Nommadians, Ray felt she'd suffered some form of inverted narcosis. She'd hauled herself from warm waters to find herself intoxicated on dry land, believing none of the solid world real.

During those two remaining evenings they ate together, but said nothing. Fari had withdrawn into himself, almost enough to convince her to stay, so she tried not to notice what was happening, a difficult task. Although he kept his back straight and his thoughts lively, physically he'd wilted. His skin was pale, his eyes red. He obviously wasn't sleeping. He spoke in a low monotone, not saying much, and when he did his lips barely moved. Even his hair, loosened and free, fell in a subdued mass, making him seem like a despondent lion, weathered and aged. He picked at his food. The waiting staff, used to his wide grin and excitable nature, turned from Ray to Fari and back, understanding deep in their eyes. They spoke gently, calling him *brother*, or *sir* if they were women, treating him with trained attention as though he were sick. The sight of him keeping upright, attempting to withhold his emotions so she'd feel better about her conclusion, broke Ray's heart.

At night, separated by narrow space, she tried to stifle her tears. He was awake, she knew. It wasn't fair. Nothing made any sense. She'd long dreamed of leaving the city behind, especially of late, yet she had no idea why she felt so strongly. Nothing she could get to grips with intellectually and decipher, only that urge to get away. Spiky excitement, nerve endings leaping static. Inexplicable love. Naunet was right about the sun, she decided, eyes heavy, focused on the ceiling, knowing there was more, unable to discern its form.

That second evening, at dinner, dessert plates smeared and empty, Ray's eyes obsessed by her mauby, the liquid brown as tea. Fari sat across the table watching her for the first time in hours.

'So aren't you going to say something?' Ray lifted her head.

'Aren't you?'

'You're the one who's staring.'

'Why shouldn't I? You're the one who's not saying anything.'

'Fari. You've virtually ignored me for two days.'

'I've let go. That's not the same.'

'*You've let go?* That's all you've got to say?'

'What else do you think I should do?' He licked his lips, paused, looked over his shoulder. Faced her again. Saw no answer in her eyes. 'Don't you think I have a right? Don't you think I deserve more?'

'For what? Behaving like this? Like I've done something wrong?'

'You're talking about *my* behaviour? Mine?'

He was slouched, speaking in a rasp, eyes darting to see if they were heard by other diners. She grew scared. He was never like this. He was calm, easy-going. She sighed, biting her lip.

'Yes, I am. Look, there's got to be a better way—'

'So when were you going to say?'

'Say what, Fari? Jesus, what are you—'

'Say you're going,' he whispered, finding her with a look so naked her cheek prickled. 'Don't take me for a joke, that's why you won't look at me, isn't it?'

She snatched her eyes from the tablecloth. Their usual waiter – a sweet young man no more than nineteen, vivid white eyes, willing expression, cirrus beard and a scattered pattern of shaving bumps on his neck – stood poised, unwilling to move his stringy limbs forward even though he'd been trained, fingers writhing like anemones. She feigned a tight smile. He stepped back.

'I haven't even decided—'

'*Bullshit!*' he spat, throwing his napkin at Ray. It hit her in the chest. She gasped, shocked more than upset. 'That's bullshit, Eraynor, and you know it.'

He got up and left.

Ray took the napkin from her lap, placed it carefully next to her plate. She sat at the table until her heart calmed, her temples cooled. She rose, twitching a smile in the general direction of anyone who might look, aware all the attention in the dining room was on her. She wondered what stories they'd created. Left them behind for their room.

Outside their door, Ray stopped. She steeled herself, even when she thought she'd heard him, dismissed the sounds, maybe callously at that point, about to insert her key card when she saw a stern-faced, pig-tailed maid two doors away, alert. When the woman realised she'd been seen, she ducked her head and entered the room she'd been cleaning. Ray second-guessed, pressing her ear against the door. Fari's cries were loud, unrestrained. They clawed at her heart. He was beating something, it sounded like the wall.

Ray backed away, leaving the hotel and going to the beach. Where she belonged.

She stayed past dark, looking out to sea. Couples took moonlit walks past her, saying goodnight. She nodded, smiling with plastic rigidity. She wrapped her arms around her knees and flexed her bare toes, savouring the rub of granules against her skin, listening to the water. It spoke to her. Always had. Part of her was sorry, mostly she wasn't. She was happy and it had nothing to do with Fari. For the first time.

On the main road, walking back, a car horn repeated, disturbing her peace. First she ignored it, but when the vehicle pulled up a few yards away she felt a twinge of fear, gazing at the oncoming traffic. When she next looked back, a hand waved from the parked driver's side, a head leant out. Richie. She sighed, throwing a desperate look at the glowing hotel sign, the room lights and warmth of her own bed. Her island oasis. But it was no good. She walked to the passenger-side door, let herself in.

He drove to the spot where they'd first met, Cray's, frequented by men and women who favoured night life, not that Ray had known it then. The place had been loud and shadowed, jammed with locals and tourists, Passa Passa dancehall thumping, just what she needed to fill the gaps. Fari was a good travel companion, yet overly calm and measured. His conservatism, her rock back home, seemed out of place here. Ray wanted to shake things up, she knew it before they left.

Her boyfriend had gone for their drinks and started a conversation with Richie at the bar, finding him friendly in his understated, drawling way. Before long he'd joined their table. They talked of the ocean and the art of diving, interests shared by all, dividing the conversation three ways until the bar closed. They covered everything: favourite dive spots, hottest clubs, most annoying tourists and loneliest beaches on the island. With every topic exhausted, they spoke of their lives.

The next morning, a tangerine sun rising above the underlined sky, they'd stood on the beach opposite their hotel waiting for the motorboat. It didn't belong to Richie. He'd borrowed it from his workplace, which also rented out jet skis, speedboats with inflatable banana trailers and glass-bottomed boats. It also rented Richie, which was why he'd arrived at mid-morning for their final dive instead of their usual dawn start. He'd taken an elderly Italian couple for a tour around the island with a breakfast stop at the raging waters of Bathsheba, coming back to the west coast in time for Ray and Fari. He charged mate's rates, so it made perfect sense to dive according to gaps in his schedule. Richie seemed like the type of man who talked more than he thought, but was honest. Fari trusted him completely.

This time, tagging behind him in Cray's, Ray wasn't sure what Richie wanted. He went to the bar, further surprising her, coming back with a pair of tall glasses. Tequila sunrise. Not her favourite, but a clear indication he wasn't trying to get her drunk, so she didn't mind. His eyes still sparkled, although dark thumbprints lay beneath them. They clinked glasses, Ray forgetting to drink, only remembering it was bad luck when her glass hit the table. She put the straw to her lips. The liquid was thick, artificial. Richie frowned at the orange and red, shrugged and took another sip, smacking loudly, turning the glass from side to side. He looked up, noticing she wasn't drinking.

'Nice?'

'It's all right.' Ray watched his response. 'You don't think so?'

'Tourists love ah tequila. Thought I'd see why.'

'Not for you?'

'Nah, suh. A Cockspur man, me.'

'I don't blame you, not at all.'

They listened to the Soca, Ray moving her shoulders despite herself. He didn't say anything else. Something had shifted. He was dredging up courage, his eyes and the way he watched her said it. The way he looked at her before always filled her with unease. Now it made her feel wanted. Nothing like desire, in fact, far from it. More like reverence. As if she were a relic he'd dived long and deep for, searching wrecks and unseen places but surfaced without, only to find it washed up on the beach, as though the ocean had presented it just for him. She felt bathed clean with saltwater, scrubbed by brine and rough contact until she was smooth and polished, restored. She smiled at the thought, her body turned from Richie, knees pointed at the wooden dance floor. She sipped hard, grimacing.

'Him all right?'

'Who?'

'Fari.' He frowned. Who else? 'Him say anyting bout me?'

'No. But he forgives you.'

'Him say that?'

'No.' Richie's expression collapsed. Ray felt terrible. She sipped again, embarrassed, the straw barking emptiness. 'I know he doesn't blame you. It's me he's angry with. I'm to blame.'

'You not going?'

'Yes. I am.'

His head was down, stirring ice with his straw. She was glad she didn't have to see his eyes.

'Male and female work best. Try convince him.'

'Is that why you never went? Because you don't have a partner?'

He kept stirring, taking test sips, stirring again. Nothing more than melted ice and tequila fumes in his glass. Bass throbbed through her ribcage, warming her insides. She waited, willing herself not to move to the beat.

'Try convince him, do.'

'You can tell me. It's OK.'

His head lifted. His eyes were piercing, like sunlight on sea. The hurt was all his, blazing to the back of her skull. It made her lose grip. The glass squeaked from her fingers, almost toppling until she strengthened her hold.

'I caan conceive. I would go otherwise, honestly. I would.'

She held on despite the intensity, seeing him and clutching tighter, feeling cold against her palm, welcome chill. She released the glass, grasped his hand.

'Richie, I'm sorry.'

He nodded, not stopping, head moving like a marionette, the smile returning after a while.

'Me know. Otherwise you wouldn't go, right?'

Ray grinned across the table. Of course not. She hadn't thought of it like that.

He took her back to the hotel and Ray let herself inside their room. Fari's body was stiff under the duvet. She brushed her teeth, climbed in. Curled up, closing her eyes. She felt the cover move, heard him turn, and his hands were on her, so she turned to meet him. They pulled each other's underwear free, made love. They were crying, placing kisses all over each other. 'They won't take me on my own,' she said, and he shook his head, saying they would. They needed women more than men, he was sure. Ray knew it was possible. And if it was, she had to. Afterwards they calmed, on their backs, breathing slow, pushing each other away. She tried to sleep. Couldn't. She got up, dressed, curled on the small sofa bed and closed her eyes. At one forty-five she got up, pulling on her shoes. She blew a kiss towards Fari, going before her sobs disturbed him even more.

The stillness of the night was comforting. No one to see her guilt. She stifled her cries against the back of her hand, remembering the colour of Naunet's and the Nommo's dark palms matching their knuckles. She thought of her children being like that. Amphibious when their mother was not. Shit. She had no equipment. How was she going to reach Hanoa? She hadn't thought of that. Ray kept going, down the incline of beach, kicking yellow puffs, slipping off her shoes and holding them in hooked fingers. The tide exhaled beyond her. She looked. There were voices, formless and distant, no one in view. Overhead, the constellations shimmered among the thin veil of Milky Way. She got closer to the water, which had eaten half of the beach, and there they were, rising like modest titans, Mesi and Okoro. They were naked as before, though she hardly noticed, she was so happy. Each had diving equipment dangling from their hands, gifted by Richie she realised. She needn't have worried. Obviously they'd think of that. She was smiling, walking faster, splashing seawater.

'Thank God,' Ray said. 'Thank God.'

'*Yewande* . . .' Okoro greeted, arms wide. He stopped, trouble reaching his dark eyes. They looked over her shoulder, mouths open.

'What's wrong?' she said, even as she knew.

'Fari?' Okoro's tone was light, eyebrows lifted. Ray saw disappointment, felt early jealousy. They didn't care about her. They wanted him.

'He's not here?' Mesi peered behind her as though she were intentionally blocking her view. Ray's heart cried silent pain.

'You must be a couple. Male and female work best.' Okoro's eyes were wide. Yes, there was sympathy. He saw her emotion. Yet he shook his head, unwilling. 'We tried before. With one. It doesn't work. Two is all.'

The words didn't come. Her head dropped as she tried to think of a reason, or argument. He would have known. They might not have accepted his argument but Fari would have known what to say. He always did, whereas she . . . Ray looked up, eyes misty. 'I really—' She stopped, swallowing tears. 'This is everything I've wished for. I can't imagine going back. I can't. I mean it. I really want to do this. There's got to be a way.'

'Ah,' Mesi said. 'He's here.'

She didn't understand until she followed Mesi's gaze. Twisting, there was Fari, locks alive and bouncing as he jogged, heels spitting sand, hotel lights surrounding him in aura. He was there, with her. She threw her arms around him, laughed. He squeezed her waist, pulling her into his warmth.

'You're not going anywhere without me. You're not,' he repeated, burying his head in her shoulder, useless words she could hardly hear falling from her mouth.

They released each other. The Nommo were smiling, seawater lapping at their calves, a tame beast.

'The ancestors are pleased,' Okoro said. 'Now we must leave.'

They suited up, made a quick gear check and looked over each other's. Ray kissed Fari roughly, feeling solid teeth behind lips, then pressed her head against his chest. The soft pounding made her smile. She squeezed harder.

'Ready?'

'We are,' he told Ray.

They followed the Nommo into high tide. When it reached their chests they threw themselves forward, going under. Five metres down, Ray took Fari's hand. They made their descent into the blue.

THE SANKOFA PRINCIPLE

Eighty seconds after the prototype WiSP[1] drive came online, *Mimas 4* blinked out of existence. Saturn probes searched the immediate region for traces of its arrival, macro or subatomic, yet found nothing. Ten years would pass before EASN[2] finally declared the craft and its entire crew destroyed. What happened afterwards became the greatest occurrence in space exploration history.

A cylindrical shape just shy of sixty metres, a curved groove spiralling its length like a giant, headless screw. The surface, black as the expanse between galaxies, betrays equally unfathomable depths. Even when inoperative the drive is forever in motion, much like the human heart when the body is at rest. The WiSP never sleeps. It's programmed to spin clockwise eternally, elegant and pure as a ballerina. The translucent liquid-cooled surface ripples with trapped artificial light. The machinery is practically noiseless until its true purpose is engaged. It's

---

1 Wormhole-induced Subatomic Particle
2 Euro-Asian Space Network

mesmerising to see first-hand, believe me. The WiSP. *Mimas*'s lost soul.

Much of the story behind the WiSP's creation is classified, which makes a detailed examination of its origins supremely difficult. Research undertaken leads to silence, unreturned calls, redacted or destroyed documents, university posts long vacated. Voids, if you will. It's obviously all very apt. There's a beginning, but no end. A call, but no response.

This is what we laypeople know. Since 19__ it had long been postulated that the black hole, for all its magisterial deadliness, could in fact be a source of discovery. Everyone knows the basics. A black hole is a region of spacetime exhibiting such strong gravitational effects that nothing – not even light – can escape. General relativity predicts that a sufficient compact mass can deform spacetime to form such a hole. The boundary between this region and the area in which normal gravitational rules apply is called the event horizon. The area in which the hole exists, a singularity.

Kerr's theory of the Einstein–Rosen bridge predicts that if an object were to fall into a black hole, it might be sucked down a tunnel, and through a 'white hole' or 'ring of fire' on the other side, to emerge into a parallel multiverse. Essentially, what this theory suggests is that gravitational forces that exist within the hole could break down matter and remake it anew. That being the case, interstellar space travel utilising the power of such forces began to be seen as a conceivable pursuit.

The observation of gravitational waves emanating from a collision of two black holes by the LIGO[1] collaboration in

---

1 Laser Interferometer Gravitational-Wave Observatory

February 2016 proved that radiation could escape a singularity. A second sighting later that year confirmed it.

Ever since, a challenge was set. How might we harness the powers of spacetime distortion in order to serve our urge for exploration? Was it even possible? When the adequate technological advances were made nearly eighty years later, we sent probes to Earth's nearest event horizon, Sagittarius A. Not to find out what was on the other side; that was of little interest. But to examine the gravitational processes that cause the breakdown of spacetime as we know it, and the ability to survive them without perceptible change.

Following those probes, scientists were assembled from around the world. They were locked behind high walls that housed enough buildings for a small town, forming gated cities made up of families, lovers and close friends. Still, even they couldn't go beyond the inner sanctum of research buildings where scientists, engineers and academics worked from sunlight to sundown every day. All were monitored for every hour of their existence via cameras, voice-recording instruments as delicate as butterfly wings, or implanted DNA chips. Any mention of a wrong word, or a strange mannerism, and soldiers turned up at the door flanked by needle-thin sec-bots, armaments glistening in mandarin sunset. Sayonara. Or so they said.

It lasted generations. Research, exploration, colonisation, further research, published papers. We made gains, had major setbacks, won back ground. Countries formed coalitions that came and went. The USA had been a player, once. The New Civil War put paid to that, along with much of the Deep South. Only a crater the size of western England to show for their efforts. The UK took part too, but before long they also retreated into the distance like a stationary figure. By the time Leyton,

Anis, Bai and Emilia were born and came of age they were the best team for the job, and their regions of origin were joint-principle players. No warped sense of guilt or history there.

Two hundred and four years from that first discovery, a plume of radiation escaping a half-moon sphere. Shorter than the length of time between Newton's 1687 opus *Principia Mathematica* and the grasped ability to free ourselves from gravity's grip, some might have argued.

And they'd be right.

Because in August 2220, after countless trials and deterrents, scientists finally reached the conclusions they had craved.

A four-person crew. Two women, two men. One couple married, the other common-law. No children. No living parents. EASN made that mandatory, it wasn't a secret. They'd tried separating people from their immediate families for extended time periods. It drove their astronauts mad.

Two women, two men. All *fuego*, according to my wife. Neither of us was sure if EASN made that mandatory too, but it certainly helped sustain public interest. Global media being what it was, we knew everything. Where they were born, how they grew up. Where they were educated, how they met. Where they trained and how they did it, what takeaways they liked, what came back up, all being unwell, what time they went to bed. What movies they watched, their favourite songs. Hell, we even knew if they were having regular sex (they weren't – at least not in their own relationships). We knew it all from A to Z and the Network encouraged us. We'd long forgone ideas of privacy. It was the price that came with the future, someone had said decades before. We were chipped and moni-tored and we liked it that way. The crew were young, we were bored for the most part and it was habitual. There they were, every day. And so were we.

The *Mimas 4* crew members, in no order of importance, were:

Leyton Shaw: 27, married to Anis Creighton-Shaw; Jamaican-British, 6' 3", Professor of Physics at Trinity College, Cambridge. Keen football player and 21st-century film enthusiast. Position: Research Scientist. Rank: Lieutenant.

Anis Creighton-Shaw: 33, married to Leyton Shaw; Ghanaian-British, 5' 11", Professor of Astro-Physics at Trinity College, Cambridge. Former pilot for the Ghanaian Air Force, Wing Chun 2nd Dan. Position: Research Scientist/Pilot. Rank: Captain.

Bai Liu: 30, common-law husband of Emilia Jonas; Chinese-French, 6' 1", Professor of Engineering, ENS, Paris. Tennis enthusiast with a love of the dramatic and written arts. Position: Chief Engineer. Rank: Lieutenant.

Emilia Jonas: 32, common-law wife of Bai Liu; Euro-German, 6' 0", Professor of Computer Science, ENS Paris. Mountaineering expert, a keen passion for geology. Position: Navigator. Rank: Executive Officer.

These were the brave men and women who carried our thirst for knowledge on their shoulders. They peered into the frontier, looked back at us and whispered. *Yes. It's safe.*

It's safe.

The *Mimas 4*'s crew were our extensions, in as much as they shared our wonder. Of course they were also our betters but it never showed until that final day, far from Earth, the starcraft a lone vestige of solidity beneath their feet. Leyton was very much the joker. He couldn't help smiling, even when he spoke, and had a favourite string of cowrie shells he took everywhere that were always running through his fingers. Unsurprisingly, he also had very little stress. Anis was way more serious than her husband, only because she cared so much. Often she would look into the tiny camera at the world, frowning at some distant problem, and our hearts would ache with the need to solve it on her behalf. Bai was hyperactive, talked fast and moved even quicker. He and Leyton formed a bond far beyond their years together, while women Earthwide wrote interzone messages proclaiming love for the soft-spoken Frenchman. Emilia was the hippy of the group, delighting in soft electronic music and wading through waist-high grass. She and Anis were often inseparable.

They worked tirelessly over a four-year period until launch day at the Vikram Sarabhai Space Centre, Kerala, August 25th 2220. We followed them on that final night until they woke at 4 to prepare for an 11 a.m. launch. It was warm, the sky clear and winds calm, as predicted. Leyton and Anis slept curled together. Bai lay on his back dressed in a faded blue NASA T-shirt and boxers, snoring. The sheets beside him lay flat and empty.

There was a flurry of camera angles and shots as, in a manned studio far away, some maddened production manager screamed at his director to find Emilia Jonas so the world would know what she was doing the night before world history fragmented from its known trajectory for ever. We screamed at the vid-gel right along with him.

Three long hours. By then, it was 2 a.m. An eagle-eyed line manager saw tracks in the sand, tracing them to a beach, the breadcrumbs of discarded hemp trousers, a thin jacket. Satellite imagery zoomed in. The tree. Emilia lay prone, nightdress billowing in the sea breeze, high on a thick branch, blonde hair trailing like a willow, the curled Gye Nyame tattoo on her right shoulder exposed, dead to the world.

Everyone calmed down after security guards were sent to

retrieve her body and she jumped awake, alarmed by the lights and the shouting and the dogs tugging their handlers into a stuttered trot: weapons drawn, pointed in all directions, in search of the unthinkable. She'd been sleeping. Just sleeping. Someone, the line manager perhaps, focused a camera on the empty Kingfisher bottle at the root of the tree. It remained there a full minute. Emilia only wanted one last night by the ocean, to hear the wash and wane of the tide, the call of night birds and chorus of insects. Just like anybody else. Just like us.

Rumours were she'd been taken to task for her negligence, only to bite EASN's head off in return. We never knew the truth. The cameras went black for an hour, the longest they'd been on standby in any of our lifetimes, we recalled during those minutes of dark screens and perplexed faces. What the hell? When they came back clear lines had been drawn. The *Mimas 4* crew didn't pay us any more acknowledgements. They stopped looking into cameras and blowing kisses. There were no telltale winks, or thumbs up when they passed us. No more would we catch their whispered asides, or self-conscious, muttered commentary. We were on our own.

And so they kept their focus on the jobs they'd been assigned, becoming the machines EASN programmed for so long. Just when the Network wanted them to display their humanity, they chose to withhold it. Maybe they weren't angry, just nervous. No one will ever know. There's nothing to say they even opened up to each other, let alone us watching from afar. That came later. When it was too late.

By all accounts it was a perfect launch. The equipment performed much like the crew, exactly as it should. The ground staff checked their read-outs with typical efficiency and kept banter to a minimum, unsmiling and taut. Lift-off occurred practically to the second. Hoses disengaged, scaffolding swung, smoke and fire breathed from engines, and it was up, slowly at first, then it caught hold of the sky, clawing spaceward with more excitement, more vigour. First the size of a cruise ship, then a building, then a house, then a car, then a bike. Then a scooter, a pencil, a ring. A star.

Mimas 4 became the embodiment of the new world after decades of dark centuries. It promised all was right for the species, asking no more than our adoration, our love. Its disappearance almost sent the world back into the abyss from which we'd barely managed to crawl. We rocked side to side, poised on the edge of exhilaration, one firm push from plummeting into our past.

An open book laid flat. The wings of pages catching sunlight from a window, my dark curtains thrown aside. A beam of light, thick and slanted. Within that half metre or so of space, a multiverse of shifting, spinning motes turning at separate velocities. Some fast, free-falling, dizzying; some slow and feather-like, eternal. Me lying on my back watching flecks of human skin, mostly mine, marvelling not just at what I saw but what I'd read. So vivid, even now. Closing my eyes, imagining. Atoms breaking down from a construction of solid forms to the invisible. Firing like rockets across unimaginable spaces. Arriving, reassembling.

I was eight years old and that three-page article caught my imagination like a flame. Ten to twenty years' time, they wrote. A mere ten to twenty years. We could travel to other planets in the time it took to cross the city. With the right technology we might even travel to far-reaching solar systems and galaxies. Ever since I'd first learned about the real constraints of space travel

– muscle and bone loss, one-way trips to other worlds, the dangers of breaking Earth's atmosphere at the peak of what were essentially huge bombs – I'd been filled with melancholy. Why couldn't we travel to the stars? All the stories I'd read made it seem easy. In those fictional worlds all problems were solved. Part of the reason the memory of that day was so arresting is because I'd finally read a factual article about space travel that was optimistic about exploring the cosmos. There would be a man or woman on Mars, providing the WiSP drive worked. Maybe even a colony.

I read other articles in *Space and Time* that summer, but nothing stuck like the knowledge that the WiSP might exist. What I didn't know, but half guessed in my excitement, was that an article on the drive meant it was close to reality. They were preparing the world, step by step. And it would happen in my lifetime.

At first, like any child dreamer, I wanted to go. I scoured the zone for details of how to be an astronaut. Spent hours hunched over my keyboard when I should have been in bed, or doing homework. But it was no good. I was a small child, thin, with bad eyesight and worse asthma. Too much late-night reading, my dad said. The air wasn't good, too polluted after the wars. My mum said I could always get corrective surgery as an adult, and my teenage years might take care of the rest. I lived in hope until I reached sixteen. Nothing had changed. I still needed glasses, I was still bamboo-thin, and I still used a respirator on the hottest nights. I wasn't sporty, much preferring to solve coding than be on the football field. So that was it. I still had an interest in all things interstellar, but I wasn't going to the stars. Maybe I could find another way.

I studied a bit of astrophysics in college and didn't do badly, but followed my heart and went into media and journalism at uni. I met and fell in love with Juanita during my second year. She was reading geology to keep her parents happy while she lied about her love of twentieth-century performance poetry. She was small and dark and Cuban, everything I loved. She would come to the flat I shared with two friends to cook us spicy tofu with vegetable rice. I kept my hand in by joining the _____ society while I studied, and also kept a close eye on what was going on with the WiSP. When I graduated it had fallen behind schedule, so society gossip went. The drive was the stuff of bad jokes and cryptic discussions. No one really believed it would happen.

I left university and did the right things. Got a flat, a car, moved in with Juanita. That meant I had to get a job too, which I managed with relative ease, landing a junior position on a big online paper, *The Sentinel*. I covered world affairs and politics mostly, but every now and then they'd let me at the space stuff. The Saturn probe launches were good work, and the renewed signals from Voyager One. That boosted the hopes of any interested parties, as the pictures it sent were fantastic. *There* was the initial proof that the universe was in fact a multiverse, made up of myriad galaxies and star systems forming a glistening latticework that had only been speculation until then. By the time I married Juanita the word 'universe', along with 'supersymmetry', was actually extinct.

We remained without children. Everyone wondered why, especially our parents, and it grew worse after I was promoted to a senior position, but after eight years it became a sore subject they'd rather leave alone. We didn't even know why ourselves, honestly: a generational thing perhaps? Overpopulation was such a big topic, and so much had gone wrong over land, oil and power that later generations like ours seemed to think, *What for?* It wasn't as if there weren't enough people on the planet, or we hadn't caused enough damage. Environmental issues were way more important than they'd been for the previous generation, even more so than discrimination. Anyway, what that meant for us, in part, was we hosted quite a lot of parties. Probably two or three a month. We always had an open house: I'd invite people from work and Juanita would bring people from the arts – editors, agents, directors for stage and screen, big-time producers and poets from all over the world. She was quite famous by then, travelling, winning prizes and taking residencies in tropical places. The people we invited would often bring friends. Many nights, we had no idea who was there.

It was the winter of 2202, I think, when I got talking with this small, grey-haired guy who seemed a bit out on his own. He had a sallow, orange tan that didn't suit, and was munching on a Quorn mince samosa, looking at the loud-talking people as if they were diseased. I went over with a mind to introduce him to someone else, but he seemed so sad and unable to cope with the art of conversation I soon realised that dumping him on anyone would make me a neglectful host. So I got him a cup of wine and steered him out towards the garden, where it was quieter and I could actually hear what he might say.

We found a small bench that thankfully wasn't damp. The night was cold, thick with moisture, our breath stark white. His face was narrow and thin. He kept squinting at unseen objects, though he didn't wear glasses, or at least didn't have a pair with him. He wore a thin mustard jacket and a light brown shirt that hung from thin, drooped shoulders. He ate like a mouse, the samosa held between tiny hands, turned clockwise, nibbled, turned again. His legs were so slight the material of his hemp trousers hung from his thighs, leaving flattened material where flesh should have been.

We lived quite close to the airbase. Every so often a broad-winged plane roared by, lights blinking silent code. After the second, I raised my cup.

'To our moral defenders,' I said. I must admit, I was pretty drunk. The man said nothing, nibbling. His cup sat by his ankle. I tried to keep my eyes away, but it was tough. Mine was almost empty and I wanted more.

'Don't like them much, do you?'

His eyes were grey, I noticed. Grey and watery as the English Channel.

'Not particularly.'

He lowered his head, going back to the samosa. I tried not to sigh aloud. This was getting ridiculous. I sipped the last of my wine and mentally gave up. I was thinking about going back inside when he said:

'They're not defending anything.'

I waited to see why. Not that I had anything to say.

'They're a security measure. They don't get involved with our external affairs, what little there are.'

'Really?' Shifting sideways on, I put my cup down. Held out a hand. 'Richard Pearson.'

'Harry Devonald.'

His fingers were like clay, damp and sticky. I let go.

'That's very specific. How'd you know so much?'

'Up until tonight, I worked there,' Devonald crooned, a soft lament. I felt my heart stop, my instincts kick. A story perhaps?

'What happened?'

Grey eyes blinked.

'They accused me of something I didn't do. Something I wouldn't.'

I looked around the garden and half-open back door, cracked

with light and voices, made sure we were alone. My mouth hung open, breath swirling. He looked at me, weighing me up, no doubt.

'It's this,' he said, taking something from his pocket. Square and thin, tiny even in his hands. A circuit board. Soldering glinted in dim light.

'I thought you said—'

'I didn't,' he interrupted, voice firm for the first time. 'I didn't. They came to my desk. It was in my hand and I just . . .'

Didn't let go. Dangerous choice.

'Can you tell me what it does? Should you?'

He sighed a plume into the night, looked up. I didn't think he would say anything until he did.

'There's a project. Decades old, possibly centuries. To build a starcraft—'

'A starcraft? D'you mean the *WiSP*?'

Devonald whipped around to face me.

'What?'

He was up, stumbling, one hand on the bench. He kicked over his drink, shook wine from his foot, cried out. I forced myself not to rise.

'Harry, hold on.'

He hissed something wordless, exasperated, and ran back into the house, slipping on cold paving slabs. I thought he'd fall, but he held on to the door frame and was gone.

I relaxed against the bench, swearing to myself. Idiot. So close.

Later we learned that Devonald had met a school friend we also knew at a pub not far away, just hours after being escorted from the airbase. The friend, a huge beast of a man named Alex, had spied Devonald nursing a full pint of ale alone. He'd approached his friend hoping to catch up, only for Devonald to tell him the whole story; how it had been for years without family or friends after his wife died from spinal cancer, diagnosed not long after they'd been contracted to the base. The trips he'd made to the perimeter wall, the money he slipped to guards who let in local women to take care of lonely men's needs. The quiet, barren rooms formerly used for interviews, one wooden table, three chairs, where it all took place. The banter between himself and the women, nothing remotely classified as far as he could remember, but the chip . . . Perhaps the chip said different. The shock of guards pulling him from his desk, rough hands at his back, pushing him down aisles. Big as he was, Alex cried when he told us how scared Devonald had looked at that empty table, and how he'd thought that being at a party, among people, might have cheered him up. Made him feel less alone. I listened, unaware yet that our chance meeting had reawakened an interest in the WiSP that would last the rest of my life. Juanita sucked air between her teeth, holding my hand tight. None of us were chipped back then. It wasn't obligatory at that point, thank God. That, too, would come later.

Nothing lives on Saturn. As beautiful as it looks, it will always be a dead, cold world. Its atmosphere, composed mainly of ammonia, is gaseous. Its interior, silicon rock and liquid hydrogen. This made the sixth planet a perfect target for *Mimas 4*'s maiden journey. Far enough to pose a challenge, close enough to reach with probes, silent enough to register even the faintest subatomic charges and, under the best possible conditions, perhaps rejuvenate a planetary graveyard.

The first probes, launched centuries before, were mere fly-bys, intersolar tourism so to speak, taking low- and eventually high-res photos of the planet and moons for extensive mapping.

Later missions were exercises in fact-finding, an exploration of methane lakes, a search for life. When none were discovered, Saturn was written off as a lonely outpost, great for chemists and physicists, bad for biologists. The probes that followed had been nothing more than monitoring stations, early-warning systems and the humble beginnings of docking stations for proposed interstellar exploration.

There are four monitoring stations in current operation around the region of space occupied by the ringed planet. One orbits a fixed rotation above the north hexagon. Another hovers the empty space between two moons, Titan and Rhea. Yet another lies opposite its sibling, an array of sensors and antennae attuned to the furthest reaches of the solar system. The last floats beneath the southern pole, isolated beneath the vast Cronian planet.

The stations' secondary mission is to chart chemical and geographic changes on Saturn's surface, moons and rings, while monitoring the surrounding region for rogue meteors, or, perhaps even more dangerous, a hostile alien species. The first and most important mission is to monitor the performance of the WiSP. Put basically, the drive is designed to construct an inner wormhole. Radiating outwards, it breaks *Mimas 4* and then itself down into subatomic particles, which are fired to a pre-programmed location where it reassembles both, hopefully without harm. The probes are designed to serve as navigational beacons, tracking every micro-instant of the craft's arrival just beyond *Mimas*, one of Saturn's sixty-two moons, from a jump point 0.3 AUs[1] from Earth's lone satellite. Four unmanned tests took place, which means there were three previous incarnations of *Mimas* before

---

1 Astronomical Unit

the final manned flight. Of the first two, the drive and its computers burned out hours before each jump. The third sent the craft shy of the asteroid belt, while the last was right on target. Eager to dispel even the slightest chance of failure, EASN prepared their most successful starcraft for the first manned test flight to Saturn.

The craft's design is exceptional in its beauty. Ninety metres from tip to exhaust, twenty-one metres high, with a wingspan of seventy-five metres. Varied TPS[1] materials cover the entire craft, one of few sustainable relics from NASA's twentieth-century shuttle programme, a source of protection from the heat of re-entry and the cold of space. The bow contains a small flight deck and observational area. The amidships house the airlock, research hot desks and the living quarters of two small cabins, a kitchenette, twin WCs and shower facilities. The lifeboat bay, comprising four boats, is in the aft. Behind those is the WiSP, followed by the main rocket engines. TPS materials colour the craft honey-brown. From the exterior it looks like a poised bird of prey. *Mimas* is by far the royalty of EASN's starcraft line, treated as such by the governing body and general public alike. No other craft has received as much attention. No space programme is funded as richly.

The very real dangers of that maiden flight were rarely addressed, in public at least. Everyone was aware of the risks, the *Mimas 4* crew members most of all. Each journey since the dawn of space exploration has come with its own dangers, and yet none were so formidable as this. The possibilities of certain death far outweighed the probability of the craft returning intact and the crew alive. Everyone on Earth expected, although no one

---

1 Thermal Protection System

said as much, that the men and women we looked up to wouldn't survive. No one was prepared for what actually happened, however: that they would disappear from our known multiverse.

In the ten years after *Mimas 4* ceased to exist, the programme withered in its wake, dying from apathy. The only research done, so they said, was into what had happened to the craft and why. Test simulations were run on a prototype WiSP, though none provided answers. From what little I learned, nine out of ten simulations had *Mimas* arriving at Saturn as programmed. A tenth showed the anomaly, its disappearance. The computers couldn't tell what caused it, where *Mimas* went, or for how long. Just that it happened.

A year after Leyton, Anis, Bai and Emilia were officially declared deceased, EASN suspended the WiSP programme indefinitely. The line was that they never stopped looking, and that might have been true, if they'd only known how to attempt a search. The very idea of trying was impossible, borderline insane, besides being no way to sell a product to countries and governments of the world. Space was too vast, the possibilities endless. Instead they concentrated efforts on sending astronauts to planets in conventional ways. Rockets, five-mile-long generation crafts, cryogenic hibernation. None were entirely successful, or reaped anywhere near the data and commercial rewards they'd hoped for, but at least they weren't global adverts against the very possibility of a manned space programme.

Fifteen years after the starcraft blinked out of reality, it had faded from our memories like a dream.

Then, on October 17th 2235, *Mimas 4* returned.

The decks and cabins are cold as death. A sustained hum of machinery surrounds us. Our feet echo on metal, and the yellow lights above and below are dim, presumably on standby, making distant objects hard to define. *Mimas 4* is remarkably like any other starcraft I've seen, in person or on screen. It's so ordinary I keep finding myself wondering why I'm here.

We're escorted by a knot of burly EASN staff, not exactly guards, although they perform the same purpose. Possibly picked for height and a distinct lack of emotion, they talk very little and barely make any physical movements or facial expressions. They shepherd us along the confined expanse of corridors, heads low, instructing us to do the same. Every so often there's another generic EASN staffer in a hemp jumpsuit standing by a locked door, a rifle in two hands, pointed at the floor. They ignore us, much as we stare. Sometimes I look at the others shuffling beside me, craning their necks in wonder, fingers twitching with an unconscious ache for the camera or touchpad. I feel their pain, although I'm grateful to be here at all, and try not to be too upset by the loss. They can sense it, discomfort leaks from our skin along with our sweat and makes them wary, I can tell. I keep whatever I see on repeat inside my head, a litany for Juanita I tell myself, so I might play it back into my notebook when I'm back in the shuttle, hurtling to Earth. It's my only consolation, and I'm willing to take it. They're going through the motions because they have to. They want us to do our jobs, but they've been warned the fact we've been chosen means that we're the best. And so they should be on their guard. Watch everything we do. After all their attempts to clean up, we might see more than they wish.

The woman beside me is small, elf-like, the collar of her dark coat pulled tight around her ears. Her red hair is cut short and square, her skin is pale. Freckles pattern her nose. She is far too serious for talk. She walks fast, trying to keep up with our EASN chaperones. Her name's Roberta Miles.

The man is taller than me, a lot thinner. His face is gaunt from the vegan diet we've endured since the '82 ban. It doesn't do him good. He needs a protein infusion and perhaps a bit more fat. His eyes are too close together, red and drooping. His teeth are large, chattering spontaneously in the cold. From the colour of his blue lips you'd think he's about to faint, if you didn't know they'd been like that on Earth. He's one of those types who are always aware of people. On the ground he gave me a thin smile, now he's trying to keep up with Roberta and I've been forgotten. He said his name's Wade Kennedy.

The only historic event that comes close to what I'm doing is the discovery of the abandoned *Mary Celeste*. Juanita hoped reading about the ship might have prepared me for what I'd see. I felt as much when I researched its history on the zone, but I think she was wrong. Accounts from the crew of the *Dei Gratia*, who found the ship midway between the Azores and the coast of Portugal in 1872, spoke of missing sails and damaged rigging, ropes hanging limp over the side. Personal items scattered, papers missing. Unlike the *Celeste*, *Mimas 4* is launch-pad ready, oiled and new. There's a smell of clean bed linen, marred by an unpleasant odour of fresh hemp leather. Surfaces gleam, and from what we've been told there's nothing to suggest anything has been taken or is missing, besides the four humans previously on board.

Speaking of the crew, there is one similarity with that derelict nineteenth-century vessel. All four lifeboats have been jettisoned. Every single one.

Another hulking EASN staffer, body turned sideways into an open door, pale light flooding his left side. The corridor opens into a wider area. Beyond us, panoramic windows frame the expanse of space and a spilt glitter of stars. A crescent bank of excitedly blinking monitors and computer arrays lie beneath the window. In a left-hand corner, I see an enticing peek of the cratered moon. Almost dead centre, the glistening jewel of Earth. We journalists stand in shock, feeling the enormity of distance perhaps for the first time. We huddle, each individual need placed into perspective by the magnitude of what we see.

There are plush high-backed seats made from imitation animal hide, right down to the intensified smell. Roberta gags, a hand over her mouth and nose. Wade's nose wrinkles but he says nothing. Most seats are located under the windows, at computer monitors in four locations around the crescent bank of metal. There are hemp-cloth passenger seats, set aside and behind the empty space of the main deck, four alcoves of three places. On the left, nearest the windows, there's a temporary vid-gel set up, the thin black branches of external speakers. We're being guided in this direction and we arrange ourselves and sit. I'm unlucky enough to have the middle position, hunched between the others; still, I really don't mind that either. I've always dreamed of this moment. After years spent imagining what it might be like, I'm on board *Mimas 4*. I'm not nearly vain enough to believe EASN followed my work on this story, but they were surely informed about my decades of interest, as here I am, an old man with a youngster's curiosity.

Staffers bustle around the vid-gel while we wait, lifting eyebrows at each other. I can smell the toothpaste on Wade's breath, the damp-rain smell of Roberta's coat. The gel is equipped with built-in wireless connectors, but they have yet to come online I assume. We've been told nothing about what we are about to see or why we're here, only that we've been invited aboard to report the craft's condition to the world, and that its crew members remain missing.

Staffers mutter and move from the vid-gel to the bank of window monitors. I drift, thinking of the drive. Our first stop on *Mimas*, the huge screw-like mechanism was ghostly, inspiring. Like being in the presence of some alien, godly creature was to the ancients, had those mythical spirits existed. I had felt myself sway as I watched the drive turn. My forehead prickled and my eyes filled with exploding colours. It was like we were communicating, the WiSP and I. The weight of compressed air almost forced me to my knees.

A blond-haired staffer finally stands, turning towards us. We stand alert. His shoulders are double the size of mine, hair stringy and flat. His cheeks slack, green eyes emotionless.

'Thank you all for agreeing to attend this viewing. We're indebted to you for making the time in your busy working schedules. What you're about to see are the last known recordings on *Mimas 4* following the Saturn jump of 26th August 2220, 12 p.m. IST. After your viewing, you may ask any questions. Thank you.'

He steps aside, along with the other staffers. While we mutter and stem our shock, the screen floods with bright colours. The recording begins.

It's the same flight deck. The window of space is smeared white with stars. All four crew members sit at various work stations around the bank of twinkling monitors, Anis in the centre, Bai to her left, Emilia to her right. Leyton's strapped into an alcove of passenger seats and, from what I can tell, they're the same seats that we're sitting on some fifteen years later. Their backs are facing us, apart from Leyton, who is sideways on. Anis barks information at Bai, and the Frenchman responds with dry certainty. Emilia speaks once in a while, but mostly scans her monitor. They are feeding each other data that concerns bringing the WiSP online. There's a throbbing hum that grows louder, a rattle and thump of machinery, a whine of metal that strains the black branch speakers. Leyton's eyes close. He looks at peace. His cowries fall into his lap.

The hum and rattle and thumps grow louder, and the camera begins to shake. Anis shouts data over the noise. Emilia's fallen silent. Bai chants numbers and percentages in a constant stream until the picture shudders like an earthquake. The roar is so loud we can't hear what they're saying. There's a strange noise, an elongated whine like grinding metal and the vid-gel is dark. Finally we notice white numbers at the bottom-right corner of the screen. A mission clock, running ever since the recording started, which counts a further fifteen minutes after the blackout before Wade says, 'Are we meant to just sit here watching a dark screen?' One staffer, a young girl newly graduated from tech school perhaps, replies, 'We'd really love you to see the whole thing.' She's blushing, her eyes lowered. Roberta tuts and chews a thumbnail, lips twisted. 'They want to reassure us nothing's been doctored,' I say, the wise elder, and they get it, sitting back. After twenty minutes of dark screen and silence, more young staffers bring orange juices, plates of hot food. Bamboo and sweet potato red curry with sticky rice. 'Tastes organic,' I say. 'Better be,' Wade snorts. The speakers rumble like an aeroplane.

Forty-five minutes pass before the picture's back. It occurs with no fanfare, or even a crash of returning matter. They're just there. Everything looks normal, apart from one thing – they're in the wrong part of space. Earth glows before them. The moon is further in its orbit, but they know she's there. The crew look at each other. They seem confused. They haven't moved. We're not sure if they're aware of how much time has elapsed, or whether they think none has. They check their own bodies, look over monitor read-outs. Anis and Bai take some time to report green, while Emilia says nothing. Leyton's eyes remain closed. He's sleeping, the string of white shells light in his fist.

When Anis asks Emilia for a status report, her navigator doesn't answer. She asks again. Still no answer. Emilia's looking frantically from the monitor to the expanse of stars and back. Anis peers over her shoulder, coming closer. She too falls silent.

'What's wrong?'

Bai's standing. His smile is tiny, receding.

'Wake up Leyton,' Anis says. 'Wake him up and tell him to come and see this.'

He does, and thirty seconds later her husband joins her. There are howls, cursed disbelief. They double-check their instruments and yet there's no need, all the evidence they can wish for is outside the bridge windows. The obvious is apparent, although, until Emilia voices it, easy for us slow-witted journalists to overlook.

There are no satellites, dead or functional. No EASN dry dock station, or GRIDS.[1] No space debris, the eighteen million or so hunks of floating rubbish that have orbited our planet for centuries. There's nothing because they don't exist. They haven't been invented.

This takes the crew about an hour to ascertain, and a further hour to confirm. During that time they go from worried to practically delusional with fear, and truth be told we do too right along with them. It's the most compelling viewing we've

---

1 Global Responsive Intersolar Defence System

ever had the privilege to watch, that's for sure. We're leant forward in our seats, occasionally sipping juice, or whispering for more ice. The crew check everything; all known architecture, the global physical topology (of which they find none), land and oceanic geography, the immediate constellations surrounding Earth. Bai flops back in his seat. His face is red from effort, and he's sweating. The others won't look at him. They know. We all know.

'So where are we?' says Emilia.

He spins in his seat, staring at the emptiness of Earth, space, and avoids her question.

Much later, after Anis gives the crew an hour's grace to deal with the reality of their position, we journalists learn that *Mimas 4* has not been fired across space as intended, but time. Their position at the moment of recording was four hundred and twenty-six years in Earth's past. 1794.

What this means dawns on each crew member separately. There are cameras throughout the craft, forever on standby, made functional by motion and heat sensors, even in the cabins. As above, so below. It's easy to tell Anis and Leyton bear the full impact of their discovery. They don't rest, and pace their cabin, often at opposite ends. Anis spends ten minutes on her bunk staring at their cabin wall. Further camera angles reveal what holds her interest – a strange painting of a black crescent bird with thin legs, arching its back to reach a beak towards its feathered tail. They type conversation to each other using hand-helds, in an effort not to be recorded perhaps. This is useless, they must know. The devices can be tracked through their chips, but it means the cameras don't hear what they say, and so neither do we. Once, they hold each other and cry mute tears.

Bai and Emilia sit on their beds. He looks at the ceiling lights.

She bows her head, scratching at the blue tattoo on her shoulder. She throws an object across the room, it's difficult to see what. Bai tracks where it lands, hands in his pockets. He sighs.

When they meet on the flight deck their body language has changed. Leyton doesn't smile. His posture is stiff, combative. His eyes dart, and he's standing, while the other sit at their positions and don't look at each other. His string of cowries is gone.

'You know what this means? If we're right?'

'We're right,' Anis mutters. 'All the instruments say so.'

'Well?' he says to the others.

'Look, we get it,' Bai says, 'totally. So what do you propose?'

Leyton doesn't speak, just looks jittery.

'Say it,' Anis orders. An accusation.

'I'm thinking I've got to go down there. I've got to help.'

Emilia swivels away. Bai kicks the metallic bank with a heel. Anis glares at her husband. Her eyes are wet and red.

'That's crazy,' Bai says, and Anis barks sarcastic laughter. 'We're only lifeboat-equipped. If something happens on *Mimas*, you can't come back.'

'I know that.'

'We don't even know how we got here, or what the drive will do.'

'Yes, we talked about this,' Leyton says to his wife. 'But what choice do we have? They're enslaved. Suffering. I could stop that. We could stop that. We've got superior weaponry, we've got this ship.'

'What are you suggesting, we turn the ship's weapons on those people?'

Emilia sits forward, an arm outstretched towards the windows.

'If we have to, or if I don't come back. It's an option.'

'Not for me. Bai?'

He shrugs, runs a hand through his hair. '*Merde.*'

'Yeah, exactly. But I can't sit here chewing vegetables and waiting for some miracle to occur that might get us home. My ancestors are down there, dying—'

'They're ours too,' Emilia says, her eyes bright. 'We're still one people, don't let your brain go back as well as your body.'

'All the more reason,' Leyton snaps. There's something in his eyes that's quite smug, it must be said. He folds his arms and stares Emilia down. 'How can we allow this to happen when we know better? Would we let this continue during our time?'

'Of course not.' And yet Bai's fidgeting gives away his unease with the question. He swivels half-rotations. 'Anis? What do you think?'

She bites her lip, smoothing the material of her jumpsuit, a palm surfing her thigh.

'It's suicide. We should wait. EASN will send a rescue party—'

'*How?*' Leyton explodes, catching himself. Anis waits, tense.

'They will find us,' she says, this time to the walls. 'Besides, there's no guarantee our weapons are advanced enough to go against several navies. Let alone what changing history will do to our present.'

No one has an answer to that. They retreat into their own thoughts, isolated. The mission clock moves forward one second at a time. We barely breathe.

'I have to take that risk. You know how many people are dying, right now. If I can stop one slave ship—'

'You might not be born.' She lifts her head, taking measure of him. 'One life saved might mean yours doesn't occur. Have you thought about that?'

Leyton's jaw is rigid. His hands clenched, empty.

'So be it.'

He walks out.

We watch the recording for another two hours. In this time, there's frantic typing on handhelds, the beeps of received messages. It's certain Leyton prepares a lifeboat regardless of his crew's misgivings. We see him wandering from the bay to various supply stations, stocking carry-bots with essentials. What's less easy to see is what the others make of this, or why they've agreed to silence. Video logs are commonplace on short- and long-haul missions, and yet they act as though they have no intention of carrying out the necessary protocols. Why? It's unheard of. Everything else they do is with the strictest adherence to regulations. They know they're facing the risk of being court martialled when they arrive home. Nevertheless, to a person, they isolate themselves in various places. The galley, their cabin, the WiSP drive bay, where they type, far from each other, refusing to log. It's the damnedest thing to watch. None of us can work out why.

Two and a half hours pass until they meet in the lifeboat bay. Emilia, Bai and Leyton suit up, helmets in hand. Anis does not.

They're stiff and formal. They hug, one by one. Anis and Leyton kiss without warmth; it's easy to tell how she feels. Though they don't talk much besides procedural discussions, from the look of things the plan is for Anis to stay aboard, maintain communications, and be ready for a possible pick-up if assistance is needed. They attach their helmets, enter the lifeboat. Anis swipes her eyes as if she's angry with her own body. She steps out from the bay and lets the countdown procedure run its course.

A frozen screen. A staffer steps forward. The thickset blond, blocking the vid-gel with his body.

'My apologies. The next recording of significance comes after seven days. For some unknown reason, at this stage the WiSP drive begins to reboot. It was initially suspected this had been done by Anis, or even possibly Emilia, but there are no records to support this. The countdown to the drive's re-engagement has a ten-hour window. It would seem from the recordings Anis did everything in her power to stop this from happening, but could not. She finally uses the lifeboat to escape and join her crew. We still don't know how the remaining two boats were jettisoned, as once *Mimas* returned to our present time all communications had ended.'

We sit, squeezed together on comfortable seats, staring at the empty deck where all this took place, unable to imagine. The staffer clasps his hands.

'Perhaps you'd like to view the final thirty minutes?'

I really wouldn't, and ignore the question. Wade and Roberta say yes. The giant nods to the left. He steps away from the screen.

It's awful, a nightmare. The camera shudders. Thunder makes the speakers vibrate, our ears ring. For some reason the lights blink on and off in time with the rhythm of a warning klaxon that never occurred during the first jump. Anis is clearly distraught, moving from monitor to terminal trying to work against the craft's motherboard array and failing, her face a sea of tears, cursing, screaming at the ceiling, pounding keys and, when that doesn't work, even the screens, but the WiSP will not be denied. After ten minutes she decides. She runs to the lifeboat bay, suiting up. From what we can tell she had foresight enough to stock the boat for an emergency, either during the ten-hour window or before. She internally primes the locks and starts disengagement. Forty-two seconds later her lifeboat blasts from the starcraft's side and Anis Creighton-Shaw is never seen again.

How do I feel about WiSP? As you might imagine, I've been asked that question many times, particularly after the article, the bestseller, and all that followed. It's been quite a whirlwind, not a time of deep contemplation by any means. I've met heads of state and royalty, and dignitaries by the hundreds. I'm sure you'll forgive me. Yet, and perhaps only Juanita has come to know this, there are nights when I relive my time aboard the starcraft. The hollow thud of feet against the deck and muffled weight of reconstituted air in my nostrils. The chill dankness of cold seeping through my outerwear, a monotone chorus of machinery. I sometimes shudder, or if I'm asleep I wake gasping, the thrum of the drive fading. Or else I'll be in the car and we'll hit a bump, and I'm reminded of that final thunder before the WiSP brought *Mimas 4* back against its crew's will. I find myself wondering, what would I have done? Would I have been as brave?

Rocketing to Earth, orange flames licking our shuttle and lighting our windows like sunset, I was struck by jigsaw-piece thoughts that formed an odd type of picture. I turned them mentally this way and that, peering close, making conclusions even as I gripped my seat belt and prayed for guidance.

Leyton's cowrie string. Anis mesmerised by her cabin painting; many months later I learned it was actually the Ghanaian symbol Sankofa, which in the Twi language means 'Go back and get it'. Emilia's Gye Nyame tattoo, also Ghanaian, meaning 'except God' or 'only God', high on one pale shoulder. Bai's puzzle piece took more time, yet I eventually found it back on Earth, after many months of research. His family is originally from the Shanxi province, northern China, an area known not only as a seat of

Asian civilisation, but for thirty-eight pyramid burial structures, many of which contained the mummified remains of humans. It's speculated those ancient people were African migrants who left their continent over one hundred thousand years ago. Though conflicting research exists, the centuries-old discovery of shared African and Asian DNA corresponds with a theory I formed on my journey through the fiery atmosphere of my home world.

I've already written of my belief that the WiSP might actually be guided by something more cosmological than physiological. More spiritual than scientific. That deep within our cells, on some subatomic level, our very blueprints, our coded DNA, could be subconsciously activated in order to command the WiSP to visit the places we intend within the core of our beings, over-riding the pre-programmed wishes of board members and committees. The scientific proof underpinning epigenetic inher-itance is, like ancient beliefs, centuries old. 'Cherry blossom' mice and holocaust sufferers alike were both found to have a knowledge of trauma that was passed through their DNA. Could it be that a form of this genetic reshuffling brought about the occurrence on *Mimas 4*?

When I dared to suggest as much in an amended edition to my bestselling book, *In the Footsteps of Mimas*, EASN, a handful of undocumented WiSP boffins, and my fellow journalists Roberta Miles and Wade Kennedy, all admonished me in print. I have never bothered to restate my arguments, or refute theirs. I'm an old man. These days at least, I've no heart for a fight.

And yet some nights I find myself in my garden sitting on the very bench where a harried scientist once kicked over a glass of red wine, and ran. My ears sing with the hum of mechanisms. With my eyes open, I dream. I gaze at the moon and imagine where such a power could lead us. Is it right to admit I can't quite see that far? Would it be allowed? Juanita sometimes comes out with a chilled glass of white, asking me to find the intermittent glow of the *Mimas* 5 orbital build. I search the heavens with a finger although, as much as I try, one glistening star looks much the same as another.

LINK

Aaron felt it for the first time, a pulsing at the back of his skull, firm pressure between his eyes. A throbbing ache behind his ear, low ringing. He'd made a call the night before, half believing nothing would come of it, only to wake up with sensation invading his head. An answer. There were others. He called again during breakfast, his mum fussing around as usual, and felt three stronger replies from three directions. The back of his skull, between his eyes, behind his right ear. He relaxed into the warm, steady pulsation, chewing until there was nothing left but lonely oat kernels, Mum going on about him doing the housework while she was at the hospital, Aaron ignoring every word.

He should have known what to expect before he got there, might have if he'd thought about it harder, but he'd been more concerned with his own nerves alongside the jarring pain of the too-bright, too-loud veneer of normality, a glistening, shifting bubble. The cheap glow of budget clothing stores. The counterfeit stall selling defrosted E-number cakes they claimed were organic and homemade. The row of fruit and veg stalls, the lightweight shack of the CD hut, its walls of thin black material, rippling as the masses walked by. People, too many, walking too fast or slow, darting through gaps in the crowd or halting right in front of him until he swore and sped past the lurching granny sideways on, guilty for subscribing to group consensus. He hated the old centre during the day.

It was almost a relief to swerve into the pissy oasis of the car park entrance, a small enclave leading to oil-dark steps. He climbed past two hunch-necked olders, puffing a ripe blunt, stench of smoke and urine filling his head, making Aaron cough, them stare. He trotted upwards until he met swing doors, pushing into the expanse of the first floor. Breathed deep, tasting exhaust fumes, smog. Sighed. He wandered across concrete, taking the steep incline of driveways instead, up and up until he reached the sixth floor.

They stood by thin railings looking at the streets. The down-turned meringue peaks of the bus station awning, the glass underground entrance and panoramic Westfield steps, the six-times-removed hum of the crowd. There were three, of course. Two girls, one boy. It took a moment before he clocked that he knew them. Not well, not to talk with, just from around. Live anywhere your whole life and you're bound to see the same faces, *Groundhog Day* for real, only less dramatic, more tedious. Crossing the street to the corner shop, standing in line for Maccy D's, sitting rows from each other on the bus. Only one he'd ever wished he could talk to, or thought about longer than the time it took to walk by. But he knew all three as surely as the silent boasts of tags on street signs, or missing digital letters on the countdown. They all belonged to the bits, were all home.

The tall kid wore a school blazer, was lanky and broad with a face like a pinched raisin, the lopsided mini-Afro of a younger. The 'fro looked like a disabled black dorsal fin, making his screw face infantile; a man's aggression beneath a toddler's hairstyle. Aaron stifled a laugh. The girl was short and BRIT-Award thin, a few years older than himself, blonde hair tied back, falling to her waist, brown leather jacket with bare zips, sensible shirt, trousers and flat shoes, the dark rings of a part-time weed smoker around her eyes. He'd seen her going in and out of the dentist's opposite his GP surgery for long enough to assume she worked there. She was hard-faced and gaunt, smoking a withering fag, looking more like thirty than the early twenties she really was.

The other girl was a manifestation of dreams. Tall as Aaron, tight storm-cloud jeans betraying a curve of hips, snug roll-necked grey top tucked in at the beltless waist, as gorgeous above as below. Aaron saved the best for last, after he'd taken in the rest – deep brown skin, unblinking eyes, lips maintaining a perpetual pout. The slim denim jacket, blue LDN fitted and rare matching Nikes that told the world she was not only down, but prided herself on originality. Normally the type he sneered at inside his head, knowing he felt unworthy, except she was here and that made her different from the others, a woman of substance rather than image.

All three lived within a square mile and passed each other randomly at least once a week, possibly more.

He approached, only really seeing her, heart leaping at the odds of her being one of them. The others lost clarity and focus, became peripheral. He was smiling, and she noticed, recognition curving her lips upwards, Aaron drawn by the strength of a connection he'd not known existed until now. He almost reached out a hand towards her, managed to stop himself (too soon, way too soon), pushed his glasses up on his nose and widened his grin.

'Oh *hell* nah, not him too, are you lot bloody serious?'

Old Girl, expression wrinkled, shook her head with even more violence than her words, hair whipping her back and shoulders.

Tall Kid spat laughter. Dream Girl's smile didn't exactly grow, but didn't disappear. *Damn it. Skinny bitch.*

He ignored her, stopping before them, eyeing the younger two without saying anything. Actually he didn't know what to say but an older cousin had told him silence could make him look confident if he pulled it off right.

'Are you shittin' me? You lot seriously trying to say that's him?'

They stared him out, daring him to say the real reason he came up to the sixth floor acting like he knew anything. Dream Girl seemed uncertain. Tall Kid's swaying body, hard eyes and clenched fists made him look as though he wanted an excuse to spark him, and would probably enjoy it too.

'They're not *saying* it's me. I am, because it is. I called you. Last night I said I could feel you, all of you, and I meant it. Now I want to know why.'

He let that sink in, concentrating on the white trail scribbled across blue sky behind their heads, fading into wisps then nothing but molecules, hearing low gasps, mutters, feeling the atmosphere change. Dream Girl and Tall Kid relaxed. Old Girl felt it too, sucking hard enough on the fag to hollow her cheeks and make her eyes bulge, enhancing her death stare, which roamed in all directions until she threw the blazing stub at his feet, where it exploded into a bouncing trail of sparks. Aaron refused to move or acknowledge what she'd done. He stared into her eyes, waited.

'Have fun on yuh play date then. I'm off.'

And she was, brushing his shoulder lightning fast, muttering curses all the way to the fire doors, which clapped sudden thunder after her. He scratched his head, turned to the others.

'What's her problem?'

'She thought you'd be older.'

'How'd she know I'm not?'

Both smirked. He felt himself grow hot and tried to shake it off. Be cool. He had to be cool.

'She thought we'd all be.'

That was better. Tall Kid stepped forward, eclipsing Dream Girl with his broad body, but Aaron could see her aura glowing on all sides. He imagined he could even feel her heat. Then the fist was high, up in his face.

'Limo,' Tall Kid said, less hard, practically smiling. Except he couldn't quite do it, could only manage a sneer.

'Huh?'

'My name. Limo.'

'Oh cool. I'm Aaron.'

They connected knuckles, Aaron wincing at the force of contact as always, teeth clenched trying to hide it. He never understood why they couldn't just shake hands, or at least slap fingers.

'Christie.'

Damn, bruv. She was even hotter close up. Teardrop hazel eyes, long dark lashes, brown skin underlit with red infusion, cute dimples on both cheeks. She smelt of something sweet, consistent. He smiled as much as he dared without foiling his cool, and didn't know how to greet her so he settled for doing nothing, disappointing himself. It speared him deep inside to think she might have felt the same way. He fought against his insecurities again.

'She's not even that much older than us.'

All nodded, conceding defeat. Old Girl's view had won, right or wrong. She'd left them feeling like the kids she claimed they were.

'So what now?' Christie said.

Aaron didn't even have to think about it. He'd been doing enough of that last night, nursing that very topic like a sore muscle. His first troublesome thought was their obvious opening question.

'Show us.' Aaron pointed at the railings. 'Down there.'

They walked that way. Bodies bent, they looked at the streets below. The nearest were the hordes waiting by the lights for traffic to slow to a stop so they could cross. Christie went first, seeing as she'd asked. He tried not to snatch a peek at the blue jeans stretched taut against her bum and thighs, to keep his eyes on the road, but it was tough.

'Which one?' Limo propped on his elbows, searching the crowds.

'Him,' she said. 'Bald guy, blue suit.'

'Don't point,' Aaron heard himself, bit his lip. Granddad.

'Sorry,' she said, lowering her hand, shooting him a look that he felt, didn't see. Not malice, regret. It made him like her just that little bit more. She understood he wasn't being an arse, only cautious.

'Just so they don't see us,' he told her, still feeling bad.

'Sure.'

'He's crossing,' Limo warned, and then her attention was back. Her threaded eyebrows lowered.

'No he's not,' she muttered.

The green man was flashing, beside him yellow digital numbers fell from ten. Blue Suit stopped in the middle of the crossing, head pivoting. A small kid bumped him, looked up in shock and went around, dragged by the hand and momentum of a woman who was probably his mother. The surge of pedestrians flowed around Blue Suit like a river around a stone, slowing to a trickle until he was alone. The green man disappeared. The count reached zero. Blue Suit remained in the centre of the crossing. Limo sniggered, covering his lips. The red man returned and a BMW revved, leaping forward. Blue Suit looked perplexed but stayed where he was. Horns beeped. Drivers got out of cars. It was all getting too much when Blue Suit did a strange robotic turn and went back to the shopping centre side of the road where he'd started. A driver made to follow – red in the face, trackie bottoms and XXL T-shirt. Christie grunted surprise, leant forward. The driver walked back to his car just as purpose-fully as he'd left, got inside and roared away. Blue Suit blinked into the faces of his fellow commuters as if they could tell him what had gone wrong. Christie backed away from the railings.

'Classic,' Limo said, slapping brick with an open palm.

'Well done,' Aaron said, meaning it. She gave a teeny smile, something less focused in her eyes. This time he tried to avoid them.

'My turn,' the kid said, a little too eager for Aaron's liking. He watched him, not the road.

Hunched like a cat, slowly licking his lips, the kid's chin rested on the cradle made by his folded arms. When he saw what he wanted he rose, stiffening. 'This'll be bare joke,' he grunted through half-closed lips, nearly too low to hear. Aaron saw pure concentration, more focus than Christie.

'Don't do that.' He heard her say. '*Don't.*' Then she turned away from the street below. Aaron alerted, slipped into the space next to Limo.

A gathering of boys about the kid's age. Blazers and thick school jumpers, pointing. Work commuters passing, heads turned as if to view an accident, still walking towards the crossing, shaking their heads. A woman, megaphone in one hand, Bible in the other, placard at her feet – JESUS SAVES – calling God's vengeance, pointing at the homeless man with his arms and legs wrapped around a lamp post, hips moving, slow grinding, rubbing against hard, grubby metal. Peals of laughter reached them. Aaron gritted his teeth, said nothing. When the British Transport Police approached the homeless guy Limo let him go, bringing him back to face heavy hands on his shoulder, protesting as he was led towards a waiting patrol car.

Limo slapped brick even harder, creating solitary, one-handed applause. Aaron looked back at Christie. She frowned at her box-fresh trainers, arms wrapped around her own body.

'That's not funny,' he told him.

'Is to me.' Limo towered over Aaron, concrete hard again. 'Each to his own, innit?'

Aaron tried a look that said he was beneath some school kid's drill-based posturing, turned back to the railings.

'Fair enough,' he said beneath his breath, tuning out Limo's rigid face and grubby blazer.

The air filled with perfume. Christie had come closer, but he focused on the streets and another homeless dude. This one was sitting by a wall just beyond the totem pole of train station signage, a series of varied transport symbols stacked on top of each other. Behind the dude, who stared into space oblivious to the hordes tramping by him, stood a quartet of bright ATMs.

'Him,' Aaron said, tilting his head. He heard their complaints, felt them jostle him on both sides, trying to see past the disgusting *Day of the Triffids* sculptures the council put up during the Olympics – to hide the old centre from the world many had said. Probably to hide the people too. Now the shimmering yellow and green petals worked in reverse, blocking Westfield and all routes out of Stratford. He silenced the thought. Concentrating, he found his target.

She was a young businesswoman who might have been going home after a long day in the office. Brunette, legs tanned, suit well fitted. Tall and broad-shouldered, possibly eastern European, but that was just a guess. He made her type in more cash than she needed without a receipt. When the wad spat from the machine he made her take it quick, walk three steps and drop it into a homeless dude's lap, gasps of shock exploding like cloudburst from spectators, then had her sprint towards the bus station as a 25 rounded the corner, pulling up at stop B. Knowing what was good for him, homeless dude shot to his feet as if the ground was electrified. He gathered his dog, loose change and blanket, shuffling off before any spectators fully reacted to his luck, disappearing into the backdrop of commuters. Unable to find him, Aaron let the woman go, turning his back on her wheeling on the spot, heels tap-dancing against the pavement.

'*Sick!*' Christie came closer still, deliciously embracing him, even kissing his cheek. Aaron blushed, shivering at the warmth. 'Proper sick! I love it!'

'No problem,' he said, trying to stare out Limo, who wouldn't allow it. The kid was vex, no doubt. His bottom lip stuck out, his eyes tracked tarmac. His arms hung, huge fists useless by his side.

'So what, you lot on a link ting now?'

She let Aaron go. Immediately, he missed her. They stood apart, looking as guilty as people who had actually done something wrong.

'No.'

'It ain' even about that, Aaron done a good thing. Why you goin' on weird?'

'Yeah, carry on.' Limo honestly looked hurt, as though Aaron's actions were an affront to his moral centre, an act that had to be purged in some way, perhaps by the undertaking of more evil. 'I see how this'll run. You lot are on some couples vibe, an three ain' magic. Later, yeah?'

And he was gone too, arms swinging, leg limping, fire-exit doors flapping until they closed. The silence afterwards was awkward, dense, Aaron unsure what he should do next. He didn't want to say it but the urge was sweet, compelling enough to take the risk.

'He's not wrong, though, is he?'

He turned to face her, seeing that bright, beautiful smile. She sized him up as though he'd pleased her.

'No, he's not,' she said and took Aaron by the arm, leading him towards the swing doors.

They went back to his, seeing as Aaron's mum was mopping floors and sterilising hospital surfaces until late that night. He tried not to think about it, the hard work she was forced into just so he could have a painless education. Her only reward a future that saw him comfortable, a good job, wife, house, two good, beautiful kids. Aaron dismissed those vague, misty images with more purpose. Too far, too distant. When he asked Christie where she lived, she pursed her lips, head twisting to follow the exhale of a passing bus, breathed, 'Not far.' Aaron smiled. He got it. Enough said by her hand in his, the slip of her arm between his inner bicep and ribs. What more did he want?

They didn't even run to catch the 25, just let it idle to allow people on, an old Asian lady struggling to step upwards like a toddler. When they finally got aboard and tapped Oysters, the driver snapped alert, looking from Christie to Aaron as though they were mythical, like he already knew their secret. Aaron bowed his head, hid his grin. He walked her to the raised back seats, radiator hot, thrumming. Christie put her head on his shoulder. It was all he could do not to look each and every passenger in the eye, to ensure that they took note. This was him. With her.

His room was dark and tidy, which always made Aaron wonder why his mother caused such a fuss about housework. He made sure the place looked like his personal space, even cooking on occasion. He was responsible. He owed Mum that much. Christie slow-spun, taking in posters, his pinboard, the jammed bookcase and full shelves, his tiny writing desk beneath the window, his DVDs. He sat on the bed, swallowing nerves. When she'd made the whole three-sixty, bending to inspect book covers and cut-out newspaper clippings closer, her neat eyebrows were arched in surprise.

'You march?' she said, pointing at the largest poster. A red star superimposed with black letters: LBR – and underneath that, an explanation, London Black Revolutionaries.

'Yeah, course. Not every one,' he said, blushing, chin touching collarbone. 'But sometimes. You?'

'Yeah, course.'

He tried not to show his pleasure. 'I didn't think you'd be political.'

She shrugged, walking over. When she sat, springs gasped and the mattress indented, taking Aaron with it. He moved towards the wall.

'Sorry,' he said. 'It's a bit old.'

'Don't be.'

She took his hand. She was staring in a way that made him feel weird, intense and unblinking, but she was so beautiful he felt himself doing the same.

'Which way you votin'?'

'Huh?'

She peered at the poster and he shivered.

'Remain.'

'Course.'

'Course.'

She kept peering downwards, running her hand across his. He wanted to close his eyes, her touch made him sleepy, but was worried that might say more about him than he wanted her to know. He tried to sit up straight. She was the first girl he'd had up to his room in four years.

'This is nuts.' Half laughing, coughing to hide it. 'We only just met.'

She slid soft fingers along his bare arm, focused on what she was doing. Her lips shone, parted. She leant forward until she'd pushed beneath his T-shirt, reached his shoulder.

'Uh huh,' she said. Perfume clouded him. Their lips met.

Nothing but sensation. No sound, no feeling, not even thought. Everything happening on the inside, like closing his eyes in a dark room only to see the delicate, butterfly swirl of phosphenes. Something composed of nothing. Like falling, a feather not rock. Like nothing to push against and nothing to hold, a lightness he'd always felt inhabited his body were it not for bones and liquid and muscle and soft tissue. Were it not for himself. He might have smiled, tried to, but as the feeling glowed and expanded there wasn't the familiar stretch, the noise of separation, a touch of hard teeth against soft lips. Everything had flattened, merged, spread like clay. There was no way to tell what belonged to him, or anything else. There wasn't anything else. Only touch.

He was on the bed, head fuzzy, ceiling spinning. A quick

check; he was fully clothed. Another; Christie was gone. He sat up, palms flat against the mattress, checking every dark space and crevice as if the ability to shrink had been added to her powers. He squinted his desk from a formless blob back to its original shape. Found his glasses splayed on the bed, put them on. An open book face-down by the empty chair. He checked the spine: *Other Britain, Other British*. No other sign of Christie.

There was nothing left but to put out a call. He did so tentative, a little scared of what he might learn. When the pressure returned between his eyes, a soft migraine, he closed his eyes, lying back. Allowed a smile to touch his lips. He curled on the bed, sensation pulsing at his forehead, and that's how his mother found him when she opened the bedroom door just before 2 a.m. Sleeping fully clothed, a pillow clutched to infinity beneath his nose, still smiling.

He put out a call at breakfast before his morning classes and heard nothing. That didn't faze him. He wolfed down bran flakes and left the house before his mum woke for her customary coffee and low-energy grumbles. He sailed through his lectures with an enthusiasm that made staff and students alike look twice, wondering if he was the same person they'd seen for almost a full term. In the afternoon, when he powered from the building with secondary-school force, his classes done for the day, a trail of smiles, head nods and raised fists bubbled and frothed in his wake.

She leant against the lamp post directly outside his college. Short denim skirt, tights and Tims, slim tank top and bright furred gilet. Hair pulled back and gleaming, frost-chip eyes and high cheekbones. Nearly every guy who passed her turned to get a better look, and those who didn't stiffened, walking self-consciously, swag depleted. Christie seemed lost in another world until she saw Aaron and stood to attention, overjoyed at something as mundane as the mere sight of him. Damn. She even had a lollipop, ruby gleaming, which she gave a final lick, crunched into shards and pulled from her lips, dropping the white stick behind her, grinning.

'*Hi*,' she sang, embracing him. A collective gasp rode the air. Her perfume, a tang of something sensual, something her. The scent of flavoured sugar on her breath. The dark of his closed eyes felt good, like the night before. He wallowed.

'How you doing?' he said, letting go to look at her. *Damn*.

'Good.' She was jittery, blushing. 'Thought we could do something. At the polling station? You voted?'

'I haven't.'

She sent a quick image across real-time vision. He watched, sightless, nodding. Pretty good idea.

'We can hang out after if you like.' Head ducked towards dark pavement, giving him the zigzag line of her centre parting. 'Maybe go Nando's? My treat?'

Aaron was in love.

The polling station wasn't far, an old church he'd ignored most of his life, signs outside stating its new, temporary persona. A tall woman with thin lips, cornrows and a council ID hanging from a poppy-red ribbon smoked and shivered against the damp wall, eyes distant. Christie waited not far from the woman while Aaron made his mark and slid his vote into the ballot box, joining her after. They leant against open church doors, playing sullen-eyed teenagers, nothing more on their minds than the time on their hands. They didn't have to do much. Just a simple look in the direction of anyone who passed, a gentle probe inside their heads, a nosey around. If the person was voting their way they left them be. If they were going against their interests, or unsure, a suggestion was planted. Often, when that happened, the person would jerk, frown as if they'd forgotten something and continue on, a little more determination in their step than before.

The Tall Woman went inside after fifteen minutes. When she came back an hour and a half later to see Christie and Aaron still there and a number of people halt, jerk and look puzzled, she turned towards the teenagers, uncertain suspicion in her eyes.

Aaron didn't see her until Christie nudged him twice. He watched the Tall Woman for a long while, pushed out a command. She jerked too, harder than the others, all scrutiny blinded. Opening her cigarette box she fumbled one to her lips and began to smoke hard, non-stop. Finished it and started another. And another. When they left the polling station around 10 p.m. she was smoking cigarette butts she found on the grass, one after the next. Her colleagues beside her trying to pull at her arms while the woman elbowed them away, kept searching.

They bought a whole lemon and herb chicken and double large fries to share, taking it to the shopping centre where they found a place to sit huddled by closed Holland & Barrett doors. Around them, the swish and clatter of roller skates and skateboards, white noise beneath drill pumped by youngers outside Costa watching their mates with grim, negligent pride. Others with their backs pressed against JD Sports glass, or sat on benches lacing up, speeching fresh-faced teenage girls or staring into space meditating on their next move, carnal or athletic. Afropunks mostly, hair mixtures of blues, reds, oranges and a rainbow of chemically enhanced colours, shaved close or flowering in full bloom, beaded, loxxed, weaved. Straight-haired blondes and brunettes styled much the same, long hair tied thin to avoid accidents. A trio of girls in khimars, skates rattling trains, rolling west, all laughter and shouts and streaming dark material until they went unseen, trailing ghosts of echoes. Ripped and rolled-up jeans, exposing bare knees and glistening ankles, polished Doc Martens and fresh Tims. A reflected haze of bodies on floor tiles, coloured wheels pulsing like distant landing lights. Some spun on the spot, ballerina-slow, trapped in worlds belonging to them alone. Others leapt for harsh ceiling lights, wheels erupting noisy landings, wobbling but upright, expressions betraying they expected no different.

In their midst, pedestrians crossed from one side of Stratford to the other. Late-night students, red-eyed workers, young lovers, families pushing bully buggies, their walking children finding a grip wherever they could. Silver-screen aficionados, shambling drug addicts and their alcoholic cousins, pensioners bored to blindness by dull four walls. Skaters wheeling through everybody, unseeing, perhaps uncaring. A handful of high-vis security guards stood to one side, serene as though dreaming white light and ambience. Homeless men and women set up for the night, laying sleeping bags flat, clutching steaming teas. The cinema-sized flat screen above the West Mall showed boy bands and London Met ads on continuous rotation.

Christie motioned at the Nando's bag. He tipped it towards her and she burrowed for fries, stuffing a handful into her mouth. Raised voices barked loud. People stiffened, looking. There, just beside the lime-green lettering of Osbon Pharmacy, they saw him.

'Christie . . .'

They got to their feet.

'It's him, right?'

Craning to see, one hand on his arm. 'Yep.'

'We better go over, in case.'

She seemed reluctant, yet moved with him to the central area where Limo, even taller in huge black skates, loomed over a broad man much older than himself. The man had lank black hair plastered to his head, a dusty red hoodie and a rolled-up *Metro* in his fist. Both shouted at each other, Limo pointing in his face, the man gesticulating with his paper. Aaron couldn't make out what was going on, caught between the thin girlfriend trying to pull the broad man away and Limo's friends tugging in the opposite direction, the kid shrugging them off, shouting, 'I didn't touch you, though,' louder each time.

In one swift moment the broad man's face changed. Eyes narrowed, his face seeped red until he was spitting: 'Who the *fuck* d'you think you, are, eh? *Eh?* Wait until mornin', you'll see, you lot'll be sent back where you come from pronto, d'you hear me? This is *my* country. *My* country.'

Maybe he didn't really mean it. Maybe it was only a counter-reaction to what the kid was saying, brought on by the vote and the intensity of the argument, but Limo stopped shouting as though he'd been slapped. His expression lost all animation, blanking until he regarded the man with no more interest than a frayed bootlace.

Christie tensed, Aaron felt it. The broad man turned on a scuffed heel, brushing past his confused girlfriend walking towards the marigold Amazon lockers on the northern end of the mall. He stopped and smashed his head against the metal, again and again, the sound of it like someone beating a tin drum. People screamed. Security guards ran over, trying to grab his arms, one pushed away by the man, falling and skidding across the polished floor on his arse. He got up and tried again with more of his mates and they were all pushed back even harder. The metal lockers banged, rocking steady time, growing dented, smeared red. Limo's friends backed away, their expressions pale and sick.

And the kid stood there, focused on the man butting the lockers, a sneering half-smile twitching at his lips.

Aaron stepped forward, not even thinking until he felt a hand on his forearm. Christie shook her head, eyes holding his. He frowned *why not*, and she shook her head even harder. A surge of anger swelled in his chest. Why not? When he turned back Limo had seen him, his smile broader, eyes dilated, the whites seemingly larger. He winked at Aaron and let the man fall, unconscious. The watching people gasped, rushed to his side. The man's girlfriend had long fainted, but no one noticed her. Limo spun on the spot, skating away with long graceful strides, the lights in his boots blinking. Aaron watched the glittering red, blue and white. His body grew light, and the spiral ascent opened in his head. The shopping centre faded, returned, faded, returned. Prickles of rage burned his eyes.

Christie saw his anger, he knew that. She grasped him by the shoulders and led him away from the people and the fallen man. He let her walk him outside, into cold night, towards the bus stop where she pushed him aboard the first 86 to pull up, guiding him to the upper deck. She sat him in the space behind the stairs by the window and leant against him so he could feel her warmth. Aaron saw dull lights, slow-walking people. He felt so tired. He wasn't even sure what was wrong; all his energy had left him. Somewhere further along the main road she hauled him down the stairs and onto the pavement, crossing roads until they came to another stop. They climbed aboard the next bus. She sat him down, putting her arms around him to quiet his shivering. He had a vague sense of where he was. His body felt loose and floppy, no bones.

He blanked out completely after that. When awareness came back they were entering a house, hers he guessed. A featureless hallway with one framed picture; an aerial shot of a beach, an orange and red outlined word in a corner: Bantayan. He had a vague memory of two people; a snub-nosed man in a blue-checked lumberjack shirt, red-eyed, tiny brown marks dead centre on his lips, sucking on the tiniest roll-up Aaron had ever seen; and a plump woman, lively in a fading way, wearing a little blue apron and regarding him as if his presence was of little importance. There were names, a round of nods before lengthy silence, yet Aaron didn't understand the words. He was tugged upstairs before he had time to ask if they were her parents. He might have even said it, but he didn't remember Christie answering, or even sure whether he'd actually voiced the question. The next thing he knew a door was closing. He sat on a sagging single-bed mattress pretty much like his own.

The room was dark, very warm. That strange redolence in the air like nothing he'd known, pleasant and enveloping. Like the undercurrent Christie brought whenever she was near him, yet stronger, richer, headier. He tried to see the walls and objects in the room, to get a better picture of who she was, but struggled to find anything to hold on to, just vague black forms and a light from the hallway that disappeared when Christie shut the door. He thought she'd flick the switch, waited for ever for the click, the quick ache at the back of his eyes, a sudden reimagining of the formerly blank space. He felt a dip then solid warmth beside him.

'We gonna sit in the dark then?' His tongue felt thick. He could barely free the words. She snuggled next to him, hair tickling his ear. It bothered him that he couldn't move. Speaking felt uncomfortable.

'I always wanted to go Philippines.'

She giggled, kissing him beneath his ear. He closed his eyes.

'You're Filipino, right?' Mumbling, barely able to free the words.

She did it again, a trail leading to his lips, turning his chin and kissing him fully. Everything inside him relaxed.

He was there again, floating in darkness he remembered, and this time it was better because of anticipation. When the free-fall came he let himself stretch and surge, be carried wherever the flow took him. This time he went deeper, a sensation like rich, soft liquid removing every physical sense of who he was until he was enveloped by it and he moved without will. He heard a low creak, similar to crickets only it sounded synthetic. Then something else came, hotter, a little searing. Later, he would think it was like steaming water being poured into a cooling bath, followed by the rapid awareness it wasn't that at all, more like hot water being poured inside himself from the top of his head to his toes. Except there was no head, no toes, and the water was scalding, painful, and he tried to open his voiceless, mouthless lips to scream only to find it was impossible; he had to wait until the pain faded into the dark of the room.

The bed. The dark, nothing further. He tried to crawl, to find something solid he recognised by touch. When his fingers brushed objects there were only corners and right angles, rectangles and squares, flat surfaces nothing like household items or objects someone owned. Even the bed, when he went back, had no legs, just a smooth, cool material akin to plaster reaching from the mattress to the floor. He frowned. Crawled to the bedroom door. Fright built inside him as he imagined there might not be a handle, he might be trapped, until he eventually found it, opened, could stand.

The passage was wreathed in shadows. A blurred arc of light below was enough to see down the stairs. He stepped quietly, trying not to make any noise in case Christie's parents were sleeping. Perhaps she was watching TV or had crashed out on the sofa. If the last were true, he'd leave and call in the morning. A sudden loudness erupted from the television, something about the vote that caught his attention. He tried to descend fast without making a sound. At the living room door he stopped, peeking around the frame, self-conscious. He didn't know these people, barely knew Christie. White light flooded the room. Farage filled the screen, baring teeth amid flashing lights and bouts of applause, saying it was Independence Day for England, and he listened, feeling that falling sensation again, only quicker and now, inside his own body, solid, rooted, causing him to slump against the door frame.

His eyes were drawn away from Farage's face towards the sofa, which seemed to be moving. It wasn't the sofa that was moving: it was three strange, writhing masses in a row that were on it. Not matter, not as he knew it, these were spheres of persistent energy, patterns shifting and swelling on each surface like plasma on the photosphere of a star, waves rippling, tendrils emerging, testing the air every so often before receding into the central mass. When he dared to take a step closer he saw discarded flesh laid in a draped pile beneath the rounded balls of energy like snakeskin. Fanned hair and glimpses of clothes flopped from sofa cushions onto the carpet. He realised the husks were the shed carcasses of *them* – Christie and each of her parents, the skins creased and partly inside out, veined and pale.

The spheres eased into deeper colours, darkening. Somehow, they rotated. The closest ball to Aaron reached out a slow, probing tendril. It curled like smoke, stretching towards him.

He ran. Out of the door and into the street, down the empty orange-lit road. He sprinted across roads, feet slapping pavements wet with morning dew, night buses bathing him in stark light. He didn't stop, and didn't pay any mind to whether they were following. There was no point. They knew where he lived. They also knew where he was *right now*. He and the creatures were for ever linked. He'd thought he was smart, the leader, the one who'd called them all, when really, from the start, it was her.

He collapsed against a lamp post, slid to its concrete root and when he could stand again he walked. His lungs burned, his legs weak. The streets were shimmering lake water. The high road stretched into the distance.

There was nothing else to do but go home, let himself in, and wait. Aaron shivered at the thought of his mother asleep in her room, snoring loud enough to be heard downstairs. He walked, alert to every sound, craning frightened looks over his shoulder whenever he heard a noise. No one was ever there.

In the kitchen he poured cold water and sat at the table, the silence a solid force. The walls ticked and the sporadic creak of floorboards made Aaron wonder if they could teleport. No matter. Not now. There was nowhere he couldn't be found. After an hour he heard shuffling at the back door. A hazy shape formed in frosted glass, blurred as her true form. A series of soft taps against wood. One, two three. He got to his feet. His hands shook as he unlocked the back door.

She looked the same. Just as beautiful, not frightening, or perhaps there was something in her eyes. Not shy, downcast, only steady appraisal. That was it. She studied him without pause, without feeling.

'Sorry you had to see us.'

He lowered his head, not wanting to remember his panic, heart thudding, seeking pounding escape from his chest.

'We were going to tell you. You woke sooner than we planned. I knew you were strong from the start.'

Aaron looked at the ground. On another road, not far away, a car changed gears, engine fading.

'So what now?'

'You come with us. We'd prefer by choice.'

He released a sigh, his swirling breath.

'OK. OK.'

She said nothing, did nothing, not even nod. Just stepped back to let him pass.

They took the bus. It was dawn, a trickle of commuters seeping through glass station doors and past the shuddering arms of barriers. On the tube Christie sat next to him, back stiff, face blank. They did not touch or talk. He kept his chin tucked into his chest. She was like a carving, or better yet a mannequin, more anatomically correct, more real. He looked from the corner of his eye to see if she'd react to anything, but she sat motionless, life-bled. It was eerie. He wondered if the other commuters noticed. They seemed buried in their papers, and he didn't want to risk a better look in case she suspected he was up to something, trying to communicate what they were doing, that he wasn't going along entirely willingly.

At Westminster she stood and he followed. Up escalators, out through barriers, into the streets and the morning crowd. The sun cracked the sky pale orange and red. The clouds were dark-bellied, gloomy. They walked along Whitehall at a rapid pace, Aaron treading fast to keep up, but she kept on and didn't look at him once. Halfway down the long, wide road, they stopped outside black gates. Two policemen stood on either side eyeing them. A sign above their heads said what he'd feared: Downing Street.

'Here?' He stood directly in front of her, a vague challenge, trying to see beyond those deep-water eyes. 'Seriously?'

She turned towards him, her unfeeling expression fathomless. It scared him. He backed away.

'OK. OK.'

Someone brushed his shoulder. He started, turned. Limo and Old Girl. Their faces blank, unseeing. Other young people were by their side, equally blind and entranced. They pushed forward, Aaron following. They walked up to the barrier, all of them, and the policeman guarding the street stepped aside, opened the gate, let them enter.

At Number 10 they did the same thing.

THE DIFFERENCE
BETWEEN ME
AND YOU

The difference begins around midnight when stark light invades his window and the thunder of machinery erupts. Geoff rises and walks across the room. He stands to one side, shielded by musty curtains. There's a routine clang of metal on metal that's shrill as a high-pitched voice, and an equally repetitive thud of helicopter blades. He hears shouts, the raw scrape of tools. Something pounds the earth, making his sash window frame rattle and Geoff step away, pressing his back against the cool wall. He pushes one hand against his lips so hard it begins to hurt. He realises what he's doing and returns to his desk.

He doesn't know what to do. He plays with the black mouse on its mat. He gnaws loose skin beneath his thumbnail. He throws back his head, sighs deep and swears between clenched teeth. In a fit of anger, he swipes at his phone. One knee bounces. Phone unlocked, he touches favourites and calls home.

'Mum?' He waits, scowling. 'Hello? Yeah, it's me. I know you know, I'm just saying. You all right? Yes, it's late. No, nothing's wrong, it's just . . . Look, they've started . . . The wall. Yes. I don't know. Right.'

She doesn't have much to say beyond the platitudes most parents grow used to, especially those who've long drifted from the practice of daily calls with their child. He tries not to get too upset with his mum and dad for their lapses, yet if he's honest the passage of time is beginning to scare him. That relentless creep towards an unseen future of *before it happens* and the *who knows?* after. The realisation he's seeing some measure of his own fate. He's noticed little changes in their manner, a lack of reasoning, the forgetfulness, an inability to move as well as they once did and their shortened tempers, all transmitted by phone or Skype these days, but even when he visits he sees so much he'd rather not. Markers of time. They'd crossed a line before Geoff had been fully aware, tipped over an unseen edge into slow decline. He'd seen it coming too late, worrying for scant seconds before replacing the weight loss, the greying hair and sporadic amnesia with more immediate problems, mainly his own. And now there was this.

'Don't worry about it, yeah? I'll get it sorted. I know they said but there's got to be a way. I'll see about it in the morning and let you know when I do. I know. Well, at least you and Dad are OK. That's the main thing.'

He blanks out when she talks about the banal realities of her life, only to realise and snap out of it. What's he doing? What was he just telling himself? He nods, shuffles his mouse, picks at his jeans.

'Bye Mum,' he says when she trails off. 'I'll call soon, OK? Love you.'

He doesn't wait for her reply and cuts off the line. Lightning brightens the room. This time, he won't look.

★

They're out there for the rest of the night. Radios playing bland pop, pounding tools that echo across the bare expanse of moist, sodden earth. The tinkle of fallen nails and grunts of heavy goods vehicles over a random whirr of drills. The searing noise of a cutting machine makes Geoff start, half rise. He'd dreamt of a circular saw, a fountain of sparks, some tough material or another shorn away, bending like paper. He sits up, drinks his bedside water and stares at drawn curtains. He can ignore the bastards but they won't go away.

Morning brings relative quiet. Geoff eats granola to a background noise of occasional hammer blows and various mechanical devices, although he also hears birds and the roar of planes. He spoons cereal, chewing thoughtless mouthfuls, pushes the bowl away and stands. He grabs his keys, his ID and leaves the flat. The door slams behind him, shuddering in its frame.

The stairs are dark, the grey walls cold. Faded graffiti is smeared in bleached patches all the way down. He pushes the icy steel bar out of his block and into the bright of day. Altostratus clouds veil the sky. The sun's dull, as if hidden behind ground glass. Geoff pushes his hands into the pockets of his denim jacket, hurrying along the black gravel path, slipping on the odd mud patch. It's cold and he's hunched against a growing breeze. The pop music's louder, irritating. He turns the corner.

Egg-speckled columns, somewhat like motorway struts, are placed in a single-file line, spaced maybe four hundred metres apart, it's difficult to tell. They stand high, towering over the building that contains his one-room flat by at least another half block, perhaps. Geoff understands last night's need for loud machinery even as he marvels at how this was done. The columns hike across the shattered remains of the worn town, far into the greying distance. Between each T-shaped strut there's an odd, shimmering trick of the light that reminds him of childhood, the translucent film of bubbles he blew as a boy.

He's stunned to a halt by this seemingly insubstantial barrier. For years they'd threatened to build a wall and eject those who sought to destroy their way of life, to safeguard and protect freedom as if it were a stolen foreign jewel, seen but never touched. They made plans and held referendums, argued for and against although in truth there was never any question. And while London burned and terrorists murdered innocents, people grew ever more fearful. The iron will the city was so proud of grew brittle with rust. Only a matter of time before it snapped, fell away. Exposed to the elements, quickly corrupted from outside by political businessmen who barely lived in the city. And so that final vote, to expel not only foreigners but also the less wealthy, had been enough to make it keel and die. Those who'd voted against couldn't imagine how right they were when they said the results might possibly last for ever.

He turns away. Not far from where he walks a lumbering group of pre-adolescents test the wall by throwing stones. The transparent material sparks and glimmers with each contact, a hissing snake. Stones chip into pieces and fall to the mud as though they're striking concrete. Geoff wants to give the youths a dirty look, but instead he does his best to ignore them. Idle workmen see what's happening and chase them away.

He over-emphasises his strides so he can make headway over loose soil. Gravel scrunching, escaping underfoot, he keeps his hands in his pockets, trying not to fall. He passes workmen in hard hats, their frames squat and shoulders broad, suited men gathered around ATM-sized computer banks analysing dark screens of information, and the inert figures of lifeless machines: diggers, flatbed trucks, others he's never seen. Beyond them, a larger group of people mills, growing to a knot of crowd. There's no shimmering film here, just open space. Geoff gets close before he sees it's actually two separate groups. The nearest, stood with their backs straight, are dressed alike. Coming behind them as he does, without his glasses, he has to squint before he sees they're army. The further group are dishevelled and broken. Geoff notes mucky faces, the single-file queue. Many are covered in blankets, hunched. Some limp away from the soldiers to gather beside a white bendy bus at the bottom of a grassy incline. Civilians, he tells himself. Rejects.

He circles the soldiers, pushing to the front of the queue. The waiting people shuffle and give him bad looks, but even now they do that typical English thing and remain silent. Three soldiers dressed in fatigues, two men and one woman, stand by a makeshift desk and computer set-up, scanning IDs and finger-prints against names on the screens, checking them off, sending the relevant person on their way. Geoff forces a smile to his lips. Be calm, he warns himself. Another four soldiers are poised in varied positions of battle readiness, hands on rifles, scanning the crowd. As Geoff moves closer, the largest steps towards him.

'Can I help?'

He feigns another smile at the giant of a man, all lips, no teeth. The giant looks through him. He imagines the man's thinking of the best place to put a bullet if he makes a sudden move. The man is blond, wide-faced, cheeks flecked red.

'I'm all right, actually. Just wanted a word with Lieutenant Parks.'

She looks up from the screen. Her eyes widen before she composes herself.

'Mr Morgan. Are you OK?'

'Yes, I am.' He's less sure now, thrown by their need to

negotiate the moment as strangers rather than what they are. If anything. 'Is it all right to speak for a minute? Won't take long.'

Parks turns to the giant. She blinks, lips pursed, and he steps back into position. Her colleagues try to keep their attention on the civilians. She leaves and Geoff follows, walking down the incline until no one's close, between the bus, the people, the shadow of his block and the closest strut.

'What're you doing?' she's hissing. 'You trying to get us both in trouble?'

'No, I just . . . I didn't know you'd be here. How would I?'

She softens, more like the woman he knew by lamplight in the empty confines of his local. Her deep eyes are still gaunt and hard, exposed by the tightness of her wrenched-back hair, but her shoulders fall. The tiny mole to the left of her lips makes her mouth look like it's pouting when she's really not. She snatches a glance behind her.

'So what do you want?' she says, less accusing even though her hands are on her hips. She peers at Geoff like he's a foreigner.

'I need to get home. To my parents. They—'

He can't say it. Instead, he toes crumbling earth. Parks sighs, breath whistling in time with the low wind.

'Look. We're getting concessionary passes,' she says. 'For when we're done. Two a man. I don't need them, so . . .'

Parks looks at the civilians. She'd told him that night, about the lights out at eight, the shared bedroom and unfeeling care-home staff. The waiting for adoptive parents that never arrived. Geoff floods with elation. He barely stops himself from hugging her.

'Thank you. That's—'

'Go home. Stay there. I'll come round at twenty-three hundred hours.'

She pivots, going back to the desk. Geoff tries not to stare at her rear, the twin curves easily visible beneath her loose fatigues. He moves away.

A woman he's never seen before leans face-forward against his block wall, arms covering her head, body trembling and bent. A limp hoodie falls halfway down her back. He sees the peach strap of her vest, the black bra strap beneath. Her skin's pale, her deltoids ridged, although small. She's a sorrowful void against rough walls.

He can't very well ignore her, not after Parks's kindness. Geoff trots down the incline onto the path, standing beside her for a series of useless moments.

'Hello?' he says after some time, one hand raised above her shoulder. 'Hello?'

She ignores him. Behind her, former Londoners trail onto the white bus, heads turned to watch. Geoff eyes the soldiers. They're busy filing people through the open gate.

'You'll miss the bus. You need to get to the displacement centre or you won't be rehoused.'

The woman sobs louder. She's tall and skinny, her hair masculine short. She wears tight jeans and that thin hoodie. She must be cold.

'Look, do you want a cup of tea? I might be able to help. I know a way to get back into the city.'

She doesn't react for some time and he's about to give up when she lifts her head. Her eyes are tower-block grey, saturated by red. Her nose runs in delicate strings. She doesn't seem to care. She hiccups, stares.

'Come. Let me get you inside, I'll explain there.'

Geoff sweeps an open arm towards the path. When he leads, the woman follows.

★

She perches on the edge of his sagging three-seater, a mug in both hands, focused somewhere behind him. Geoff sits opposite at his desk, misted by his own steaming mug of tea. When he asks how she'd come to be ejected from the city she speaks, her voice tinged with a Spanish accent. A CEO husband heading one of the big five housing associations, a six-bedroomed relative palace in Golders Green. A near-perfect son about to begin secondary education at a leading private school. She could have remained a housewife and claimed her husband's income on the census, but she'd started her own cleaning business, as that's what she did when they met, and she was proud not to rely on him. Little did she know when the vote was taken there'd be two strikes against her, one for her country of origin, another for her lack of personal wealth. She'd been blacklisted without anyone's knowledge until the declaration of section one eight two. The night before last, the government implemented that order.

They're silent when she's finished. Now she's told him who she really is, the difference between them is startling. Her thin, sitting upright and taut with the muscle that comes from hard work, him podgy, slumped in his office chair. Her thick with an accent that makes her speaking voice difficult to decipher, him concise, well-thought-out and clear. He finds it tough to imagine her wandering a six-room mansion, or dropping the son off at school, hurrying him through the gates. She doesn't look the type, more like an immigrant fallen on hard times in a drug dealer's jacket. It seems odd that even with all Geoff's upbringing and education he should end up here, in this flat, and she there. The difference produces an acid burn in his stomach he can't entirely put down to not having eaten since breakfast, or the tea.

'What do you do? Is that your work?' she says, indicating the laptop.

'I'm a journalist, actually. For the local rag. Only I haven't written for them in a while.'

The truth was they'd let him go. Budget cuts, they said. He'd been living on meagre funds borrowed from his parents for the last nine months. Stubborn, not wanting to leave. And now this.

But of course he can't say that. Scraps of truth lodge between his teeth. He clenches his jaw.

'I have an army friend down there; you might've seen her,' he tells the woman. 'She can get passes. She'll be here at eleven.'

The woman shifts, uncomfortable. Her face is drawn with lines beneath the bare light.

'And you'd give me one?'

'Of course.' He stretches his lips in another toothless smile. 'Why else are you here?'

Her eyes are opaque. She's trying to keep them open, obviously struggling.

'Thank you. Thank you . . .'

'No trouble at all,' he sing-songs. 'You can pull out the sofa bed if you want. I'll take the laptop in the other room. I won't disturb you.'

The woman looks confused until he gets up, removing his laptop from its stand. She takes off her shoes, swivelling horizontally. She's lying down and doesn't have on socks.

'What's your name?' he asks from his bedroom door.

'Nuria.'

'I'm Geoff,' he says, pushing the door closed.

He writes an article for a friend's blog, something inane about the falling teenage pregnancy rate in his locality. He makes a good attempt at getting back into it until the outside begins to call, distracting him from the white screen. He grunts and shuts the laptop, banishing words. He walks over to his bedroom window. Voices float on thermals. Civilians stream from the makeshift checkpoint. Three bendy buses stand in line, doors open, engines purring like idle cats. The soldiers corral their charges towards the vehicles and he can't see Parks but knows she's there, performing the job he can't quite believe is hers. The magnetic wall shimmers purple and blue under sodium lights like trapped nebula beneath glass, a series of installations extending for ever north.

Geoff checks on Nuria. She's sleeping, comatose. He makes a bowl of cereal and sits at the desk, watching. That good feeling, the one that came with the elation at finding a way into the city and giving aid to a fellow human being, gives way to something else. He can't quite recognise what, but a thought rises. His lone voice. *Who's the victim?* it asks. Geoff's spoon is poised. He waits for an answer. Me and you, of course. Me and you. He shakes his head, attempts a laugh. All he expels is a soft rasp, more like a wheeze. He shuffles in the office chair, eats another spoonful. Me and you, he thinks, me and you.

Even so, he can't quite picture the balance. Although he's well aware it's not entirely accurate, Geoff eats cereal and imagines a pair of antique scales tipping against him every time.

The knock comes just before eleven. He pads out to answer as Nuria's still curled up, snoring like a child. When Parks follows and sees the woman on his sofa all colour leaves her face. She gestures, harsh whispering. He puts a finger to his lips, beckoning her into the bedroom.

'Who the fuck is she?'

She's flushed, breathing hard.

'Jesus, Parks. She needs a pass, that's all. I thought you might help.'

'And what's she giving you?'

He shakes his head, tutting disappointment.

'I told you to call me Rasheda anyway.'

'Do you have them? Please.'

Her chest heaves. Geoff keeps his eyes on her face. He tries to push away his memory of how she looked in dim light, unclothed beneath his faded bed sheets.

'Please, Rasheda.'

She sags again, and then he feels bad. He'd thought her tougher than this. Tonight he sees she actually cares, only it's too late.

'I've only got the one anyway.'

Geoff hears birds, the engine thrum of the bendy bus.

'What?'

She stares into his eyes, not letting go.

'Obviously they know my circumstances. Some of the guys needed more, what could I say? You're lucky they gave me this.' Rasheda holds an orange envelope, tilting it at him. 'Good thing too. Considering.'

'I'm not sleeping with her.'

'That's not my business,' she says, looking at his unmade bed, the scattered books, papers and clothes, the undrawn curtains. 'You can do what you like. Can't you?'

The muscles of her jaw protrude. She looks at the window.

'This is just silly.'

'D'you think?'

Dark eyes flash.

'Don't you?'

She stares him down. He drops his gaze, grits his teeth.

'Will I see you in London?'

Geoff knows the answer, yet she has grace enough to smile. Rasheda gives him the envelope.

'Probably not,' she says.

He gathers the important things in a rucksack. Laptop, novel, notepad. He tucks the flimsy pass into an old Oyster wallet, pockets both and puts the orange envelope face-up on the coffee table with Nuria's name printed in black felt tip. He hasn't told her much. Just that the flat's hers if she wants it, that he had to leave immediately, where the folder is with information about the boiler and all other household appliances. He hasn't said he's sorry. He wants to, only he doesn't know how to word it, everything he writes feels wrong. Geoff feels his hands tremble and tightens them into fists. He puts his house keys on top of the envelope, slipping out before Nuria wakes to find him standing over her, the difference between them alive and naked in his eyes.

UTOMA

Today is my one hundred and forty-six thousandth dawn. As always, it's spectacular. I go into the garden, my daily ritual. There's a hum of escaping insects, the soft breath of wind, the expanse of green and silent land. To the south, the hazy orb of Utoma City. To the east, a dark undulation of hills merges into a marble-blue sky fissured with growing light. I pause to watch this tender seepage, the rise of our sol. I'm amazed.

My qualia is to separate bindweed from roses, creeper from fig tree, and so I begin. Destroying one species so another might thrive. I try not to think of it like that, but as I'm sure you can tell I'm in a reflective mood, never mind the glowing beauty of sunrise, or perfume of surrounding flowers. The M'Rec is a pleasant whirr, a reminder. In the old days I barely noticed, but today I'm especially conscious I'm talking to you for the first time since the beginning. You hear all, my every thought. It wasn't something I cared about, but today the noise is especially loud. Odd. I hardly ever think about the beginning either, only I do now for no clear reason except the obvious. It's strange.

And there it is again. That rustle among the hedgerow, the low snuffle of a creature picturing that she cannot be seen. If I look in that direction she stills, but if I turn back to the weeds or move away from the hedge she stirs again, and sometimes I'm quick enough to catch rippling leaves from the corner of my eye. I feel the urge to go closer, not to catch her, just to gain a better look, but I've tried that before so I know what it will cause: fierce eruption, the pattering weight of padded feet and harsh, panting breath. A streak of dark fur darting into the long grass two hundred metres beyond my hedge perimeter. I'm curious, of course. I've never seen the creature; in fact, I very rarely get close to any animals. Avians beat frantic wings skywards, cawing with fear. Mammals are either disturbed by my heavy feet, or catch my scent yards away, disappearing long before I arrive. Even insects never land anywhere near us, but dart into the unseen distance, zigzagging in primal fear. It's a curse we all live with, though for me, a lover of nature, it makes me aware of what most deny. This particular creature seems unlike the rest. Although I try not to look, I feel her eyes on me, weighing my worth. I'm desperate not to fail.

I dig earth with cupped hands, extracting the weed and its roots, throwing it onto the pile of ugly vegetation behind me. Although the work is calming, I feel an urge grow. The creature is bolder. Teasing perhaps. I try to keep my thoughts on bindweed, yet it's impossible. The creature pushes a long snout out of the bushes; I can see from my rear-view. Her eyes are like the pollinated centres of sunflowers, yellow and black in the centre. I suppose she wants to talk. It certainly looks that way. Why else would she come back, day after day? Slowly she pokes her head further. First eyes emerge, then a broad, flattened skull, finally twitching ears and a long thick neck. Her tongue hangs low, ridged and dripping with a translucent liquid that steams as it hits swaying grass. She's a huge beast, magnificent. I've never seen one like her. She steps a great clover-shaped foot onto my territory.

I turn and leap, covering the distance between us, some sixteen metres, in one bound. By the time I land she's already disappeared from the hedgerow. Jazari. When I leap onto the arid land beyond the creature runs into the metres-high grassland that marks the wild, fogged by dust, feet scrambling, ears low, her tail a sharp, straight line. She disappears into the whispering grass and that's the end. I've lost sight of her, maybe for ever. I look around in case anything witnessed what I'd done, but the land is bare for miles. *Couple*. I shake damp earth from my fingers and wait. Nothing moves. I give up, leaping back to my side of the hedge.

The appearance of the creature and my handling of her are unsettling. I'm not a being of impulse, far from it. I've suppressed my predatory leanings to such a degree I've erased all but the faintest remains of pogroms. I know my temperament is not the same as yours, it's why I moved from the city and into the land. You still curse The Others' name routinely. In Utoma City, when I was there, they were treated with violent apathy, disgust. Then they were few, their sightings rarer than creatures, but I heard and saw enough to cause me to wonder why this was, to realise I was the anomaly, not you. What knows which turn of circumstances created me like this? None are like me, and my course of action became clear soon after my daymark. I had little possessions, only the seeds collected over time if you remember or care to track that far.

At your leisure, you may track to the first time I set down beyond the Old Town and saw the remains of their lives. That huge, incomprehensible marker: W LC ME TO MI TON KEY S. Untidy rectangles, once gardens I assumed, overrun and wild. Warped furniture thick with dust; beds, tables and chairs, useless things of that nature. Cracked and picture-less frames, the portraits most likely destroyed centuries ago. Fragments of their pasts blown through shattered windows carried to unknown places by the wind. It was fascinating for me to think of what this might have been long before us, and though I knew it was useless to you I stayed awhile, because it was necessary for me. I'd found something I hadn't known I wanted. I'm a being of nature, that's on the Bank, nothing new to any of you. I derive pleasure from the organic so it follows I might be curious about the natural world which came before us. That's why I do my best to recreate what they once had to the best of my ability. Not to live as they did, obviously. That's impossible. No; I find myself by absorbing what remains of their past.

Some of their leavings come to good use. The chair with its long curved boards instead of legs, which I found in an upstairs section and brought into the lower, has been a comfort throughout these years. Even though I have no need to sit, it's good for contemplation. I push back; the chair allows it; the chair pushes forward in turn; I follow. The motion is extremely soothing. The light grows brighter in my cool dark section, and I push the chair into a steady rhythm. I think about the creature and what led me to behave like that. The predatory instinct doesn't live in us, not any more, but there is something about the urge to capture the creature that's very unsettling. I thought I was immune to the ways of those before me. Yet I didn't let her come to me. I didn't.

I know what I'm leading to. Bo. It's only in these times I feel I really need it, and though it's often little help, this brooding alone won't get me anywhere. I push my chair, and think, until I slam my feet on the wooden floor. I walk outside into cloudless sun. Distant hawks circle overhead, broad wings outstretched, a plea. Smaller birds chatter in the trees, flitting from branch to branch. The sounds of organics are so consuming I almost forget what I'm doing. I focus, bend at the knees, and bound.

It's further into the wild than my land, although that doesn't mean it's organically inclined despite the work it's been given. While I appreciate Bo's need for solitude I don't understand its sneered distaste for the natural world, or why it chooses a barren, infertile waste to call its own. As far as I can tell it has no feel for its qualia. I believe the work is more suited to me. The journey is a good two-hours' bound, and in time the abundant grasslands are left behind until I'm travelling over grey earth, baked dry by lack of foliage, dusty and cracked like rotten vegetation. Plumes of clouds explode beneath my feet as I take off, hit the ground. Trees are crumbling and withered. Nothing stirs for miles except the breeze. Death's mute voice is every-where.

It would be easier if I were airborne, I know that. Sometimes I wish the modifications had been fitted before my daymark, but you can't choose your specs. Anyway, it goes against my beliefs to excrete substances that damage organics, so I bound without complaint. It's not exactly difficult, although it is wearing on the joints. That's why I only travel to visit Bo, or Old Town, avoiding permanent damage.

If I close my eyes and imagine, I could almost be avian. One push from my bent knees, an abrupt straightening of the legs and I'm thrust high into the air, fine earth swirling below. The wind howls and buffets my body. The ground disappears; with the right weather conditions there are even wisps of cloud. On a sol-filled day like this, it's a beautiful way to travel.

There are many techniques for a bound. I favour hands laid flat against my sides, legs together and feet pointed towards the earth for optimum speed, chin tucked into my chest, even though it limits visibility. At peak trajectory I change to the crouch position, knees and arms bent as though I'm about to sprint; this slows descent. Some like to roll into a ball then arrow their body towards the ground, arms outstretched, palms together, assuming a crouch position closer to the earth. To me this is madness. I prefer the slower method, straightening the right leg just before landing so the force is absorbed through a greater body mass. After, I stand upright, legs together, to bound again. Before long a rhythm builds and I'm hardly aware of what I'm doing.

Below, there are often large mammals in the wild, fat and slow. Their bellies rock from side to side as they hear my rapid whistling descent from above, trying to run. Not so much where I bound now, in the land Bo chooses to remain. In mine I've often seen the waddling black and brown creatures once consumed by The Others, even bred. Field could tell me what they're called, but the truth is they're ugly and I have no interest in them, so I never ask. I accept the truth of my assembly. I was not constructed to be scientific, or curious. I was made for a love of inanimate organics. This is my qualia. The pursuit of experience in this field, nothing more. That has been Banked, I'm sure. It's the reason I don't know why I pursued the creature in my garden. The flash of urge was just that: bright, momentary. When it left me, I was blinded, startled.

For my final few bounds, the land gains definition. Small black dots on flat grey. From my heightened view they resemble blight on an otherwise featureless stem. They grow and recede, grow and recede, becoming more distinct with every descent, almost magically forming flat-roofed buildings, observation decks, concrete walls, patches of grass and high fencing. When flowers begin to take shape below my feet, I smile. I land in a final explosion of earth, and there it is, by the tall, partially opened gate, waiting.

We take to the observation deck, as is our custom, on the roof of Building One. There are four warehouse spaces, each built to house various breeds of organic life. This main building is dedicated to sections of flowering vegetation. Building Two houses bacteria farms. Three is where trees are cultivated. Four is empty, for now. Bo prunes fuchsia while I watch, spraying them with liquids. The sol has passed its optimum point, and is already falling. The change in temperature is one degree, will likely drop a further two by the time the star descends for the evening. The night will be cool with a touch of welcome rain.

Bo has its back to me. The snips of its tools are the only sound. There are no creatures for miles and the insects have gone elsewhere. They will return when we are inside the building, after they deem it safe. I've seen them do this from our windows.

'Why speechless?' Bo says, without turning from the vegetation.

'I'm not sure.' In reality I sensed it didn't want to be disturbed. Track previous days and you'll see there are many occasions when I've spoken aloud only to receive no answer. 'You seem busy with your organics.'

'You should be celebrating, no? On your daymark? Isn't that traditional?'

'Not for us,' I say, even though I know its response. It scoffs loudly. I try to ignore what I hear.

'Don't start that again.'

'I'm not. It's pretence, you know that.'

'You say that as though The Others never did so.'

'You say that as though we should do everything they did.'

It makes another noise of exasperation, gets to its feet. I'm very unsettled when it does that. Just another pretence, another way of acting like something it's not. We are not they. Is that hamoi? If so, too late. The Bank already knows. Bo's taller than I, hair fanned around its face in a false dark halo it grew after seeing historical records of The Others on the Field. It wears cut-off trousers favoured by their kind at the time of the Percipi, shorts it calls them, and thin almost-clothes on its upper half that reveal both arms. Told me it was *cool*. All because they constructed its carapace with a heavy dose of melanin. I mean, mine is too, but you don't see me going off wrapping my head in thick fabric, or wearing robes that fall to my toes, or painting a red dot in place of my daymark. I know this behaviour's encouraged but Jazari forgive me it's infuriating. We have no need to grow protein from our heads. That's precisely the reason I'm void of the stuff. What purpose does it serve other than looking foolish? The idea is ridiculous emulation, nothing more, I hope you won't find this blasphemous but you know how I feel and I can't help it, we are not and will never be them.

It's looking at me now, one corner of the lip tugged in an irritating smile. I shift from side to side.

'Is this because of the dog?'

'The what? What are you talking about?'

'The dog. The creature you tried to catch. That's what it's called.'

'How do you know?'

'It seems to bother you a bit, that's all. Don't worry, they're many. They populate your area. Live up in the hills mostly, quite a large group. The Others called them packs.'

'Yes, but how do you know what she's called?'

'The Field. It's all there, I keep telling you. You shouldn't be so single-minded.'

It's scanning, curved pruning tools limp in its hands, and those eyes never leave me. I picture its image of me bent over in the small cloth chair being processed, recorded, sent to the Bank simultaneously with mine.

'I've had other things to do,' I say, looking at the parched grey expanse of the plain. The stillness.

'Really?'

'I have no need of a creature. A dog.'

'Perhaps you'd like an exploration.'

'I have my vegetables.'

'Something more complex perhaps. More able to communicate.' Bo takes the seat beside me, puts down the tool. 'I would.'

There's a softer, calmer look in its eyes. I feel a sense of ease growing as it sits, and settles. Not mine, its.

'I'm not built for such things. Neither are you. It's against our programme.'

It twitches somewhat, as though affected. More pretence. Words don't harm us. We're logical beings, most of the time.

'Some say otherwise. We think, laugh, converse, enjoy, feel. Why wouldn't we develop beyond our original programme? Isn't that what we are built for? To experience?'

'Not me,' I say, sitting back, grasping the arms of my chair. 'I'm happy as I am.'

'This type of thing is usual in Utoma. They breed them to know nothing but us. They explore, learn. There are even competitions. They become accustomed to us.'

'Field said that's impossible.'

Bo thinks, one finger pushed against its chin. Even such a simple gesture is annoying.

'The information might be encrypted. Although, if a dog is visiting you, the Bank will give you access. You should ask.'

'I have no need for a creature to fill my time. I have you.'

It throws back its head, laughs so loudly I jump. I feel my teeth clench and I grip the chair tighter waiting for it to finish. This takes time.

'I'm sorry . . .' it says between pealing chuckles. 'I'm sorry. I forget who you are sometimes, it's foolish . . .'

'What.'

Bo turns and leans back, scanning me, all in one practised move. It's so fluid even I see it as one of them for a moment. I delete the thought.

'What d'you mean?' it stutters.

'*What* I am. Not who. We're not Other. You can convince yourself if you like, but don't keep trying to convince me.'

Even though I'm unsure? The thought is off and bounds into the distance before the desire to snatch the words back are produced, were such a thing allowed. Away via Memory Recorder to Utoma City. To be dissected and analysed by their bots, maybe charged with the offence of hamoi. Blasphemy. I expect Bo to be angry, but it's nodding like it understands.

'All right. All right. This must be difficult for a young mod to grasp. You'll learn. It might take time, but you will. No one can help their lesser station in life.'

That sounds like an insult, though I don't know what it means. Lesser is never good. Bo's language is another consistent annoyance.

'Are you deliberately talking in riddles?'

It makes another of its noises, this time a sigh. I use the temporary pause to make a quick connection with Field. The page superimposes on my in'screen. I blank.

Begin search . . .

What is the meaning of 'station in life'?
Does it mean religion?

Loading . . .

. . . 'Station in life' as in:

Nonetheless, seams can make borders 'semi-permeable membranes', relatively more or less porous to people, depending upon their nationalities and stations in life, to economic exchange, to the passage of ideas . . .

That expression is considered 'dated' today, though a convenient catchphrase in flowery speech and writing.

{M'Rec Hub Bank}

Different stations in life

4.1 [*count noun*] • One's social rank or position

 . . . *we are defined by our jobs* . . .

In a broader sense, perhaps, status, standing, locus standi, position.

{M'Rec Hub Bank}

What determines 'station in life'?

Your 'station in life' includes such things as age bracket, marital status, whether or not you have children, whether you are a priest, religious or layperson, perhaps your work status (i.e. if you are an employer or not).

{cut in'screen}

Darkness lifts. I return to Bo. It's scanning again, this time with a frown cast across its handsome face. Even the swirling, circular daymark stamped on its forehead is beguiling, easy to view; under normal circumstances I struggle to take my eyes away. I blink to focus on what I'm trying to say. I'm leaning forward. My volume is raised.

'Why am I lesser? I'm not ranked high enough to understand your warped ideas of hierarchy?'

Bo sits back, shaking its halo. It glistens in sunlight like the night skies of the wild.

'Augo. Come on. Are you angry?'

'Of course I'm angry. You're saying I don't have the capacity to grasp simple propaganda. You're calling me unintelligent.'

'No! Come on, why would I? I'm stating a fact. Look, listen a minute, don't argue. You and me, we're friends. Right? That much is clear. But at the same time we're different. I'm Binary Organic, you're Augmented. I'm daymarked earlier, sure, but that still gives me a forty per cent greater capacity on the back end, which works out an extra ninety million terabytes. That's fact. Your qualia. You're smart, I just have a greater capacity, hence our different stations. Look, man, that's how Jazari made us . . .'

I sit forward, and something snaps. The urge breaks loose, blanking my hub again, surging from my mouth.

'I'm *not* a man, and we don't have different stations in life, the simple fact being neither of us are alive! We're coupling machines for Jazari's sake! Coupling *machines*!'

Silence. Bo's still hand is raised mid-gesture, its face all hard angles, protruding cheekbones, grizzled spots of protein on the cheeks and chin. Eventually it relaxes. The hand falls, it sits back, its legs protrude. If I could name one thing it has a greater capacity for, I would instantly say patience.

'Look. It's your daymark. You're one hundred and forty-six thousand days old. Congratulations. That's a fantastic achievement, but you're fresh off the line. Haven't even liv—' It stops, gulping back the word, smiling a white-toothed grin. '*Existed* yet. OK? I'm two hundred and ninety-two thousand, double your age. It took time to learn how to navigate this place, and it will take you time too. If all the worlds' histories were a day, our kind only existed in the last half a minute, do you know that? *The last half a minute*, Augo. Be cool and you'll get there, young spark.' Bo flashed bright enamel. 'You will.'

I'm looking at it, seeing glistening fervour and thinking *my Jazari*. It really believes we live. The grin is growing, making it look almost like wandering fantasma, those rogue, crazed, unprogrammed beings that roam the wilds, and I'm thinking about the harm false programming can do to hub wiring, corroding and shorting. I can't take it seriously or bear to see its expression much longer because it actually makes me afraid, even though I realise that thought's going to be Banked, is forbidden. I'm about to turn away, in fact I already have when something amazing happens. I see a darting presence from the corner of my eye, click to rear-view/front-view merge so I catch the thing from both angles and I see him, there's no doubt, this part is real.

Bo sits up, back straight, body imploring, eyes wide and full of deep-held belief, when a fly swoops down and lands on its still wrist.

One moment. That's all Bo has before the fly perhaps realises he's made a mistake, or feels the quivering hum of internals and lifts into the bright sun again. Yet I saw the insect land and take off, and most importantly Bo felt him. Its eyes flood with liquid saline. I know it's a mechanical trick, but the response that sets it going is emotional nonetheless, therefore real. It feels this too. Bo lifts its chin, watching the creature zoom over the compound, buzzing loud enough to fill our surrounding void. The event is undeniably huge, monumental, will be Banked and monitored for thousands of days to come. Bo might even be visited by high-ranking Utoma scientists, the compound forensically analysed for clues as to why such a thing happened here.

'Did you see that?' Bo whispers. It sounds on standby.

'Yes.'

'I can't believe that. It's like a picture. Thank Jazari for the Bank.'

'Yes.' I say. 'You'll be famous!'

'Can you believe that? Can you?'

It looks like the young spark, not me, fists clenched on knees, mouth agape, hardly able to stir.

'Hardly. That was a miracle.'

'I'll go down in history!'

'You will.'

'For the second time!' it blurts, seeing my confusion. The smile falters. When the expression returns it is forced, subdued. It looks at the white concrete roof. A leg twitches. Another piece of information I haven't been told. Perhaps because of my low station?

'Thank Jazari. We are Ificans proud,' it murmurs at the hardened floor. 'Might beyond measure.'

'Measure beyond might,' I say.

And now my fear has returned.

It doesn't need to tell me, although I sense it will. We descend into the building, which is dark and overly warm. Bo cultivates vegetation in the main section. Each time I come its growing something new, and I want to examine its product, but we never spend enough time before I have to leave. This may be design. There are huge looming organics with wide hanging leaves connected to an array of machinery at the furthest end. Smaller flowering vegetations powdered with rich perfume, their colours glowing even in the dark. The scent of damp earth is a balm. We wind through aisles with vegetation beds on both sides, pushing by the thick leaves of bigger organisms. One particular vegetable catches my eye; it bears oval, dark seeds covered in thick, coarse fur. I reach for her. Bo looks back, sees me.

'What's this?' I ask.

'Sapodilla.'

'What's its use?'

'They produce a resin we use for mechanical production. They never tell me how, I don't ask. I just grow them.'

'I've never seen it.'

'I'll give you a few seeds before you leave. Sapodilla needs plenty of heat, so you might need to readjust your generator.'

We move on. I'm scanning placards as we pass. *Bromeliad*, *heliconia*, *poinsettia*. The colours and variations are a dream, red the most dominant, until I see a small tree of green bananas and almost cry out *Wait*, but Bo won't stop, taking me to the back exit and out into the dusty central compound. There's a cool of the shadowed buildings that's pleasant. The breeze is slight and of low degree. I strain my ears for insects, but there aren't any.

We walk across the compound, straight all the way to the next building, the smallest. The walls say BUILDING FOUR in tall black letters.

It told me this was empty. The building was always empty. There's a large double door, digitally locked. It's metal, inches thick, reflecting our blurred images, a cloud of various colours and no features. Bo sight-reads its daymark for entry. The door clicks, slides open.

This warehouse is cooler than the main building. The door slithers closed. I register the instant rhythm of machinery, whirrs and sighs and a bubble of warm liquids. There are machines on metre-high tables everywhere. They fill the warehouse. Some are thin, bare, glistening arms that hold and lift, some no more than hand-shaped metallic dispensers of medicines, barrel-shaped needles in place of fingers. Some are petite boxes with wheels instead of legs, a hub power no greater than insects, programmed by ideals even less noble than instinct. There are thick rectangles lined against the wall, dead and weak despite their array of lights, metallic zombies. Where in the hierarchy are these poor beings? These slaves to our higher wills, our voiceless counterparts? Surely each is only a hub, the inclusion of semi-organic materials and the illusion of choice away from ourselves? I gaze into dim light only to be reminded of the city I left behind, the machines I thought were days in the past.

Bo moves on. I follow, unenthused. This is already more horrible than I'm prepared for. It's already shown me hell. Before us, tables are lined with docile mechanical beings trained on numbered glass domes placed in rows throughout this section. There are hundreds in the relatively small area. Each has a dim red light cast behind it, the same collection of mechanics servicing his needs. Each bears a tiny zygote, pink and alien, floating in thick transparent liquid. Their heads are huge, lowered, the hands flat and the black dot of their unseeing eye like a grim, featureless daymark. A network of red and blue veins runs throughout the body and the soft grey hub, or brain as they called it, the pulsing heart. They are disgusting, ugly. I begin to see why we curse them. We are not made in the image of these morbid beginnings.

'This might be why it landed . . . The fly, I mean,' Bo says. Its volume is low, words hushed.

'Why do you think that?'

I'm struggling to speak against my disgust. Is that also hamoi?

'I carry the seed.'

I'm not sure I believe. I'm scanning too hard, I know this; anything else is impossible. My every thought and action feels forbidden.

'I thought there wasn't any.'

'They kept some, of course. They had to. We need the material. They produce them from organic DNA and insert them into my organs. I carried them for ninety days.'

'And the egg?'

'A female Bo.' It grins with success. 'They brought her especially from Utoma City. They're pure genius.'

'But why? We can farm.'

'Too precarious by far. Too dangerous. We lose those and our kind is finished. No flesh, no hair, no blood, no internals . . . No exploration of any kind. Think about it, Augo. We need procreation. We need autonomous life.'

'To farm.'

'Yes, of course to farm.' It frowns again. 'What would you suggest? That they roam free?'

'No,' I say, eyes firm on its. 'Of course not. That would be hamoi.'

I'm not sure it's convinced, because it scans me for a long time. I think it'll let the question go and we can leave the too-cool, too-dim warehouse, until it goes on, spewing whole passages, all the data I've heard. We are supreme beings, blessed by Jazari. The next evolutionary step, *Uto Sapien*. When The Others wiped out *Homo neanderthalensis* they proved their inability to live with another humanoid species. The *Uto Percipi* was a justified response to prospective genocide. A reminder, as if I needed one, of the one million, eight hundred and twenty-five thousand-day peace, no fights, insurgencies, battles or wars, unheard of historically. Our pre-ordained divinity.

'And when we finally locate Jazari at the centre of the universe,' Bo almost sings with devout emotion, hands clasped the edge of the metal table – it leans forward so the light of the glass dome catches one side of its face; the ridiculous protein style it wears gleams – 'when we locate him we will be proven correct and eternal, now and forever . . . Might beyond measure, my Ifican brethren.'

'Measure beyond might,' I say, without thought or a desire for meaning. The words have become void, never more so than now. It's gazing into the glass dome, at the floating zygote, overcome by a fixed expression of standby. I'm reluctant to break its focus, but my own question beats at my lips, and I have to. 'So . . . Are you coupling? With the female?'

It spins to face me. More silence. I think I've caused offence until it shakes its head. It wasn't angry, only thinking.

'Good question. Very good question. Not me. Probably not any of us for a hundred thousand days or more. But one day. Who knows?'

Thank Jazari. My fingers are clenched and I let them fall apart, feeling the glands do their work, spreading liquid over my palms. I've never liked that sensation, never will. It puts a hand on my shoulder. I want to pull away but I'll be sent to the city if I do. I know this. I root myself firm.

'I'm a father,' Bo says, shaking me back a little, forward a little. 'I'm a father to all these Others and there'll be so many more.'

I smile, knowing I must.

We stand together outside the compound gates. Night is on its way, sol falling behind us. Bo hands me something. Small and dark, a handful. Seeds. They are light for something with such potential weight. It looks into the growing dark.

'Usually you stay longer.'

'I want to avoid fantasma.'

The wind throws grey dust about us. We are unmoving.

'Be careful in the wild. It can be dangerous.'

It seems haunted now, less exuberant. Maybe I should have stayed. When I find myself tracking automatically to those glass domes backed by red light, I picture my own meagre cultivation, the silent lives of the organic community I raise. I'm not sure whether it means me to feel unsettled, but I do. I put the seeds in my pocket, lower my head.

'Congratulations on your success and thank you for sharing it with me. We're on the verge of a new beginning, surely. Jazari bless you.'

'Certainly, brethren,' it says. The expression is rigid as it scans me. No smile, no enamel. It knows, I'm thinking. But then you already do. My future, positive or otherwise is sealed, Banked.

I put both legs together, bend my knees. In one bound I am

high. I scan over my shoulder. Bo is a tiny dot, no bigger than the insect that landed on its wrist, receding. I turn, tucking my chin into my chest. I soar.

Against my own wishes, I picture Building Four. Glass domes and hundreds of prototype Others. Mindless worker machines keeping them alive. I hear myself whisper under the rush of wind, shaking my head to blank the image. I do not want to see our work. I do not believe our cause. I do not. I close my eyes tighter. If I force hard, the image discontinues, replaced by my hedgerow, morning dew, rustling leaves.

So be it. Let all in Utoma know – I will do as Bo has. Make the creature, this dog as it calls her, come to me. I will coax it, not with meat or attempts to be quicker or stronger, but by letting it know I am not shaped by our history or the terrible places it leads us. That is theirs to keep. I will not use it for exploration, just companionship, and if I ever have to, I'll leave for the wilds. I raise my volume above a whisper, speaking over buffeting air. I will do better. I will.

ACKNOWLEDGEMENTS

Really lucky to have trusted friends, allies and loved ones on this journey.

To the higher energies, give thanks always.

Thanks to Sharmila, Senen, Nya, Mum, Arvind, Tara, Sunil, Anj and Manu for your eternal encouragement.

Thanks to Brook Stephenson, Jenn Baker, Kelvin Black, David Monteith, Drew Sinclair, Sherin Nicole, Mark Isherwood, Conor Montague, Sarah Hall, Peter Hobbs, Julia Bell, Dave McGowan, Tom Bullough, Matthew Cunningham, Rich Blk, Rachael de Moravia, Rukhsana Yasmin, Will Mackie, Joelle Taylor, Toyin Agbetu, Ra Page and Comma Press, George Sandison, Ashish Ghadiali, Margie Pope, Kit Caless, Hannah Knowles, Aa'Ishah Hawton, Leila Cruickshank, Katie Huckstep, Jamie Norman, Francis Bickmore, Jamie Byng, Saba Ahmed and all the good folk at Canongate. So happy you chose me! Everyone at the Arvon Foundation who heard these stories, often more than once! Thank you Valerie Brandes and Jazzmine Breary. This was an extremely long haul but all of your support kept me going.

To Crystal and Jason, I truly appreciate you! Thanks for allowing me to join the Own It! family.

Immense gratitude to FlyLo for gifting me such an awesome

title. And many thanks to Michael Salu for your beautiful cover design.

Thanks to the Society of Authors foundation and the Taner Baybars award, along with Arts Council England for their generous support.